Str

Grabbing his side, he tried to haul himself to his feet. The floor swayed out from under him, the lamplight tilting crazily. He groaned, caught the bedrail, felt the iron frame jolt at his weight. Rosie's eyes drifted open, focused, and jerked wide. She sucked in a breath just as he clamped his hand over her mouth.

"Don't scream, Rosie," he croaked as the bed seemed to turn on its side and his feet began to drift on cotton clouds. "Please. It's me. It's Bart."

Her skin and lips melted under his palm as black curtains blocked his vision. "Bart!" he heard her gasp. Then the curtains wrapped themselves over his head, and his feet floated out from under him. He tumbled like a falling oak tree across his Rosie's soft body.

Diamond Books by Catherine Palmer

OUTLAW HEART
GUNMAN'S LADY

GUNMAN'S LADY

CATHERINE PALMER

DIAMOND BOOKS, NEW YORK

This book is a Diamond original edition,
and has never been previously published.

GUNMAN'S LADY

A Diamond Book / published by arrangement with
the author

PRINTING HISTORY
Diamond edition / May 1993

ISBN: 1-55773-893-9

Diamond Books are published by The Berkley Publishing Group,
200 Madison Avenue, New York, NY 10016.
The name "DIAMOND" and its logo
are trademarks belonging to Charter Communications, Inc.

PRINTED IN THE UNITED STATES OF AMERICA

10   9   8   7   6   5   4   3   2   1

For Bolivar friends, new and old,
especially Zanetta Roam, Linda Roller,
and Linda Tappmeyer

My thanks for research assistance to the Arthur Johnson Memorial Library in Raton, New Mexico; the Raton Chamber and Economic Development Council; the Estep Library of the Southwest Baptist University in Bolivar, Missouri; and the Southwest Regional Library, also in Bolivar.

Deep appreciation to those who turn my dreams into realities: Judith Stern, Patricia Teal, and Tim Palmer.

GUNMAN'S LADY

*One
· ·

April 1883—Raton, New Mexico Territory

While trying his damnedest not to bleed to death, Bart Kingsley decided he had *not* gotten himself shot on purpose. No man in his right mind would do that kind of a chuckleheaded thing.

Besides, it took a fair amount of brain to accomplish what Bart had in the last two months—tracking down a fugitive woman who'd given herself an alias. Trailing her halfway across the frontier. Locating her at last in a two-bit mountain town where she'd gone to work as a waitress in Fred Harvey's railroad restaurant. Yes, sir, Bart Kingsley had his wits about him.

But then, just two minutes ago, Laura Rose Vermillion had walked into her dormitory room and sat down on the bed Bart was hiding under. When she lifted her black skirt and he caught sight of those pretty little ankles he remembered so well, he had to admit he wasn't a hundred percent certain he hadn't leaned just a hair into the path of that sheriff's bullet.

Odd thing was, nobody had ever yet shed a drop of Bart's mixed Apache and White Eye blood. Not his stepfather, who'd sure tried enough times. Not Laura Rose's pappy, who would have liked to, whether he ever had the guts to pull the trigger or not. Sure as hell not any of the string of lawmen and bounty hunters who'd tried to gun Bart down and had found themselves eating cold lead for supper.

But here he lay, his blood soaking into the edge of

1

Rosie's pink hooked rug, a bullet jammed into one of his innard parts that had been hurting like the devil for close onto an hour, an armed Pinkerton detective snooping around outside and probably about to track him to Rosie's dormitory window. All this because of a woman he'd tried to forget for six long years.

Laura Rose. From underneath the bed Bart studied those ankles as she unlaced her stiff leather shoes and worked her stocking feet around in tiny circles. God didn't make many ankles that slim, that fragile, that downright luscious. Rosie had ankles worth fighting for.

Not that Bart had ever fought for them.

No, sir, there was no way he could deny that when push had come to shove, he had skedaddled out of Kansas City as if a scorpion had been crawling down his neck. Of course, he'd been only seventeen years old at the time, but that excuse didn't hold much water. Even as a kid he'd been strong as an ox and more stubborn than any mule.

He could have stayed in Missouri and fought Rosie's pappy, he could have pulled out the certified marriage license he still carried with him everywhere he went. He could have argued his case in court as her pappy had threatened to do. But Rosie's father wasn't a highfalutin university professor for nothing. After the shouting, the warnings, and the threats had failed to make Bart waver, Dr. Vermillion had resorted to the only weapon left in his arsenal—the truth.

Under the bed, Bart grimaced as he probed the seeping wound in his side. The physical pain seemed almost easier to bear than the memory of Dr. Vermillion's damning words. He shut his eyes for a moment, fighting the instinctive self-contempt that had made him silent and withdrawn as a boy—battling the shame that inflamed his angry loneliness as a man.

Breathing steadily, he willed a wall of iron around the fragile hurt inside and forced himself back to the present. He could see Rosie's feet moving around the room now—small feet for a woman as tall as he knew she was. A ragged hole in the heel of one dark cotton stocking showed a round patch of tender pink skin.

"Etta, come in here, would you?" She had opened the door to her little room and was calling down the echoing hallway. Bart wished he could shrink farther into the space beneath her bed, but it was mighty hard to fit a six-foot-three-inch, two-hundred-pound man under a frail iron bedstead in the first place, let alone ask him to melt into its shadows.

"Do you smell anything odd in my room?" Rosie was asking her slipper-footed neighbor. "I noticed it the minute I came in from the restaurant. It's sort of a leathery, dusty odor—not unpleasant, but all the same, sort of raw and wild."

Beneath the bed, Bart bent his head and took a whiff of his fringed buckskin jacket. He couldn't remember the last time he'd had a good wash. Come to think of it, his hair probably needed combing in the worst way, and his boots hadn't been polished since he took them off that horse thief he'd shot dead in Little Rock.

"Phew!" Etta exclaimed. "I hate to say it, but the smell's probably coming from your own shoes, Laurie. These regulation laced boots Mr. Harvey expects us to wear cause the worst sorts of problems after a day of hurrying around a busy restaurant. I swear I've gone through two pairs of stockings a month since I've worked here."

Bart saw Rosie lift one foot and heard the little gasp that followed. "Jiminy Christmas, would you just look at this, Etta? A perfectly awful blister right on my heel!"

"What did I tell you? You'll have calluses in a month and corns before you know it. Someone should write a letter to that Mr. Harvey and tell him how we suffer. Listen, you soak your foot in a basin of salt water. I'll fetch some vanilla from my room."

"Vanilla?"

"Put a drop in each shoe and set them in the hall all night. By morning that scent will be gone, you'll see." Etta paused a moment. "Although I must admit your shoes really do have the strongest odor I've ever smelled."

As soon as Etta left, Rosie sat on the bed again and examined her sore foot. "Jiminy," she whispered. "Corns!"

In a moment she had bounced up and was padding to the window. Bart heard the sash drawn up and felt a blast of chilly air. At the same moment the sounds of male voices drifted into the room from the street below. A bridle jingled. Horse's hooves stomped the hard earth. Bart stiffened, his heart suddenly pounding in double time.

"What on earth are you doing, Laura Kingsley?" Etta cried as she reentered the room. "You'll catch your death with night breezes coming in like that! Don't you know how dangerous it is, us up here in the mountains and all?"

Turning his head with some difficulty in the tight space beneath the bed, Bart watched as Rosie stood on tiptoe to lean out the open window. Laura *Kingsley*, Etta had called her. The name Rosie had taken to calling herself sent a warm thrill down Bart's spine.

"I just want to air out the room, and— Etta, what's going on outside? A whole bunch of men and horses are right below my window downstairs. Men aren't supposed to be this close to the Harvey dormitory, are they? I thought that was against the rules."

"Ma'am?" The word was shouted from below the second-floor window. "Excuse me, ma'am, but have you seen a wounded man about these parts?"

"Shut the window!" Etta hissed. "Quick! Shut the—"

"Wounded?" Rosie was still on tiptoe. "Listen, sir, I'll have you know men aren't allowed near the dormitory. It's against Mr. Harvey's regulations. You'd better take your horses out of this yard before the sheriff comes over here and arrests you."

"I'm the sheriff of Colfax County, ma'am. Sheriff Mason T. Bowman. This fellow here's a detective from the Pinkerton National Detective Agency out of New York City."

"Jiminy!"

"I told you to shut that window," Etta whispered.

"Don't mean to frighten you ladies, but we're in search

of a desperate outlaw. This man was wounded just about an hour ago in a gun battle downtown—shot once or maybe twice by a Colt revolving pistol. He's lost a lot of blood, and we think we've tracked him as far as this here backyard.''

Shot *once*, Bart corrected silently under the bed. He might have needed an excuse to get close to Rosie, but he wasn't such a damned fool as to let two bullets plug him.

''We have reason to believe this man is heavily armed and dangerous. He's a hardened criminal with a price on his head in the state of Missouri. He could be lurking anywhere around. Take my advice and keep your dormitory windows shut tight and your bedroom doors locked.''

''Yes, Sheriff Bowman.'' Rosie's voice was hushed. ''We'll pass the word to the others.''

''Much obliged.''

Bart could see both women's feet over by the window. Rosie had curled her toes up tight and was stepping on one foot with the other.

''So what's this man done, anyway?'' Etta called out.

''You name it. Robbed banks, trains, stagecoaches. He's a horse thief and a cattle rustler. And he's wanted for murder.''

Under the bed, Bart frowned. He was *not* a horse thief and cattle rustler.

Rosie and Etta were giving little feminine gasps of horror out the window. ''Murder! My stars!'' Etta said.

''That's right, ladies. This is a wanted man.''

''What's his name?'' Etta called.

''Goes by two or three aliases—Injun Jack, Savage Jack, and Jack King—but his legal name's Bart Kingsley. He ran with Frank and Jesse James and the Younger brothers for a while before Jesse got killed last year. He's been on the loose ever since—going solo, so to speak. The detective here is after him for three train robberies in Missouri. He's been trailing Kingsley since he nosed onto him in Kansas City.''

Kansas City? Bart thought. The Pinkerton detective had been tracing him since Kansas City? Rosie, of course, had left a trail a mile wide, but Bart didn't think he had left any clues to his own whereabouts. Damn. Maybe he was a chuckleheaded fool after all. No wonder the sheriff had winged him with that bullet.

"Well, if we see anything suspicious, we'll send for you right away, Sheriff," Etta was calling out the window.

"Sorry to trouble you. Good evening, ladies."

"No trouble at all, sir. Thank you for alerting us." Etta slammed the window shut and fumbled with the metal clasp. "A murderer! Can you imagine, Laurie? Right outside the dormitory, too. Why, the other girls will be scared half out of their wits at the thought! I'm going to tell Annie and Mae right away. Won't they just swoon? . . . Laurie? . . . Laura, are you all right? You're as pale as a ghost, honey."

"Oh, Etta."

"What is it? What's the matter, Laurie? Don't be scared of that outlaw, now. The sheriff will probably have him rounded up by morning. Look at you, Laurie, you're trembling."

"Etta, I want you to open my wardrobe door right this minute and look inside. Wait—take this!"

"A gun! You're not supposed to have a gun—it's against regulations! You could get fired! Have you had this in your bag all along?"

"Take it, Etta. And look in the wardrobe. Please!"

Bart clamped his jaw shut as the two pairs of feet crept past the bed toward the large oak wardrobe.

"What if he's in here?" Etta whispered.

"Shoot him! Just shoot him right through the heart."

Bart scowled. Well, that was a fine attitude.

"The wardrobe's empty, Laurie."

"Etta, don't leave. Don't leave me here alone."

"Good Lord, honey, you're just trembling like an aspen tree in springtime. That man's not going to get in here. I've locked your window, and you can bolt the door after I'm gone. Put a chair under the knob if it'll make you feel better. Honest, I didn't expect you to be so lily-livered, Laurie. You've seen men in the restaurant who must've been outlaws. Remember the day that lawman came through on the train with the fellow who'd strangled a woman in New York? You volunteered to wait on that table!''

"Etta . . .'' Her breath sounded shallow. ''Etta . . . I know that man. I know the man who was down in the yard.''

"The detective?''

"No, the outlaw! The killer. I know him. Or at least I think I used to know him. I knew someone by that name.''

"Injun Jack?''

For a moment the room was silent. Then Laura Rose let out a ragged breath. ''Bart Kingsley,'' she whispered. ''I think I was married to him.''

"Etta, don't you dare tell them what I said about that outlaw!'' Laura Rose whispered as her small room quickly filled with wide-eyed young women, most of them still in their waitress uniforms. She could hardly believe her friend had spent the last few minutes shouting the news down the dormitory hall.

"There's a killer outside!'' Etta had hollered. ''Everyone come quick—a real live murderer!''

The bevy of excited, breathless girls scattered themselves over the pink quilt on Laura Rose's bed and perched on the two wobbly chairs. ''An outlaw?'' they babbled. ''Right outside in the backyard! How do you know? I thought I heard someone shouting. The sheriff's men! Sheriff Bowman is so handsome, don't you think? Laurie, tell us all about it!''

Laura Rose studied the sea of expectant faces around her. How young they all were, like buds not yet opened. Soft eyes, pink cheeks, tender skin, and hearts full of hope, these girls had come west with their dreams still tied up in neat little packages. They knew so little of real life. It would take time before they understood, as she did, that dreams were woven of a fragile, easily unraveled fabric.

"There was a shootout downtown,'' she explained simply. ''The outlaw got away, and the sheriff thinks his posse might have tracked his blood to the yard downstairs.''

"He's bleeding?'' someone said with a gasp.

"The sheriff peppered him!" Etta crowed. "He's a murderer, a horse thief, a cattle rustler—the worst kind of fellow. There's a price on his head in three states!"

"Jehoshaphat!"

"And he must be part Indian, too."

"A half-breed!"

"Oh, what difference does that make?" Rosie snapped, irritation and uncertainty bubbling inside her like a hot caldron. "Whoever the man is, the sheriff wants us to keep our windows and door locked tonight. So you girls had just better head down to your rooms and do as he says."

Their excitement now subdued, the young women began to slip out into the hallway. "A half-breed murderer," someone whispered. "Will you stay in my room with me tonight, Annie?"

"They'll have hunted him down by morning, girls," Etta announced as she ushered the rest of the women out of Rosie's room. "With a handful of bullets in him, how long can he last, anyway?"

After shutting the door with a thud, she hurried to the bed and plopped down beside Rosie. "I swear my heart is just about to pound right out of my chest! I could barely hold my tongue after what you told me, Laurie. You think you were married to the outlaw? Heavens to Betsy, tell me all about it this minute!"

"Etta," Rosie breathed, trying to still her own heartbeat, "I don't want to talk about that. It's all in the past."

"Oh, Laurie, how can you just up and say you were married to a murderous outlaw and then not tell me, your very best friend in all the world, the whole story?"

"I wasn't married to an outlaw, Etta."

"But you just said—"

"The Bart Kingsley I knew in Kansas City was no killer. He was just a boy. Seventeen. And I was only fifteen. It happened a long time ago. It probably wasn't even the same Bart."

"You got married when you were fifteen years old?"

Rosie studied Etta's incredulous face. Two bright pink spots lit up her cheeks, and her hair had escaped its roll to form a wildly frizzy blond spray across her forehead. Blue eyes sparkling, she licked her lips as if eager to sink her widely spaced teeth into this juicy tale.

"I said I don't want to talk about it," Rosie repeated, feeling hot and miserable and for some reason close to tears. She laced her fingers together and buried them in her lap as she found the flood of memories washing through her.

"Oh, Laurie, please tell me," Etta begged.

"But it's not like you think . . . not romantic and wonderful. It was all a terrible mistake."

"Was he mean to you? Was he cruel? Could you tell he was going to become a killer one day?"

"Of course not! Now that I've had time to think about it, I'm sure I couldn't have known the Bart Kingsley they're hunting for. At least . . . I don't suppose it could be the same man."

"But it *might* be," Etta stressed. "Think how scared you were when you first heard his name—same as yours. You were certain it was the same man."

With a sigh Rosie untangled her damp hands and smoothed down her black cotton skirt. Right now she wanted nothing more than to untie her soiled white apron, slip off her stockings, and soak her sore feet in a basin of water. She didn't want to think about her past. She didn't want to remember Bart . . . Bart Kingsley. . . .

"He was very handsome," she said softly, unable to look at Etta. "My Bart Kingsley had green eyes . . . strange green eyes with threads of gold. And straight hair, black as midnight. He was skinny—rail thin—but strong. Oh, my Bart was *so* strong. He was always kind, too. Very soft-spoken and polite to everyone. He loved animals. All kinds of stray dogs and cats from around the farm used to follow him wherever he went. He didn't mind a bit. When he sat down to rest from his work, there'd be one cat on his shoulder and another one on his lap."

"He worked on your father's farm?"

"In the stables. He was wonderful with horses, and he loved his work. He could break and train them with such gentleness. It was almost magical the way they obeyed him.

And you should have seen him ride. My Bart could do anything on a horse.''

''What do you think turned him into a cattle rustler and a murderer?''

''It couldn't be the same man,'' Laura Rose snapped. ''The more I think about it, I'm quite sure it couldn't be the same person. The Bart Kingsley I married never hurt anybody. He wouldn't even say a harsh word if someone was cruel to him.''

''If he was such a kind boy, why would anyone be cruel to him?''

''The other farmhands taunted him sometimes because . . . well, because he was part Indian. His real father was an Apache.''

''An Apache!'' Etta cried. ''But the sheriff just told us that outlaw they're hunting for goes by the name of Injun Jack. I'll bet it's him, Laurie. How many men could fit that description?''

''A lot,'' she shot back sounding more defiant than she felt.

''So you got married to him when you were fifteen. Did he kidnap you? Or did you actually keep house together . . . and everything?''

At the withering look Rosie gave her, Etta quickly changed her tack. ''Was it a church wedding? I just don't see how you could bring yourself to marry a savage Indian. Did you get a . . . a *divorce*? And why are you working as a Harvey Girl? Harvey Girls aren't supposed to be married—it's against regulations. You could get fired.''

''We were only married two weeks before my father found out about it,'' Rosie explained, eager to get rid of her curious friend and be left alone to sort out her thoughts. ''Pappy was furious. He and Bart had a long talk, and that was that. Bart left the farm that afternoon.''

''He *left* you? Just like that?''

''There was a short note.'' Her voice grew thin and wistful as she thought of the special place in the woods that had been their own secret bower. The place they had first touched, first kissed, first held each other. The place where she had found the note. "Bart wrote that he realized the whole thing had been a mistake and that we were both too young to know what we were doing. He said that he'd begun to realize it right away after we got married. He said . . . he said he didn't really love me after all, and I should forget about him. He told me just to consider that nothing had ever happened between us."

"Nothing?"

Rosie lifted her eyes. "*Nothing*. So there . . . I wasn't really married to him at all. Not in the Bible way. Our marriage didn't count. And that's the end of the story, so if you'd please just leave me alone now, Etta, I want to go to bed. I have the early shift tomorrow."

"You've got that blister, too," Etta added, her voice sympathetic as she gave her friend a quick hug.

Pulling out of the embrace, Rosie stood and smoothed the rumples in the pink quilt on her bed. There were probably lots of Bart Kingsleys in the world, she thought. Besides, she was about as far as she could be from Kansas City and the life she had shared with him. No one was going to find her in Raton, New Mexico. Not her pappy. Not the man who had been her husband for the past three years. And certainly not Bart Kingsley.

"Lock up now, Laurie," Etta said from the doorway. "I've put your shoes out in the hall. You'll see how much better everything will be in the morning."

Under the bed, Bart watched as Rosie bolted her door and set a chair under the knob. She really was afraid. Afraid of Bart, the murdering outlaw? Or afraid of *him*, the Bart who'd married her and then had run off and left her high and dry?

It wasn't going to matter much either way if he up and died right under her bed. Lord, how his side burned! He knew there were all kinds of important parts to his innards, like kidneys, lungs, a liver, and so on, but he didn't have much of an idea where they were located or what would happen if one of them got a bullet in it.

What he needed was to slide out from under this bed,

wash his side with some clean water, and try to take a look at the damage. He needed ointment and bandages. He needed a drink. His mouth felt like the inside of an old shoe.

But he couldn't risk scaring Rosie by edging out into the open. She'd put up a holler; then all those girls would come running, and that would be that. The sheriff would cart him off to jail, the Pinkerton agent would haul him back to Missouri, and the law would hang him high. A half-breed Indian who'd robbed trains and banks with the Jesse James gang wouldn't stand a chance in court.

Bart swallowed against the bitter gall of memory as he recalled the years he'd squandered. And now, after all this time, he'd found his Rosie again. So long ago she'd been the one bright spot in his life. Once again she was his only hope.

He studied her feet as she peeled away her stockings. There'd been a time when she had let him hold those feet, rub away their tiredness, kiss each tender pink toe. Her black dress puddled to the floor, only to be whisked up by her long-fingered hand. In moments a soft white ruffle-hemmed gown dropped over her ankles.

She began to hum, and Bart worked his shoulders across the hard floor in hope of a better look. The thought of dying this close to his Rosie without ever really seeing her again sent an ache through him. He tilted his head so the pink quilt covered just one eye and left the other exposed.

There she was, sitting on a chair, her back turned to him. She had let down her hair, a shining mane the color of milk-laced coffee. As he watched, almost breathless, she began to pull a brush from the dark chocolate roots to the sun-lightened sheet that fell well past her waist and over her hips. Long and straight as summer wheat, her hair was so thick Bart wondered how she ever managed to work the brush through it.

"Forty-eight, forty-nine, fifty," she counted in a soft, whispery voice. She swung the mass of hair across her shoulders and began to brush the other side. "Fifty-one, fifty-two, fifty-three . . ."

She had put her feet into a basin of water while she worked on her hair, and Bart could see those bare ankles again. He shut his eyes, swallowing the lump that rose in his throat at the memory of the first time he'd caught a glimpse of her bare legs. They had been down at the swimming hole where he and his stepbrothers liked to fool around. But this was an autumn afternoon, too chilly for splashing around butt-naked, and Bart's stepbrothers were nowhere in sight.

Rosie had agreed to meet him at the swimming hole, and he'd been waiting for her like a horse champing at the bit. When she finally came, she was all sunlight and laughter, her head tilted back and her brown eyes shining at him with all the love in the world. She had plopped down onto the grassy bank, unlaced her boots, and taken off her stockings. Then, while he held his breath, she had lifted the hem of her skirt and waded right into the icy pool.

Great heavens, how he had stared at those pale curvy legs and those thin little ankles. And like a boy of seventeen, out of control, he had felt himself grow hot and tight-chested and swollen up like a bull in rut. She hadn't known, of course. His prim little Rosie was the essence of innocence. From the water she had waved and beckoned him to join her. But he hadn't trusted himself even to stand up, for fear she'd notice the rigid bulge in his britches and run off like a scared lamb.

Under the bed, Bart suppressed the urge to chuckle at the way she had scolded and teased him for being lily-livered about wading in cold water. Then she had sauntered back onto the bank, pulled up her stockings, and laced her boots. They had sat together in silence for such a long time that Bart had begun to fear she really was mad at him about the wading. So he did the only thing he could think of—he grabbed her, kissed her right on the mouth, and then ran off lickety-split like the devil was after him.

"Ninety-eight, ninety-nine, one hundred," Rosie said now from the chair. She lifted her feet out of the water and dried them with a soft white cotton towel. Once more she checked the bolt on her door. She padded across the floor and tested the window latch. She crossed to the wardrobe. Breathing heavily, she jerked open the door. After a moment she shut it again and let out a sigh.

"Dear God," she said, falling to her knees beside the bed, "please watch over me tonight. I'm so scared. Don't let it be Bart out there, dear Lord. Please don't let that horrible killer be *my* Bart."

She was silent for a long time, and under the bed Bart held his breath. Eyes squeezed shut, he found himself praying along with her, as if he could will away the truth: *Don't let me be that Bart, dear Lord. Please don't let me be that killer they're after.*

"Dear God, help me to like Etta as much as she likes me," Rosie prayed. "Give me patience, and please don't let her blabber about the things I told her tonight. Bless Pappy, but don't let him find me—at least not until I've started teaching school and gotten myself established here in town with a house and enough money so I can keep Pappy from hauling me back to Kansas City. Bless Nana and Gramps. Bless Callie, James, and Bessie. Please don't let them worry about me, dear Lord. Bless . . . bless Dr. Lowell and help him to understand how hard I tried to be a good wife."

Bart's eyes flew open. Dr. Lowell's *wife*? His Rosie was someone else's wife? But she was married to Bart Kingsley! How could she be married to another man, too? She was Rosie—*his* Rosie! He felt as if he might black out.

"Forgive me, Father, for my sins. My many sins," she murmured in a voice so low Bart could hardly hear it. She sniffled. "And take care of Bart. Amen."

The bed creaked as she climbed into it. Lying underneath, Bart could feel the wooden slats sag just a little onto his chest. For a long time she lay sniffling under the pink quilt. She turned over on her side, then tossed to the other side. Since she hadn't blown out the lamp on her dressing table, Bart could see her shadow on the opposite wall as she twisted the coverlet in her hands.

He felt sick. Dizzy with loss of blood. Dry as a desert bone. And knotted up inside like a tangled vine. Rosie had married someone else! When? How long had it been? Why hadn't his half brother told him?

Some other man had touched and stroked and *used* his Rosie. Damn! But she had run away from the fellow, hadn't she? All the same, how could she have gone and married another man when she knew good and well she was married to him? Hell, he had the license to prove it! He wanted to shake it in front of her face and shout, Why? Why, Rosie?

But she could simply throw his question back at him. Why, Bart? Why did you run off and leave me? Why is the sheriff hunting you down? Why did you kill and rob and throw in with a gang of outlaws? Why, Bart?

Above him he could hear her breathing grow steady, her tossing ease, and the bed cease to groan. He touched his side and found that the blood had finally begun to clot over the ragged, burned hole in his skin. But he knew he had to get out from under the bed. He couldn't go on much longer without water.

Should he just slip out the window and hope the posse had given up hunting for the night? Should he leave Rosie sleeping, never to know the cause of the bloodstain on her pink hooked rug?

He ran a dry tongue over his lower lip. Quietly, ever so silently, he began to shrug his shoulders across the wood floor and out from under the bed. The pain in his side flared up instantly, movement relighting a fire inside his gut. Clenching his teeth, he scooted his hips clear of the iron bed, then dragged his legs out into the open.

The world swung like a bucking bronco as he rose onto his elbows. Dizzy, he shook his head, but the foggy clouds refused to roll back. Fighting to keep from grunting in pain, he rolled up onto his knees. His breath came in hoarse gasps.

There she was! His beautiful Rosie, sleeping like an innocent babe in her bed of pink. Her dark lashes fluttered with the movement of her eyes beneath their shut lids. Damn, she was prettier than ever. Rounded cheekbones, a straight, delicate nose, and full lips barely parted.

Grabbing his side, he tried to haul himself to his feet. The floor swayed out from under him, the lamplight tilting crazily. He groaned, caught the bed rail, felt the iron frame jolt at his weight. Rosie's eyes drifted open, focused, and jerked wide. She sucked in a breath just as he clamped his hand over her mouth.

"Don't scream, Rosie," he croaked as the bed seemed to turn on its side and his feet began to drift on cotton clouds. "Don't scream, Rosie, please. It's me. It's Bart."

Her skin and lips melted under his palm as black curtains blocked his vision. "Bart!" he heard her gasp. Then the curtains wrapped themselves over his head, and his feet floated out from under him. He tumbled like a falling oak tree across his Rosie's soft body.

*Two
. . . .

Faster than a cat with its tail afire, Rosie pulled herself out from under the deadweight of the unconscious man. She grabbed the oil lamp from the dressing table across the room and nearly doused its flame as she swung back to the bed to take a closer look.

Clamping a trembling hand over her open mouth to keep from crying out, she scanned the man's torn, bloodstained buckskin jacket and faded trousers. He wore low-heeled leather boots caked with dried mud, and his long, uncombed black hair fell in a tangle over his broad shoulders. He lay face down, his nose pressed into a rumple of pink quilt and clean white sheets. Every breath he took sounded like a dying train engine as the air struggled in and out of his lungs.

Gnawing at her lower lip, Rosie kept her eyes locked on the man while she fumbled in her bag for the pistol Etta had held earlier that evening. The cold metal felt reassuring as her fingers clamped around the gun, and she hugged it to her breast. On tiptoe, she edged around the bed, intending to get a look at the intruder's face.

Bart, he had called himself. And he had known her name—her real name! "Rosie," he had whispered. She was almost sure that was what he had said before he collapsed on top of her. But this shaggy bear draped over her bed couldn't possibly be the Bart she once had known. She lifted the lamp until its yellow glow spread down his entire frame.

No, she thought with relief, this certainly wasn't her Bart. Her Bart had been much shorter. This man more than filled up the bed. Her Bart had been as lanky as a young colt, but the stranger's weight made the metal bed frame sway down in the middle. The scrolled iron head- and footboards bent inward as if they, too, wanted to take a closer look.

Certainly her Bart would never have let his beautiful shiny hair get into such a state as this. Why, the tumbled mop couldn't have been washed in months! Two six-shooters and a fair arsenal of cartridges hung on belts at his waist. His buckskin jacket was spotted and stained as though the man never took it off. No wonder her room had smelled so odd! All evening this great malodorous hulk of an outlaw had been hiding under her bed.

Shivering, Rosie pointed the gun at the man's head. What on earth was she going to do with him? Her eyes traveled down his body again, and she had to marvel at the immense breadth of his back, solid as a granite cliff. His legs might have been a pair of thick pine trunks, smooth and straight beneath his worn leather britches. And his arms! Like great slabs of pure roping muscle, they strained against the confinement of the jacket. If he regained consciousness, she wouldn't stand a chance against such a brute!

The wisest thing she could do was just cock her pistol and shoot him if he so much as twitched.

"Okay, mister," she said, jamming the pistol against his skull. "Okay, I've got you now. Don't even think about trying anything on me, you hear?"

He didn't budge.

She began chewing on the inside of her cheek. What if he was dead? A dead man, right on her very own bed! Swallowing, she bent toward him to listen for the ragged breathing that had sounded so loud only moments before. She couldn't hear a thing. Dear Lord! Still holding the gun, she set the lamp on the floor and lowered her head to his back. Could a person make out a heartbeat through such a rock-solid hunk of flesh?

"Rosie . . ." The moan came from somewhere deep inside his chest.

Her head shot up, and she jabbed the pistol barrel back

into his temple. "D-don't move," she said. "I've got a gun pointed right at you."

She knew she should call Etta and the other girls, but her door was bolted. She had even put a chair under the knob! Maybe she could tie the man up with something and then run for help. She glanced around the room, spotting nothing more useful than her worn black stockings and the black silk ribbon she usually wore in her hair.

A muffled groan welled out of him.

"Well, go ahead and wake up the place," she said quickly. "Mrs. Jensen will come running from her room just down the hall, and then you can tangle with her."

"Rosie," he murmured again.

She watched his mouth form her name. Her real name.

"What?" she tried to answer, but no sound came out.

He turned his head so that his face emerged from under the quilt. "Rosie . . . help me."

Her hand shook as she placed her fingers on a hank of his black hair, then lifted it away from his face. "Oh, dear God in heaven, please no," she mouthed as she dropped the hair over his ear.

But there was no mistaking the sharp angle of the man's high cheekbone, the smooth golden plane of skin that sheered down from it, the straight line of his nose with its perfect petal-shaped nostrils. There was no way Rosie could deny that she had seen those sun-bronzed lips, curved just enough to tempt, yet outlined with firm masculine ridges that could so easily become taut and uncompromising. She recognized the man's chin, square and jutting in that proud way she had always admired. And she knew his jaw, corded with sinew and rigid with bone.

His face had changed, grown more masculine, more severe, more angular. Yet it was exactly the same—the color, the shape, the underlying tension. Then he opened his eyes. Green eyes, shot with golden threads, just as she remembered.

Rosie's breath hung in the dry arch of her throat. She dropped the gun carelessly to her side as she took a step backward. "Bart?" she breathed.

"Where are you, Rosie?" Grimacing with pain, he lifted his head. His emerald eyes flashed in the light. "Rosie?"

"Bart . . ."

"Rosie, I think I'm gonna die."

"You're bleeding." It was a stupid thing to say. Of course the man was bleeding! He was bleeding all over his jacket and her quilt and who knew what else? And he was Bart! *Her* Bart.

She knew for a fact that this dying man on her bed was Bart Kingsley. And yet she also knew for a fact that he *couldn't* be. This was a huge shaggy-maned outlaw with a bullet in his side. This man was wanted for murder.

"I got shot," he mumbled from the bed. "Rosie, I need water."

Unable to move, she stared down at him. She had always thought that if she ever saw Bart Kingsley again, she would slap his face just as hard as she could. She'd make him sorry for running off and leaving her the way he had. She had planned out a list of names she would call him. And she had imagined that if she'd owned a gun, she wouldn't think twice about shooting him right through the heart. He deserved it, coward that he was. Traitor. Chicken heart. Lily-liver. Yellow-belly.

But Rosie didn't slap Bart or shoot him or call him names. She didn't do a single thing she had thought of during all the sleepless nights. Instead she set the gun on a chair and forced herself to walk to the washstand. She poured a glass full of fresh, cool water, carried it to the bed, and knelt at his side.

"I gotta turn over," he whispered. "Help me, Rosie."

She didn't want to touch him. *No,* she couldn't.

"Please, Rosie," he whispered.

"Here, raise your head if you can." She slid her hands under his shoulders and heaved him over like a sack of flour, then sat on the bed and lifted his head into her lap.

"Damnation!" he muttered through clenched teeth as he grabbed at his side. "Hurts like hellfire."

"Hush your cussing and take a drink of this water."

His face contorting with pain, he forced himself up onto

his elbows and sipped at the water. He hadn't taken more than a mouthful before his shoulders fell heavily and his head thumped onto her thighs.

"Damn that Pinkerton son of a—"

Rosie clamped a hand over his mouth. "You stop swearing this minute, Bart Kingsley!" she snapped. "You're turning the air in my room blue. Bad enough you had to sneak in here and bleed all over everything, and smell like a pair of old leather shoes and scare me half out of my wits . . ."

But she couldn't finish. His warm hand slid down her arm and covered her fingers where they lay on his mouth. Against her palm, she could feel his lips moving, pressing lightly into her skin. She jerked her hand away and stuffed it under her bottom.

"What are you doing here, anyway?" she demanded in a harsh whisper, miffed that her heart was slamming against her ribs worse than it had been when he'd fallen on top of her. "This is Raton, New Mexico. Nobody passes through here but miners and homesteaders and such. And how did you come to climb in my window and hide under my bed?"

He didn't answer for a long time. His eyes had shut again, and he was drawing deep breaths. She could see that his chest was bare beneath the buckskin jacket. Smooth copper-hued skin roped with muscle formed a landscape of mesas and valleys, sharply defined and as solid as stone. Her gaze traveled to the ragged hole in the side of the jacket, the soft leather stained with red blood, the dark powder burn, the torn flesh.

"I came looking for you, Rosie," he said suddenly, and her eyes darted to his face. "I tracked you down."

"I don't see how. I changed my name."

The trace of a smile softened his mouth. "Kingsley."

She flushed. "Well, it was the first thing I could think of when the man asked me the day I applied for the Harvey job. I hadn't thought that far ahead, and . . ." She trailed off, feeling foolish.

"Laura Rose Kingsley."

"Jiminy Christmas!" She pushed his head off her lap and

stood over him with her arms crossed. "I have a good mind to call for the sheriff this minute."

"No, Rosie! They'll haul me back to Missouri and hang me."

"Hush, unless you want to wake up the whole dormitory." She stared at him for a moment. "Besides, the law should hang you if you've done all the wicked things Sheriff Bowman told Etta and me tonight. You rode with Jesse James. You robbed banks and trains, stole cattle and horses, killed people."

"I'm no stock rustler."

"Oh, *that's* a relief!" She could hardly believe he was lying on her bed and as much as admitting to murder. Brushing her hair from her shoulders, she scrunched up her toes. "You don't look a thing like you used to."

"It's been six years. I grew up."

"You grew up into an outlaw."

He closed his eyes and said nothing. What could he say? Rosie was right, of course. He'd grown up into a man, and he'd done every damned thing he was accused of, except for rustling cattle and horses. The James brothers had a policy against that. Their grievance wasn't with their fellow Missourians—down-home southern farmers and ranchers like them. No, Jesse, Frank, and the others had set their sights on northern institutions such as banks and trains.

In a way, Frank had once explained to Bart, he and Jesse were just continuing to fight the war the way they knew how. They had been guerrillas, taught to raid by William Clarke "Charley" Quantrill and "Bloody Bill" Anderson, under whom they had served until the end of the war.

But when most of the Confederate guerrillas returned to their homes and civilian labors, the James brothers and their pals, the Youngers, had elected to continue raiding. Footloose wanderers had joined up along the way, men who had come and gone as part of the gang during its sixteen-year reign of terror across the Midwest.

Bart clenched his jaw. Oh, he had known every one of the fringe members of the James-Younger gang: Clell Miller, Bill Chadwell, Charlie Pitts, Bud McDaniels—all of them dead now, killed by lawmen. Andy McGuire, Arch Clements, Dick Burns—all lynched. And others who were serving time in prison or, like him, hoping to escape the law: Bill Ryan, Tucker Basham, Dick Liddil, Clarence Hite, Hobby Kerry, Jack Kean.

His pals, those men had been. They had accepted the half-breed homeless boy when no one else would. They made him part of their group, fed him, boarded down with him at night, saw to it that he had clothes and boots . . . and guns. They laughed at his jokes, listened to his stories, taught him to shoot. Together they spent hours playing checkers, drinking whiskey, swimming in the river, hunting deer and squirrels. Oh, they had a fine time, Bart and the boys.

Until the day that was burned into his memory like none other: October 7, 1879. Glendale, Missouri. The Chicago & Alton train.

Bart swallowed and opened his eyes, knowing that light always erased the haunting blackness of his past. And there was his Rosie, standing in a circle of golden light, gazing down on him with her velvet brown eyes.

"Rosie," he whispered, hardly able to believe he was really looking at this woman who had grown more beautiful than ever. Maturity had sculpted her face into a masterpiece of porcelain skin, delicate cheekbones, a fine straight nose, and lips the color of roses. Rosie, his prim and proper educated high-society lady. Rosie, the tree-climbing, pond-wading, horse-riding love of his youth. His Rosie.

"You're going to have to leave," she announced, shattering his reverie. "I'll help you to the window."

But she didn't move toward him, and he couldn't stop staring at her. Had her hair always been that long? That shiny and thick? Why couldn't he remember the old Rosie as easily as she seemed to remember the old Bart?

"Well . . . it's getting very late, and I have to work the breakfast shift tomorrow."

He placed a hand over his side. "If I leave, the detective will find me."

"I guess he will."

"He'll take me back to Missouri."

"I reckon you're right."

"But I won't get a fair trial. Not a half-breed like me."
Her brown eyes darted to his face. "Even if you did, would you be cleared?"

"I might be."

"But you robbed trains."

"It was Jesse's idea. His plan, his guns, his horses. I went along for the ride. Just to help out."

Her eyes told him his explanation wasn't good enough. "And you killed people."

"People who were trying to kill me first."

"Oh, Bart, how could you?" Her voice sounded loud in the quiet night, and she quickly lowered it. "How could you stand there and shoot somebody? You just pulled the trigger and shot people dead, ending all their hopes and dreams. You took away everything! Memories, promises—"

"Rosie!" He grabbed her arm and jerked it with such strength that she stumbled forward. "Rosie, let me stay here tonight. Just this one night. I promise I'll leave tomorrow."

"Great stars, you can't stay in my room! What if someone walked in on you? Etta almost always comes to fetch me in the morning. And who knows what Mrs. Jensen does all day? I suspect she creeps in and out of our rooms looking for infractions of her precious rules. If she saw you, she'd drop over in a dead faint. Then I'd lose my job lickety-split!"

"Please, Rosie." His hand slipped from her wrist to her fingers. "Don't turn me out."

If he had said anything else, she would have forced him to the window at gunpoint and made him climb right out into the cold. But how could she turn him out? The Bart Kingsley she knew had been turned out far too often in his life—taunted by the farm boys; beaten, whipped, and burned by his stepfather; neglected by his own mother. He'd worn ragged shirts and trousers, and boots that had pinched his toes and rubbed blisters on his heels. In the winter he'd had no coat. In the summer he'd had no hat. The school-marm had refused to allow him in her class. The preacher had made him sit outside on the church steps to hear the sermon.

No, Rosie knew she couldn't turn him out. Not tonight. Even if he had become a train robber and a killer. Even when he had a price on his head. Even if it meant losing her job.

"All right," she said. "But in the morning I expect you to skedaddle."

"Sure thing, Rosie."

Once the decision had been made, there was nothing left but to treat the awful hole in his side that had been staring at her. She went to her trunk, lifted the heavy lid, and pulled out the bag of pills, lotions, and cures she had taken from the chest in her home in Kansas City.

Dr. Lowell—though he had been her husband for three years, she had never gotten past calling him by his formal title—had often left samples of patent remedies lying around after salesmen brought them to the office in town where he treated most of his patients. Rosie had decided the medicines might be of some use to her in Raton. When she fled, she hadn't even known if the town would have a doctor.

"You'd better take one of these liver pills," she said, stepping to the bedside. "I suppose that bullet could be stuck in your liver."

"You never know." With a slight grin, Bart lifted his head and swallowed the tiny brown pill.

"Now a teaspoon of Dr. Hathaway's Blood Builder. It's guaranteed to destroy all poisons in the blood, purify the body, and invigorate the system," she read from the box.

He submitted to a spoonful of the vile stuff. "Where did you get all this, Rosie?"

She shrugged, her cheeks growing slightly pink. "You might as well take some cod-liver oil, too."

"Are you trying to kill me after all?" He swallowed and nearly gagged. "I'll be damned if that doesn't taste like a hell of a—"

"Hush your swearing, Bart. You never used to cuss."

He watched her bend over him as she worked at the buttons on his jacket. No, he hadn't always cussed. There had been a time when he had hardly said a word, keeping his frustration, anger, and rage locked inside him. But if he hadn't allowed himself to swear, neither had he permitted the good words inside to come out. Now all he could think about was how much he wanted to tell Rosie what it meant to see her again. How beautiful she looked. How black the years without her had been. How soft her long hair was as it brushed against his hand.

"Jiminy," she whispered. "You're going to need a doctor for this."

"No, I can't go to a doctor."

"Well, it's an awful mess, and I don't know the first thing about nursing."

"You still thinking about being a teacher, Rosie?"

She glanced at him, her eyes giving him the answer. "I've got to get this jacket off. I'll fetch my scissors."

"Don't cut it!" He grabbed a handful of nightgown to stop her. When she swung around, the cloth flattened against her chest. He noticed the round swell of her breasts, their taut peaks jutting up in the chilly air, and he forced his eyes to her face. "This jacket is all I've got, Rosie."

"You don't even have a shirt?"

He shook his head. "I'll work this thing off, just give me a minute." Releasing her gown, he began to shrug his shoulders and arms out of the warm buckskin sleeves.

She watched him for a moment, then knelt to grapple with the soft leather. His face was beaded with perspiration from the effort, and she hurried to pull away the garment. This close to him, she could see the clearly defined hard muscle that surrounded his flat red-brown nipples. His chest was hairless, smooth, and coppery. His pulse quivered in the hollow of his throat, and his Adam's apple moved up and down as he struggled out of the jacket.

The scent of woodsmoke and leather clung to his skin, making Rosie's nostrils flare. *That raw, wild scent*, she thought. She wished it were an unpleasant sensation, but she couldn't deny that the smell of this man's flesh stirred something visceral deep inside her. Though she tried to keep her fingers from touching his flesh, the effort was hopeless. She ended up wrestling with his big shoulders and fighting his long arms out of the sleeves.

"There!" she said, letting out a breath as he collapsed back onto her pillow. "When's the last time you took this off? Looks like it's almost part of you, Bart."

With two fingers she carried the bloody jacket across the room and dumped it into a basket in the corner. It needed a good washing with lye soap, and the hole ought to be mended. Of course, there wouldn't be time for all that, with Bart leaving first thing in the morning.

She glanced over her shoulder to find him breathing deeply, his eyes shut and his huge chest filling her narrow bed from one side to the other. Heavens, when did he get to be so big? She poured her white washbasin full of water and dumped in a palmful of salt for good measure. It would sting, of course, but the salt would cleanse the wound better than anything else she had on hand.

Heaving the basin into her arms, she trudged across the floor and once again sat beside him on the bed. His green eyes opened, reminding her that even though he didn't look like her Bart or act like her Bart, he *was* her Bart.

"The water's cold," she informed him, keeping her eyes focused steadily on the bullet hole in his side. "And it's salty. Now bite your tongue and don't you dare start cussing at me, or I'll let you clean up this mess yourself."

She wrung out a cotton towel and covered the wound. He flinched but said nothing. Dipping the cloth in the water, she again blotted his skin. *Dear Lord*, she breathed in silence as she studied the damage, *don't let him die on me. Much as I've wanted to kill this man at times, please keep him alive till morning.*

"How's it look?" he grunted.

"Terrible. It's positively a perfect round hole right in your side."

"Can you feel the bullet?"

"I'm not sticking my finger down in you!"

"All right, all right, Rosie-girl."

"Jiminy," she muttered, dabbing at the fresh flow of blood.

"Will you at least sew me up?"

She lifted her head. "Are you crazy? All I've got is my sewing needle and thread. Besides, what if the bullet decides to come out on its own?"

"Rosie, it's not coming out unless someone takes it out. And if you don't sew up that hole, I'm liable to bleed to death. I reckon if you'd do that for me, I wouldn't ever ask another thing of you."

"Why should I trust a murdering outlaw?" she asked, rising to fetch her sewing basket.

"Especially one who ran off and left a girl two weeks after he married her," Bart finished, because he knew that was what she was thinking.

"We never were married," she said softly as she looked through her box. "You said so yourself."

"You found the note?"

"Of course I did." She selected a spool of fine silk thread and her tiniest needle. Her fingers were shaking so badly she didn't know how she was ever going to thread the needle, let alone stitch up Bart's skin. She wished he hadn't brought up their youthful lark. Long ago she had pushed the memory of that awful day into the back of her mind.

Huddling by the lamp, she managed to push the thread through the needle's eye and tie one end in a knot. If only he hadn't tracked her down. If only he hadn't crawled into her bedroom all shot up and bleeding and in need of her help. Now she was stuck with him come hell or high water. But only until morning.

"It's going to hurt," she said as she set the sewing box on her bedside table, then placed the lamp high on the box.

Before she could begin, he caught her hand and held it to his chest. "Rosie," he whispered.

"What?" She looked into his green eyes, her breath unsteady.

''Thank you, Rosie-girl.''

She dropped her gaze. ''You won't be thanking me in a minute.''

Why couldn't she make herself look at him as easily as he looked at her? she fretted. He was practically devouring her with those emerald eyes of his. And why did the sight of his face draw her back through time with a haunting ache that wouldn't go away in spite of everything she knew about him? Biting her bottom lip, she bent over his stomach and squeezed the edges of the raw wound. Oh, Lord.

She had to concentrate on tending the wound. What if this was a mistake? What if bullet holes needed to breathe or something? On the other hand, look how much blood he was losing. She took the first stitch, then blotted his skin. Concentrating, she took the second stitch. In the middle of the third stitch, she felt his hand slide into her hair.

She glanced sideways. Eyes squeezed shut, he had arched his neck backward, and his face pointed at the ceiling. His hand had closed over a hank of her hair and she could feel him working it between his fingers.

Running a dry tongue over her lips, she focused on the wound again. If he needed something to hold on to, how could she deny him? But his arm felt so hot, burning hot as it rested across her shoulder. And the way his fingers were sifting through her hair made every nerve in her scalp tingle.

She poked the needle into his skin. He jerked. A fourth stitch. A fifth. She wiped away the blood with a towel. It didn't seem like such a large hole now that she had sewn it up so neatly. Maybe she should take one more stitch, just for good measure. She worked in the final loop of thread, knotted it, and looked for her scissors. Spotting them on the chair at the other side of the room, she leaned over and took the end of the thread in her teeth as she always did at the end of her darning.

But the moment she severed the silk, his hand clamped down on her ear, pressing her head hard into his belly. ''Bart!'' she gasped.

"Rosie, we *were* married," he murmured. "We were."

She stared at his leather trousers, the beltless loops, the swell beneath the buttons of his fly. His heartbeat drummed in her ear, and she could feel the rise and fall of every breath he took.

"You were my Rosie," he whispered, relaxing the hand that had covered her head. His fingers slid through the hair at her temple. "Once upon a time you were my Rosie-girl."

She closed her eyes, fighting tears. His fingertips stroked across the down on her cheek, feathering her skin with the lightest touches she had ever felt. Something warm and curling slid into the bottom of her stomach and began to throb ever so faintly. One of his fingers touched the arch of her eyebrow and smoothed her soft hair. Another found her eyelid and rested lightly there a moment before fanning down to her lashes and cheek.

"Remember, Rosie, how you shinnied down the oak tree by your bedroom window that night," he was saying, his voice almost inaudible, "and we hustled ourselves over to Reverend Russell's place? You had on a white dress, and you'd pinned bunches of lilacs and rosebuds in your hair. The reverend was drunk, as usual, but we hardly noticed because we were so scared and excited to finally be getting married—"

"No!" She jerked her head up and rubbed a knuckle under one eye. "That was all just a child's game. We were kids. You said so yourself."

Pushing away from the bed, she fumbled her needle and thread into the sewing box and hauled the pink-tinted water back to the washstand. Six years ago she had convinced herself that she had never married Bart Kingsley. She'd never told a soul. Her pappy—the only one who did know—had never ever mentioned Bart's name again.

The disaster had been put away like one of Pappy's old university textbooks. Hidden on a back shelf. Forgotten. Denied. Denied so completely that Pappy had arranged for Rosie to marry Dr. William Lowell. Denied so totally that she had silently submitted, as she always did, to Pappy's will. Denied so thoroughly, that every night when she lay in Dr. Lowell's bed in his big fancy house, she didn't give Bart Kingsley a thought.

She didn't remember the way he had held her hand, gently weaving his fingers through hers. She didn't remember the way he had touched her face, his green eyes memorizing her every feature as though it were precious beyond belief. She didn't remember his mouth moving against hers, his lips exploring and his breath ragged.

"Rosie," he said from the bed. She straightened and knotted her fingers against her stomach while he spoke. "I don't play games, Rosie. You know I never have."

"All I know is that you'd better get some rest if you're going to have enough strength to climb out that window in the morning." She rinsed her hands in clean water, then went to the wardrobe for a blanket. "I guess I'll sleep on the floor. You've made a mess of my sheets anyway."

Standing by the wardrobe, she suddenly decided to tear up an old petticoat she had brought from Kansas City. The strips of clean white fabric would make a good bandage for him. As she ripped the cloth, she determined that she simply wasn't going to listen to the man anymore or think about anything he said. He was part of her past, her long-forgotten past, and come sunup he would be back in the past where he belonged.

"You're still bleeding a little, so I'm going to put this around you," she said, sounding more matter-of-fact than she felt. "Seems silly to sew you all up and stop the bleeding when a doctor is going to have to cut you open again soon to take out that bullet."

"I reckon you've done me such a good turn I won't even need to see a doctor, Rosie."

She laid the bandages across his stomach. "You can't go around with a bullet inside you for the rest of your life."

"I sure as hell can." At the arch look she flashed his way, he felt himself grow quickly uncomfortable. "What I mean to say is, most of the men I know have been shot so full of holes you'd think they'd leak every time they took a drink.

They usually carry a few lead souvenirs around inside them just to make their stories ring true.''

"I don't believe you. Why, a bullet would fester and such, wouldn't it?''

As she smoothed the cloth bandage over his skin and behind his back, it was all he could do to keep from taking her shoulders and pulling her down against him. Just the touch of her lips against his would cure any ill he could ever have. As she worked at tying the fabric, her long straight hair draped over her shoulders like a cape, the ends of it cool against the bare skin of his stomach.

"That's a fine bunch of friends you have, Bart,'' she was saying as her fingers straightened the edges of the bandage. "Men with bullets lodged inside them. Great ghosts, who ever heard of such a thing?''

"Cole Younger's been wounded upwards of twenty times in his life. He reckons he's got a good fifteen bullets buried in him.''

"Cole Younger!'' she snapped, straightening suddenly. "So you really are pals with those outlaws, just like the sheriff said. Oh, Bart, how *could* you?''

"Rosie, it's not like you think,'' he said, reaching for her. But she had already swung away from him. After marching to the wardrobe, she bundled a blanket against her chest. Beside the bed, she knelt to pull her pink hooked rug into the center of the room. Bart waited for the gasp of horror when she saw the blood-soaked wool. Sure enough, a moment later she nearly woke the whole dormitory.

"Jiminy Christmas!'' she cried. "Bart Kingsley, you have ruined my rug! And I brought it all the way from Kansas City on the train because it was the only thing I ever liked out of that whole ugly house my husband bought—''

Catching herself, she clamped a hand over her mouth and stared at Bart. He watched, aching inside from a hurt far worse than the wound of a bullet.

"We *weren't* married, Bart,'' she said in a hushed voice, as if speaking the words could make them true. "We never were married, you and I . . . were we, Bart?''

When he didn't answer her, she spread her blanket on the

bare wood floor. Then she curled up against herself and pulled what was left of the cover over her body. Bart studied her small, rounded form for a moment, then lowered his head to the pillow. In the darkness he could hear her crying.

*Three

. . . .

If Rosie thought Bart would hop right out her window at
the first light of dawn, she was badly mistaken. She woke to
find him sprawled half on and half off her bed, a sheen of
feverish perspiration covering his naked chest. His long
arms and legs writhed in the agony of a dream from which
she could not seem to wake him, though she urgently
whispered his name again and again. Finally, afraid his
moans were going to rouse curiosity, she put her hand on his
damp shoulder and shook him.

"Bart, wake up!" she pleaded. When he didn't budge,
she began to worry that he had slipped into unconsciousness. She pushed at him again, more firmly this time.
"Bart!"

At once he sat straight up and grabbed her arms in a
powerful, blood-stopping grip. "Rosie, don't let them get
me!" His wild green eyes were filled with some unnamed
terror. "Don't let them . . . Don't let . . ." He winced at
a sudden pain, then sagged back onto the bed. "Ah, hell.
Damn that good-for-nothing sheriff—"

"Hush!" Rosie ordered. She glanced at the door, wondering how thin the wood-frame walls in the two-story
Harvey House actually were. Could the voice of a feverish
man carry from room to room? She brushed her hair back
from her face and heaved a sigh as she studied the massive
figure on the bed. If cussing wasn't such a terrible sin, she'd
be tempted herself. What on earth was she going to do with
this hulking giant?

Now, in the light of day, it seemed utterly foolish of her

not to have sent for Sheriff Bowman at once. It wouldn't be long before someone would either hear—or smell—the intruder. Anyone with half a brain would march right down the hall to Mrs. Jensen's suite and confess the whole thing. The truth of the matter was, Rosie mused, she didn't owe Bart Kingsley one iota of kindness. He had wooed her, misled her, tricked her, abandoned her, and now he'd endangered the one sure thing in life—her job as a Harvey Girl.

"Rosie?" he was murmuring. "Rosie?"

She chewed on her lip. He tossed his head from side to side, his long black hair a tangle on the white pillow. She realized with surprise that he'd never even taken off his boots the night before. But if she pulled them off, that would mean she intended to let him stay. She certainly *didn't* want him to stay!

On the other hand, he was far too ill to climb out a window and make his way to safety. If she called the sheriff, everyone would wonder why she had let the outlaw sleep in her bed all night, for her bloody sheets would bear witness to the fact that he hadn't been hiding under her bed forever.

"Oh, dear," she whispered to herself. Hurrying to the small table that served as both vanity and writing desk, she checked the gold pocket watch she had taken from Dr. Lowell's jewelry chest the morning she left Kansas City. Six-thirty! The uniform inspection bell would ring in a mere half hour. Then she would have to rush downstairs to eat breakfast and prepare the dining room for the eight o'clock breakfast train. Could she just go off and leave a feverish, groaning man in her bed?

Pressing her fingertips against her puffy, tear-swollen eyelids, she made her decision. She'd let him stay through the first shift; then she'd return to her room before the lunch trains came through. Since she would be free until the one o'clock shift, there would be time to check in on Bart. If he was the slightest bit better, she would insist that he leave.

"Rosie?"

"What?" she shot back almost before he'd finished

saying her name. She swung around to find him staring at her, his green eyes bright with fever.

"Rosie, I promised I'd go this morning," he said softly. "I'll need my jacket."

Her shoulders sagged. "Oh, Bart, just stay where you are for the time being. You're in no shape to go anywhere."

"No, Rosie. I made you a promise." He heaved his legs over the side of the bed and struggled to lift his shoulders. For a moment he sat hunched over, staring at the floor and breathing heavily. Then he hauled himself to his feet.

Rosie watched him sway like a great tree about to topple at the blows of a woodsman's ax. *He means to do it*, she thought. *He actually means to keep his promise to me.* One of his long legs started to crumple, but he grabbed the iron footboard and forced himself upright again. His guns and cartridge belts seemed to weigh him down as he shuffled across the room toward the basket where she'd thrown his jacket. During the night the bandage she'd wrapped around him had become stained with a dark red blotch that revealed the inadequacies of her medical skills.

He propped one big brown hand on the windowsill and bent to pick up the torn buckskin. "Rosie," he said, turning to her, "I'm sorry. Sorry I messed up your sheets and your rug. Sorry about when we were kids and how much I hurt you back then. I'm sorry I made you cry last night—"

"Oh, for Pete's sake, Bart!" She dashed across the room and jerked the jacket out of his hands. "You're delirious, plain and simple. You're just rambling on and on like an addled parrot. Now get back to bed this instant. I'll check on you after the breakfast shift."

"No, Rosie!"

"Damn it, Bart, let go of that windowsill and grab on to me before you fall down with a crash and bring Mrs. Jensen running into my room."

Aware that she had let an impious word slip out of her mouth, Rosie clenched her teeth and heaved Bart against her. *Well, he drove me to it*, she thought. *He and all his ridiculous apologies.* If he hadn't been so sick, she'd have given him what-for. She didn't need anyone's apologies for the way her life had turned out. She'd made her own choices and now she would live with them.

"Get in this bed," she snapped, "and don't get up until I tell you to. You're going to make me late for inspection, and then where will I be?"

Working quickly, she tugged off his boots and set them on the floor. My, but they needed a good airing-out and polishing. She pulled the sheets and blankets over his chest and tucked the edges under the mattress.

"Now rest!" she ordered, thinking that he looked more like a big papoose than a wounded outlaw.

Brushing her hands together, she dashed to the washstand and grabbed the basin of water she had used to clean his wound the night before. She hurried to the window, unlocked it, and tossed the pinkish water to the ground, where it landed on the spring-green grass with a noisy splash.

"Mornin', Laurie!" Etta called from a window down the way where she was tossing out her own wash water.

Rosie waved and ducked back inside, her heart thumping. Leaving the window open to freshen the room, she didn't allow herself the usual peaceful interlude during which she loved to gaze out over the little town of Raton and the encircling range of high, snow-capped mesas she had grown to love.

Instead, she quickly scrubbed her face, hands, and arms with a bar of Ivory soap and a thick cloth. She used the wardrobe door to screen herself from Bart while she tore off her nightgown, hung it on a hook, and dressed in her uniform. Black stockings. Chemise. Corset—oh, she had to hurry with the irritating laces! Black skirt. Black shirtwaist buttoned up to the neck.

Rushing to the hook by the door, she grabbed a freshly starched white apron and tied it around her waist. In a trice, she buttoned the white bib to her breast, arranged her collar, and pinned on her badge and number: Laura Kingsley—#2. But there wasn't time to appreciate the fact that in two short months she had worked her way almost up to head waitress.

Her shoes were outside the room! Jerking the chair out from under the knob, she opened the door just a slit.

"Mornin', Laurie!" Annie called as she hurried down the hall to empty her chamber pot. "Sleep well?"

"Sure," Rosie answered, grabbing her shoes and shutting the door with a bang. She was never going to get away with letting Bart stay in her room! People were everywhere.

Trembling, she laced her tight boots, then set to work on her hair. A quick flourish of brush and comb tamed the long brown tresses into a smooth, straight sheet. Bending over at the waist, she tied a ribbon around the hank to form a long tail that dragged on the floor. Straightening, she wound the tail into a thick glossy knot and pinned it to the top of her head.

Oh, there was a time when she had taken pride in the fluffy fringe of fashionable curls that had graced her forehead, Rosie thought as she glanced in the small mirror over the table. She once had a lady's maid who arranged her hair and pinned on one of the innumerable feathered, flowery hats Rosie had always worn while calling on ladies of her social circle. She used to don gowns of silk and velvet, slippers and gloves of soft kid, and necklaces and bracelets that sparkled with diamonds, emeralds, rubies. But now Rosie knew she wouldn't trade her severe black and white Harvey Girl uniform for all the lace, ruffles, taffeta, and ribbons in Kansas City.

"Uniform inspection!" The voice in the hall sounded so close that Rosie nearly jumped out of her skin. A bell rang, followed by the sounds of doors opening and shutting.

Breathless, she flew across the room to the bed where Bart lay. He was staring at her, his eyes taking in every move she made. "Now, don't do anything foolish!" she whispered, smoothing the sheet over his chest as though he were a sick child and not a gunslinger. "I'll be back around mid-morning after the last breakfast train. I'll try to bring you something to eat. Just stay in bed and rest, you hear?"

He caught her hand and brought it to his lips, but she jerked away and fairly scorched across the room to her door. Opening it just a wedge, she slipped out into the hall and shut it quickly behind her.

* * *

During her breakfast with the rest of the Harvey establishment, Rosie was in a dither just waiting for Mrs. Jensen to come storming into the kitchen screaming about the outlaw in Laura Kingsley's room. Fortunately Rosie knew the coming morning's work would be demanding. She would have neither the time to stop and think about what she'd done nor the energy to stew over dire possibilities.

In charge of coffee preparation, Rosie hurried out of the kitchen to fill the large silver-plated urns with fresh water the train had brought in the night before. Fred Harvey insisted on fresh water in all his establishments. Everything had to be done to exact measurements, for Harvey coffee was famous all along the Santa Fe railroad line. When the aromatic coffee was boiling hot, Rosie went to her work station—a grouping of four tables that were her sole responsibility.

Though she had done exactly the same thing after the last customer left the night before, she ran a damp cloth over each of the tables, checked the supply of salt, pepper, sugar, and jellies, and dusted every single chair.

"Did you sleep okay last night?" Etta called from her own station by the long twelve-paned windows that faced the platform and rails. "I was sure worried about you, Laurie."

"You worry too much, Etta," she responded, attempting her usual cheerful demeanor. Loaded down with plates, cups, saucers, and silverware, she began to set her tables.

"I guess that outlaw will be long gone by now," Etta continued.

"If he's smart he will." Rosie folded the heavy white linen napkins one by one. "Of course, if he was smart, he never would have gotten himself shot in the first place."

"We'll find out when Mr. Adams comes in for breakfast. That fellow always knows what's going on in town."

Charles Adams, the proprietor and editor of *The Raton Comet*, loved to boast that his eight-page weekly newspaper never missed any local story worthy of coverage. Rosie pictured the shock he would have if he knew that the scoop of the year lay just overhead in Room Seven.

"Attention! We've got twenty-two omelets coming in on the eight-o'clock train," Tom Gable announced from the kitchen. As the manager of the Raton Harvey House, he commanded total respect. Every girl instantly stopped her work to listen as he informed them of the food order that had been wired ahead from the train. "There'll be fourteen hotcakes and six biscuits and gravy. Thirty-three coffees and nine milks."

Rosie smiled for the first time that morning at Mr. Gable's wording. She sometimes wondered if he thought of the passengers not as people but as walking omelets and hotcakes. On the other hand, he was stringent about his staff treating the passengers with utmost courtesy, almost as though they were royalty.

"We have fresh orange juice this morning," Mr. Gable continued. "The first course will consist of a fruit plate. Second course will be Fred Harvey's famous cinnamon rolls. Third course will consist of diners' orders. Oatmeal is available, if desired. Remember, there will be a large number of local patrons joining us for breakfast. Now back to work. The first train is scheduled to arrive in seven minutes."

With a collective gasp, the five Harvey Girls, the head waitress, the cashier, and the desk clerk rushed to complete their preparations. Rosie knew that back in the kitchen, the new German chef, the cook, the baker, and all the baker's helpers would be frantically squeezing orange juice, turning omelets, stirring gravy, and checking the ovens for the biscuits and cinnamon rolls.

As tired as she was at the end of each day, Rosie loved her work as a Harvey Girl. Respected, protected, well paid, she couldn't have found a better situation in which to make a new life for herself. But thanks to the encroachment of her past, she was also aware that at any moment everything could come tumbling down.

A blast of steam followed by a deafening *whooo* set the whole staff scrambling to their positions. In moments the platform and the dining room floor began to shake. Glasses rattled. Cups shook. Spoons tinkled against knives. Rosie turned to the row of long windows, her heart pounding as it always did with the arrival of the first train.

Hisss. Steam billowed across the platform as the enormous black and silver engine of the Atchison, Topeka and Santa Fe train rolled into the depot. The brakeman set the brakes, and the train squealed in protest. Chunks of red-hot coal spilled from the firebox. Railway men rushed to stomp them out. The smell of oil, smoke, and boiling water enveloped the Harvey House.

Like wraiths, the passengers descended through the steam onto the platform. Their hats askew and coats not quite settled, they stretched, waved, and stared at the blue sky after the long ride. Children scampered to the rails to inspect the big engine. Tails wagging, a pair of dogs known to the whole town as Tom and Griff trotted through the crowd. Then one of the busboys stepped into the crowd and raised his large brass gong.

"Breakfast is served," he called, giving the gong a hard whack with a stick. "Breakfast is served!"

Rosie stood silently, hands behind her back, as the passengers walked into the dining room and took their seats. The moment one table had been settled, she started around it.

"What do you care to drink this morning?" she asked. "We have coffee, milk, or orange juice."

As each patron stated a selection, Rosie quickly arranged the cup according to the code she had been taught. The cup on the right side of the saucer indicated coffee, upside down and tilted against the saucer signaled orange juice, and upside down and away from the saucer meant milk.

Annie followed Rosie from table to table pouring the selected beverages without saying a word. The customers, of course, were totally mystified as to how she knew exactly what they had requested. But this was all part of the Fred Harvey mystique, and it made his employees feel proud to carry this air of magic about them as they served.

While the diners were munching on apple wedges,

oranges, and grapes, Rosie went around her station taking orders for omelets, hotcakes, and biscuits and gravy. The moment each person had finished the first course, a busboy arrived to sweep away all used plates and silverware. Instantly Rosie placed a thick, steaming cinnamon roll at the empty place. The dining room filled with the spicy-sweet aroma that seemed to rouse the passengers even more effectively than the famous Harvey coffee did.

When the cinnamon rolls were all consumed, Rosie arrived with trays of hearty breakfast fare. Standing motionless, hands behind her back and the required smile on her face, she kept her eyes constantly roving her station for the slightest possible indication that she was needed by a diner.

On most mornings she was so absorbed in her work that she never gave anything outside it a second thought. But knowing Bart lay upstairs in her bed, Rosie found her concentration wandering. What if he took it into his head to try to climb out the window? What if he lost his balance and *fell* out?

She glanced uneasily through the long side windows, suddenly fully aware of the impossible situation she was in. Outside the front of the red board-and-batten Harvey House lay a long porch, a row of widely spaced trees, and the depot and train tracks. Behind the building was the small fenced private yard for the House's female employees, and beyond that stretched the town of Raton. Now that Rosie thought about it, how on earth could Bart ever hope to escape in broad daylight? He'd be spotted immediately.

But how could he stay in her room for the rest of the day? Someone would find out for sure! And what if his fever grew worse? She lifted her head, listening for thumps, bumps, and moans.

The silence was almost worse than the anticipation of noise. What if Bart had *died*?

She wrung her clasped hands behind her skirt. If Bart died, she would never have the chance to chew him out the way she'd always intended. On the other hand, she'd never learn exactly why he had followed her all the way from Kansas City. She would never know for sure how he had fallen in with Jesse James and his gang. She'd never be able to tell him how strange it felt to see him again . . . how she had never really thought she would . . . how miserable her life had been after he went away . . . how awful her marriage to Dr. Lowell had made her feel . . .

"All aboard!" The bellow jerked Rosie back to reality. Her passengers were hurrying out of the dining room, having left the table littered with coins that lay among the debris of their breakfast. A mere thirty minutes after the train had pulled into the depot, it chugged to life again and eased away.

The moment the train was out of sight, Mr. Gable bounded into the dining room. "We've got sixteen omelets coming in on the eight forty-five!" he called. "Twelve hotcakes and eleven biscuits and gravy."

Rosie had no choice but to scramble to clear her station and prepare for the next breakfast train. There was no time for worry, no time for weighing consequences, and no time for desire.

Somewhere along about ten o'clock, Bart felt his fever break. Bathed in sweat, his body suddenly began to cool. The hammering in his head eased. The room stopped spinning.

He lay still for a while, aware that his side still felt like hell and his mouth was as parched as a Kansas dust storm. He could hear the sounds of clinking glasses, laughter, and chatter coming from the dining room below. The unbearably tantalizing aromas of cinnamon, bacon, and freshly brewed coffee drifted up through the floorboards and swirled around his head. His stomach growled at the thought of tasty food in a good restaurant like Fred Harvey's.

Harvey . . . Raton . . . *Rosie was downstairs!* The reality of it hit him like a sledgehammer. He lifted his head. Yes, this was her room! Her hairbrush lay on the table. Her clean starched aprons hung by the door. He'd found her.

He let his head drop back onto the pillow. But Rosie didn't want him. She'd made him promise to leave. She had spoken of the man she'd married—her husband. And all

Bart had done was bloody her rug and her sheets, smell up her room with his old leather jacket and dusty boots, and put her in a position to lose her job.

He had no choice but to get out of her life.

With a grunt he hauled himself off the bed and dragged his legs to the window. He'd be damned if he had enough wind in him to blow out a candle. Sucking in a deep breath, he lifted the lace curtain.

Lord-a-mercy, the town was twice as big as it had looked in the dark the night before! Right from Rosie's bedroom window he could see a post office, a bank, a shoe shop, a bakery, an undertaking parlor, a laundry, and enough saloons to keep the whole town drunk as hillbillies at a rooster fight. There was the Five-Cent Beer Saloon, the 1883 Saloon, the Mountain Monarch, the Bank Exchange, the Progressive Saloon, the Cowboy's Exchange Saloon, the El Dorado, the Green Light, the Lone Star, the Dobe Saloon, and O'Reilly's. And those were just the ones Bart could make out.

A church or two had elbowed out some holy ground in among the saloons. A meeting hall, a hotel, and a water tower near the bank showed that the town of Raton, New Mexico, meant business. The whole place swarmed with people—folks heading in and out of the hardware stores and mercantiles, a milkman stopping off at every house in town, men loading wagons with lumber from Hughes Brothers' Carpenter and Building Supply, and women carrying bundles out of D. W. Stevens, Dealers in General Merchandise.

Bart brushed a hand across his forehead. There was no way in heaven or hell he could climb out of this second-story window and not be spotted immediately. He let the curtain drop and sagged onto the sill. If he couldn't leave this morning, he'd leave right after sunset for sure. In the meantime, he'd make up for all the trouble he'd caused Rosie.

"I'll see you at one o'clock," Rosie called to Etta, who was draped over a chair.

"Lucky you! My feet are killing me."

"Why don't you prop them up on the lunch counter?"
With Etta laughing at the absurd idea she had proposed,
Rosie swung into the kitchen. She knew it would be no
problem to load a plate with food, but how could she explain
a sudden insatiable hunger to Mr. Gable, who was always
protesting that she ate like a bird?

Trying not to attract attention, she stacked a cinnamon
roll on top of a plate of hotcakes, and grabbed a glass of
milk. Then she sashayed out of the kitchen as if she were
doing nothing out of the ordinary. But the lightness in her
demeanor quickly faded as she climbed the stairs to her
room. What if Bart had gone? What if he was still there?

She glanced from side to side down the empty hall before
tapping twice and then turning the knob. Slipping into the
room, she stared at her bed. It was empty!

"Howdy, Rosie."

At the sound of the deep voice coming from the direction
of the window, she nearly dropped the breakfast. Whirling,
she clutched the edge of the warm plate against her stomach.

"Bart?" she whispered.

The half-naked man seated on the windowsill looked
nothing like the pale papoose she had tucked away earlier
that morning. His bronze skin gleamed as it stretched across
the muscles of his broad chest and thick arms. A towel hung
around his neck. His hair, still damp at the ends, had been
washed and combed away from his face.

For the first time Rosie fully saw what time had done to
the boy she had loved—and, great ghosts, it was all
heavenly! From the raven eyebrows that slashed across his
forehead to the burning emeralds of his eyes, from the
straight slant of his nose to the sensual tilt of his lips, from
the squared turn of his chin to the solid trunk of his neck,
Bart Kingsley was all man. Taut, sinewed, hardened man.

Disconcerted, she tore her eyes away and focused on the
changes that had occurred in her room. On a makeshift
clothesline that stretched from a nail in one wall to the
wardrobe door on another hung a pair of dripping leather
trousers, a wrinkled buckskin jacket, its fringes making neat
puddles on the wood floor, and a set of white sheets.

"You washed," she said.

"Everything but the rug." He stood, and she realized that he wore nothing more than one of her thin cotton towels around his waist. "I didn't have enough water for that."

"Oh . . . no, of course not." Without meaning to, she focused on the place where the ends of the towel were tucked around his waist. Then her eyes wandered down to the clearly visible lump between his thighs. And she looked at his long bare legs, nut brown and corded with muscle. Her gaze rose again to the swollen place, and she swallowed.

"I saw an older woman leave the building earlier this morning," he was saying. "I decided it must be your Mrs. Jensen, so I took my chances and headed down the hall to fill a washtub. The water was cold as a witch's—"

He caught himself and stopped speaking. Rosie's head snapped up, and she felt herself flush with heat, not from Bart's slang, but because she was sure he'd seen her staring at him so openly.

"Cold as a witch's fanny," he finished.

She gave a little shrug and forced herself to meet his gaze. "Cold water's the best thing there is for taking bloodstains out of cloth." She held out the plate. "I brought you something to eat."

"Thanks. I'm hungry. The fever broke a while back, and I reckon I'm on the mend."

"That's good to hear."

"Yep, I guess I'll be able to head out of here pretty soon." With his green eyes locked on her face, he took the plate. "I might ought to wait until dark, though. The town looks pretty busy. I'd be much obliged if you'd allow me to stay in your room a while longer, Rosie."

At that moment she would have allowed him to do almost anything he wanted. Never, never had she seen a man like this. His whole body seemed to fill and dominate her room with a powerful presence that threatened to overwhelm her. In contrast, her husband had been a short man with hair that grew over his chest and onto his back in a thick mat that obliterated any sight of muscles and ribs or the round brown nipples so obvious on Bart.

If she hadn't known his veins ran with both white and Indian blood, Rosie might have mistaken Bart for a pure Apache. With his copper skin, short towel-loincloth, and long black hair, he could have passed for a mighty warrior straight out of a dime novel. But he was too tall, and his eyes were too green to deny the heritage of his English mother.

"Rosie?" he asked. "*Can* I stay?"

"Oh . . . well . . . sure." She patted at an imaginary wisp of hair. "Unless you want Sheriff Bowman nabbing you first thing."

"No, I don't want that. I take it you don't, either?"

"It doesn't matter to me one way or the other if he catches you," she said, turning to reach for a clean apron. "I just don't want everyone wondering what you've been doing in my room all this time."

"Yeah," he said in a low voice as he sat on the edge of her bed. "Sure thing."

Unable to watch him eat, Rosie busied herself straightening her dressing table. She hated for things to be out of place and in disarray. Whistles signaled the arrival of the lunch trains as they began to pass through the station. On the platform beside the depot, the brass gong called the passengers inside to eat.

"You reckon I should hang for my crimes, Rosie?" Bart asked without preamble.

Rosie glanced up from unwinding the long brown hair from her brush and coiling it into her porcelain hair receiver. "How should I know? You'd have the answer to that surer than I would."

"Well, I've been studying over it for a hell of a long time, and I'll be damned if I can figure it out." He lifted his head. "Excuse my ripe language. Cussing's a hard habit to break."

"Okay," Rosie said. She felt a strong need to calm herself, even though she knew a casual observer would find

little out of the ordinary in this conversation between a man
and a woman. Still, it was hard to hear Bart swear, and even
more difficult to know that he wanted to tell her about his
crimes.

"Here's the thing," he was saying. "It's sure enough
true that I did some mighty bad deeds a while back. Deeds
a man should hang for, if the truth be known."

Rosie was pulling hair out of her brush like a mad demon.
She didn't want to hear this! She didn't want to know all the
terrible things Bart had done. How could the boy she had
loved commit crimes he could die for? How could this man,
with his beautifully honed body and gentle ways, deserve to
hang?

"What I keep on pondering," he was saying, "is the
notion of forgiveness. Remember how the reverend used to
preach on it over at the Methodist church when we were
kids?"

Rosie tried to swallow the lump that suddenly formed in
her throat. "Sure, I remember." She also remembered the
way the minister had refused to let Bart set foot inside his
precious church. She remembered finding the young half-
Indian squatting on the cold stone porch steps as he
followed the sermon in a little black Bible he'd gotten
somewhere. She remembered a lot of things about the
preacher who had rejected a boy whose craving for spiritual
knowledge had shown so plainly in his thin face.

"Remember the things the reverend used to say about
how God could forgive us for anything we did, if only we'd
ask Him?" Bart asked, studying his now empty plate.

"Yes," Rosie whispered.

"And remember how he told us we ought to forgive other
people the wrong they did, just like God forgives us?" He
lifted his head. "Rosie-girl, you reckon anybody could see
their way clear to forgive me for what I did and let me get
a fresh start on things?"

When she didn't answer, he chuckled bitterly. "No, I
expect not. That's probably asking too much. Sheriffs and
lawmen and bounty hunters aren't in the forgiveness busi-

ness anyhow. They'd as soon shoot a man dead as let him try to make a new life for himself.''

Rosie set her brush on the table and ran one finger over the soft bristles. ''Are you thinking about making a new life, Bart?''

''I didn't come all the way to Raton, New Mexico, to rob trains—you can bet your bottom dollar on that.''

''Why did you come?'' She heard Bart let out a breath, but she couldn't bring herself to look at him.

''About the time Bob Ford shot Jesse James in the back of the head, I was doing some figuring. I got to looking over the years of my life, and all I could see was a great long tunnel. A black, cold tunnel. There was only one sliver of brightness in the whole thing. One spot of light.''

Turning, Rosie saw that he was staring at her with a look she couldn't read, a look that sent her pulse skimming and her stomach curling into a warm, throbbing ball.

''That light was you, Rosie,'' Bart said. ''It was you. And that's the reason I came to Raton, New Mexico. I came to find that light again, to see if it was real, to see if I could touch it, to see if it could shine away some of that darkness in the stinking black pit I've made of my life.''

Oh, Bart, she wanted to say, *I forgive you. I forgive you*! But the one-o'clock lunch train pulled into the depot with a whistle and a rush of steam that obliterated every sound in the tiny room. Rosie felt her chair shake and saw the lid of her hair receiver tremble on its bowl. And she was thankful— so thankful—she hadn't said anything to Bart.

The reason was clear. As she left her room and hurried down the stairs to the lunchroom, Rosie saw the faces of her angry father, her disappointed husband, the doctors who had said she would never bear children. She saw the wreath of roses and lilacs she'd worn in her hair the night she married Bart Kingsley, the glade where she'd cried her eyes out over him, the bed where William Lowell had violated the chapel of her body—the body she had promised to another man.

Rosie realized that with all these things, a blackness had crept into her own life. A blackness so intense she had fled from it on a midnight train to a frontier town where no one could ever find her again. A blackness so dark she was not at all sure that even a flicker of light remained—the light that had been Laura Rose Vermillion. The light Bart had come seeking.

*Four

. . . .

Minutes after the last lunch train pulled out of Raton, the sheriff, the newspaper editor, and the pastor of the Methodist church strolled into the lunchroom looking for a bite to eat. Because Rosie was always stationed at the main counter, there was nothing she could do but abandon her cleanup chores and serve the men.

"I'll have a ham sandwich, Miss Kingsley," Reverend Cullen announced as he flipped back the tail of his short fitted jacket and sat down on one of the round stools. "And a dish of that wonderful Harvey ice cream."

"I'll take the same," Mr. Adams of *The Raton Comet* added.

"Might as well make it three. After being up all night and combing the woods this morning instead of eating breakfast, I'm hungry enough to eat my own horse."

The other men chuckled at the sheriff's comment. Rosie tried to make herself smile as she knew she should. If Mr. Gable caught her quaking in her boots at the sight of Sheriff Bowman, she knew she would be in trouble.

She had always liked working the lunchroom better than the dining room. The slick counters were easy to keep clean and tidy, less walking was required, and without the camaraderie of the square dining tables, passengers quickly got down to the business of eating. But right now Rosie would have given almost anything to have been assigned to the dining room.

"You got any of that orange juice?" the sheriff called out when she was halfway to the kitchen.

53

"As always," she replied brightly.

Etta was chatting with the new German chef when Rosie swung through the double doors. The buxom little blonde took one look at her friend and gave a quick gasp. "Laurie!" she cried as she hurried to the board where Rosie was pinning the lunch orders. "You're positively green around the gills, honey!" She grabbed Rosie's shoulders and turned her around. "Are you coming down with something? Heavenly days, I hope it's not typhoid fever! Or yellow fever! Have you seen those alleys out back of the local hotels and restaurants? Why, there are dead dogs and hogs, garbage from the kitchens, decayed vegetables—a regular breeding ground for yellow fever—all the way from Clark to Cook avenues between First and Second streets!"

"No, no, Etta." Rosie placed a calming hand on her friend's arm. "I expect I'm just tired after all the excitement last night."

"Well, get on up to your room and take a nap. You've got a good two hours before the first dinner train rolls in."

"I can't. Three locals just walked into the lunchroom, and they're out at the counter," Rosie explained as she filled a glass with fresh juice. "They're asking for sandwiches and ice cream."

"Sakes alive, you'd think they'd have heard the last train blow into town. Don't they know we're trying to clean up?" Etta glanced at Stefan Braun, who was already slicing half-inch-thick slabs of ham. "I'll take your shift, Laurie," she said in a low voice. "Go on, now."

Rosie saw the melting look Etta had given the young chef. Even though associations among Harvey employees were totally against regulations, it was clear to everyone that Stefan had gone sweet on Etta. And the feeling was mutual.

"No, you finish up in the kitchen," Rosie said, giving Etta an elbow in the ribs. "Besides, that silverware could use another coat of polish, if you ask me."

With a quick wink, she picked up the tray now loaded with sandwiches and drinks, and returned to the lunchroom. The three townsmen had removed their felt hats and leather gloves and propped their elbows on the counter. Now they were deep in conversation.

"Three ham sandwiches." Rosie set the plates in front of the men. "And fresh orange juice for you, Sheriff Bowman."

"Bart Kingsley's a regular skunk," the sheriff said, completely ignoring her, "a no-good half-breed sidewinder who's mean enough to have a reserved seat in hell."

"Now, that's not for you to judge," Reverend Cullen countered as he picked up his sandwich. "Only the good Lord knows for certain who has a reserved seat in which eternal dominion."

Rosie stepped back against the coffee island and wished she were invisible. With her hands locked behind her back, her bosom couldn't help but thrust forward, which made her badge seem to stand out like a proud banner announcing her name: Kingsley.

She had a notion to head for the kitchen in the hopes that none of the men would take notice, but it was against the rules to leave a counter unattended. If there were three people she didn't want to be around on this upsetting day, they were the nosy sheriff, the inquisitive newspaperman, and the righteous minister.

Sheriff Bowman gave a loud snort as he addressed Reverend Cullen. "You didn't hear all the things that Pinkerton man told me before I put him on the train back to Kansas City this morning, Preacher. The gunslinger's got a file as thick as this sandwich, and the things he's done are enough to make your hair curl."

Mr. Adams cleared his throat. "If you gentlemen don't mind, I believe I'll take a note or two on the subject of Raton's most prominent outlaw."

"Go ahead, Charley, but don't put down who said what. Them Pinkerton files are supposed to be a secret, you know."

"Did the detective think Kingsley really did skedaddle last night?" Adams asked.

"He's gone, all right. We lost track of him right outside here. The Pinkerton fellow wanted to search the girls' rooms, but I set him straight on that one. Tom Gable would have a holy fit if I let any man set foot upstairs—let alone some stranger who meant to open wardrobes and trunks and such. Ain't that right, Miss Kingsley?''

Rosie broke into a prickling sweat at the mention of her name. ''Men sure are forbidden upstairs, Sheriff.'' She gave him a weak smile. ''But it's Mrs. Jensen who would have the holy fit.''

''Ain't that the truth! Now there's a she-bear nobody'd want to tangle with.'' The sheriff grinned at his own joke. ''Besides, I reckon the minute some stinkin' outlaw set foot in one of the girls' rooms, there'd be such a hollerin' and bawlin' it'd be noisier than a breedin' jackass in a tin barn.''

''Sheriff, your language!'' the preacher admonished. ''I beg you to take consideration of our female company here.'' The elderly man gave Rosie a kind smile, his blue eyes soft and warm. ''I'm sure you don't want to cause any more consternation in the Harvey dormitory than our outlaw has already caused the young ladies.''

''Sheriff Bowman,'' the newspaper owner put in, ''why don't you tell us about this fellow just in case he decides to reappear? I think the citizenry of our fair town deserve a full report. If the outlaw should come back into Raton, how would we know him?''

The sheriff wiped his thick mustache with a napkin, then picked his teeth a minute before answering. ''The Pinkerton fellow didn't have no picture to go by, but he did have that file. Besides what I already told you men on the way over here, there's the fact that Bart Kingsley is . . .'' He glanced up at Rosie, then lowered his voice to a whisper. ''He's a bastard.''

''Sheriff!'' the minister exclaimed.

''Sure enough?'' Adams was quickly scrawling notes in the little book he had pulled from his back pocket.

''Mother's said to be some kind of a''—Bowman leaned closer—''a whore.''

''And his father?''

''Old Man Trouble's only son.''

Adams chuckled. ''An Indian, I hear tell.''

"Apache."

"Good Lord."

At that the preacher slid his empty plate to the edge of the counter and thumped his hand on the counter top the way Rosie had seen him do in church. "Now, gentlemen, there's been quite enough swearing and defamation of character around here. A man can't be held responsible for his lineage. And, Charley, I trust you'll refrain from printing Mr. Kingsley's unfortunate heritage in your newspaper."

The sheriff eased his big shoulders around and poked the preacher with a beefy finger. "Kingsley ain't responsible for his family tree, but he's sure as hell accountable for them three trains he robbed over in Missouri. Bein' as how Raton's a railroad town, I don't intend to let nobody mess with my territory."

"Well, of course not," Reverend Cullen said, leaning backward a tad.

"I'll have you know that, during the robbery over in Winston, two men was killed—William Westfall and Frank McMillan. Now, I ain't sure who exactly it was that pulled the trigger, but I can tell you one thing: no low-down sorry half-breed bastard of a train robber is gonna get away with nothing while I'm sheriff. If I have to, I'll shoot him on sight."

"I hear there's a price on his head," Adams added. "Fifty dollars?"

"That's right."

"And fifty dollars would go a long way toward that new house you're building over on your farm."

"But you hardly even know what the man looks like," Reverend Cullen protested. "You couldn't have gotten much of a look at him in the dark last night."

"I saw him well enough to shoot him. Besides, he's half Apache, ain't he? I reckon that'll make him red-skinned and black-haired. I reckon he'll have them high cheekbones and a chest like a barn door. I reckon he'll be packin' a belt full of guns and wearin' some kind of buckskin getup like the one he had on last night. And I reckon it won't be too long before he slips up and lets on who he is. That's when I'll put a window in his skull."

With that, the sheriff stood and palmed a nickel onto the countertop. "Good afternoon, gentlemen," he said, settling his hat on his head and striding out of the lunchroom.

Rosie began gathering up plates and glasses as fast as she could without dropping something. Her hands trembled so badly she was sure someone would take notice. But the Reverend Mr. Cullen and Mr. Adams pulled on their gloves and dusted their hat brims as if she were invisible.

"Don't pay the sheriff any heed," Adams said as they stood. "He's just fit to be boiled because he lost that outlaw's trail last night."

The minister waved a hand, dismissing the issue. "He probably needs a good night's sleep is all." He turned to Rosie. "Miss Kingsley, that was a delightful repast. You may convey my deepest compliments to Herr Braun."

"Yes, sir."

"And will I see you in church this Sunday?"

"I would imagine so, sir."

Rosie was fairly scrubbing the varnish off the countertop as the two men left the lunchroom. Oh, but she felt ill! Downright sick at her stomach. The sheriff was right—Bart *was* an outlaw and a killer. How could she deny it when he'd admitted it himself?

The more she thought about it, the more Rosie began to understand that Bart was the cause of every trouble she'd ever had in her life. If it hadn't been for him asking her to get married, she'd never have disobeyed her father. Then Bart had run off and left her to carry the burden of what they had done. If it hadn't been for him, she might have accepted Dr. Lowell and been a better wife. She wouldn't have felt so guilty and ashamed of her past. If she hadn't had Bart to compare her husband with, she might actually have grown to like Dr. Lowell. Maybe if she'd cared for her husband, he wouldn't have felt the need to do the things he'd done to her—the shouting and shaming . . . and the other cruelties. If Dr. Lowell had been kinder, she wouldn't have been driven to run away from him. And she wouldn't be fighting for her future with such slender hopes!

Bart was the reason she was green around the gills and shaking like a leaf. If he hadn't tracked her down, everything would have gone just as she'd planned. But he had followed her all the way to Raton, he was up in her room, and the sheriff intended to kill him!

Rosie wrung out her washrag and scrubbed the same patch of counter for the third time. Bart had told her she was the only light in his life. But she didn't feel like a light anymore; she felt more like a snuffed-out oil lamp—black, empty, and cold. Finally she admitted that Bart himself had been the one who had turned down the bright wick of her dreams, doused her flame, and blown away the final sparks. Her fire had gone out, and it was all Bart Kingsley's fault.

She picked up her tray of empty plates and started for the kitchen, determination growing with every step. Well, she hadn't come all this way and worked this hard to let some gun-slinging outlaw ruin her hopes—no matter how good he looked with a thin white towel wrapped around his waist.

In a mere three years, the town of Raton had grown from four ragged tents to a row of inhabited boxcars to a full-fledged bustling community. As Rosie marched down First Street, she felt a surge of pride in her new home. Her black and white uniform set her in crisp contrast to the ragged coal miners and rough-hewn cowboys on the street, and she held her head high. Maybe she did have an outlaw in her bedroom, Rosie thought. And maybe she had taken some unhappy paths in life. But none of that doomed her to failure.

Ever since she could remember, Rosie had loved children and had wanted to teach them. Pappy, of course, wouldn't hear of such an absurd notion. Schoolteachers were "working women" and therefore far beneath her in social status. She could almost see his face, his dark eyes snapping as he lectured her from behind his huge desk.

"Working women are socially suspicious," he had informed his stubborn daughter more than once. "They're just one step away from the very cellar of society—prostitution. My dream for you, Laura Rose, is marriage to a prominent man, a bevy of healthy children, and success as a full-time homemaker.''

Rosie had to smile as she crossed Rio Grande Avenue onto Second Street. Pappy would be downright apoplectic if he knew she had taken a job as a waitress! Women who worked in eating houses were at the bottom rung of the job ladder. Considered coarse, hard, and ''easy,'' they were usually believed to be doubling as women of ill repute.

One look at Fred Harvey's establishments, however, had convinced Rosie otherwise. Here in Raton she was held in as high esteem as any other reputable female. Men tipped their hats; women greeted her with genuine smiles. Rosie and the other Harvey Girls were invited to every community picnic, baseball game, dance, and opera show in town. The fact of the matter was, in the two short months she had lived here, she had had more wholesome, refreshing fun than she could ever remember in her twenty-one years of life.

Never mind about Bart Kingsley, Rosie thought as she climbed the wooden steps to a small one-room structure at the corner of Clark Avenue and North Second Street. She had come to Raton to build a new identity. Fred Harvey had laid the foundation for her, and now Mr. Thomas A. Kilgore would open the door to freedom.

Her knock caused a shuffling of feet inside the building, which could more easily have been termed a shack. In moments a middle-aged man with a walrus mustache pulled open the door.

''May I help you?'' He looked at her through a pair of thick spectacles that threatened to slide off the end of his nose.

''Mr. Kilgore?'' Rosie asked, suddenly nervous before the imposing man.

''Indeed. And your name?''

''I'm Miss Laura Kingsley, sir. Recently of Kansas City.''

He scanned her uniform, his blue eyes intent beneath his bushy brown eyebrows. ''You're employed at the Harvey House.''

"Yes, sir. But I've come to speak to you about a teaching position."

The eyebrows lifted. "I'm conducting class at the moment, Miss Kingsley. Would you kindly return this evening?"

Rosie swallowed. "I'm afraid this is my only free time today, Mr. Kilgore. I work all three shifts, and the first dinner train will arrive shortly."

"I see." He pushed his spectacles onto his nose and regarded her for a moment. "Well, come inside, then."

Rosie had been peering around his shoulder, but she could see very little in the dimly lit room. Now she followed Mr. Kilgore through the door to find more than twenty young faces turned in her direction. Each child was standing beside a chair. Each pair of little hands was folded neatly, and each small mouth had been clamped shut.

"Students, may I introduce Miss Kingsley?" Thomas Kilgore announced.

"Good afternoon, Miss Kingsley," the children replied in unison.

"Good afternoon, students. I'm pleased to meet you."

Rosie suddenly felt light-headed to be standing in the place she had dreamed of for so many years. A schoolroom, with desks and flags, slates and readers, inkwells and chalk dust. The children looked exactly as she had pictured them—some clean and neat, others ragged and dirty; some bright with intelligence, others more dimly visaged; some giggly and mischievous, others solemn. What would it be like to stand before them and open doors in their young lives? To guide small hands over the forming of the alphabet, to encourage thin voices in recitation, to dry tearful eyes and bandage skinned knees, to enlighten and comfort and praise . . .

"Students, you may be seated," Mr. Kilgore stated as he gave the children a quick scan through his spectacles. "Grade three, continue your history recitation without me for the moment. Minnie, you may lead the group. The rest of you, carry on as you were."

"Yes, sir," they said.

As young heads bent to work, Mr. Kilgore led Rosie to his large oak desk at the front of the small room. Though the crowded school was shabbily outfitted with hand-made desks, curtainless windows, and an ancient pot-bellied stove that smelled of soot and ashes, Rosie loved it at once. She knew she should concentrate on her mission, but she couldn't keep from imagining herself—clean, neat, carefully dressed, and fresh-faced as spring—in charge of the classes.

"Now, Miss Kingsley," Mr. Kilgore addressed her in a low voice as he seated himself behind the big desk. "You have stated that you are interested in a teaching position. May I ask what qualifications you have?"

Rosie lifted her chin. "I have completed high school, sir, and I've taken several college courses. In all subjects, I received excellent marks."

"College!"

"My father is a professor at Park College in the town of Parkville, in Platte County. It's near Kansas City. I attended the institution where he is employed, and I studied Latin, art, music, and science."

"Science . . . my goodness." He ran a finger down the length of his thick mustache. "Do you hold a teaching certificate, Miss Kingsley?"

"No, sir. But I have no doubt as to my ability to pass public examination by any school board."

"I see. And what brings a woman with your qualifications to this remote New Mexico Territory?"

"I came here to work for Harvey House," Rosie said, reciting the plan she had formed so many months ago. "I intended to become established in Raton and earn enough money to support myself while seeking out the employment I will make my lifetime career—the education of children."

"Hmm," he said, then gave one of his older students a warning look. "Manford Wade, I suggest you return to your study of the elements of grammar." When the red-haired boy had dipped his nose back into his book, Mr. Kilgore returned his spectacled gaze to Rosie. "Miss Kingsley, I founded this school with the intent of forming a much larger institution. My wife and I have high hopes of establishing an independent school district in Raton according to territorial law. As you can see, we suffer from overcrowding here, and I fear my students are lagging behind other pupils of like age who have enjoyed better school privileges. At my request the school commission recently voted to extend our school term in order to give the students better preparation as they continue in their education. A good many of these boys and girls will one day attend high school, and some will even want to go on to college. We want them to be able to compete with their peers."

"Wonderful," Rosie said, impressed with the man's dedication.

"The voters of Precinct Six have petitioned an election for this purpose, and it will take place the last Saturday of the month. If it passes, the school term will continue through July."

"July! That should allow plenty of time for the students to make up what they've missed."

"Should the election turn out favorably, however, I'm afraid I will be without a teacher. My regular instructor, Miss McMichael, has . . ." Here he paused to survey the room; then he leaned closer toward Rosie. "Miss McMichael has elected to return to Chicago as the bride of a young lawyer of her acquaintance," he finished in a whisper.

"I see." Rosie gave the man a look of sincere sympathy, but her heart swelled with excitement and hope.

"I am, of course, eminently qualified for the position of instructor, and I often work with the older pupils. But I prefer to manage the business and community aspects of my school."

"I do understand, sir." Rosie could feel her heart thudding so heavily she was almost sure her badge must be dancing on her breast. "And I would be most honored to fill the teaching position your difficult situation has made available."

He pulled at his mustache for a moment before responding. "Can you return tomorrow morning, Miss Kingsley, after I've spoken with my wife? I will discuss the possibilities further at that time."

"Oh, yes, Mr. Kilgore. I'll leave the Harvey House right after the last breakfast train pulls out of town. And thank you, sir. Thank you for considering me."

Light-headed with optimism, she shook his hand firmly before making her way among the clustered desks to the front door.

If she was ever going to get Bart Kingsley out of her room and on his way, Rosie knew she would have to find him something decent to wear. As a Harvey Girl, she earned the satisfying sum of seventeen dollars and fifty cents a month plus tips, room, board, laundry, and travel expenses, which left plenty of money for spending. Of course, Rosie had saved nearly all of her income, since she planned to buy a small house after she became a teacher. But if it meant she could safely send Bart out of her life, she was more than willing to spend a dollar or two on a new shirt for the man.

After the evening trains had pulled away and the dining room had been set in order, the Harvey Girls climbed the long stairway to their dormitory hall. Though it was well after ten, Rosie felt as wide awake as if it were morning as she clutched the shirt she had purchased and opened her bedroom door.

"Bart?" she called softly, unable to see anything in the darkness. Again she felt that strange ambivalence. She hoped he was finally gone. At the same time she feared that he had left her once again.

"Over here, Rosie." His deep voice came from the corner by the window. "I was just waiting until you came in. I wanted to say good-bye."

She let out her breath and made her way to the dressing table where she lifted the glass globe of her lamp. *He was still here.* "I don't know why you waited around," she said, belying her own sense of relief. "The sooner you leave, the more of a head start you'll have on the sheriff."

"I don't need a head start on him."

Rosie struck a match and lit the wick. "Why not? He's still after you. As a matter of fact, he was in the lunchroom at noon talking about how wicked you are and how you deserve the price that's on your head."

"I reckon I do, Rosie."

He looked dark and looming in the shadowy corner, so she lifted the lamp. She saw that he was dressed as he had been that morning, in his buckskin jacket and leather trousers, but the man standing by the window was not the wounded, bleeding wreck who had crawled out from under her bed. His long hair black and shining, he wore an air of confidence that emanated from his broad shoulders and glowed in his smile.

"I reckon I deserve a lot of things," he said, "but I'm not aiming to reap them in this lifetime."

She shrugged, hoping to make him see how little she cared what he did. "As the Good Book says, 'Sow the wind and reap the whirlwind.'"

"That about sums me up, huh?"

"All I know is, if Sheriff Bowman gets his hands on you, he's going to shoot you dead. He wants that reward, Bart."

"Then I reckon I'd better not let him get ahold of me." Still smiling gently, he walked toward her.

She winced at the thud of his boots on the hollow wood floor, but it was the nearness of the man that made her face go hot and her mouth dry. "W-what are you going to do?" she stammered.

"Right now I'm planning to say good-bye to the only woman I've ever loved."

"I . . . I mean after you leave. Where are you going?"

"I'm glad you care this much about me, Rosie."

"I don't care. Not a lick. But I think I should know where you'll be, just in case."

He stopped a mere two feet in front of her. "In case what?"

"In case . . ." She moistened her lips. "In case I should ever need to know what became of you. Last time you just went off without leaving a clue. I know now that you were running with an outlaw gang. Is that what you're planning to do again?"

His eyes left her face and trailed to the badge on her bosom. "Kingsley," he read, lifting a hand to touch the metal. "I reckon a man who's got a woman wearing his last name ought to think of something better to do with his time than bank robbing."

She pushed his fingers away from her badge, but as his hand fell, it brushed across the rise of her breast. At his touch a burst of sparks sang through her skin, and Rosie caught her breath. Flushing, she tucked her lower lip between her teeth and turned to put the lamp on the table.

"You made that same sound the first time I touched you," he said in a low voice. "Remember, Rosie-girl? We were kissing in our special place by the stream. You gasped when my fingers found you . . . but you didn't pull away from me. Remember, Rosie?"

Her eyes trained on the lamp, she shook her head. "I'm a married woman, Bart, and you'd better leave my room right this minute."

"You're married to *me*, and I have every right to stay here as long as I want."

"No, you don't!" She whirled on him, her brown eyes dark. "I've been married to Dr. William Lowell for three years, and—"

"And you've been married to me for six. We loved each other back then, Rosie."

"We were children! We didn't even know what love was."

"And you're telling me that you do now? Is that why you hightailed it to New Mexico? Is that why you ran off and left your rich husband?"

"You don't know one thing!" Her voice sounded hoarse, and her eyes stung with unshed tears.

"I know one thing. I know I aim to make a new life for myself. And finding you is the beginning of it."

She crossed her arms over her chest and stared at the ceiling in hope that he could read nothing on her face. Oh, why couldn't this confusing man just leave her as he had before—with no farewells, no speeches, no tenderness? Why was he standing so close, smelling so good and looking like the devil himself? Why did her heart have to hammer and her throat swell up in a lump? And why, oh, why did she long to feel his hand stroke her just one more time?

"We're both trying to start over, Bart," she went on when she trusted herself to speak. "But if finding me is the beginning of your new life, it could be the end of mine. I don't want any reminders of the past. I want freedom from my old life. I want to be a new person, independent and strong. I want to be alone, Bart. Alone!"

"Rosie," he murmured, unlocking her arms and letting his big hands slide down to take hers. "Rosie, don't push me away. Give me a chance."

"I don't live that way anymore. I don't have to do what you or anyone else says."

"I know you've always done what people told you to—your pappy, the fellow you married, even me. But I'm not telling you to do anything, Rosie-girl. I'm asking. Please . . . give me a chance."

She swallowed and studied the design on the border of her pressed-tin ceiling. "A chance to . . . to what?"

"To touch your face, Rosie." He ran the tip of one finger down her cheek. "I want to know the feeling of your hair in my hands and your breath against my skin."

He cupped the back of her head and drew her closer. She could feel his thighs brush against the front of her skirt and send a liquid heat roaring through her. She could hear herself drawing uneven breaths as a voice inside her screamed protests at the insanity of allowing him this much freedom.

"Remember how I used to pull the ribbons from your braids, Rosie," he was saying, defying everything reason demanded, "and I'd untwist your hair until it hung loose around your shoulders? You used to laugh and scold me because I could never put your braids back the right way, and you worried that your pappy would find out what we'd been up to. But I knew you didn't really care, because you would always lean against my shoulder and let me slide my fingers around your head. You'd tell me how my touch tingled on your skin and made you shiver in secret places."

As he spoke, he slipped his hands up through the puff of loose hair around her face and eased through the bun she had so carefully knotted that morning. And oh, how she tingled and shivered. Those secret places only Bart had been able to stir came to life for the first time in six years, and Rosie closed her eyes at the sheer power of the need rocking through her body.

As her hair spilled down her back, she felt her breasts lift and tighten. When his hands wove around her neck, she sighed and moved against him. But the surge of his male body thrusting urgently against the soft skin of her thighs brought her to a sudden sharp awareness.

"Bart!" Her eyes flew open, and she jerked the fabric of her skirt around her legs like a protective cape. She knew what that rigid pressure signaled. She had felt its pain all too many times in the past three years of her marriage, and she never wanted to know such ravishment again. "Bart, you'd better leave."

"Rosie?" Confusion darkened his eyes.

"I—I have to work the early shift tomorrow."

"I've scared you, haven't I?"

"Of course not. I just got to thinking about how tired I'll be if I don't get a good night's sleep. And you ought to head out while the moon's up."

She looked into his face. She desired him, and she loathed him. She feared the feelings he evoked in her, and she craved them. She hungered for his touch, yet the thought of it terrified her.

"So, good-bye, Bart." She forced the words out. "It was

good to see you again, and I sure hope your wound heals up.''

Before he could see the quiver in her lower lip, she spun away from him and hurried to the hook where her aprons hung.

*Five
· ·

With shaking fingers, Rosie fumbled to release the buttons on her bib. She didn't like anything to do with the ways of men with women. She didn't want to know that she had stirred Bart, and she certainly couldn't allow herself to accept what the touch of his hardened body had done to the secret places inside her. He must leave now!

But she had barely formed the thought when she heard him moving close behind her and felt his chest brush against her shoulder blades. "Rosie," he said softly against her ear. "Rosie, I don't mean to upset you, girl. I just want you to know that a day hasn't gone by without my thoughts going over and over those times we spent together. I want you to understand how I felt while we were apart. Rosie?"

His hands circled her waist, and he turned her to face him. She kept her eyes on her uniform, her fingers working at the bib buttons. She couldn't make herself look at him, but she could feel his breath stir her hair.

"You're all a-tremble," he whispered as he covered her hands with his own. And then he was sliding each tiny pearl disk from its mooring.

The pressure of the movement bathed each of her breasts in a pale, pulsing glow, and she could feel their crests bead inside her chemise. She shut her eyes, half reveling in the sensation and half filled with recrimination for the liberties she was allowing him.

"Did I ever tell you how crazy I am about your ankles, Rosie?" he asked as he let the bib fall from her bosom.

She shook her head because it was all she could manage.

71

. "When you were about fifteen, you used to take off your stockings and wade in the swimming hole. You were so innocent and prim about it all, but seeing you that way just about killed me." Now his hands had taken her badge, and he began unpinning it. "Once you slipped on a mossy rock and fell in the water, remember? It was the first time I'd ever seen the shape of your body, Rosie. Your long legs . . . your little waist . . . your breasts."

"I-I bought you a shirt today," she inserted quickly. "I decided against a collar, since they cost twenty cents each."

"Your body has changed a lot in six years. Your shoulders are straighter, and your arms seem more slender to me." As he spoke, his hands moved over her until they eased gently over the peaks of her breasts. "You're more beautiful than ever, Rosie."

"Bart." She knew she should keep talking about shirts and collars, but all she wanted was the pressure of his palms warming her bare flesh as they once had beside the swimming hole. "Bart, I . . ."

"I've been half loco missing you, girl." As he worked open the buttons down the front of her shirtwaist, he could hear his own breath grow short at the sight of her milky skin. Oh, he wouldn't hurt or frighten his Rosie for anything in the world. But he couldn't abide the thought of leaving her again without knowing the way her skin felt, without holding her and telling her the things he'd needed to say for six long years. Even though she had told him to go a hundred times, she was having just as much trouble breathing as he was. Maybe she wanted him, too. In spite of what she said, maybe she had missed him just a little, and maybe she'd thought about him now and then. Maybe she'd wanted him just as much as he'd wanted her.

When he glanced down at his hands, he saw his long bronzed fingers slipping over the swollen globes of her breasts, dipping into the sharp shadow between them, drawing ever closer to the lacy edge of her chemise. He felt exactly like the gangly boy he'd been the first time she had discarded her veil of primness and let him explore her bare young body. Hot as a firecracker now, he let his fingers slide over the soft fabric and begin to circle the small round pebbles jutting up above her corset.

With the slightest movement, he knew he could graze the crests of her nipples and send flames shooting through her. But she was still trembling so, and her hands were locked behind her back as though they'd been handcuffed. Was he hurting her? Or scaring her to death? Did she dislike him but not know how to tell him?

"Rosie," he whispered. Her eyes, dark brown and liquid, fluttered open. "Rosie-girl, will you put your arms around me the way you used to? Will you hold me just once before I go?"

"Oh, Bart, I can't."

"Because you married another man? Is that what holds you back from me?"

She nodded as his hands left her breasts and rose to cup the sides of her face. "But it's not like you think . . . not that I feel loyal to him."

"Then what, Rosie? Tell me, girl."

"It's just that I made a choice to leave him, and I don't want to be with a man in that way ever again." She straightened her shoulders and looked him square in the eye. "I can't have children, Bart—you might as well know. The man I married is a medical doctor and, after examining me, he told me I was as barren as a desert. He sent me to all kinds of other doctors, and every one of them agreed I'd always be childless. Since having children is the only reason I can think of for . . . for going through all that rigmarole, I simply decided I'm going to be a spinster for the rest of my life."

His face softened, and he crooked up one corner of his mouth. "Rigmarole?"

"You know very well what I mean." Pulling out of his arms, she walked across her room, sat on the edge of her bed, and began unlacing her boots. "All that sweating and grunting and such. I used to just despise the gleam that came into that man's eye. And every night I had to face such unpleasantries."

"Every night?"

"As far as I'm concerned, God made beds for sleeping in. For two months now I've had the most blessed nights of rest since I was a girl. So you can see as plain as the end of your nose that I don't intend to put my arms around you or any other man."

While she tugged her boots off her sore feet, he came and hunkered down on one knee beside her. Taking her blistered foot, he set it on his thigh and began rubbing her reddened heel and each sore toe. If it bothered him that Rosie had spent time in bed with another man, he thought, it bothered him a hell of a lot more to realize that whatever the villain had done to her had killed the spark of feminine response he'd once loved so much. Well . . . maybe not quite killed it. Squelched it.

He looked up at her to discover that she was clutching her skirt again. Her white-knuckled fingers were balled up into fists, and she was chewing on her lip. Scared, that's what she was. Downright scared! Finally he understood that she wasn't frightened of *him* so much as she was of her own memories of a man too demanding and callous to think how she might feel about his nightly invasion.

"Rosie, you reckon I could get me a job here in Raton without raising any suspicions?" he asked, warding off her trembling with a change of subject.

"I doubt it. The sheriff surely saw you before he shot you."

Bart kept rubbing her foot, trying to keep his hands away from her little ankle. "Not too well. It was mighty dark out in the street. I reckon he must have caught a glimpse of my jacket and my hair and figured I might be the man he was looking for. When he hollered my name, I made the mistake of turning around, and he commenced firing at me."

She studied the top of his bent head. My, what a thick mane of hair the man had. And how clean it smelled. But she forced her thoughts back to the conversation. "If you walked into town," she said, "the sheriff would probably shoot you again."

"What if I got a haircut and put on that new shirt you gave me?"

"A haircut?"

He lifted his head. "Would you cut my hair for me, Rosie?"

"Oh, I don't think . . ." The very idea of touching his hair sent a shiver down her thighs. "I doubt it would do you a lick of good. Your skin is as brown as a berry, Bart, and you've got those high cheekbones. The sheriff said he'd be on the lookout for a man with a face like yours."

"Would you cut my hair anyway, Rosie? I reckon I'll give the straight life a chance."

"But here—in Raton?"

"Why not?"

"Why, Bart?"

Raising his head, he slid his big hands over her hips and up to her waist. "Rosie, there's something you ought to know about me. Once upon a time, all it took was a few harsh words to send me scampering. But I've changed in six years. I learned to do right whatever I set my mind on. If I meant to break a horse, I'd have him gentle as a kitten in no time flat. If I aimed to rob a train, I'd rob it plumb dry. If I shot a man, the bullet went clean through his heart."

"Bart!"

"Well, that's the facts, Rosie. I came to Raton to find you and make a new life for myself. So if you'll just give me a haircut, darlin', I'll get on with it."

What she was doing cutting Bart Kingsley's hair at midnight, Rosie would never know. As she combed and snipped away at his coal-black mane, she berated herself over and over again. Crazy—she was just crazy, that's all! She should have sent him off long ago. Instead, she'd let him whisper in her ear, unbutton her shirtwaist, stroke her breasts, massage her foot. And now she was actually cutting the man's hair so he could stay in Raton and make her life miserable!

"Reckon there's any chance I could pass for a gentleman dandy just off the train from Chicago?" He was seated on her chair as he studied himself in her silver hand mirror.

"Bart, you look just like what you are—an outlaw. A big, brawny gunslinger."

"Maybe I'd better leave my six-shooter and holster with you."

"Don't you dare! Bad enough I have to hide a bloody rug and a pile of chopped-off black hair without adding an arsenal to it."

He chuckled. "You've really done me a good turn, Rosie. Much as my side still hurts, I don't believe I'd have made it this far without your kindness."

Softening, she shook her head and ran her brush through his hair. Why was it God gave some men such fine, thick, healthy tresses? Now that his hair stopped just above his collar, she could fully see the tremendous breadth of his shoulders. Of course, the buckskin jacket still made him look like a savage fresh off the warpath.

"Maybe you ought to grow sideburns," she said, brushing tiny hairs from his back. "Most men have them these days. Or a mustache."

"I don't expect I'd have much luck with either of those."

No, she thought, remembering the smooth skin of his hairless chest. Bart was sleek and silken, his bronzed flesh stretching tautly across his frame. "Well," she said with a sigh, "in spite of the haircut, you still look like an Apache to me."

"Does that bother you, Rosie?" he asked, turning quickly and catching her hands. "Does my blood make a difference to you now?"

As she gazed into his green eyes, she saw that he had become the little boy again, wounded and shamed by the cruelty of others. "I always told you to be proud of who you are, Bart. I don't give a barrel of shucks about your blood, and I never have. It's what's inside a man—what he chooses to do with himself—that makes him who he is."

"But I chose to make myself an outlaw, didn't I? No matter what I dream about, the fact is always going to slap me in the face: I'm a no-good half-breed outlaw."

Rosie knelt beside his chair. "When I knew you on the

farm, Bart, you never hurt anything. You were always kind and gentle.''

"Not a soul on the face of the earth would call me gentle now, that's for sure.''

"What happened to you, Bart? What changed you?''

"Hell, Rosie,'' he said, lifting her between his legs and settling her onto one thigh. He held her tight against his chest as if her embrace could ward off the realities of his past. "I can't afford to turn back and try to study the things that happened. All I know is that I'm looking to make a change. I've dug myself a grave and I'm just one foot out of it. There's something I've been searching for all my life. I don't know what it is exactly, but I'll know it when I find it. The only thing I'm sure of, Rosie, is that whenever I'm near you, I'm close to the answer.''

"Oh, Bart, I can't mean so much to you! I have to get on with my own life and find what *I'm* searching for.''

He drew back and looked into her eyes. "What are you looking for, Rosie? Tell me that.''

"Freedom,'' she whispered. "I'm looking for freedom.''

"Don't tell me that, girl,'' he murmured, his face twisting with pain as he pulled her hard against him and kissed her mouth. He cupped her head and covered her soft cheeks and warm sweet neck with the urgent caress of his lips.

In his arms she trembled, and he knew it was a shiver not of fear but of desire. Rosie had told him she wanted freedom, but her hands had slid around his back, and her breasts were pressed against his chest. She said she wouldn't respond to a man, but her mouth had found his shoulder and her damp lips were pushing against his skin with a demand she couldn't deny.

"Rosie, my Rosie-girl,'' he whispered.

"Oh, Bart, why did you run off and leave me?'' Her words were spoken into the bare flesh of his neck. "And why did you ever come back?''

"Shh, darlin'. Stop your frettin' now, and let me love you the way I used to.''

"Bart . . .'' But he was already extinguishing her protests in a rush of liquid heat as his hands worked their magic

on her bare shoulders and his lips taunted and lured her
mouth. As she willingly succumbed, a brief wash of
memory soothed her uncertainties. "Let me love you the
way I used to," he had said—and Bart had never taken her
in the terrible way her husband had. Between the two young
lovers there had been only hours of sweet teasing and
exploration, only ardent kisses and murmurs of desire.
There had been avowals of devotion, heedless hunger
tempered by moral restraint, the playful discoveries of the
uninitiated.

Oh, yes, Rosie would let Bart love her the way he used to!
Even now, as his fingers trickled over her shoulders, sliding
away her garments and lighting trails of fire over the swell
of her breasts, she recalled the way it had always been
between them. Stolen pleasures, gentle caresses—and
never, never the utter plundering and brutality she had come
to expect from a man.

"Bart," she whispered into his ear, "remember the way
I used to dampen your neck and make you wiggle?"

Did he remember? Even now as her tongue explored the
sensitive skin beneath his collar, he felt a familiar weakness
slide through him and leave him breathless. Still holding
her, he slipped to the floor and lowered her gently. Yes, the
wooden boards were hard beneath them, but they had never
used a bed for their tender ministrations. Lying now side by
side, they searched for comfort in each other's eyes—green
and brown—the years of pain erased.

"You always wore a little cotton chemise," he said as he
continued running the tips of his fingers back and forth over
the outer rise of her breasts. "You hardly filled it up."

"A pair of thimbles, you used to say."

He smiled. "Not anymore."

"Grapefruits, maybe?"

"Watermelons, more like."

"Oh, Bart!" Giggling, she covered her mouth to block
the sound. How they had laughed together in the old days!
Everything had seemed so light and carefree. But now he
was slipping the straps of her silky chemise from her

shoulders, and she realized that they were no longer children.

She felt an unexpected intensity, almost a craving, in her need for his touch. Something strong and driving wound its way through her when his fingers lowered the edge of her undergarment and she saw her own breasts, creamy white and lightly etched with a delicate blue web, as they blossomed into his palms. The catch in his breath told her that he, too, was unprepared for the moment when her womanhood was revealed to him.

"Rosie-girl, you're all grown up now, aren't you?" he murmured as he began to stroke the full pink tip of each breast. "Do you still want to giggle when I play with you like this?"

Giggle? No, not at all. Barely able to breathe, she felt all at once a rush of hunger that zipped from her nipples to her stomach to her thighs. Her toes went weak, and her fanny began to ache. Suddenly she realized that somewhere in her secret places a new sensation had been born—something throbbing and damp that made her hips begin to sway and her pelvis start to press against his.

As she ran her hands down his back and slid them over the waist of his denims, she felt his mouth begin searching her neck. Unable to stop herself, she cupped his hard buttocks and pushed her stomach against his. Instantly she knew she had made a mistake. There it was again—that undeniable evidence of male dominance!

Oh, if she kept on touching him like this he would want to rip her clothes away and force himself on her. He would plunge into her again and again until tears wet her cheeks and her fingernails cut into her palms. Then he would grunt, roll away, and begin snoring while she crept to her washstand to administer the cool ablutions that were her only solace.

"Bart," she whispered, hoping to stop the madness before it went too far. "Bart, please!"

But he was already sliding her skirt up her thighs, his big hands warm and urgent. His mouth covered hers again, and before she could think, he began to run the tip of his tongue along her closed lips. My goodness—what was this? she thought, amazed that her fear of his approaching hands had vanished in the utter pleasure of his kiss. His tongue, damp and sensual, traced the tight seam of her mouth, then moistened the pillow of her lower lip.

"Taste me, Rosie," he murmured, his mouth never leaving hers.

Tentatively she parted her lips and slipped her own tongue against his. Fire! Flames of delight shot through her body as she allowed herself to toy with this pliant, moist part of him. When she thought she might die of the sensation, he slid his tongue deep into her mouth and began to explore. Suckling him, she ran her hands through his hair and pulled his mouth harder against hers.

His fingers slipped beneath the band of her knickers and began to stroke the petal-soft skin of her lower belly. Reeling, she pushed her breasts against his chest and thrust her tongue into his mouth. With a groan of pleasure, he sifted his fingers through the soft triangle of curls between her thighs.

"Bart!" she whispered, drawing back. He was so near her secret privacies! "Bart, please stop."

"Rosie?" He lifted his head and met her eyes. "Am I hurting you, Rosie?"

"No," she said in a rush of breath. "No, it all feels . . . it feels wonderful. I remember so well how we used to play—and how much I liked it. But you never touched me. Not there. And, Bart, I don't want that. I don't like it."

"Are you sure, Rosie?" he asked, sliding one finger through the curls to gently touch her throbbing place.

She sucked in a gulp of air. "Oh, yes, I'm sure. It . . . it scares me."

He shut his eyes and struggled to control himself. Dear heaven, but she was creamy with readiness for him! Even as she begged him to stop, her hips pushed against his hand and her breasts were tipped with hard mauve pebbles of arousal. He would never do anything to hurt or frighten his Rosie—never! But she lay in his arms, panting with desire, her brown eyes heavy-lidded and her hands belying everything she said.

How he needed her! His own body felt like a brand of fire, hot and demanding. But he knew it was this very urgency that terrified her.

"Rosie," he said into her ear, "tell me which part scares you. Is it the kissing?" He began to suckle her again, all the while exploring her damp secrets with his fingers.

"No," she answered in a shaking breath. "I like the kissing." With his free hand he cupped her breast and began to fondle her nipple. "Is it the way I hold you? You used to love it when I touched you here. Is this what scares you now?"

For a moment she couldn't speak, carried away as she was by the unbearable ecstasies he was working on her body. "No, not that," she managed finally.

Still kissing her mouth, still rolling her nipple between his fingers, he slipped apart the velvety folds of her hidden treasures. Her thighs spread involuntarily, and she lay in limp surrender as his hand stroked and caressed her.

"This, Rosie?" he whispered. "Does this frighten you?"

But she couldn't answer. Her body was riding on a wave of tingling pulsations. Hips dancing, she arched her back into his touch. Her lips parted, and he filled her mouth, their breath mingling. Higher and higher she rose on the crest of the wave, unable to speak or think or see beyond the zigzags of lightning that streaked across her closed eyelids. His fingers taunted her, drawing her near to a dizzying brink, then easing away to leave her gasping and craving more. She clutched at him, lost in the sea of brilliant lights.

"Bart!" she cried as her body suddenly began to slide over the edge of the crest.

He covered her mouth with his as she gave a sobbing exclamation. Her skin erupted in a wash of shivers. Ripples of throbbing undulations tore through her, and her hips rose and fell in a dance of release. Gasping his name, she surged and swayed endlessly as his fingers prolonged her pleasure. At last the waves began to wash away into tiny rhythmic eddies. Her toes curled and her thighs stretched, and her breath escaped her chest in an enormous sigh.

"Bart . . ." She was so spent she couldn't even open her eyes. Her body lay limp in his arms as he slipped his hands around her shoulders and kissed her cheek.

"Is that the part that scares you, Rosie-girl?" he whispered.

She lay in silence, soaking up the smell and the feel of the man who had never left her heart. Finally, as sleep drew a warm blanket around her, she mouthed the words he needed to hear.

"I never knew about that part, Bart," she told him as her eyes drifted shut. "That part was brand-new."

The touch of a hand on her shoulder brought Rosie out of the purple twilight of sleep. She smiled and reached for the callused brown fingers that had brought her so much pleasure. Instead she discovered the hand to be small and cold, shaking her roughly.

"Laurie! Laurie, wake up! You're going to miss uniform inspection."

Sitting bolt upright, Rosie stared at the frizzy pouf of blond hair and the wide blue eyes. "Etta?"

"Well, who did you expect?" Etta shook her head. "Come on, lazybones. You've got ten minutes flat before Mrs. Jensen gives you what-for."

Unable to respond, Rosie glanced at the floor by her table. The mat of sheared dark hair that had been scattered across it was gone. She looked to the window. The buckskin jacket no longer lay in the basket. The holsters and six-shooters had vanished from the shelf. There were no heavy boots on the floor and no leather trousers hanging on a line overhead. Only one thing out of the ordinary ruffled the stillness in her room—the white curtains dancing in the breeze at her open window.

"When you didn't poke your head out to dump your wash water this morning," Etta was saying as she grabbed Rosie's blankets and jerked them back, "I thought sure you were sick again. . . . Lord have mercy, girl, you slept in your uniform!''

Rosie slid out of bed and brushed past her friend. Where was Bart? In the closet? Under the bed? Or had he climbed out the window sometime during the night? She began to button her shirtwaist where he had drawn it apart during their loving. Or had she imagined that? Had she just invented Bart altogether?

"Laurie, you can't wear that uniform. It's all wrinkled!'' Etta pulled open the wardrobe door, and Rosie let out a gasp. But it was empty. "Mr. Gable will have a hissy-fit if he sees you looking like that. And your hair—it's all tangled. Are you sure you're not sick?''

"Etta, just leave me alone for a minute,'' Rosie said quickly, guiding the girl out the door into the hall. "I'll set things right by inspection time.''

"You've got less than five minutes!''

Rosie shut the door and leaned against it, breathing hard. "Bart?'' she called in a whisper. When she didn't hear an answer, she ran to the bed, knelt, and peered beneath it into empty blackness. "Bart, where are you?''

The inspection bell began to ring. A sudden chill poured through her veins. He was gone. Bart had left her again! Dear Lord, how could she go through this another time!

"Laurie!'' Etta was pounding on her door.

Rosie ran to her table and grabbed her hairbrush. No, she hadn't imagined him. She drew a long black hair from the bristles and laid it carefully on her crocheted doily. Bart had been in her room. He had held her and loved her in a way she'd never dreamed! And now he was gone!

"Laurie, here comes Mrs. Jensen!''

Frantic, Rosie bent at the waist and jerked the brush through her hair. In moments she had tied the ribbon, twirled up the bun, and pinned it in place. Then she tossed a clean apron over her wrinkled black dress and buttoned the bib while jamming her stockingless feet into her shoes.

"Coming!'' she cried, bolting through the door and snapping to attention just as Mrs. Jensen approached.

"Miss Kingsley, how rare of you to be untimely,'' the

elderly woman said as she lifted her monocle to inspect Rosie's face. "Mr. Gable will not be pleased."

"I beg your pardon, ma'am." She knew there would be no room for excuses.

Mrs. Jensen lifted a parchment-skinned hand and pecked at Rosie's cheek with her small birdlike fingers. "At least you're not wearing cosmetics."

"Of course not, Mrs. Jensen. I would never do such a thing."

The monocle was lowered. "Your dress is appalling. Is it even fresh?"

"I'll change it at once, ma'am."

"And I see that you haven't bothered to lace your boots."

Rosie stared at her hopelessly tangled shoelaces. "No, ma'am."

"You'll scrub the hallway walls after the breakfast trains, Miss Kingsley."

Rosie started to nod, then remembered her appointment at Mr. Kilgore's school. "Oh, I can't! I have to . . . to . . ."

"Have you found other occupations more interesting than your employment at Fred Harvey's House, Miss Kingsley? If so, I shall be happy to report to Mr. Gable that he may immediately hire your replacement from the long line of young women waiting in Kansas City and Chicago for just such an opportunity."

"No, ma'am. It won't ever happen again." She lowered her head, knowing she couldn't afford to lose her job as a Harvey Girl, even though she had hoped to get the teaching position. "I'll scrub the walls directly after the last train."

"Good morning, Miss Kingsley." The starchy matron turned and marched back down the hall, her monocle swinging at her waist.

Rosie fumed as she washed the yellowed walls of the dormitory. Her pappy, her lady's maid, Dr. Lowell, Mr. Gable, and Mrs. Jensen—everyone she had ever known had tried to control her life. And they'd succeeded!

Soapy water dampening her cuffs, she sniffled back the

tears that had threatened all through the breakfast rush. Bart was gone. When she'd returned to her room to change into an ironed dress, she had searched every nook and cranny of the little place. Bart was gone, along with his boots, guns, jacket, britches, and even the shirt she had bought him.

Her heart fluttered a little every time she thought that he might actually have gone into town to look for work. But the spark of hope was quickly quelled by the reminder that for six long years Bart had not been a working man. He'd been an outlaw. And for all his talk about haircuts and new shirts, he still looked like an Indian. She had no doubt he had either left town—or been shot.

The sheriff didn't come in for breakfast, and neither did Mr. Adams of the *Comet*. It was all Rosie could do to keep from approaching her minister. But the Reverend Cullen was visiting with the Baptist preacher, and none of the other locals said a word about town news.

The time passed when Rosie should have been at Mr. Kilgore's school, and her heart sank even further. Such a responsible man would never hire a teacher who couldn't bother to show up when she'd promised. What kind of an example was that?

The lunch trains started through the depot just as Mrs. Jensen approved Rosie's newly scrubbed walls, and she rushed down the stairs to her station. Swallowing the knot in her throat, she served up sandwiches and soups and plates of fresh fruit by the score. She scooped tips into her pockets, scrubbed countertops, and pasted the Harvey smile on her face.

But as she stood with her hands locked behind her back and her eyes scanning her station, she felt sick with unhappiness. Bart had loved her last night. He'd given her something she'd never even imagined possible. The memory of his touch was so strong it rocked her off balance every time she allowed it to creep through her thoughts.

Then he had gone away. And Rosie knew why.

Oh, dear God, she *knew* why Bart had run off again! Last night she had been no better than that scoundrel Dr. Lowell.

She'd taken everything Bart had to offer her, every pleasure he awakened her to, and then she had fallen asleep!

Bart must have lain there for a long time thinking about how bad he felt and how empty and unsatisfied he was inside. Then he must have put her into bed, strapped on his guns, and climbed out the window to start his new life without her. How could she blame him?

*Six

....

Buttery afternoon sunlight gilded Rosie's hand as she lifted it to knock on the schoolroom door. From inside the small frame building she could hear thin, high-pitched voices lifted in song. Someone strummed a guitar in a futile attempt to regulate the tempo. When the guitar hit a discordant twang and the choir dissolved into a medley of giggles, Rosie squared her shoulders and rapped at the open door.

In a moment Mr. Kilgore peered around the frame. His eyebrows lifted above his thick spectacles. "Good afternoon, Miss Kingsley. We had agreed on a midmorning meeting, had we not?"

"Yes, sir," Rosie answered, trying her best to sound confident. "My services were unexpectedly required at the Harvey House during the morning, sir. Please accept my apology for the delay."

He pondered for a moment, then dipped his head. "Of course."

At his kindness she felt a surge of assurance. "May I come in?"

"As a matter of fact, Miss Kingsley, I'm afraid our appointment is not necessary after all."

Rosie's pasted-on smile waned. "I beg your pardon?"

"After discussing your situation with my wife, I came to the conclusion that your services will not be of use to us here at the public school."

"But why not? I'm perfectly qualified."

"On the contrary." Mr. Kilgore glanced over his shoulder at the bustling classroom, then stepped out onto the stoop and spoke in a low voice. "After assessing our interview, I realized that you have neither a teaching license nor any professional recommendations. You have no experience in teaching and no training whatsoever."

"I assure you I can obtain the license, Mr. Kilgore. As for experience, how am I to acquire it unless someone like you is willing to employ me? I have the education, the dedication, and above all the sincere desire to become a teacher. I've left my home and family, every security in life, with the single aim of educating children. Sir, I promise you would not be the least disappointed were you to hire me."

His face softening, Mr. Kilgore gave Rosie a gentle nod. "I appreciate your enthusiasm, Miss Kingsley. Such earnestness is admirable indeed. But I'm afraid you simply lack something I have decided is most essential to any teacher in the town of Raton, New Mexico."

"And what is that?"

"A husband." When her mouth dropped open, he shrugged. "In the short time I have owned this school, I have lost both of my teachers to the lure of matrimony. Mine is not the only scholarly institution to suffer such a fate. The Raton Free School's teacher, Miss Bella Roux, recently departed for Chicago to marry a Mr. Daniel Tine. Miss Harliss opened a school in town, then closed it after one year and moved to Hutchinson, Kansas. In fact, the only successful schools in the Raton district are the pay school operated by Mrs. Belle McCord, Springtown's log-cabin school taught by Mrs. Bobb—both of these instructors are happily married to local men—and mine. Neither of the other two schools is in need of an extra teacher, and based on their example and my own experience, I have made up my mind to employ only a married woman."

"A husband has nothing to do with the success or failure of a schoolteacher, Mr. Kilgore," Rosie protested.

"In Raton it does. As you well know, this town is populated with railway men, homesteaders, and cowboys— every one of them eager to find himself a wife. I wager that each of you Harvey Girls will be wed within the year and carted off to railroad towns or ranches across the West. No, Miss Kingsley, I'm afraid I'm going to have to insist on employing a married woman as my new schoolteacher.''

"But I have no intention of ever marrying, sir!'' Rosie responded hotly. ''I plan to remain a spinster for the rest of my life. I assure you I would be loyal to your school.''

"A woman as fetching as you? I can't imagine the local cowboys leaving you alone for a minute, my dear. Why, you'd need but to bat those big brown eyes and you'd have your choice of husbands. I'm sorry, Miss Kingsley, but you're simply too great a risk.''

"But Mr. Kilgore!''

"Good afternoon, Miss Kingsley.'' He gave her the slightest of bows, backed into his classroom, and shut the door on Rosie's dreams.

For a long time she stood on the stoop and listened to the young voices inside the school. She could hear the children reciting multiplication tables, singing the alphabet, and reading stories from primers. The shuffling of restless feet and the scratch of chalk upon slate drifted through the open window beside the door. The scent of early lilacs carried from across the street on the mountain breezes, yet to Rosie even the sunlight weighed heavily on her shoulders.

Her dreams came to an end. Her hopes had just been crushed. She had worried for hours that she might lose the teaching job because she'd missed the morning interview, but that had had nothing to do with it. A husband—that was what she lacked. To Mr. Kilgore and the local citizenry, a husband would prove her stability; a husband would endow her with the labels she needed of matron, wife, mother. With a husband she would shift from the role of silly, flirtatious girl to that of reliable, permanent homemaker.

But Rosie didn't want a husband.

As she started down the steps onto the street, she reviewed the list of men who had pushed their way into her life. Dr. Lowell would be the most stable sort of husband Mr. Kilgore could ever wish upon a teacher. But of course Rosie could never confess to that abominable marriage. Her husband would have her carted back to Kansas City in a second if he ever found out what had become of his wayward wife. No doubt her desertion had placed him in a horrifying social position and had probably endangered his professional standing.

Plenty of men in Raton had made passes at Rosie, asked her to dance, and escorted her to picnics. Wanting to seem like the other girls, she had gone along with these attentions to some degree. But she had always pushed away any serious advances with the excuse that eventually she wanted to become a teacher—and good teachers were always *single*!

Mr. Kilgore was probably right: she could bat her eyelashes and have a husband in no time flat. But what a price to pay for a teaching position! Not for anything in the world would Rosie trade her freedom for the imprisonment of marriage.

As she headed for the Harvey House, she studied the townsmen delivering goods to the mercantiles, swabbing saloon floors, marching in and out of banks, and driving cattle to the stock corrals by the depot. None of them had the broad-shouldered, rugged physique of the one man Rosie actually might have considered allowing on the fringes of her life. Bart Kingsley was gone; she had no doubt of it. The town felt empty to her, devoid of the presence she felt sure she would sense were he there.

With a sigh she climbed onto the porch of the Harvey House and fixed her eyes on the distant blue mesas. She didn't want the abusive Dr. Lowell for a husband. She didn't want a cowboy or a railwayman, either. Even if she wanted Bart, she couldn't have him, and she might as well accept that she never would. Now she had lost her chance at the teaching job.

As the first dinner train whistled through the distant pass, Rosie molded her lips into the Harvey smile, locked her hands behind her back, and hurried to her station in the dining room.

Any small hope Rosie might have held that Bart was in town faded as the days turned into weeks, and the month of

April headed for May. Raton came to life with sweet wild grasses that greened the patchy yards around newly white-washed clapboard houses. Lilacs, roses, and violets brought from the East blossomed among budding native piñon, aspen, juniper, and cottonwood trees. Mrs. Bayne's Milli-nery and Dressmaking Shop produced wondrously trimmed hats, bonnets, and gowns for the Easter church services. Driving wagons laden with seed plows and cultivators, farmers headed out to their homestead claims. Coal-burning stoves shut down, the air cleared, and the fresh smells of spring cleaning, baking bread, and wet laundry permeated the town.

True to Mr. Kilgore's prediction, spring fever took its toll. Annie up and married a cowboy from the J. R. Jones ranch, and she moved out of the Harvey House to take up her new job raising hogs. Mae fell in love with a brakeman from Chicago who wanted to marry her and take her back to the big city. But she was also crazy about a welder from C. A. Fox's hardware and tin shop who aimed to make her his wife and settle her in a quaint little house in town. Etta and Stefan Braun failed to keep their ardent romance a secret, and Mrs. Jensen was in favor of firing them both. It was only Tom Gable—who knew he couldn't find a better chef than the young German—who kept them employed at the House.

Rosie dragged herself to town picnics, horse races, and egg hunts with the rest of the Harvey Girls, but it was all she could do to keep her chin up. One afternoon, the sheriff dropped by with some news for the coffee drinkers in the Harvey House lunchroom. The Pinkerton Agency had sent word that Bart Kingsley had been rounded up in Albuquer-que and carted back to Missouri to face the judge. He'd be hanged, Sheriff Bowman assured anyone who asked him. A man with a record as black as that outlaw's would be left gargling on a rope, for sure.

So that was the end of that; Rosie had to accept it. Bart Kingsley really was no good, after all. He had come into her life twice, toyed with her twice, and left her twice. Not only that, but she had been fool enough to believe everything he had told her—twice. All his sweet words and gentle ways had been a sham. His tender touch and fiery caresses had served his own selfish aims. How she had managed to fall for such a man twice, Rosie would never understand. She certainly wouldn't let herself act so lamebrained ever again.

In fact, as April wound to a close, Rosie decided she would pursue her goal of teaching just as she had planned. If the resolution to extend the school year passed during the coming election, Mr. Kilgore would be in need of a teacher. And if not he, one of the other school owners in town might be looking for a determined young spinster, though all her inquiries at the other schools had come to nothing.

Still hopeful, Rosie scheduled an appointment with the district school board in Springer, hours away by rail. On Friday, April 27, 1883, she used her free vacation train pass to travel south to Springer, where she sat for examination.

"You have passed with distinction, Miss Kingsley," Commissioner Jerome Troy announced as he handed her a crisp certificate that afternoon after she had sat through five hours of grueling questions. "Any school in the district would be proud to employ you."

All the way back to Raton on the train, those words curled through Rosie's thoughts. As the engine struggled up the mountains to the tiny town that marked the famous pass, her determination grew. She would have that teaching job! Mr. Kilgore's school had the finest reputation in the area, and with her exemplary performance on the exam, she would secure a position there.

The moment the train whistled into town, Rosie smoothed and dusted her city skirts, descended onto the depot platform, and marched straight to First Street. By the time she turned onto Second Street, her heart was pumping harder than it had the whole time she'd been facing the school board. She climbed the schoolhouse steps, tucked stray wisps of hair into her knot, and knocked on the front door.

"Well, Miss Kingsley," Mr. Kilgore said when he looked out the open window. He came to the door and cracked it, but he didn't invite Rosie in. She hardly cared.

With a flourish of pride, she unrolled her certificate and held it up in front of her chest like a banner.

"I have passed my teacher's examination with distinction," she announced. "Commissioner Troy informed me that any school in the district would be proud to employ me."

Mr. Kilgore tucked away a tender smile and pretended to inspect the certificate. "My goodness, these are high marks," he commented. "Mathematics, Latin, history, geography, grammar . . . well, well. And French! You certainly have proven yourself here, Miss Kingsley."

She beamed. "My education has been of the highest order."

"I see that. Yet it takes more than a good education to score marks like these. You must be a very intelligent young woman."

"Intelligent and determined. I've returned to request your reconsideration of my application for a teaching position, Mr. Kilgore."

He let out a breath and chuckled lightly. "Persistence is indeed a virtue. But all I need to do is take one look at you in that lovely blue dress, Miss Kingsley, and I find myself assailed by doubts. What is your marital status these days, young lady?"

"I am single, sir, and determined to remain so." If Rosie expected this to reassure Mr. Kilgore, she was wrong. His smile sagged, and he shook his head.

"I've told you I won't hire an unmarried woman, Miss Kingsley. You're too much of a risk. Why don't you take your certificate back to Kansas City and seek out a position? Or, if you're determined to stay in the West, go to Albuquerque or Santa Fe. I'm sure they're desperate for young single schoolteachers."

"But I've made my home here," she protested. "I belong to a church; I have friends; I'm part of a community that I love. I've invested my savings in Raton's banks and I've struggled to prove myself a decent, reliable worker in this town. How can you ask me to start all over, when you're in need of a teacher yourself?"

"I don't know that the school election will pass tomorrow, Miss Kingsley. If it does, my wife and I will make the effort to conduct classes ourselves for the next three months. If not, there will be no need of a teacher here anyway. I'm sorry, my dear. Truly I am."

Once again, he shut the door on Rosie. She stood outside, fingers gripping her skirt and jaws clenched against threatening tears.

"I will have that job, Mr. Kilgore," she whispered over the lump in her throat. "I'll have it no matter what you think of me."

Discouraged but undaunted, Rosie hurried back to the Harvey House and climbed the stairs to her room. Having taken the day off for her trip to Springer, she still had several hours to herself while the other girls waited on the dinner-train passengers. Though she had thought the free time would be a blessing, she discovered that her mind insisted on traveling down a wayward track.

As she sat on her chair by the window, Rosie couldn't keep back the memories of those hours she had spent with Bart. How badly she had been fooled! He had told her he'd come to Raton to find her, that she'd been the one bright spot in his life. And so she'd sewn him up, fed him, boarded him, clothed him—and allowed him liberties with her femininity. Then he'd taken his new haircut and his new shirt, and he'd left her.

They had spent such a short time together, but Rosie knew she would never be the same. In those brief hours with Bart, she had fallen under his old spell. She had trusted every word from his lying lips. She had trembled at the sight of his rugged body and the feel of his sensual caresses. Worst of all, she had allowed him to touch her in a way no man ever had. Certainly the callous Dr. Lowell had never taken her to such heights . . . or such depths.

Dabbing a silk handkerchief into the corner of her eye, Rosie stood from the window seat and went to her dressing table. She spread her rolled teaching certificate and slid it into the edge of the oak frame around her mirror so that she could see it from any part of her small room. She might be a fool when it came to Bart Kingsley, but she was brilliant in every other area of her life.

As she changed out of her city clothes into her white nightgown, Rosie decided that she had taken enough of what other people dished out. She had come to Raton to get a teaching position, and by golly, she would have one.

"Dear God," she whispered as she folded her hands and knelt by her bed, "I've made some whopping mistakes, as You very well know. There was all that with Bart . . . and then there was Dr. Lowell . . . and then Bart again. I'm sure You can't be any too pleased with me. But, Lord, I had good intentions in coming out here to Raton to be a schoolteacher, only now Mr. Kilgore says he doesn't want me. I know he needs me, Father, and I know I'd do a good job for him. Dear God, please work out this problem. Give me a sign, Lord, and I'll do whatever it takes. Just show me a sign. Amen."

As she slipped between the cool sheets, stretched her tired legs, and shut her eyes, Rosie felt the first peace she'd known since Bart Kingsley crawled out from under her bed three weeks before.

At one o'clock in the morning the screaming whistle of the switch engine woke every sleeping soul in the town of Raton. The firing of guns shattered the night's silence. Shouts and cries echoed through the streets.

"Fire! Fire!" someone hollered below the Harvey House dormitory. "O'Reilly's Saloon is afire!"

Rosie bolted out of bed and ran to the window to discover the ebony sky lit with an orange glow. Red sparks shot upward to mingle with the stars and then vanish. Smoke billowed over shingled rooftops. The members of the newly organized hose company, decked out in black boots and yellow rain slickers, galloped past the Harvey backyard.

"Laurie!" Etta was hammering on Rosie's bedroom door. "Laurie, there's a fire in town! Everyone's going out to see it. We've decided to wear our peignoirs!"

"I'm coming!" All thoughts of her troubles extinguished

by the excitement, Rosie grabbed her lace-edged white robe and pulled it on over her nightgown as she tore open the bedroom door. "O'Reilly's Saloon is a frame building, Etta!"

"I know! It'll go up like a matchstick. The whole town might burn down. Oh, isn't this thrilling!" Etta, frizzy blond hair bouncing around her shoulders, was dancing up and down the halls while she waited for the other girls to assemble. Even Mrs. Jensen, ruffled nightcap in place, had pulled on her boots, grabbed her monocle, and started marching toward the stairs.

"Onward, girls!" she bellowed. "A Harvey employee always aids her community in times of distress."

Etta giggled and nudged Rosie. "She wants to see the fire as much as any of us!"

Like a flock of angels, the white-clad Harvey Girls floated down the backyard and hurried across the street. Gray smoke hung thick in the night air, tickling Rosie's nostrils and mingling in her loosened hair. She clutched her shoulders against the chill but noted with relief that no wind had sprung up to blow the fire from building to building.

It seemed as if all the citizens of the Gate City had emerged from their homes to view the spectacular blaze. Children clung to their mothers' nightgowns. Fathers lugging buckets of sloshing water trotted toward the saloon. Tom and Griff, the town dogs, howled every time the switch engine whistle blew, and young boys climbed onto rooftops for a better view.

While the Harvey Girls gathered under the awning of Page Palmiter's Bank Exchange Saloon across the street from O'Reilly's, Rosie sucked in a breath at the awesome inferno. Against the bright orange fire, silhouetted men shouted, waved, and tugged heavy hoses. Streams of water shot into the fire. The saloon hissed, steamed, sparked, and groaned.

"There's Page Palmiter!" Etta cried, pointing out a local saloon owner. "Mae just heard that he's the one who first spotted the fire at O'Reilly's."

Rosie could barely make out the popular man who was

bravely kicking down O'Reilly's door to spray water on the blaze. She recognized a good many townsfolk: the Adams brothers, who had elected to fight the fire rather than take notes for the *Comet*; Sheriff Bowman with his deputies; Judge Moulton, the justice of the peace; Reverend Cullen, the Methodist preacher, and Reverend Craigmyle, the Baptist minister; Mr. Bayne, whose wife ran the millinery shop; and Dr. Kohlhouser, the local physician.

"There's Stefan!" Etta gasped. "Oh, Laurie, I hope he doesn't get hurt!"

Rosie could see the young German's blond hair backlit by the blaze. He was unrolling hoses from the hose cart. "There's Mr. Pace, the postmaster," she said. "He's helping Stefan."

"Who's that with them?"

A stocky, long-haired man had just climbed onto the hose cart and was shouting orders left and right. His hooked nose wore a faint sheen, and his high cheekbones had turned pink with heat.

"That's Cheyenne Bill," Mrs. Jensen announced, her starchy voice unable to hide the fascination she obviously felt for the man. "He doesn't eat at the House often, but he's famous in town."

"Is he a real Indian?" Etta asked.

"No one knows. He works odd jobs, and he's very popular at glove contests. I understand all the men in town regard him highly and are known to wager large purses on him."

"Jiminy," Etta whispered. "And who's that Indian with him? His brother?"

Mrs. Jensen squinted through her monocle. "Never seen him before in my life."

Rosie turned to focus on the tall, broad-shouldered silhouette of the man who had leapt onto the hose cart beside Cheyenne Bill. The stranger's short black hair glistened in the firelight, and his thickly muscled arms gleamed like bronze. He pulled at the tangled hoses, his long body moving with sleek pantherlike grace. Then he straightened, tossed a length of hose to a waiting fireman, and lifted his eyes to the stars.

Ice washed through Rosie's veins.

"He's an Indian, all right," Etta said, oblivious of the stricken look on her companion's face. "Why, except for the haircut, you'd think he'd walked right out of a tepee. Oh, look, Laurie—the saloon roof's caving in!"

But Rosie gave the shuddering, cracking building not a moment's heed. Her eyes were fastened on the tall stranger who had slung his arm over Cheyenne Bill's shoulders and was gabbing like a best buddy. The shorter man shook his head, laughed out loud, and began hollering to the other townsfolk.

"It's a lost cause," he shouted. "Let 'er go, boys!"

As the crowd of men dashed to safety away from the collapsing saloon, the stranger was lost in the throng. But Rosie didn't need to see him again to know who he was.

Bart Kingsley had come back to Raton.

"I'd open the Bank Exchange for you fellers," Page Palmiter was saying, "but me and my cook are just too tuckered out to fix up a meal this time of night."

"Who cares about a meal, Page?" someone shouted in return. "Open 'er up for the whiskey! Couple snorts of snake poison ought to be good for what ails us!"

As the men laughed, Tom Gable elbowed his way out into the street and held up his hat. "There are too many women and children here for you to turn this into a moonshine party. Come on over to the House, and my gals will fix you up with some hot coffee and cinnamon rolls."

"How-dee!" someone hooted. In moments a stampede for the Harvey House was under way. Children in nightshirts, women in nightgowns and robes, and soot-blackened men abandoned the charred saloon as though they'd completely forgotten it, and began dancing down the street.

"Lord have mercy," Mrs. Jensen shrieked as the full impact of Tom Gable's invitation hit her. "Skedaddle, girls! You've got mouths to feed."

Rosie had completely lost sight of Bart. Hand in hand, she and Etta raced down a side street. The other girls were close on their heels, and one of them swung around to yell at Mrs. Jensen, whose large bosom was undulating with every step as she tried to keep up.

"What about our uniforms, ma'am?" Mae called.

"Forget them," she puffed. "The whole town's outfitted for bed, so you might as well be, too."

"Will they expect fresh orange juice?" someone else cried. "And what about fruit plates?"

The young women scampered up the back steps and into the kitchen to find Stefan and the other cooks already slamming hot oven doors. The blond chef shouted orders in German which nobody could understand, and wore a grin that made him look like a jolly cook just popping out of a cuckoo clock.

There was no time to think. Rosie and her companions rushed out into the empty dining room and lunchroom to take up their positions. Amid the ringing of the gong, the front door burst open, and two hundred laughing, chattering Ratonians poured inside the Harvey House. All formality went by the wayside as the waitresses hurried from table to table to pour hot coffee, milk, and, yes—freshly squeezed orange juice that was being pumped in the back kitchen by three young baker's boys.

In no time the smoky-smelling room filled with the aroma of cinnamon, sugar, raisins, and hot yeasty bread. As Rosie came out of the kitchen, she ran smack-dab into Etta and nearly dropped a whole plate of rolls. In spite of her jitters, she laughed, lifted her tray a little higher, and wove her way among the crowded tables.

This was why she so dearly loved Raton! The families, the chatter, the camaraderie—everyone in town turning out to fight a fire, then heading for a midnight meal as though it were the commonest thing in the world. How silly and loose Rosie felt to be dressed in her nightgown and robe! How delightful to scamper through a room where she was usually obliged to stand like a stiff soldier! The lunch counter was crowded with children and youngsters who had managed to escape their parents. Rosie patted sleepy little boys on the head and tucked napkins under the collars of wiggly little girls.

"Hello, Miss Kingsley," a mid-sized fellow called out. "We saw you at school today. Or was it yesterday?"

Amid a cacophony of giggles, Rosie waved at the young redhead she recognized as Mr. Kilgore's troublemaker. "And you'll be seeing more of me soon, I wager, sir."

"Are you going to teach us, Miss Kingsley?" a blond, blue-eyed girl asked.

"Lord willing, I am." She glanced at Mr. Kilgore, who was surrounded by a cluster of children at the counter. "That is, if things work out the way I hope they do."

"Miss Kingsley!" The shout came from Mr. Gable, who was standing in the doorway between the two eating rooms. "We've got fifteen cinnamon rolls in here. Can you come help out?"

"Sure thing!" Rosie wiped her hands on her apron, gave the children a wink, and headed into the dining room. But the moment she saw who sat at the central table, she longed to back right out and run up the stairs to her room.

"Right here, Miss Kingsley," Mr. Gable said, pointing out the large table around which crowded a group of Raton's prominent townsmen. "Eleven cinnamon rolls at this table and four over here. They're asking for coffee, too."

For a moment Rosie thought she wouldn't be able to make her legs move. She was staring into a pair of green, green eyes that sparkled like rainwashed leaves. The buckskin jacket was gone. So were the heavy holsters and six-shooters. But she recognized the collarless white shirt, the thick black hair, and the confident smile.

"Miss Kingsley!" Tom Gable shouted.

Jumping to attention, Rosie half ran into the kitchen and grabbed a tray of steaming rolls. It *was* Bart! But how could that man be Bart? Bart had left Raton weeks ago. Bart had been captured in Albuquerque and sent to Missouri to be hanged. Bart had run off and left her again—hadn't he?

She pushed between two men and stood at the large round table. Wedging the tray against her hip, she began setting the thick, six-inch-in-diameter rolls at each place. Shaking, she nearly dropped Bart's roll onto his plate, but he said nothing and didn't even look at her.

When she reached the other side of the table, she glanced up from her tray to find him watching her again. But his face bore no sign of recognition.

"Miss Kingsley, you got any refills on this coffee?"

Rosie looked toward the sound of the voice and saw Sheriff Bowman holding out his empty white cup. *Sheriff Bowman—at the same table with Bart!*

"I reckon most of us worked up a powerful thirst fighting that fire," the lawman continued.

"I'll say I did," the man Mrs. Jensen had called Cheyenne Bill affirmed. Swarthy, cocky, and grinning from ear to ear, he eyed the other gentlemen. "I reckon I organized the whole affair from start to finish."

"Chances are you lit the dang fire in the first place," the sheriff said with a laugh as Rosie filled his coffee cup.

"Would I do a thing like that, now, Sheriff Bowman?" The Indian feigned a hurt expression. "You just ask my cousin Buck here. We was over to the Mountain Monarch playing billiards right up until we heard the switch engine whistle blow."

Rosie's eyes darted to Bart, who had just set his coffee cup in its saucer. "The worst of it is, *I* was winning," he said.

"Naw!" Cheyenne Bill clapped Bart on the back and began to guffaw. "You boys reckon I should call up a glove contest to settle this matter between me and my cuz?"

"You wouldn't want to spar with the Terror of the Wicked West, Buck," the sheriff said. "Ol' Cheyenne Bill would drive you into the ground like a stake."

As if a signal had been given, all the men at the table chorused: "Cheyenne Bill is a hard, hard man."

Amid the ensuing hoots of laughter, Rosie fled to the kitchen. Bart *was* back! But why? Oh, why now? She leaned against a cupboard and clutched at her churning stomach. He was pretending not to know her. But how long had he been in Raton? How had he managed to become the "cousin" of this famous Cheyenne Bill whom everyone seemed to admire? When had he changed his name from Bart to Buck? And how on earth had he managed to delude Sheriff Bowman?

She pushed her heavy, loose hair behind her back and stared at her feet. Bart. He was a liar, a user, a trickster, an outlaw. And he was the handsomest man in the entire world! Oh, those green eyes. With his short hair and white shirt, he might have passed for a white man, except that his high cheekbones and coppery skin gave him away at once as an Indian. But he certainly was not a Cheyenne! He certainly wasn't named Buck.

And he most certainly *was* back in town.

"Miss Kingsley!" Mr. Gable bellowed. "Three more cinnamon rolls just walked in the door!"

Rosie straightened her shoulders, lifted her chin, and hurried back out into the dining room. But the big table had emptied, and Bart Kingsley had vanished just as certainly as he had returned.

*Seven
. . . .

If any day in Raton could be given over to a little extra
sleep, a fishing trip, or a train ride to Springer for supplies,
it was Saturday. And after all the excitement over the
Friday-night fire at O'Reilly's Saloon, Rosie wasn't sure
how many men would haul themselves out of bed to cast a
school election vote. Only a scant number of townsmen
appeared at the Raton Harvey House for breakfast that
morning, and Rosie feared the inactivity didn't bode well
for sending Mr. Kilgore's free public school into an extra
three-month term.

Tired and on edge after the busy night, she scrubbed her
dining room station after the last morning train had chugged
away from the depot. The exhilaration of the evening before
had gradually faded during the long hours in which she had
lain awake turning the reappearance of Bart Kingsley over
and over in her mind. When she made up her mind to leave
the House and hurry out to First Street toward the voting
boxes, Rosie had to admit she had been driven out into the
brisk morning by more than a desire to watch the men cast
their ballots.

Trying not to seem too obvious, she scanned the front of
every adobe, frame, or brick building she passed. She
peeked surreptitiously into windows and glanced through
open front doors. She scrutinized every carriage that rattled
past her down the street. She carefully inspected every rider,
tradesman, and merchant.

Page Palmiter and some other men were surveying the
blackened ruins across the street from the Bank Exchange

Saloon. Wisps of gray smoke curled into the blue sky to be wafted toward the distant snowy mesas. Dr. Kohlhouser's enormous brindle mastiff, Griff—all one hundred fifty pounds of him—had busied himself sniffing around the broken kegs and bottles. Griff had a well-known fondness for hard spirits and had been known to knock a man flat to get at his whiskey. He also was a tremendous salivator and could be tracked around town by the trail of wet drips he left wherever he went. Griff was accompanied by Tom, who was part St. Bernard and part something else nobody was sure of. Tom belonged to W. A. White, Raton's popular photographer, and was a favorite among the schoolchildren.

Among the charred beams, a group of boys played picket, the local form of hide-and-go-seek. Rosie recognized one of them as the young redhead who had hailed her during the midnight snack at the House.

"Mornin', Miss Kingsley!" he called as he leapt over an empty beer keg. "Them sure was good cinnamon rolls!"

"Why, thank you, sir," Rosie answered, lifting a hand to wave. "How's the picket game?"

Before the fellow could answer, another began to jeer, "Manford Wade is sweet on Miss Kingsley! Mannie has a sweetheart!"

At that moment Griff took it into his massive head to chase the taunters down the street. Tom took up the pursuit with equal fervor. Rosie watched the boys yelp and holler, their scrawny legs churning as they ran around a corner and disappeared. Only paces behind them scampered Tom, while behind him galloped the loose-lipped Griff, ears pricked forward, tail wagging, and foamy slobber flying in a spray around his head.

Mannie had ducked behind a blackened porch post to escape the onslaught. Now he grinned at Rosie with a smile that seemed to spread from ear to ear. "Where are ya goin', Miss Kingsley?"

"I thought I'd take a look at the voting booths." She paused and studied the boy's sparkling gray eyes and bright red hair. "I'm hoping Raton will decide to keep you in school another three months, Manford."

"Three months is a long time. It'll be hot in the classroom, and most of us boys will be workin' on the farms or in the mines."

"Maybe so, but Mr. Kilgore believes that if you want to keep up your studies, you'll need those extra months of school."

Mannie stuck his hands in his pockets and squinted up at the tall starched-and-uniformed woman who faced him on the muddy street. "I'm a good reader, Miss Kingsley," he averred. "I wouldn't mind keeping a book handy this summer. But I don't cotton to figures. When it comes to numbers, I'm as chuckleheaded as an old prairie dog."

"If the proposal passes and your father allows you to stay in school, you'll have the chance to really concentrate on your mathematics."

"I don't have a pappy, and my mother don't care a lick about arithmetic. She needs me to bring in a good wage come summer. You understand about that."

"Yes, I do, Manford." Rosie gave him a smile. "Working is very important. And so is school."

"Ah, shoot. I reckon you're right." He kicked his heel against a charred window frame that lay on the sooty ground. "So you're gonna go have a look at the voting. Mind if I come along?"

"Not at all. I was hoping you'd join me."

Rosie suppressed the grin that tickled her lips as the youngster swaggered along beside her. Clearly Manford Wade regarded himself as a fine gentleman—not one to be swayed by the teasing of his mates. Unlike the ragged boys he had been playing with, Mannie wore his shirtsleeves buttoned at the wrists and his tails tucked into his pants. Though the elbows and knees of his clothing had been patched and repatched, he might have been a city dandy the way he held his head up and strode proudly down the street.

"You made them cinnamon rolls, Miss Kingsley?" he asked as they crossed toward the line of men gathering outside McAuliffe and Ferguson's Hall. The hall served as a popular gathering place, and it was the scene of many public events. Dances, socials, school plays, meetings, dramas, operas, grand balls, and even church services took place beneath its roof. This weekend the hall housed the ballot boxes where the men of Raton would cast their votes for or against the extended school term.

"No," Rosie answered Manford. "The baker at the House is in charge of all the breads we serve." She thought for a moment and then made an announcement that would have curdled her father's blood. "I'm a waitress, Manford."

The boy was oblivious. "Them cinnamon rolls sure was tasty. Wish I could have me another right this minute."

Rosie stepped onto the wooden walkway and glanced at the faces of the men in the line. Bart was not among them. It occurred to her once again to wonder if she had simply dreamed she'd seen him sitting at the table with Cheyenne Bill and Sheriff Bowman. Surely those green eyes belonged to the man who had held and caressed her only weeks before. But where was he now?

"You reckon women ought to get the chance to vote, Miss Kingsley?" Mannie asked.

Rosie trained her attention on the boy. "It's difficult to say, Manford. I was brought up in a very conservative household. According to my father, women aren't meant to assert themselves so boldly in public affairs. Until recently, I held with that thought myself and considered the suffragettes to be the worst sort of brazen troublemakers."

"That's perzactly what my mama says about 'em."

"But, Manford, just think how wonderful it would be if I could vote in this election. If women could vote on school issues, the resolution would have a good chance of passing."

"Not my mama. She'd vote against it. She wants me in the mines come summer."

Rosie was just formulating a response to that statement when someone brushed past her elbow.

"Mornin', Miss Kingsley. Sure enjoyed the food at the House last night."

Rosie swung around to find Bart Kingsley already half-way past her. He and the stocky Cheyenne Bill were headed for the end of the voting line, and their determined stride gave her no opportunity to respond.

Instead she simply stood stock-still and watched Bart. He greeted several of the other men, squared his shoulders, hooked his thumbs in the pockets of his britches, and took up his position to vote in the school election of Raton. Bart—a wanted outlaw! Rosie clamped her mouth shut and tried to make herself listen to Mannie, who was opining on the possible results of women ever attaining the right to vote.

"'Spect we might even get to the point of havin' female lawmakers," he was saying. "Just try to imagine a lady sheriff. *That*'ll give you a laugh."

Rosie nodded, but she was watching as Bart listened to Cheyenne Bill, who was bragging about the way he had organized the hose company to fight the fire. Bart was dressed as he had been the night before, in the white collarless shirt she had bought him, a pair of denim trousers that looked almost brand-new, and the old boots she recognized from having pulled them off his feet not many weeks before.

Any sign of the bullet wound in his side was gone. So, too, was the long-haired, savage demeanor that had made Bart seem so wild and raw. He might have passed for any other of the Raton men, save the color of his skin and hair, the distinctive planes of his face, and the fact that he stood a good three inches over the heads of his companions.

"And what about a lady governor?" Manford was asking her. "Now that would just about do in the territory. Ain't no way a woman could manage all them governor-type jobs and be sucklin' babies, cookin' meals for her man, warshin' clothes, ironin', weedin', hoein', sweepin', moppin', cannin', and such as that. Not a chance."

Rosie pulled her attention back to the boy. "It would be a challenge, but I don't imagine it would be impossible."

"Shoot, my mama says if women got to vote, first thing you know they'd be turnin' into men—smokin' cigars, drinkin' whiskey, wearin' britches, cussin', and shootin' up saloons instead of bein' the entertainment. My mama thinks a woman's place is right in her own house with her own kids and her pots and pans and warshboard.''

"Not every woman hankers to cook and clean, young feller," Bart put in, his deep voice a startling contrast to the youth's contralto.

Rosie's head shot up, and she realized that the voting line had moved forward enough that Bart and Cheyenne Bill were now standing next to her.

Manford stared at the tall, green-eyed stranger. "Who're you?" he asked bluntly.

"You can call me Buck. I'm Bill's cousin."

"You're a Cheyenne, too?"

Bart smiled. "Reckon I must be part Indian somewhere along the way, don't you?"

Manford nodded. "Sure looks that way to me. You just came to town, didn't ya?"

"About a week ago. I'm working at the livery stable over by the depot." Though the words were spoken to the boy, Rosie knew the message was meant for her. "I've claimed a homestead out near the mesa, and I'm fixing to start building my dugout this afternoon."

"No kiddin'? You reckon you could use some help? I'm damn good with a shovel."

"Hey, you'd better watch your language in the presence of such a fine lady as Miss Kingsley here." For the first time since he'd joined the line of voters, Bart looked directly at Rosie. He tipped his battered black felt hat. "Mornin', ma'am."

Rosie swallowed. "Good morning."

But Bart was addressing Manford again. "Yes, sir, I've got one hundred and sixty acres of prime land, and I'm aiming to grow sugar beets for cash, run a few beeves, and build myself a snug dugout to live in. I expect I *could* use a man with a shovel. What do you say we head out of town right after I take care of my civic duty here at the ballot box?"

"Golly, I better run tell my mama!" Manford hightailed it across the street before sliding to a stop. "I'll be right back, Injun Buck. Don't leave town without me, hear?" He started to run again, then caught himself. "Bye, Miss Kingsley! Hope to see ya again real soon."

"Good-bye, Manford." She took advantage of the need to turn away from Bart to wave at the flying youngster. Before she could fall under the spell of those green eyes, she set her shoulders away from the line of men and hurried down the wooden sidewalk.

She had just stepped onto the street when the first lunch train's whistle blew. Setting off at a trot, she heard a voice behind her. "Bye, Miss Kingsley," Bart called. "Hope to see ya again real soon."

The dinner crowd brought in the news that the ballot issue to extend the local school term by three months had passed by a good margin, and Mr. Kilgore's free school would hold classes from Monday morning right through the end of June.

"And he's looking for a teacher," Sheriff Bowman continued after downing the last bite of his hot apple pie. "Thomas Kilgore and his wife have declared that they're going to bring our kids up to par with every child in the East. They'd like to put on another performance at the hall, and they hope to add on to their house and every such thing as will make their school the finest in the Territory. Tom said he'd go to Kansas City to fetch him a new teacher if need be. But he's hoping to hire on someone right out of Raton."

"What about Miss Hutchinson?" someone asked.

Rosie was serving at a station some distance from the sheriff's table, but she traded beverage posts with Annie in order to hear the news. As she poured out cups of dark brown Harvey coffee, she listened, every fiber of her being trained toward the speakers.

"Tom wants a married lady," the sheriff explained. "He's sick and tired of seeing our teachers run off with some joker fresh in on the train from Denver or someplace. I reckon Mrs. Poole might do a dandy job at teaching school."

"Mrs. Poole or Mrs. Bell. Both of them's got some education."

"And what about Mrs. Towns who plays the piano at the Catholic church? She's got all that music talent."

"Sure enough. She could organize a choir."

Rosie had knotted her fingers together behind her back, and she wasn't even trying to wear the Harvey smile. What these men were saying was true—any number of married women in town could take that teaching position, though none of them could possibly be as qualified as she. Her initial elation on hearing that the school term would continue for three months faded quickly during the ensuing discussion.

Once again Rosie's thoughts ran through the list of men she might persuade to marry her on the spur of the moment. What a ridiculous thing to have to do to get a job! Maybe Mr. Kilgore had been right, and she should take a train to Albuquerque to look for a teaching position. But she didn't want to work in Albuquerque; she had made her home in Raton. If she hadn't been serving dinner to a trainload of guests, she would have stamped her foot in frustration.

Did she want to stay in Raton just because Bart was back? No, of course not. She'd intended to make her life here long before he showed up. Besides, Rosie told herself, hadn't she convinced herself that Bart was every bit the shameless, lying outlaw everyone thought he was? In fact, he'd probably told a whole tangle of lies to get that livery stable job and to persuade the townsmen to like him so well. But why on earth had that local character Cheyenne Bill decided to adopt Bart as his cousin?

Oh, it was all too confusing. Rosie studied the sheriff and his pals as they sat around comparing potential teachers. "I'm the best teacher for the job," she wanted to shout. "Married or not, I deserve that position!" How could Bart swagger into town and casually pick up a well-paying job he was good at, while Rosie had to work her fanny off in a restaurant, then face the reality that she couldn't have what she wanted because she wasn't married?

Well, she *was* married! Twice married, as a matter of fact. And one of her husbands was right here in Raton. The angrier Rosie got, the more an idea that had sneaked into her thoughts began to make sense. If Bart could lie his way into town, convince everyone he was someone he wasn't, get a job, and claim land, why couldn't she get what she wanted the same way? And if Bart—conniver that he was—could toy with her, why couldn't she use him, too?

Just because her father had brought her up to be moral, prim, and proper, didn't mean she couldn't grab what she deserved when it was there for the taking. Bart had been right when he'd said Rosie had always been obedient, always done what she'd been told. Well, what was wrong with wanting more out of life than that? Why couldn't she be a teacher without having to be married? And why couldn't she take on a man who owed her for all the trouble he'd caused, a man who couldn't risk anyone blabbing to the sheriff about who he really was . . . a man who belonged to her in the first place?

As Rosie looked over the heads of her customers, she saw neither coffee urns nor flowered hats nor a locomotive engine. What Rosie saw was a crowded schoolroom, rows of wooden desks, inkwells, slates, chalk, and primers. What she saw was her future.

"I'm looking for a man named Buck," Rosie stated the next morning as she stood just inside the weathered pine door of the nearby livery stable. The breakfast trains had gone, and she had left the House without bothering to change her uniform. So what if everyone found out that she'd gone to find Bart? she had reasoned. They'd know soon enough anyway.

"Buck!" the older man who ran the stable hollered. "You got a lady here wants to see you. One of the Harvey Girls. Better step to it before she gets away!"

Rosie lifted her chin when she saw Bart's head rise from behind a stall. His obvious surprise at seeing her gratified Rosie no end, and she smiled as she watched him make his way down the hay-littered walk toward her.

The air in the barn was pungent with the scents of well-oiled leather, sweet straw and oats, and dusty horses. Golden sunlight filtered in mote-filled beams through holes in the roof. A horse snuffled as someone led it out of the stable and down the back ramp toward the waiting wagon.

"Miss Kingsley?" Bart greeted her. Today, Rosie noted, he wasn't such an all-fired dandy. The sleeves of his blue chambray work shirt were rolled up to his elbows, and the fabric was damp around the underarms and collar. He wore the old leather britches that clung to his legs like a second skin. Bits of straw were scattered through his hair, and he smelled like a horse. Good thing, Rosie thought, for the moment she had looked into his warm eyes, her determination fluttered just a tad.

"Buck, is it?" she inquired.

"That's what they call me. Right, Ezra?" He nodded at the older man, who grinned, shrugged, and wandered toward the back of the stable. "What can I do for you, ma'am?"

Rosie glanced around the dusty building to make sure no one could hear. Then she took a breath and announced her plan. "You can do for me exactly what you promised to do six years ago—before you ran off like a yellow-bellied coward. You can convince Mr. Thomas Kilgore that I'm your wife, you can take me out to that homestead of yours, and you can earn a lawful, decent living for once in your life. I'm planning to take a teaching position, and just as soon as I can afford it, I'm going to buy myself a house here in town and move in. After that, I don't care what you do with yourself."

"I see." He was looking at her as if he thought she'd gone plumb crazy.

Rosie didn't mind. "You'll do as I ask," she went on, "or I'll march right over to Sheriff Bowman and tell him that you're not Cheyenne Bill's cousin and that your name is not Buck, it's Bart Kingsley. I'll tell him you're the outlaw he shot that night when the Pinkerton detective was searching Raton. I'll tell him you used to ride with Jesse James and you robbed three trains. I'll tell him that all he has to do to get his fifty-dollar reward is sashay over here to the livery stable and put you under arrest. So you just better plan on doing as I say and take me for your wife without a word of argument.''

Bart scratched his jaw for a moment. ''All right,'' he said finally. ''Since you put it that way, I reckon I could manage to do what you want.''

Rosie stared at him in surprise. She'd expected at least some form of protest. After all, she'd just ordered him to take her back into his life, and she'd threatened to turn him into the law if he didn't do exactly what she demanded. But Bart had leaned one shoulder against the side of a stall and was calmly chewing on the end of a piece of hay, all the while gazing at her with those green eyes.

''You agree?'' she asked, unable to quite believe it had been so easy.

''Well, you put it to me in a mighty tough way, Rosie.'' Bart stroked the end of the hay twig and tried his best to sound serious. He could tell it had taken a lot out of Rosie to confront him like this. She was breathing like a winded racehorse, her fine little nostrils all flared out. In her black and white uniform, she looked exactly the way he imagined a nun would look—all high and mighty, shoulders stiff and neck as straight as a board, pronouncing sentence on folks like it was Judgment Day.

How could his little Rosie know that she'd just made every dream he'd ever had come true? She couldn't possibly realize that he'd risked his life by hiding out in the wild New Mexico woods for a week while his bullet wound finished healing. She wouldn't understand that he'd put his neck on the line by coming back into Raton, confiding in Cheyenne Bill, seeking a job in as prominent a place as the depot livery stable, and taking out a homestead claim in Springer.

He'd done it all for Rosie, in the faint hope that he could pose as a stranger, woo her, marry her again if need be, and take her back into his arms forever. He had thought it would take months, maybe even years, to persuade her to trust him. Yet here she was, commanding him to marry her!

''I put it exactly the way it is,'' Rosie stated. ''Either you go along with my plan, or I turn you in to the sheriff.''

"You might get the fifty-dollar reward yourself, you know. Ever thought about that, Rosie?"

"I don't want fifty dollars, Bart. I want that teaching job at Mr. Kilgore's school." She was fit to be tied. Her cheeks were bright pink, and her brown eyes fairly flamed with determination. "Now, I don't have much time, so here's what I want you to do. Come over to the House tonight and ask Mrs. Jensen if you can take me to church."

"Church!" Bart hadn't been to church in six years.

"I think Reverend Cullen will let you in. He knows me very well, and he's a decent man. At least . . . I think he is."

"So I'm supposed to take you to church?"

"Then you're to come courting me every night next week. I'll tell Etta we're going to elope. On Saturday we'll board the train to Springer. When we come back, we'll pretend to be married."

"We *are* married, Rosie-girl," Bart reminded her in a low voice.

She shot him a look of dismay, as though his statement had thrown the first wrinkle into her plan. "Not really," she insisted after a moment. "This arrangement between us is not something I intend to go on with after I get my teaching employment and buy my own house."

"You're just going to up and walk out on your new husband? What will Mr. Kilgore and the school board think of that?"

"Mr. Kilgore will think I'm such a fine teacher by then that he won't care a lick. Besides, I imagine it won't take you long to get back to your usual ways, Bart. Then everyone will understand why I left you."

"My usual ways?"

"Oh, Bart. You don't have the ability to stick around in one place more than a few months at the most. Besides, all you really know how to do well anymore is rob trains and banks. That's easy money. How long will it be before you get tired of sweating for your pay? How long before you get a hankering to ride off in search of better things than a tiny dugout house, a field full of sugar beets, and a job shoveling horse manure?''

''What you really want to know is how long it'll be before I get tired of you, isn't it, Rosie? That's what you think I'm going to wear out on first.''

''I don't care how soon you get bored with me and decide to take off. You've done it twice before, and I've survived just fine.'' She brushed a speck of dust from her sleeve, then folded her arms against her chest. ''I don't need you, Bart Kingsley.''

He shrugged. ''Sounds like you need me pretty bad if you want that teaching job.''

''I could marry any one of twenty men in this town if I chose. But you owe me, Bart. And it's time for you to start paying.''

''Yes, ma'am,'' he said, giving her a lazy salute. ''I reckon I'll suffer through this just to get you off my back.''

''Be at the House tonight at seven.'' She turned without giving him a polite farewell. ''That's when all the courters come to call.''

''My, my, Miss Kingsley,'' she heard him say behind her as she left the stable and headed out across the depot platform. ''You sure do drive a mighty hard bargain. Yes, indeed.''

Rosie worried all through the dinner trains that Bart wouldn't come. If he bolted now, she wouldn't have anything to tell the sheriff. And without a husband she couldn't possibly persuade Mr. Kilgore to let her teach.

Precisely at seven, Etta hammered on Rosie's bedroom door. ''Laurie! There's a man come to call on you! He's downstairs talking to Mrs. Jensen, and you should just see him!''

Rosie's heart began to thunk into her ribs as she pulled a fringed shawl around her shoulders and drew open the door. ''I've been expecting him,'' she said with forced calm.

''You didn't say a thing about this to me! Laurie, I'm your best friend—how could you not tell me?''

Rosie gave her blond friend a quick hug. ''I just met him

last night after the fire. We ran into each other today in
town, and he asked to accompany me to church tonight.''

"Jiminy! He's the best-looking fellow who's ever set
foot in the House.''

"Better-looking than Stefan?'' Rosie hurried down the
hall, trying not to rush but unable to keep her feet still.

"Stefan's as cute as butter, but this man is so handsome
it's plumb dangerous! Golly, Laurie, do you think you like
him?''

"I like him well enough. He's Cheyenne Bill's cousin.
We saw him on the hose cart last night, remember?''

"The Indian!''

Rosie took the last step down into the lobby, caught one
look at the man who stood waiting for her, and realized that
the savage who had crawled out from under her bed had
been completely transformed. Bart Kingsley had begged,
borrowed, or stolen a starched white wing collar that framed
his bronzed face like a patch of gleaming snow. Around the
new collar he wore a narrow black string tie fashioned into
a bow, which set off his black hair and gave him the look of
a city dandy. The white shirt Rosie had bought him boasted
not only the new collar but also a fine black cutaway jacket
with high button fastenings and flap pockets. He had traded
the dusty felt Stetson for a bowler, which rested politely on
his knee; he had turned in his leather britches for a pair of
minutely checked trousers. From their hems emerged
leather ankle boots with contrasting shiny toe caps. His hair
was clean, and he smelled for all the world like bay rum.

"Well,'' she said, uncertain whether to laugh at the
unbelievable alteration in the outlaw or to swoon over the
sheer heady pleasure of such a handsome gentleman caller.

"Miss Kingsley.'' Bart came toward her and held out an
arm. "Mrs. Jensen has given me permission to escort you to
church.''

"How kind of you.'' Rosie gave Mrs. Jensen a quick
glance and noted the high color in the old woman's
wrinkled cheeks. Obviously the starchy matron wasn't
completely immune to the charms of a dashing man.

"Good evening, Mrs. Jensen," Bart said, bowing slightly.

"You'll stay with the others on the way to church," she called out. "And you'll bring Miss Kingsley back to the dormitory precisely at nine o'clock."

"Yes, ma'am. Of course I will."

Joining a crowd of young men and women, Rosie and Bart walked out of the Harvey House and headed for the Methodist church. It was easy enough for Rosie to remain quiet amid the bustle and chatter of their companions. But as the couples departed for their various destinations—Saint Patrick's, the newly built Catholic church; the Episcopal church, the Baptist church, the Presbyterian church—Rosie found the growing silence more and more uncomfortable.

She could feel the hard lump of Bart's bicep beneath his jacket sleeve, and as hard as she tried not to, she found her fingers slipping around to cup it. The scent of bay rum had wafted around her head like a veil, and she felt half drunk from breathing it in. His leg brushed against her skirt, tugging it slightly into her thighs. She pulled her shawl around her shoulders and gripped it against her breasts, and she discovered that against her will their tips had tightened inside her chemise.

"Fine night," Bart commented when they were strolling with only one other couple. "Yes, indeed. And it's a grand moon."

Rosie glanced over to find him grinning at the inane conversation he was making. She rolled her eyes and set one foot on the first step of the small whitewashed frame church.

"Brisk wind down from the mountains," Bart said. "Sure sets up a chill, doesn't it?"

Rosie gave him a sharp jab to the ribs. "It's windy around here, all right."

He caught his laugh and held it inside while leading her up the steps. But as she walked into the sanctuary, he couldn't resist leaning against her shoulder and whispering in her ear, "You sure look beautiful tonight, Rosie-girl."

Without responding, she kept her eyes straight ahead and made her way to the pew where she usually sat. But when she had seated herself, Rosie looked around to find that Bart had vanished. Not again!

She whisked out of the pew and marched back up the aisle. Bart wasn't going to pull this! Not tonight. Why, Sheriff Bowman sat just two pews in front of Rosie, and by golly, she would tell him exactly who had escorted her to church.

But the moment Rosie set foot on the narrow porch, her heart nearly melted. There was Bart, sitting on the stoop, his hat in his hands, just as he had done when he was a little boy. With his head bowed, he was studying a small wrinkled Bible he had pulled from his pocket.

"Bart!" Rosie whispered. "What on earth are you doing out here?"

He lifted his head and smiled. "Figured I'd be more comfortable out here. Hope you don't mind."

"I do mind! You're no outcast that you have to hide like this." She crouched beside him, her blue dress billowing into a pouf of fabric. "Please come in and sit with me, Bart."

"I'm Buck, and I'm a half-breed. I won't be welcome in there, no more than I was in the church back home."

Rosie instinctively laid a hand on his shoulder. "Please," she whispered. "You look fine tonight. Just fine."

"Fine clothes don't change the color of my skin, Rosie-girl. And much as I try to act like a dandy, I don't have the first clue about manners in church and other high-society places. My mama used to say, 'Poor people have poor ways.' She was right. Now get on back in there where you belong, and I'll meet you out here after the service."

For a moment Rosie thought about obeying, but she was finished with doing with she was told! "I'm not going in there without you, Bart Kingsley," she snapped. "Now get up off your fanny and escort me inside like a gentleman."

It was the first time in a long while that Bart had obeyed an order he didn't cotton to. It was the first time ever that he had set foot inside the lily-white walls of a church. But before he had time to ponder it, he was sitting in the fourth pew from the front, right next to his Rosie, and he was singing at the top of his lungs: " 'Oh, for a thousand tongues to sing my great Redeemer's praise, the glories of my God and King, the triumphs of his grace! Jesus, the name that calms my fears, that bids my sorrows cease. 'Tis music in the sinner's ears; 'tis life and health and peace.' "

*Eight
. . . .

When the church service ended, Bart wished he could ease right out a side door and escape for a few minutes alone with Rosie. The last thing he wanted was to be hauled up the aisle to the church door where Reverend Cullen stood shaking hands with everyone.

For one thing, Bart was feeling convicted. From the time he was a boy, he had known Methodist preachers could really lay a sinner out—and Reverend Cullen was no exception. After nearly two hours of the minister's preaching that evening, Bart was just squirming in his pew. He could envision his transgressions all stretched out across the heavens like a headline in *The Raton Comet*. Worse, he pictured God and the angels looking down on him and shaking their heads in disappointment.

Another reason Bart was hoping to bypass the preacher had to do with his uncertainties about trespassing in such a sacrosanct place. If a half-breed Apache hadn't been wanted in the Kansas City church, what would make Reverend Cullen welcome him now? In spite of the bath and shave he'd given himself and the fancy duds he had borrowed from Ezra, the owner of the livery stable, Bart knew he looked just as much like an Indian as ever.

The third reason for slipping out of church was to spend some private time with Rosie. He had never known she could be so downright cold. All through church she had just stared straight ahead. When he moved to take her hand, she had frowned at him and pulled away. Miss-Prim-and-Proper was in her element. If the angels were shaking their heads

121

over Bart, they were smiling with pleasure at Laura Rose. No doubt Rosie never felt a moment's conviction all through that sermon; she didn't have a single thing in her upright life to feel guilty about.

As he made his way up the aisle, Bart tried to steel himself for the disapproval he would read in the preacher's eyes. Sure, the elderly man had a handshake and a kind word for everybody else. But Bart didn't hold out much hope that he'd get the same reaction. He had seen too many grins dissolve into thin air when he walked into a room.

"Reverend Cullen," Rosie said as she took the preacher's hand and shook it warmly, "what a thought-provoking sermon. I was truly moved."

"All the credit goes to the Lord, Miss Kingsley."

"Of course." Rosie turned to Bart, who wished he could disappear. "Reverend Cullen, I'd like you to meet . . . This is . . . this is . . ."

"Buck Springfield," Bart said to cover her discomfort. "I'm new in town."

The preacher stuck out his hand and grabbed Bart's, giving it a firm shake. "Welcome to Raton, Mr. Springfield. I understand you're Cheyenne Bill's cousin."

Bart glanced at the ceiling, wondering if he could be struck dead for telling two bald-faced lies right inside a church. "That's right," he managed. "We're cousins."

"Splendid! I've done my dead-level best to lure that gentleman into church. Now that you're in Raton, perhaps you'll be able to convince him of the need for spiritual renewal."

"Maybe so." Bart discovered he was still shaking hands with the minister.

"And you're escorting Miss Kingsley tonight?" Reverend Cullen leaned closer, stood on tiptoe, and spoke into Bart's ear. "A fine, fine young woman, Mr. Springfield. You couldn't have chosen a better lady to court in this entire town."

"Yes, sir. I do agree, sir. Well, good evening to you." Bart detached his hand and took Rosie's. "I sure enjoyed the preaching, Reverend. It was mighty pleasurable."

Feeling hot around his collar, he lunged out into the night. Rosie was fairly running alongside him. "Bart!" she cried. "Bart, slow down. What's gotten into you?"

He shortened his stride and took a deep breath. "Did you hear what I said to that fellow? Hell, I told him I *enjoyed* his sermon! He was preaching about sin and eternal damnation."

Rosie grinned, then covered her mouth with her free hand. "Reverend Cullen knew what you meant. All of us tell him we like his sermons, even when he's been pounding the pulpit and shouting about Satan, iniquity, and the fires of hell."

Pondering this, Bart eased to a stroll and tucked Rosie's arm inside his own. It felt right to touch her again, so he slipped her fingers apart and wove his through them. He didn't know how to take the preacher's seeming acceptance of him there in the church. It was as though Bart's skin made no difference to the man at all.

"For someone who'd welcome a man like me inside his church," he said, "the reverend sure does know how to preach down sin."

Rosie gazed up at the silver moon hanging just over the white rim of a distant mesa. "You're not responsible for your bloodlines, Bart."

"But I'm sure as hell responsible for all the other things I've done. Lord, if Reverend Cullen ever found out about my riding with the James gang and robbing those trains and being wanted in Missouri—"

"He'd treat you the same, I imagine. He's often quoted the Scripture where a group of men wanted to stone an adulterous woman, and Jesus said to them, 'Let him who is without sin cast the first stone.' Everybody's done wrong things, Bart."

He started to speak, then stopped and shrugged. "I guess so."

Rosie realized how easily she had slipped into casual talk with Bart. Somehow the man had a way of drawing her out of herself to make her feel comfortable and trusting with him. But she knew good and well that he had let her down many times. He had proven himself completely unreliable. She had to remember that. She had to keep herself distant.

"No matter what you've done, Bart," she said finally, "it's a good idea for you to go to church. People will think you're honest and trustworthy. That can only help in your dealings with the townsfolk. And if Mr. Kilgore believes I've married a decent man, it'll help me get my job, too."

"You're doing all this rigmarole with me just so you can teach school, Rosie?"

"Of course. After all I've been through, there's not a man alive who could persuade me to marry him for keeps."

"Rosie, just because you had a bad time with that doctor your pappy forced on you doesn't mean another man might not treat you right."

She glanced at him. "I sure hope you're not referring to yourself, Bart Kingsley. You haven't done one right thing by me since I've known you. Now you've come to live in my town and you'll probably mess things up for me here, too."

"Not if I can help it. The sheriff thinks I'm a good man. Everyone in town believes I'm Cheyenne Bill's cousin."

"I don't see how you managed that."

He'd been waiting for her to ask about the trail that had brought him safely back to town, back to her side, but now she sure didn't seem to really care one way or the other. "I rigged it up," he said simply.

"Well, I don't expect your game will last too long. Sheriff Bowman is no fool."

He stopped and pulled her around to face him. "What makes you so sure I'm going to mess up?"

"You haven't let me down so far."

He studied the tops of the cottonwood trees lining the street. He could just make out their swelling buds outlined by the moon. The air felt as clean and fresh to him as a drink of cold water. But his gut was twisted into a knot that grew tighter with every word from Rosie's mouth.

Looking down at her, he saw those big brown eyes calling to him. He saw that sweet, full mouth just beckoning. She was a sight for sore eyes in her blue ruffly dress that gentled over her curves and stirred a hunger down deep inside him. Yet, for all her soft looks, Bart knew that when it came to him, Rosie had a chilly streak a mile wide.

"You don't believe I have what it takes to lead a straight life?" he asked.

"Frankly, no. The last time you walked the straight and narrow you were seventeen years old. All your adult life you've been living on the wrong side of the law. Don't tell me you can up and change just like that."

"I reckon I could if I had a reason to."

She pushed his hands from her shoulders and crossed her arms. "Don't make *me* your reason to change, Bart," she said. "I remember all the sweet words you said about me being the light of your life and about tracking me down and all. Well, listen here—I'm not interested in being your light or your inspiration. If you want to change, go right ahead. Just don't expect me to be part of it. I told you before: I want my freedom, and I moved out here to Raton to claim it."

"What are you so all-fired het up about, Rosie?"

"You've put me in a tangle, as usual. I don't know why I let you talk me into that wedding nonsense when we were kids, why you ran off and left me like you did, why you tracked me down after six years, why you ran off and left me all over again; I don't understand any of it!"

"Why don't you just ask me to explain?"

"I couldn't believe what you told me if you had a hundred good reasons for your behavior." She felt as though she might choke on the tears and anger that had bubbled up inside her. "You can stop blaming your mama, your Apache pappy, the boys who teased you, the preacher who wouldn't let you into church, and everyone else for the way you turned out. You're an outlaw because you chose to be one!"

"Hush, now. You're going to scare up the sheriff with all this carryin' on."

"Nobody forced you to do a single thing, Bart Kingsley! *You* decided to run off and leave me. *You* decided to join up with Jesse James. *You* decided to rob those three trains—"

Bart clamped a hand over her mouth and jerked her hard

against him to stifle her words. "That's enough, damn it!"

For an instant all her words rang true. Bart knew he was an outlaw. He was bad. He was a sinner in league with the devil. And he felt just as mean and nasty as she had made him out to be. A hot flame of bitterness curled through him as he gripped her wrist and pressed her head against his chest with his hand.

Rosie had no right to taunt and accuse him! She had no right to stand there flaunting her goodness in his face. Hadn't she been married to two men at the same time? Hadn't she allowed herself to be used and handled by someone other than her first true husband? She wasn't worthy to throw his sins at him.

"Bart?" Her muffled voice sounded timid and fearful. He could feel her lips moving beneath his palm.

He didn't want to let her go. Every instinct that had been honed over six lawless years told him to force her to do what he wanted. He could hold her down and kiss her the way he'd imagined during all the long nights alone. With his brutal strength, he could keep her prisoner for the rest of her life if he chose. He could bend her to his will, make her pay for hurting him.

She didn't believe he could ever change. So why should he struggle to control and suppress the animal inside him? Maybe he should just prove her right—show her just how bad Bart Kingsley could be.

"Bart?"

He looked down and saw her brown eyes pleading with him. Her hair had come loose from its knot, which was hanging askew on the side of her head. Long glossy tendrils, silvered by the moon, were crushed beneath his hand. Her skin had whitened beneath his fingertips. She blinked at him, and a single tear slid from the corner of her eye to trickle down her cheek.

"Damn it all, Rosie," he cried in a muffled voice, "this is killing me!" Catching her tightly to him, he replaced his hand on her mouth with his lips. The salt of her tears seeped into his mouth as he kissed and rocked and cradled her. "I'm sorry, darlin'."

"Oh, Bart, I thought you were going to strangle me or something."

"No, never. I'll never hurt you, Rosie-girl. I swear it."

She sucked in a sob, her anguish a knife turning in his belly.

"I know I'm walking right on the edge of losing what I'm trying to get, Rosie," he murmured. "I haven't been around a decent woman for years, and you're right if you think I'm a bad man. I'm used to punching anyone who makes me mad. I'm used to stealing money when I need it. I'm used to taking what I want without asking. But, Rosie, dang it, I want to change things around!"

Once he finally let her go, she backed away and stood shivering, her shawl clutched tightly at her throat. "I've never seen anybody change as much as you're going to have to, Bart," she said in a hoarse voice. "I expect it'll take a miracle."

"Reverend Cullen said miracles happen."

"God's in that business, not you."

"So, maybe God will help me." He took a step toward her. "Rosie, can't you give me a chance?"

Slowly she shook her head. "I've given you too many chances. I've trusted you too much. If you want me to believe you're a different kind of person, you're going to have to prove it to me."

"I will show you. If I can convince Sheriff Bowman I'm decent, I can convince you, too."

"Sheriff Bowman doesn't know who you really are. I do." She turned and walked quickly toward the House. "Come for me tomorrow at four. We'll go skating at the rink."

For a moment he felt elated at her words. Then he realized that she didn't want to be with him because she enjoyed his company. She was out to get what she had set her sights on: that teaching job. And her freedom.

All the next day while Bart curried, fed, and saddled horses, he thought about how close he had come to losing control of himself with Rosie. For the first time in a long while, he had actually caught himself on the fine line between peace and violence.

As a boy Bart always had kept his anger under control. He had suppressed it, turning it inward until it rankled. As a young man he had let it all out. He hadn't given much thought at all to expressing his rage with his bare knuckles. In the company of rough-hewn men, Bart had learned that he could wear his feelings like a badge—and woe betide the person who crossed him.

But he had told Rosie he wanted to change, and he did. That meant putting a lid on his urges. If she made him angry, he would have to find a way to let her know gently. He would have to learn to listen better, to be kinder, to take life more peacefully. The kind of man Rosie wanted wouldn't make himself feel good by getting drunk on a bottle of rotgut, nor would he let out his rage by shooting up a town. There were other ways, civilized ways, and Bart aimed to learn them.

As he washed and dressed in his dandy clothes that afternoon during a break between trains, Bart made up his mind to win back Rosie's heart. He knew she had loved him once. Just the memory of her at fifteen—those young brown eyes gazing into his face and her sweet girlish figure pressed so tightly against his body—told him how much she once had cared.

With his hair combed and his old boots shined, Bart presented himself to Mrs. Jensen at the Harvey House. For some reason that he couldn't quite figure, the elderly lady seemed to have taken a liking to him, and while they waited for Rosie to come downstairs they chatted politely. Bart thought the conversation was a good means of putting him in a frame of mind to be kind and gentle with Rosie.

As he heard her footsteps on the stairs, he imagined the sight she would lay eyes on when she entered the parlor— the white-haired Mrs. Jensen carrying on a la-di-da conversation with the dandy young gentleman who sat on the edge of a puffy red velvet sofa. But the minute Bart turned and saw Rosie walk into the room, he felt just as awkward and rough as ever.

Hat in his hand, he stood to meet her. My, she was a beauty! From head to toe she had dressed herself all in soft pink. She had brushed her hair up in a knot high on the back of her head and had tied it with a pink ribbon through which she had woven some purple and yellow primroses. Her small straw hat, perched just in front of the knot, was trimmed with pink feathers and bits of lace.

Her dress had a high stand-up collar, long sleeves, a draped front that came over her knees like a curtain swag in a fancy parlor, and a big bow just over the bustle. This had all been sewn out of some kind of pale pink cloth that looked mighty soft to the touch. Her pleated skirt fell to her ankles in rows of narrow pink stripes. Little trimmings all over the outfit gave it an almost airy look—lace ruffles at the cuffs and collar, lace edgings around the draperies, a row of tiny buttons down the bodice, and a pink bow at the back of the hat.

"Good afternoon, Miss Kingsley," Bart said, remembering his manners just in time. He gave a gallant little bow, and when he straightened, he found her looking at him with an engaging grin.

"Mr. Springfield, how kind of you to call." She flushed as bright a pink as her clothes when he gathered up her fingers and tucked them around his elbow.

They took their leave of Mrs. Jensen and headed down the boardwalk toward the skating rink. For a long time Bart couldn't think of a thing to say. Every phrase that crossed his mind sounded artificial to him, like something out of a dime novel.

"I hear they're planning to build a real skating rink pretty soon," he said finally. "An indoor one. Bill says there'll be a stage right in the middle of it for traveling theater companies to perform on."

"I don't know why they need that." Rosie's voice was light and casual. Bart imagined this was the way she chatted with people in her high-society circles. "Most of the dances and socials in Raton are held at Bayne and Frank's Hall. The Wallace Sisters give recitals over at McAuliffe and Ferguson's

Hall. The Williams Theatre Company performed there, and all the anti-grant meetings are held over there.''

"You know much about the trouble over the Maxwell Land Grant Company, Rosie?"

"Everyone knows about it. You can't live in Raton and not have heard about all the problems going on. Mr. McMains takes it on himself to spread the word. But I try not to get involved.''

Bart felt his heart rate speed up. "How can you not get involved, Rosie? The land-grant war is all about this part of the Territory and who has a right to settle it. How it comes out will affect the whole future of Raton.''

"I'm not interested in land issues, Bart," she said, marching ahead of him down the street. "I'm going to be a schoolteacher.''

He caught her wrist and swung her backward to face him. "Is that all you ever have on your mind—teaching school?" The moment he said it, he realized how harsh he'd sounded. He dropped her arm and stuffed his hands into his pockets. "I'm sorry, Rosie-girl. I didn't aim to be so bold with you today.''

She fiddled with the cord on her pink bag. "Teaching is all I have to look forward to," she said finally, lifting her eyes to his face.

"You balance everything in your life against it, don't you? When something comes up, you think, How's this gonna touch me when I'm a teacher? When someone says something, you think, What would I say back to this person if I was a teacher?"

"That's right, Bart," she confirmed softly, warmed by his insight.

"I'm the same way. Ever since I made up my mind to find you and become a law-abiding citizen again, I've done the same thing. I weigh things to myself all the time. Would a gentleman say this? Would Rosie like that? Is this the right way to walk and dress and eat? Trouble is, I've been out of decent circles for a mighty long time.''

Rosie smiled and slipped her hand around his arm again. "You're doing fine, Bart. Just fine.''

They approached Raton's roller-skating rink, a crude structure that had been set up in a vacant lot. Constructed of rough-hewn planks, the skating area formed a large square. Wooden seats for viewing lined the sides, and a small tented booth sat at one edge. Inside the tent, the rink owner charged Rosie and Bart twenty-five cents each for roller skates and an hour on the rink.

Few skaters were taking advantage of the early-afternoon sunshine, and the rink was almost deserted. Rosie sat on one of the benches and laced on her Plimpton's Patented Skates. Bart tried to keep his eyes on his own footgear, but he couldn't resist sneaking glances at Rosie's little ankles.

The truth of the matter was, he had never skated a single time in his entire life. If he could have chosen, he'd have suggested they walk to the park and take a stroll under the trees. Maybe then he could steal a kiss or two.

But in moments Rosie was up on her feet and swirling out across the bumpy, hollow-floored rink. Her dress fluttered around her ankles like a blossoming rose. She wore a grin as big as Lincoln County as she spun around in a tight circle that lifted the hem of her skirt clear up to her knees.

"I'll be damned," Bart muttered. If Rosie was going to expose herself in public like that, he knew he'd better stay by her side. He lunged up from the bench, rolled out onto the rink, and promptly fell flat on his backside.

"Oh, Bart!" Rosie was giggling and exclaiming in dismay all at the same time. "Don't you know how to skate?"

"The name's Buck, and does it look like I know how to skate?"

She grabbed his hand and hauled him to his feet. In moments he began to wobble, his legs spread-eagled, and he crashed onto the boards with a thump and a whoosh of dust.

"Bart!" Rosie was positively beside herself by this time. So was everyone else at the rink. Bart glanced around at all the other skaters and felt his hackles rise. "What's so damned funny?" he growled.

"It's just that you're so big and brawny," Rosie said as

she reached for his hand again. "You look as if you could wrestle a bull to the ground with your bare hands."

"I *can* wrestle a bull to the ground with my bare hands."

"But you can't roller-skate? Bart, these days *everybody* knows how to skate!"

"Not me." He eased up cautiously into a crouch, then straightened his knees. "I haven't taken a fall like that since I was first learning how to break a wild bronco."

"Here, take my hand and we'll go around together. It's easy—you'll see." With Bart at her side, Rosie began skating slowly around the fresh-air rink. True, the boards were rough and wobbly—nothing like the sanded, polished indoor rinks that were the height of popularity in Kansas City.

At home in the city, Rosie had owned her own specially fashioned skates, which had cost Dr. Lowell upwards of twenty dollars. She had gone to skating parties galore, and she'd watched every performance of *Le Prophète* when the skating ballet company came to Kansas City.

But Rosie knew she wouldn't trade all the fancy skates and shiny rinks in the world for these moments with Bart. How wonderful and rare to know him at such a vulnerable moment. He was hanging on to her like a frightened child, his jaw clenched and his eyes locked on his feet.

Bart was no child, of course. An "I'll be damned" exited his mouth every minute or so, and he towered over the other skaters.

"You're doing fine," she said when they had completed their second circle around the rink. "You want to try it alone?"

He glanced at her for the first time since they'd started. "To tell you the truth, Rosie-girl," he said, "I'm enjoying your company."

Though she flushed, she didn't move away from him, and Bart felt a thrill of victory as they swung around and around over the boards. With the late April sun shining down on her shoulders, the crisp mountain air in their chests, and the pale green aspens and cottonwoods whispering overhead, he decided things were going just right. He could feel Rosie's slender arm around his waist, her little hand cupping him just above his belt. She smelled like fresh lavender and roses, and her laughter sent a lightness to his heart.

It seemed as though they had barely gotten started when Rosie's fist dinner train whistled in the distant tunnel.

"Jiminy Christmas!" she said quickly. "I've got to go. I can't be late!"

"Why not? In a few days you're going to marry me and quit that job anyway. Why don't you stay out here with me, Rosie? We'll skate some more, and then I'll take you over to the Mountain Monarch restaurant for a bowl of ice cream. What would you say to that?"

"I'd say you were forgetting our deal, Bart Kingsley. We're not out at this skating rink to have fun. We're here to show everyone that you're courting me, so that when we do get married we won't raise too many eyebrows. Besides, I can't quit working at the Harvey House right now. I need every penny I earn so I can buy myself a house in town." She sat down on a bench and began unlacing her skates. "So you'd better hop to it and get me back to the dormitory if you don't want me to give you what for."

Rosie intuitively felt Bart's disappointment in her insensitive answer. But she couldn't let him see how much she had enjoyed the afternoon. She didn't want him to know that she would have loved to just relax with him, eating ice cream or whatever he had in mind. . . .

No, she had to continue to make Bart aware that there could never be anything between them. It might be fun to go skating with him, but she still didn't trust him. Not the least little bit.

For a whole week Rosie kept tabs on Mr. Kilgore's unfruitful search for a new teacher. At the same time, she and Bart displayed themselves as a courting pair everywhere in town. They went out to eat, attended Wednesday night prayer meeting at church, strolled down the streets of town, and accompanied a group of Harvey House employees to a band concert at Bayne and Frank's Hall.

Etta, of course, was beside herself. She kept avowing that

she couldn't get over how much her friend had changed
since the dashing Buck Springfield came to town.

Whereas once Laura Kingsley had chosen the most
severe dresses in her wardrobe, Etta explained to the other
Harvey Girls, she was now wearing those luscious things
she had brought with her from Kansas City—bright blues,
greens, and pinks; drapes, waterfall frills, lace cuffs, and
fringes; checks, stripes, plaids, and florals; taffetas, silks,
and velvets. From her traveling trunk, Rosie produced hats
Etta had never even seen—straw hats with wide brims,
small hats with upturned brims and lace edgings, tall felt
hats, and flowerpot hats.

More significantly, Etta commented on Rosie's bright
cheeks and frequent giggles. Though Rosie privately denied
any truth to the accusation, Etta insisted that her friend was
falling in love.

Of course, it was all a ruse, Rosie told herself. She wanted
everyone to think she cared for Bart in order to fulfill her
plan. Though it was easy enough to spend an hour or two a
day with him, Rosie knew she couldn't put much stock in
those moments of laughter and fun. Every night when she
went to bed, she knelt to pray that Bart wouldn't run off
before she had gotten that teaching job.

As the days passed, it became more clear to Rosie that
Bart would never last in Raton. He tried hard to keep his
rough ways hidden, but he wasn't much of a success. Not
only couldn't he roller-skate, but he didn't know a single
popular song, he'd learned his manners in a pigsty somewhere, and he couldn't make polite conversation for five
minutes without insulting the Almighty and damning two or
three things straight to hell.

When he and Rosie went out to eat at the Mountain
Monarch with a group of the Harvey employees, Bart leaned
his chair back on two legs, picked his teeth with the end of
a matchstick, and told a wild story about a bear hunt he'd
been on. Then he slipped up and started to call her Rosie
instead of Laurie in front of everyone. It took all his doing
to explain that Rosie was just his pet name for his girl.
Though Etta kept giggling and nudging Rosie to indicate

how delighted she was, Rosie knew people would mull over the event in private.

One of these days someone was going to fit the pieces of Bart Kingsley's puzzle together. One of these days someone would remember a half-breed outlaw who had come to town and been shot by Sheriff Bowman. And one of these days, someone would link that man to Buck Springfield. There wasn't a doubt in Rosie's mind.

At the same time, she knew there wasn't a moment to spare in letting the local folks think she had married him. When Rosie sat Etta down one evening, she had every intention of leading her friend to believe that Laurie Kingsley was just a besotted young woman about to elope with the man of her dreams.

"And so we're leaving on the six-thirty train for Springer," Rosie said as she clasped Etta's hands in her own. Still in their aprons and uniforms, they sat on the edge of Etta's bed. "We're going to get married at the courthouse, and then we'll come back to Raton."

Etta's eyes grew as wide and blue as a pair of morning glories. "Married! Oh, Laurie, how utterly wonderful! I'm beside myself with happiness for you."

"Now, don't tell, Etta. Not even Stefan. Promise?" Rosie admonished, knowing very well that the news would be out before she could even make it back to Raton.

"But if you get married, you'll be fired the minute Mr. Gable finds out! You know the rules. Mrs. Jensen will have an absolute hissy-fit."

"I don't care. Buck has filed for a homestead, and he's building us a dugout on his land. He's planting sugar beets, and I'm going to live out there with him."

"You're going to trade being a Harvey Girl for *that*?"

Rosie was silent for a moment before saying the words she had turned over and over in her mind. "I love him, Etta. That's all there is to it. I love him."

"Oh, Laurie!" Etta caught her friend in a tight bear hug. "Marriage! Your very own cookstove, ironing board, washtub, jam jars, and everything. And babies! You'll have scads of children. Just think—you'll be a man's wife for the very first . . . time . . ." She drew back and faced Rosie. "You've been married before, though, haven't you? You said you had a husband once."

"I told you all about that. We never were . . . intimate. I kept on living at home, and then he ran off two weeks after the wedding. It wasn't really a marriage."

"He was a half-Indian, too, wasn't he?"

"Apache. Buck is Cheyenne, and that's a lot different."

"It is?" Etta was staring at their clasped hands. "You told me that boy you married had black hair and green eyes. Doesn't Buck have green eyes, Laurie?"

Rosie could hear her breath shake as she drew it in. "I guess I'm just a sucker for a man with green eyes. Lucky thing Buck is nothing like the kid I married when I was fifteen. That boy was so skinny and short . . . and ugly," she added for good measure.

Etta looked up. "I reckon you've got a much better man in Buck Springfield. You told me the boy ran off and left you. Buck would never do a thing like that. Your first husband might have been as kind and gentle and good-natured as Buck is, but he couldn't have been half the man you're marrying tomorrow."

"Really?" Rosie whispered without thinking.

"Sure. Buck may not know better than to wear the same suit for five days in a row, but he's as good a person as a girl could ever find. He's going to build you a snug dugout and plant crops to feed your family. He works hard at the livery stable, and I've never seen him squander money—not once. If you want my opinion of Buck Springfield, here it is: he's decent, faithful, and a good provider. He doesn't have a mean bone in his body. He's fun to spend time with, and he likes a good laugh. If I weren't so stuck on Stefan, I'd be after Buck. So there!"

"Etta!" Rosie laughed.

"Go on now and get ready for your trip," Etta said, giving Rosie a little push off the bed. "Wear that blue dress for your wedding—the one that looks like ice."

"All right, Etta." Rosie pushed at the door and glanced

back at her friend. Etta was still sitting on the bed, her hands folded and her head bowed. She was staring at her knees.

"Etta?" Rosie murmured.

When her friend didn't look up, Rosie shut the door and walked down the hall to her room.

*Nine
. . . .

Bart didn't have any intention of showing his face to the justice of the peace at the courthouse in Springer, New Mexico. Such a mistake would have ensured him a one-way ticket to the gallows in Missouri. Rosie knew this, and she understood that their Saturday-morning train trip was just for show, to convince people in Raton that they'd gotten married. It was Rosie, in fact, who had set the date, and it was she who had purchased the tickets.

So when Bart arrived at the waiting train, caught her elbow, and whispered in her ear, "Happy weddin' day, Rosie-girl," she was more than a little surprised.

He was wearing a brand-new suit, and she couldn't help but think about how much it must have cost and how rarely he would ever wear it again. All the same, she couldn't deny that in his double-breasted navy jacket, white wing-collared shirt, red four-in-hand tie, gray striped trousers, and low-heeled leather boots, the man looked positively debonair. He had combed his shiny black hair and had donned a fine gray felt top hat. In one leather-gloved hand, he carried a huge wicker basket, and in the other he held a gentleman's walking cane.

"A cane!" Rosie cried, louder than necessary. She hadn't seen a man with a cane since she'd left Kansas City. It seemed that on the frontier no one thought such masculine accessories were necessary, though in the city a gentleman would rarely be found without one.

"I reckon my trigger finger looks better hooked around a

cane than it does around a six-shooter," Bart drawled.
"Besides, I knew you'd like it."

Rosie didn't want him to see how close he had come to
the truth. It was too hard to keep from flushing when he
cupped her elbow with his finely gloved hand. And she
found herself drinking in the scent of lemon balm he was
wearing.

"You must have spent all your pay and then some, Bart
Kingsley," she said in her best schoolteacher voice.

"As a matter of fact, I didn't spend a penny for this
getup."

Rosie gasped. "Bart! You *stole* those clothes?"

He threw back his head and laughed. "Get on this train,
Rosie-girl, and stop your frettin'. I broke a horse for Mr.
Loeb who owns the Star Clothing House, and I'm going to
fix his best saddle for him next week. He traded my work
for these fine gents' clothes. All except the cane. I bought
that."

Rosie hardly knew what to say as Bart helped her up the
iron steps and into the passenger car of the waiting train.
Mr. Loeb was one of the most respected men in town. It was
hard to imagine that he would actually participate in a trade
with such a man as Bart.

As Rosie seated herself beside the window, she recalled
Etta's words of the night before. To the young blonde, Bart
was no lying, untrustworthy gunslinger. Etta had labeled
him faithful, reliable, a good provider. Rosie lifted her eyes
to Bart's face, trying to see beyond the hurt and betrayal that
had built a wall between them.

Mr. Loeb trusted him. Etta was besotted with the man.
Cheyenne Bill had lied to the whole town on his behalf.
Even Sheriff Bowman had accepted Bart. Did they see
something Rosie had blinded herself to?

"You're just as soft and fluffy as a goose-down pillow
this morning, Rosie," Bart said. "Did you buy that dress for
today?"

Rosie studied her ice-blue gown, all frilly with ruffles,
rosettes, puffs, and ribbons. Actually Dr. Lowell had given
her the money to have a seamstress fashion it for a charity

tea last spring. The dress boasted not only a large bustle with billowing drapes, but also a trailing hem that gave the hint of a train.

Lifting her head, Rosie saw the look of hope in Bart's eyes. Suddenly she didn't want to disappoint him. "I'm afraid I didn't have anything to trade Mr. Loeb for, like you," she said softly, "but this is the very best daytime dress I own."

His face broke into a rewarding grin. "Thanks, Rosie."

As the train whistle blew, steam hissed from the undercarriage and the passenger car jolted forward. Bart took one of Rosie's hands and slipped his fingers through hers.

"This is sure different from the first time we got married," he said over the rattle of the wheels on the track. The train pulled out of the depot and began gathering speed for the southward journey to Springer. Musing on the marriage license he always kept folded in his britches' pocket, Bart took off his hat, set it on the empty seat beside him, and scooted closer to Rosie. "I'll never forget how you looked climbing down that sugar maple outside your bedroom window. You had your skirt all hitched up, and you were shinnying from branch to branch like you'd been born in a tree."

"I'd climbed down that maple tree enough times before to know my way blindfolded. All those afternoons I escaped my lessons and ran to find you at our . . . our place . . ." She faltered.

"I was supposed to be working the horses," he reminisced in a low voice. "But I'd get all my chores done early just so I could hightail it over to the stream. Sometimes I'd be the first to get there, and sometimes you would. You'd bring books to read to me, remember?"

Rosie nodded, lulled by the swaying of the train and by the memories of those warm, golden summer days.

"*Gulliver's Travels*," he said.

"You liked the Houyhnhnms better than you liked the Lilliputians."

"The Houyhnhnms were horses. Of course I liked them better."

Rosie smiled, closed her eyes, and leaned her head against the seat. For the first time since Bart had come back into her life, she felt relaxed in his presence. Maybe it was just that she was taking her first day off from work in months. Maybe it had something to do with the fact that they were leaving Raton and that no one would know either of them in Springer. Or maybe it was that Bart's hand around hers felt strong and warm, his shoulder felt hard against hers, he smelled wonderful, and his voice was filled with echoes of the happy days that had fled them so long ago.

"*Pilgrim's Progress*—now, there was one I really liked," Bart said. "Sometimes when I'd think about finding you again, Rosie-girl, I'd get a picture in my mind of the end of that book. Remember how old Christian would stand up and the heavy bundle of burdens he'd been carrying around would just snap and fall right off his back?"

"Christian was standing at the foot of the Cross when that happened, Bart," Rosie reminded him. "I keep trying to tell you, I'm not your salvation."

"I know that. I didn't sit on the Methodist church porch for years without coming to an understanding of where my salvation comes from. But I will say that ever since I climbed in your bedroom window a couple of weeks back, my burdens have felt a good sight lighter, Rosie."

She opened her eyes. "Mine have felt heavier."

"Damn it, Rosie, aren't you ever going to let up on me?"

Sitting up straight, she faced him. "What do you want, Bart? Do you expect me to pretend that everything about the past was as wonderful as those afternoons by the stream? Do you think I can just take up with you where I left off? Do you believe that I'm truly happier since you came to Raton and crawled under my bed?"

"I know I'm a burden to you, Rosie. I know some of the things that happened between us hurt you a lot. They hurt me, too. But I wish you could just forget about all that."

"*You* were hurt by the past?" she said, feeling the first trace of anger that morning. "What was so painful about high-stepping your way out of Kansas City and joining up with Jesse James?''

"Shh." He glanced at the only other couple in the car, an elderly man and woman at the far end. The woman appeared to be asleep, but the man was staring out the window. "If you don't learn to talk quieter, you're going to get me caught one of these days."

"You're going to get yourself caught."

"Maybe so. Maybe I'll wind up paying for all my sins by having my neck stretched. But let me tell you something, Rosie. Don't ever think I was having a rip-roaring good time through all of those six years without you. Don't think that for one second."

"If it wasn't fun, why did you do it?"

He tried to read the expression in her eyes. They were as soft and brown as blackstrap molasses. "I could lie to you and tell you I was hog-tied into becoming an outlaw. But you might as well know the truth."

"I don't want to hear it," she said suddenly, holding up a hand. "I don't want to know a thing about those evil men and their sinful ways."

"Listen here, Miss Priss, I am one of those evil men, and you might as well accept it. But you ought to know that not a one of those fellows is bad through and through. And neither am I."

"Are you trying to tell me Jesse James wasn't bad through and through?"

"Jesse was bad, but he had a good side, too. His brother, Frank, is one of the decentest men I ever met. Frank took me in and made a place for me when I didn't have a thing to my name. He's the one who set me on the right track after Bob Ford killed Jesse and things began to break up. 'Make a life for yourself like other folk, Bart,' he told me. 'Get a home, a wife, children. Find a place to live where you don't have to worry about getting a ball in the back when you go out for firewood.' That was the sort of life he aimed for himself, and I reckon he's been building it ever since the jury found him not guilty last August."

Rosie digested all this. Though she, like the rest of the

nation, knew Frank James had gotten off scot-free, she hadn't really pondered how the man had accomplished it. The sensational trial had lasted eight days and the court-house had been jammed with people. But Bart was right. Jesse James's brother had been found not guilty of the train-robbery murder of Frank McMillan.

"You think the James gang is so all-fired evil and the law is plumb perfect," Bart was saying, "but you ought to know the truth about that, too. The Pinkerton Detective Agency set a bomb in Zerelda Samuels's house. She's Jesse and Frank's mom. The bomb blew up and ruined Mrs. Samuels's arm. She had to have it amputated."

"No!"

"Yes, ma'am. Those Pinkertons have some mighty low ways."

"I expect you could even find something good to say about Robert Ford?" Rosie challenged. She knew how the members of the gang must feel about this man who had been one of their own and yet, for the reward money, had shot Jesse James in the back of the head, killing him instantly.

"Let me tell you something about Bob Ford," Bart said. "Far as I've ever been able to tell, the man doesn't have a moral bone in his body. But one time the gang got into trouble down in Arkansas. I was trapped at a train depot with about fifteen yards of open air between me and my horse. The law was everywhere. Jesse began calling the boys to head out and leave me to my fate. But Bob Ford hopped from his horse to a wagon. He pulled out his six-shooter and held off the posse while I fancy-stepped across the depot platform to my horse. Not a single bullet touched my hide. Bob Ford saved my life, Rosie. He saved my life, and I'll never forget it."

She studied Bart's handsome face and tried to understand the confusing puzzle that made up this man. Rosie's father had taught her that things were either black or white. People were either good or bad, saintly or sinful, right or wrong. Good people didn't cross the line and become bad. Bad people didn't cross it the other way—unless, of course, they happened to repent and find salvation from their sins, which, as Dr. Vermillion put it, had about a snowball's chance in hell of ever happening.

"My father taught me differently," she said. "He wouldn't have taken to your idea about those outlaws having any good in their hearts."

Bart thought back on the vain, pompous professor who had ranted and raged when he'd found out about his daughter's elopement. The words that man had said couldn't have been spoken in polite society anywhere. Finally, of course, Dr. Vermillion had resorted to his final weapon—the reality of Bart's own heritage and bleak future.

Dr. Vermillion would have classed himself as one of the good men. Rosie, too, surely saw her father as a paragon of virtue. Bart had done a lot of mean things in his time, but he would not stoop so low as to disparage Rosie's pappy, even if it meant she would never know the truth about why he had run off and left her a mere two weeks after their wedding day.

"I reckon the good Lord is the only one who can see inside a person's heart," Bart said finally. "He told us not to judge other folk, and I suspect that's pretty good advice. So, Rosie-girl, what do you say to putting the past behind us and seeing what lies ahead? Might be something good . . . you never know."

With Bart Kingsley in the picture, it might be something bad, Rosie told herself. On the other hand, he was right that she shouldn't be so condemning.

"For today," she said. "Just for today we'll let bygones be bygones."

Bart spent what little was left of the morning walking up and down the streets of Springer with Rosie while she shopped. She had brought along four crisp one-dollar bills, and she had made up her mind exactly how she intended to spend them. She was going to buy fabric to make curtains for Mr. Kilgore's school classroom, where she was sure she would soon be teaching.

With his cane and wicker basket in tow, Bart accompanied Rosie as she went from one dry goods store to another. It wasn't enough to buy just any old cloth. Rosie wanted something special, something that would cheer up the small room and bring life into the summer months. It had to be a fabric that would block some of winter's chill but also let in spring's sunshine.

Bart had started the morning feeling like a citified dude, but by the time he had stared at hundreds of bolts of gingham, silk, taffeta, cotton, muslin, and velvet in every color of the rainbow, he was about ready to take off like a wild bronco. His stiff white collar seemed to get tighter and tighter around his neck. The fancy coat he had traded for began to have the weight of a saddle on his shoulders. Even the bullet wound in his side began to hurt.

He was debating the urge to gallop out of the mercantile for a breath of fresh air when Rosie suddenly announced, "This is just what I've been looking for! Don't you agree, Bart?"

With glazed eyes, he studied the drapes of fabric in her arms. "Mighty nice, yes indeed," he said.

"It's cotton, so I can afford to buy plenty of yardage to make wonderful gathers—and just look at this pattern! Have you ever seen such lush florals?"

Bart wasn't absolutely certain what florals were, so he just shook his head in amazement. "Those are the lushest florals I've ever seen, that's for sure."

"Huge pink cabbage roses," she exclaimed. "Violets. Lilacs. Oh, it'll be just like bringing the outdoors inside!"

While Bart watched Rosie turning the fabric this way and that, it came to him that being with her like this had made his heart feel downright warm. Maybe he didn't know much about cloth and curtains. Maybe he'd never met a man who actually gave a woman's ideas much weight. Maybe shopping and chitchat were foreign to him. But one thing was clear: Bart Kingsley was enjoying the straight life.

"Would you please hold this up to the window for me, Bart?" Rosie was asking. "I'd like to see how the light comes through it."

"Happy to oblige," he said, and he carried the bolt of

flowery cloth to the front of the store. He made a sort of curtain rod out of his arm, and draped the fabric over it so that a sunbeam shot straight through the weave.

"Oh, it looks so much thinner now." Disappointment tinged her voice. "I probably should line every curtain, but I don't have enough money to buy twice the fabric."

Bart would have given Rosie every dime he owned in order to buy lining for her curtains. The only trouble was, he'd churned most of his money into his homestead, having bought a team of horses, a wagon, a plow, and a collection of tools that already seemed too few and inadequate for the job that lay ahead.

"Didn't you say you were going to ruffle up the cloth?" he asked, searching for something that might bring the smile back to her lips. With his arm still outstretched, he began to gather the rose-strewn fabric along it. "How's this, darlin'? See, the sun won't come through near so well now."

Rosie studied the fabric for a moment, at first seeing only the gathers and imagining how the curtains would look in the tiny one-room school. But her eyes soon wandered to the long, heavily muscled arm beneath the cloth. Then she took in the deeply bronzed face, the black hair, and the high cheekbones of her half-Apache escort. She remembered Bart Kingsley with his six-shooters and cartridge belt, his fringed buckskin jacket, his naked chest. At the memory, something stirred deep inside her, touched secret places that made her shiver, tightened the bodice of her dress.

Yet here was the same warrior who had caressed her so expertly, ruffling curtain fabric over his gun arm. The part of her that wanted to smile at the incongruity was quickly submerged by the intensity of his expression. Bart had shed his buckskins and gun belt along with his name and his rough demeanor. It touched her to see how very hard he was trying to fit into the roles he thought she wanted him to play—the dandy with a fine cane, the concerned shopper, the genteel suitor.

"Oh, Bart." She sighed, fighting the urge to rush to him and throw her arms around him.

"Don't fret so, Rosie-girl. Now, you just go ahead and

buy this cloth you've set your sights on. The minute I get
my paycheck next Friday, I'll give you enough money to
buy all the linings you need. Tell Mr. Puckett how many
yards you want, and I'll put it right in this basket I brought.
Then we'll go get us some lunch. How does that sound?''

Rosie's face broke into a brilliant smile. ''Thank you,
Bart,'' she said softly. ''That sounds just fine.''

Bart hadn't carried the heavy wicker basket all the way
through Springer and back for nothing. He had a plan. Once
he got Rosie out of the mercantile, he set his plan in motion.
A quick trip to the depot livery stable provided them with a
rented wagon and an old mare. A stop at the nearest
restaurant gave them a canteen of fresh lemonade, a block of
ice, and some vanilla ice cream.

''A picnic!'' Rosie said as they started out of town
toward the mountains. ''Mrs. Jensen would just have kittens
if she knew we didn't have a chaperon or a group of people
with us.''

''We're married folk, Rosie,'' Bart explained. ''We don't
need a chaperon, remember?''

''All the same . . .'' The very idea of being completely
alone with him sent a quiver down to the pit of Rosie's
stomach. The memory of the last time they were so intimate
filled her mind and set her to breathing more deeply than
was necessary. She knitted her fingers tightly together,
willing a calmness to the heavy thudding of her heart.

Bart glanced at Rosie, then took her hand. ''You don't
have to be scared, Rosie-girl. I'm not going to take
advantage of you. A gentleman would never do such a
thing.''

''Even with his own wife?'' she asked quietly, half in fear
and half in hope.

He remembered her description of the harsh way her
husband had used her for his own pleasures time and time
again. ''A gentleman wouldn't treat anybody roughly,'' he
said. ''Especially his wife.''

Still uneasy with her wayward thoughts, Rosie tried to
turn her mind to her future. It wouldn't really matter how

Bart treated her, she decided, because before long she surely would be on her own again. She had put up with her father's controlling ways and Dr. Lowell's torments for years. If Bart had a mind to boss her around or try to change her life, she could put up with it as long as she needed to because in the end Bart would leave, and she would be free to live her own life.

Of course, if he had a mind to treat her the way he had that night in her bedroom . . . with his warm fingers stroking paths of fire up her bare thighs . . . with his damp mouth covering her breast, his tongue working circles around her nipple . . .

"Did I mention that I've set my sights on a little yellow clapboard house just off Second Street?" she asked, clamping away the indecorous memory. "It's very small. Just the right size for a single lady."

Bart's focus was on the blue-gray mountains and the sapphire sky behind them. Resting his elbows on his knees, he let the old mare set her own pace along the rutted track. He had shed his jacket, and now Rosie saw the new red suspenders that held up his britches and cut into the corded muscles of his broad shoulders. Remembering those shoulders—bare, bronze, and gleaming with perspiration from struggling to control his own flaming desire for the half-naked woman who lay in his arms—Rosie flushed and glanced at Bart's face.

When he made no comment about her rambling conversation, she continued in hope that she might draw a response that would help her gauge how he felt about things between them.

"The house has a low white picket fence around the front yard," she said. "The fence needs a good coat of whitewash, but I imagine a shipment of lime will arrive at the mercantiles in Raton before long. Anyway, I've decided I'll plant flowers all along that fence—you know, tulips, hyacinths, violets, irises, roses—bulbs and some other perennials. And in the back, I'll dig a vegetable garden. With all my schoolwork, I won't have much time to tend a garden, but I think I can manage carrots and peas and such. The house isn't far from Mr. Kilgore's school, you know.''

She looked at Bart again. He had settled his hat down low over his brow, shading the bridge of his nose from the intense New Mexico sunshine. Though his green eyes were obviously alert, he still made no comment.

''There's a small front parlor with sprigs of pink flowers all over the wallpaper,'' she continued, still baiting him. ''The dining room even has a small cut-glass chandelier. I know it sounds like a costly place, but I checked the price with the brokers. Osfield and Adams are offering it, and with what Mr. Osfield told me, I do believe I can afford to buy it once I've settled into my job.'' Rosie paused a third time. ''Don't you think it sounds like a good house, Bart?''

He gave a small shrug. ''Sounds dandy. For a town house.''

Bart was thinking about the state of the small dugout dwelling he was building on his homestead—and how very far that damp hole in the ground was from a cute little yellow clapboard house with a white picket fence. There would be no fancy wallpaper in his dugout; the walls were built of rough-hewn wood planks layered against bare dirt. There would be no chandeliers; Bart felt lucky to be able to afford a few lamps. There would be no parlor, no dining room, no roses and tulips. This was a one-room shelter half buried in rough sod, and no woman who had her heart set on a city cottage could ever be happy in it.

''I'm thinking of lace curtains in the bedroom windows, with shades behind them, of course,'' she was saying as he pulled the wagon off the track and eased the mare toward a clearing beside a small stream.

Bart thought about lace curtains. In a dirt dugout, he knew, lace wouldn't last a week. His heart weighed as heavy as a millstone when he set the wagon's brake and jumped down into the ankle-high green grass. After coming around the back of the wagon, he held up his hands and felt Rosie's light weight slide into them. His palms nearly spanned her narrow waist as he lifted her from the wagon and set her feet in the grass.

"What a wonderful place you've found here!" she exclaimed, nearly overwhelmed by the stunning landscape. "Don't you just love the Territory, Bart? The sky is so big and blue, like a great canopy over the mountains. Sometimes I feel as if the sky is sitting right on top of my head! And there are so many things you could never find in Kansas City—mesas, junipers, prickly pears, and . . . Oh, look! There's a jackrabbit!"

Lifting her skirts, Rosie scampered across the ground toward the stream where a large jackrabbit had frozen in surprise, its long, semitransparent ears stiffly upright. As the froth of blue silks swished toward it, the jackrabbit suddenly took flight, hopping along the stream bed, then vanishing into the tall grass.

"Oh, how silly!" She laughed, grabbing her bonnet and gasping for breath. "Did you just see those ears!"

To tell the truth, Bart hadn't been watching the jackrabbit or its ears. He'd been concentrating on Rosie's little fanny as it swayed and swung with every step she took. My, what a bustle could do for a woman's hindquarters! As a matter of fact, Bart was having a little trouble catching his breath, too.

With all her talk about her town house and her teaching job, Rosie had fairly squelched any daydreams Bart had been having. In fact, he was thinking how blue he was feeling. But all it took was one look at that little lady high-stepping through the green grass, and Bart felt like a breeding stallion on the loose.

"He went right down into the grass just over there by that cottonwood," Rosie was saying as she approached the wagon. "Did you see? I never thought about jackrabbits much. Do you suppose they live in holes like cottontails do?"

Bart wasn't thinking about much of anything but the rise and fall of Rosie's full bosom in that scooped-out neckline of hers. The dress had been cut low enough that he could just see the dark shadow of her cleavage. Delicate ruffled lace bordered the ice-blue bodice, its white gathers lying against the creamy pillows of her breasts.

"Do you suppose they're a pest to gardeners?" she asked, stopping just paces away from him. "Jackrabbits look so funny, I don't see how anyone could take them seriously. But if they were eating up your crops . . . well, then, I suppose . . . Bart . . . Bart?"

He started. "What?"

"What's the matter?"

"Uh . . ." He rubbed a palm across the back of his neck. "I was . . . I was just wondering about lunch. Reckon you could do with a bite of a sandwich and some of that ice cream? We ought to eat it before it melts clean through the basket."

"I'm starving!" She held out her arms. "Hand me the tablecloth, and I'll spread it in the shade of that cottonwood. Maybe we'll get another look at our jackrabbit."

"Tablecloth?" He vainly searched the back of the wagon, knowing full well there was no tablecloth in the wagon, nor was there one for miles around.

"Oh, Bart! You can't have a picnic without a tablecloth." Rosie saw his hopeful expression fade, and she gave a quick laugh. "Oh, well. We'll just use this old saddle blanket. It'll serve."

"You reckon?"

"Sure! Follow me." In moments she had spread the rough woolen blanket over the grass, and was setting out Bart's picnic. It touched her to see the care he had taken with everything he had brought. There were sandwiches made with fresh bread and thick slabs of roast beef, boiled eggs, sacks of raisins, and a jar of Huffman's candies.

"*Cream* candies," he clarified proudly.

"Oh, I love cream candies."

"I know." He hunkered down beside her on the blanket and hooked off his boots. "A man doesn't forget things like that about his girl."

Rosie felt her cheeks go fiery, so she busied herself by setting sandwiches on the white plates she found in the bottom of the basket.

"I searched everywhere for some fresh fruit," Bart was saying, "but I guess it's not ripe yet. I remember how partial you are to strawberries. You suppose raisins will do, Rosie-girl?''

Suddenly unable to look at him, she began pouring glasses of lemonade. ''I like raisins nearly as much as strawberries. I don't imagine we'll have strawberries until later in May or June around here.''

''Do you still like pecan pie?''

''You didn't!'' she gasped, turning to him with sparkling eyes.

''I sure did. Mr. Farley over at the German City Bakery makes the finest pecan pie you ever sank a tooth in. Look here.'' He dug out a covered plate and held it aloft. Lifting the lid, he revealed a golden crusted pie filled with a brown molasses custard and opulent with layers of rich, chunky nuts.

Rosie sighed. ''It's beautiful.''

'' 'Sweets to the sweet.' '' Bart couldn't remember where that phrase came from, but he knew it was out of one of the books Rosie had read to him by their stream. This bold, gurgling New Mexico brook with its bed of gray rocks, its grassy slopes, and its jackrabbits was nothing like their secluded forest hideout in Missouri. But Bart was hoping that Rosie might begin to feel a little softer toward him in such a special place.

''*You're* the sweet one, Bart Kingsley,'' she said. ''This is just how you used to be—full of surprises for me, thinking of kind words to say, doing such gentle things.''

''You always have brought out my good side.''

Smiling, she popped a raisin into her mouth. It was certainly flattering to think that she could have such a positive effect on someone like Bart. When they were younger, she had never believed her influence had anything to do with Bart's character. He had been naturally generous and kind. Maybe that good side of him had been buried deep during their years apart, and now it took someone like Rosie to bring it out.

''You know,'' she said, ''sometimes these days, I get to thinking that you just invented all that stuff about being an outlaw. I mean, here you are with your fancy duds and your cane and the pecan pie and all, yet I'm supposed to believe you're a train robber?''

He toyed with his sandwich for a moment. ''Maybe you could just forget about all that, Rosie-girl. Maybe you could just pretend that I did make it all up. It wouldn't bother me a bit for you to put my past aside.''

''I can't put aside the part of the past I *do* remember.''

''Why not? Did you ever think there might have been a good reason why I went off and left you with your pappy there in Kansas City?''

She set her sandwich on the plate and studied her empty hands for a moment. ''I can't think of a single good reason for a man to run off from his bride of two weeks. No, I can't. Besides, you left that note that spelled things out clear as a bell, Bart. You said we'd just been playing at a child's game and that you hadn't ever loved me—''

''Stop!'' He caught her hands and jerked her roughly toward him so that she gasped. ''I did write that note, but not a word of it was true. Not a word, you hear?''

She stared into his troubled green eyes. ''Why did you write it, then? A person doesn't just write a letter full of lies!''

''He does if he has to.''

''You didn't have to do such a cruel thing! People were never able to cow you, Bart, no matter how they taunted. You always stood up for yourself. Don't try to sit there and tell me that someone forced you to write those awful words to me!''

''No one forced me,'' he said more gently, drawing her closer, ''but I had to write the letter all the same. I had to do it for you.''

''Why? You nearly killed me with that letter.''

''Damn it, Rosie-girl, I had to set you free to live a better life than the one I could give you. Don't you see that? I didn't have a barrel of shucks to offer you. You deserved better. You deserved a better life, a better man, than I thought I could ever be to you.''

''A man like Dr. Lowell? You ran off and left me to marry someone like him?'' Tears had filled her brown eyes.

"You were always kind to me. You believed in me, and you treated me right. So you abandoned me to a man who didn't give a hoot about what kind of a person I was? You left me to a man who tried to take away every spark of life in me, a man who forced me to act like somebody I could never be? Was that better than a barrel of shucks, Bart?"

With a groan of dismay, he caught Rosie against his chest. "I didn't know, darlin'. I'm sorry. I didn't know it would turn out that way for you." His mouth found hers, and he gentled the trembling of her lips. "If I could live that part of my life all over again, I would. If I could make things better for you . . ."

He kissed away the tears on her cheeks and eased her into his lap. She arched her neck as his mouth moved slowly down the sensitive silken skin. His fingers toyed with the knot of hair behind her bonnet, finally loosening the pins and releasing the mass of chestnut waves. As her hair spilled down her back and over his thigh, he felt her hands slide up his chest.

"Bart," she whispered, her breasts pressed tight against his shirt.

"What is it, darlin'?"

He could hear her swallow and feel the tension in her fingers as they slid through the back of his hair. "Bart, do you remember that night in my room at the dormitory?"

"It's what saw me through those two weeks in the woods until I could get back to you."

She shivered, and he ran his warm hands down her bare arms. "Bart?" she whispered again.

"Talk to me, Rosie-girl."

"You said if you could relive the past over again, you'd make things better for me."

"Yes, I would. I sure would."

"Bart . . ." She sucked in a breath that forced her breasts tighter against him. "Bart, would you make things good for me . . . right now?"

"Oh, darlin', my sweet Rosie, you know I will."

*Ten
. . . .

"Rosie, I don't want to scare you or hurt you," Bart whispered as he laid her across the blanket. "I never want to lay a rough hand on you, never. I want you to trust me and feel sure of me."

She gazed up at his face, framed by the spreading branches of the cottonwood tree. The green of the rounded leaves was matched by the emerald shade of his eyes. She could see that he meant each word he said, that he would leash every wild impulse in his body if she asked him to. And part of her wanted his restraint. She longed for the tenderness he had taught her, the gentle touch she had known only with him.

But when she began loosening his red tie, unfastening his stiff collar, and unbuttoning his shirt, an ache began inside her that demanded more than softness. Against all reason, and despite her past experiences, she suddenly wanted to know the rough pressure of his hands on her breasts, the touch of his teeth against her nipples, the hard thrust of his pelvis against hers.

"In my bedroom at the Harvey House, you showed me I could trust you," she said. "You showed me more than I ever dreamed of."

"Oh, Rosie, when you run your hands over my bare skin like that, I don't know how long I can hold back from you." His voice had lowered to a guttural growl. He leaned over her to place his mouth on the cushion of breast that swelled out of her bodice. As he spoke, his breath heated her skin.

157

"I've wanted you so bad I could hardly keep myself under rein."

"Did you really think about me after you left the House?"

"Darlin', I spent half my time swimming in a mountain stream just to cool down. You don't know what it is you do to me, girl. Back when we were kids, I just had to take one look at you and I rared up like a high-strung bull at breedin' time."

"Is it like that for you now?" she asked, though she could feel the proof of his words in the pressure of his body against her thigh. Her flush came both from the pleasure of having such influence over him and from the realization that, even now, this man was hard with desire for her.

"Darlin', you've got a hundred times what you had back in the old days," he murmured as his fingertip came down to ruffle the lace at the edge of her bodice. "When I rode over the mountains searching for you, I expected to find my Rosie-girl with her sweet brown braids and her pretty ankles. I didn't bargain for a woman whose mouth tastes like honey and whose body can fill out a dress the way yours does. I was looking for that pretty child who laughed and teased me and made my world seem okay. I sure didn't expect to find a grown-up lady with her own dreams and her own mind, a woman with twice the power over me that the little girl had."

"I don't have any power over you," Rosie protested. "The very idea! I've never had an ounce of power to my name."

"Right at this moment, honey, you could knock me over with a breath of air."

"Oh, really?" Laughing lightly, she eased up onto her elbows and blew against his cheek.

"I'm a goner," he cried, falling onto his back.

But he didn't let go of her; instead he drew her onto his chest where he could feel the sweet indentation her breasts made. If he expected coy submission again, he underestimated Rosie, for with this sudden shift in position, she actually felt a sense of the power he had spoken of. Rising above him, she slipped one leg over his thigh and settled the tips of her breasts on his bare chest. She kissed his warm skin, and as she moved downward, she allowed the crest of her bosom to trail over him.

The movement stirred her as much as it did him, for beneath her bodice, she could feel her breasts swell and tighten with need. His hands began to work apart the buttons at the back of her dress, and she shivered with the anticipation of once again knowing the touch of his fingers on her bare body.

"Bart," she whispered into his ear, "I feel as if I'm going to come right out of this dress."

"If I have my way, you are," he returned.

She smiled and ran her tongue around the shell of his ear. "I mean up top. I feel positively breathless with this tight corset and my bodice all squeezing me in."

Bart held his breath as she sat up and worked her shoulders out of the sleeves of her dress and slipped the garment over her head. At the sight of her full breasts barely encased in the thin cotton chemise, he reached for her. But she deflected his hands and began unhooking the front of her corset. In moments the stiff garment fell away, and her shoulders heaved with relief.

"Oh, this is better," she said and sighed. Wanting to tease him, suddenly aching to drive him to the brink of need, she lifted her summery chemise. As her breasts spilled out beneath it, he let out an animal groan and caught her roughly.

"Rosie," he murmured, his mouth against her breasts, "Rosie, I can't keep playing at this game of holding myself back. Darlin', I need you." His lips covered her and, as she had dreamed, his teeth nipped gently until her nipples stood out in bright, throbbing peaks. Then he began to suckle and to play with her with his tongue. Catching her breasts in his palms, he lifted them to his mouth and teased them back and forth until Rosie's parted thighs were swaying against his leg.

"I'm trying so hard to be gentle with you, girl," he said as he undressed her. Caressing the soft round pillows of flesh that formed her buttocks, he realized that she had cupped her own breasts and was rubbing their tips against his cheeks.

Don't be gentle, Rosie wanted to whisper. *I'm so hungry for you, I could die!* But if she gave in to his strength, if she let him use her body, what good could come of it? She would be giving away her own power. She would be under his control from then on.

Yet in her heart Rosie knew she had wanted to come to this isolated place with Bart. From the moment he had touched her in her bedroom, she had been ravenous to feel his fingers on her again. Could it be wrong to enjoy these moments with him, even knowing he was certain to leave her again?

All the more reason, she told herself. *If this is my one chance to feel the true pleasure of a man, let me have it all. Let me have it now.*

Lost in the swirling sunlight that poured through the cottonwood leaves, Rosie began unbuckling his leather belt. With a groan of disbelief, he shut his eyes as she unbuttoned his britches and reached inside the opening in the fabric.

"Oh, Rosie," he cried when she freed him fully into her palms. "Oh, woman."

"Touch me, too, Bart," she pleaded, "touch me the way you did before."

As she leaned over him, her naked body outlined by the sun, he slid his hands up her thighs and worked his fingers through her dark tuft of curls. "Is this what you've been thinking about, Rosie-girl? Have you been wanting this as much as I have?"

When he began to stroke her damp petals, she could only shiver in utter pleasure. Her body instantly sang, and her hips began to dance. Though she hadn't fully lowered his britches, she was able to stroke his fullness as he caressed her. Never, never, had she known such wanton craving. The delicious sensation of his mouth on hers and his fingers slipping through her moistness lifted her far beyond the bondage of her own self-control.

Gasping, moaning with pleasure, she rode his hands. "Oh, Bart, I can't bear it. I can't hold myself back."

"Rosie, will you take me inside you? Will you use my body to pleasure yours?"

His simple request quelled her every fear of this moment of union. Abiding by his wishes, she spread her knees on either side of his hips and slowly lowered herself onto him. His face went still, his lips parted, as she slipped her silken sheath over his shaft.

More to draw a response from him than anything else, Rosie lifted and lowered herself once again. He gripped her bottom as his head arched backward. She could see the muscles in his arms bunch and knot. His neck went stiff, and his thighs were rigid.

"Bart?" she whispered. She had never seen a man so completely under her control. She had always been the one beneath, the one penetrated and used for another's pleasure. Now she realized that she could make this warrior of a man do anything she wished. He had been right: she held the power.

Stroking up and down him, she felt her own pleasure heighten again, and yet the unbearable intensity of her need had faded with the absence of his fingertips. Dismayed, she gazed down at him, realizing that he was absorbed in his own rapture. Of course she wanted to satisfy him, but how could she deny her own hunger? Still pulsing with the need for his touch, she allowed her own hand to take the place of his. As she stroked herself, she felt the double ecstasy of his body filling her and her own passion rising to equal his.

"Oh, Rosie," he murmured. When his eyelids drifted open for a moment, she prepared herself to meet his disapproval of her action. Instead, he smiled and lifted his eyes heavenward. "I don't believe this," he groaned. "Rosie, woman, you have no idea what you do to me."

"I think I have some idea," she whispered, as his hand joined hers and their fingers continued to spiral her upward. "I think . . . I think we're doing the same thing to . . . to each other . . ."

With a deep growl of pleasure, he moved his hands to cup

her buttocks, sliding her over him while she continued to heighten herself. Rosie let her head drift back onto her shoulders, her eyelids sag shut, and her body ride on the ultimate crest of a wave that was so high she seemed to float above the clouds.

When she thought she could rise no higher, Bart lifted his head and began to suckle her breasts again. At the deep tugging thrill, she felt herself tighten and glide for a moment of sheer unconsciousness. And then she was sliding down and down with curls of passion washing through her, undulations of release shuddering over her body.

"Bart, Bart," she heard herself say, though her voice sounded far away. "Oh, Bart."

Savoring the moment, he held himself in control while her inner body massaged him. He watched her writhe with pleasure, her long hair swishing back and forth across his bare legs, her mouth parted with moans and mews of delight.

"Bart," she whispered, aware that he was still rigid inside her. Lifting her head, she opened her eyes.

At that moment Rosie looked straight into the double barrel of a shotgun.

"Bart!" she screamed. "Bart, it's a man with a gun!"

"Hold it now, lady," the man on the other end of the gun shouted over her shrieks. "Don't move a muscle. You under there, git up."

"What the hell . . . ?" Bart gently set the terrified Rosie to one side of the blanket and rolled onto his haunches.

"Do as I say, lover boy," the stranger barked. "Pull up yer britches and git over by that tree yonder."

When Bart stood up, Rosie grabbed the corner of the blanket and jerked it up to her chin. Half choked on fear and dismay, she stared at the intruder, who wore a faded brown felt hat darkened around the crown with sweat. His open mouth revealed a set of teeth stained by chewing tobacco. Unshaven, he had on an old patched coat and a pair of ragged blue trousers.

"Sorry to spoil y'all's fancy-dancy picnic," he said,

gesturing Bart toward a stout aspen tree close to the stream, "but I followed your wagon clear out from Springer just to get me a look at your pocketbook. I reckoned anybody dressed as much like a city dandy as you oughter have a wad of loose change, huh? Ain't I right, dude?"

Rosie watched as Bart walked slowly toward the tree. If he had been a city dandy once, every drop of Bart's Apache blood had risen to the surface now. She could see his veiled green eyes assessing the intruder, his empty hands forming the shape of his missing six-shooter.

"Then I come upon this pretty little picture here," the stranger continued, "and I decide I'll just git me two prizes in one trip. Ain't nothing' can stir a man like the sight of a hot-blooded woman. Which whorehouse did you find her at, anyhow? You must've paid damn good to get a performance like that."

At his words, Rosie curled into herself and covered her eyes with the blanket. Oh, she wanted to die. To think that this sickening man had watched her and Bart. Now he intended to use her himself. . . . She thought she was going to throw up.

"Git yer back up against that tree, lover boy," the man ordered. "I'm gonna tie you up just so's you can watch the action."

"No, Bart!" Rosie cried out.

At her shriek, the stranger turned his head for a split second. Bart instantly slammed his fist into the man's jaw. The intruder staggered backward, his shotgun firing into the air. Rosie screamed again. Bart hammered the man with another blow to the chin.

Scrambling to her feet, Rosie dashed across the clearing to the wagon. As she climbed into the back, she watched Bart pick the man up by his coat and slam his head against the tree. The stranger dropped the gun, and Bart kicked it away.

"You want some action, bastard?" Bart growled, leveling a blow into the man's midsection. "You want me to stir you up a little?"

Rosie gripped the side of the wagon and peered over the

edge as Bart pounded the stranger into the ground. Every vestige of the gentleman who had accompanied her on a picnic had disappeared. In his place was a savage warrior with one thing on his mind—vengeance.

"I'll teach you to talk about a woman like that," Bart spat as he rammed his fist into the man's mouth. "Try talkin' now, you good-for-nothing thief!"

"Ow! Ouch!" Spitting out teeth, the stranger held up an arm to ward off the blows. "Let me go. I didn't mean nothin'!"

"I've shot men for less, you little bastard."

"Don't shoot! Don't shoot me!"

Bart had the stranger by the back of the hair, and the man was bouncing up and down on his toes now. With good aim Bart kicked the man's rear end and landed him hard in the dirt. As he fell, Bart grabbed the fallen shotgun.

"I've a good mind to shoot your backside so full of holes you'll never need a privy again."

"No! I'll leave—I swear it!" As Bart hauled him to his feet, the man grabbed his bottom. "Don't shoot my ass!"

"Get on this nag of yours and get the hell out of here before I blast you to kingdom come." Bart lifted the man off his feet and hurled him across the saddle. As the air whooshed out of the stranger's lungs, Bart slammed the stock of the gun into the back of his skull. Instantly limp, the man hung over his horse, blood dripping from his scalp and mouth.

Using the rope with which the man had planned to tie him to the tree, Bart bound his assailant's wrists to his ankles beneath the horse's belly.

"Get out of here, now. *Shee-hah!*" he shouted, giving the nag a swift slap on the flank. "Take your worthless baggage out of my sight."

As the nervous horse skittered out of the clearing, its flaccid bundle flopping lifelessly on its back, Bart stood watching, with his hands balanced lightly on his hips. Though his bare chest rose and fell with the effort he had expended, he felt no pain in the hands that had battered the thief. He felt nothing but the raw male power that had been a daily part of his life for so many years.

Anger ate at him. How dare such a miserable fool think he could get away with trying to rob Bart Kingsley? He should have shot the man's head off for interrupting the picnic like that. And the things he'd said about Rosie! Bart ought to have strangled the mangy dog till his . . .

"Rosie?" Remembering, Bart turned suddenly. "Rosie, where are you?"

Her head appeared above the rim of the wagon bed. "Here," she said.

She was pale as a sheet, Bart thought as he hurried toward her. Look at her, all wrapped up in that saddle blanket! She was trembling, her eyes wide and her mouth red and puffy.

"Rosie, darlin'," he began.

"Bart, you mean, awful savage!" Though she still sat huddled under the blanket and her voice was tremulous, her brown eyes spat fire. "You didn't have to knock his teeth out!"

"What?" Bart stopped, dumbfounded.

"That man didn't stand a chance against you after the first time you hit him. But you just kept on hammering away like some kind of devil. You could have killed him, and then where would you be?"

"I *should* have killed him. Do you know what that bastard was planning to do to you?"

"He's probably going to die right out there in the wilderness. I reckon he'll bleed to death. Even if he doesn't, his brain will never work right again."

"His brain? Damn it, Rosie, that fellow didn't have half a brain to start with!"

"Oh Bart, you were just so rough with him. It was like you didn't know when to stop."

Confusion and anger still running rampant through him, Bart shook his head. "I stopped when I'd done him in. When I was sure he couldn't lift a finger against you, that was when I laid off him—and not a minute before."

Rosie sat scrunched up beneath the blanket, her eyes filled with unshed tears. "I do appreciate you protecting me,

Bart," she said, "but you were so . . . so brutal. You were like some kind of a wild animal once you got started. I thought you were never going to quit."

"I quit, didn't I?"

She lifted her head. "What if he dies? The sheriff will come for you."

Bart slammed his palm against the side of the wagon. "Damn it, Rosie, what do you want out of me? I can't be a gentleman and a lover and a protector all at the same time. I couldn't stand there like some sissy-foot and let him get away with robbing me and raping you."

"Bart!"

"Well, that's exactly what he was planning to do, Rosie!" For a moment he stared at her. Then he spat on the ground. "Shoot, I reckon I'm just what I am, and to hell with the rest of it. To hell with city duds and canes and pecan pie. I'm a man who uses his fists better than he uses his head, and I don't think that's ever going to change."

He stalked off and began to gather the scattered picnic supplies. From the wagon, Rosie watched him stuffing dishes into the basket. His jaw was set like a rock, and the muscles in his bare shoulders fairly rippled with frustration. With his copper skin gleaming in the sunshine, his black hair ruffling in the mountain breeze, and his high cheekbones gilded with light, he was every bit the Indian.

For some reason she couldn't immediately fathom, Rosie felt an uncomfortable desire blossom over her body beneath the blanket. At the sight of Bart's sinewed back bending and straightening, she felt her breasts tingle. Their tips began to ache. When he stood and she saw the fabric of his britches tighten over his pelvis, her mouth went dry.

But Bart was in no mood for passion, no matter how close he had been to his release before the intruder barged in on them. After pushing his arms into the sleeves of his shirt and jerking on his boots, he stomped over to the cottonwood tree where the shotgun lay. He grabbed the weapon, shouldered it, jerked the picnic basket up in one hand, and stalked toward the wagon.

"Your clothes are over there," he said. "Might as well

get dressed if we're going to catch the three-thirty back to Raton.''

He didn't look at Rosie as she crawled down from the wagon and hurried to gather up her tangled garments. Hiding behind the cottonwood tree, she slipped her chemise over her head and made an awkward effort at fastening her corset. She peeked around the trunk to find Bart sitting on the wagon, his hat pulled low and a frown tugging down the corners of his mouth.

Oh, why had she snapped at him so? He'd just been protecting her the best way he knew how. It was certainly true that the stranger had been planning to do terrible things to her. Besides robbing Bart and ravishing Rosie, the man might have taken it into his head to kill them both.

On the other hand, Bart *had* needlessly beaten the fellow into a bloody pulp. Maybe the man did deserve a licking. Maybe it was the only way to ensure that he wouldn't bother them again. But just the memory of Bart slamming his fist into that man's mouth made Rosie shudder. This was the side of him she didn't want to acknowledge—this sledge-hammer of a man. If he could use his bare hands to take out a gun-toting thief, what couldn't Bart do? What wouldn't he do?

As Rosie buttoned her dress, she peered around the tree trunk again. She didn't feel afraid of Bart personally—not the least little bit. But how could a woman be at ease with someone who could explode like that? How could she trust him to keep a cool head in every situation? What if every time someone made him mad he took it into his head to knock the man's teeth out?

Of course, Bart had done everything in his power to prove himself a gentleman. The memory of his fancy suit and cane, his specially prepared picnic, and the tender way he had taken her concerns into account warmed Rosie's heart as she walked across the clearing to the wagon.

"Bart," she said, looking up at him, "I owe you an apology."

He lifted his head and with one finger tipped back the brim of his hat. "Damn right," he said.

It wasn't the response she had expected, but she squared her shoulders and continued. "I shouldn't have gotten onto you when you were just trying to protect me. I should have been more grateful."

"You're right about that, too." He slapped the wagon seat. "Now get in here and sit your fanny down."

She studied the high-framed wagon and thought about her confining petticoats, skirts, and corset. "You aren't going to help me up?"

He reached out a hand. Rosie scowled for a moment, then grabbed his wrist. It took all the effort she had to haul herself up into the wagon. Her boots slipped on the bare wood; her skirt tangled in the wheel spokes; and her face turned bright red from the exertion. Bart moved not a muscle to help her any further than holding out his arm.

When she had finally settled on the seat, she spread her skirts, stuffed her loose hair under her bonnet, and crossed her arms. But when Bart started the mare with a swift slap of the reins, Rosie was forced to grab the sides of the wagon seat to keep from tumbling off.

They were almost back to Springer before Bart spoke. "I've done some thinking," he said without prelude. "For near onto a month now I've done my dead-level best to be somebody I'm not. I told you outside the church the other day that new clothes can't change the color of a man's skin. Well, they can't change what's inside him, either."

"What's inside you, Bart?" Rosie asked.

He reached behind him, grabbed the shotgun and shook it in front of her. "This is what's inside me. It's what I'm made of, see? You can dress me up in a coat and tie, but underneath I'm still Bart Kingsley. I'm a half-breed bastard who's spent every year of his grown life on the wrong side of the law. I reckon I tried pretty damn hard to be everything you could want in a man. But I messed up today. And the truth of the matter is, I'm going to keep messing up real regular, because when push comes to shove, the citified dude steps out the door, and the gunslinger walks in. I don't imagine there's a thing in the world that can change that."

Rosie fiddled with the folds of her skirt. There were a

thousand things she wanted to say to him. She wanted to tell him she liked him fine just the way he was, gun and all. She wanted to tell him she knew he could change if he made up his mind to. She wanted to say that she thought he was the bravest, strongest, handsomest man she'd ever seen. And she ached to tell him how wonderful his loving made her feel.

But to be so bold would give him the idea that she cared about him too much. Rosie knew she couldn't let herself feel strongly about Bart. He was probably right in saying that he'd go back to his old ways. And if the sheriff caught him, Bart would be thrown in jail quick as a wink. More important, if Bart's outlaw past caught up with him, he'd leave town lickety-split, and Rosie knew he would never be back.

No . . . she couldn't encourage him to keep up his efforts at change. Not when her heart was at risk.

"Bart," she said, trying to sound casual. "Bart, you just do whatever you can to look like a good husband to me for the next few weeks. Then you can go off and act any way you want."

"Yeah, you care more about that damn teaching job and that sidewinder's lost teeth than you ever cared about me." Bart knew he sounded like a pouting kid, but that was exactly how he felt. It hurt like hell to see how hard Rosie was toward him.

She sniffled at the threatening tears his words evoked. "Well, I sure never let anybody else be as forward with me as you were today," she countered. "Even that snake of a man I married in Kansas City had to force out of me whatever he wanted."

Bart slowed the wagon and let the reins sag in his hands. "Damn it all, Rosie, I meant this to be the best day of your life. I meant it to be the start of something new between us."

"There can't be anything new between us, Bart," she said, lifting a gather of her skirt to blot away the dampness beneath her eyes. "We started out wrong, and things have gone wrong ever since."

Bart thought about her words for a moment. Then he flicked the reins. "Well, if you don't think there's hope for us, if you don't believe I can change, then I reckon it's a lost cause. You were always my light, Rosie. The thought of you and your love for me was what kept me going in the blackest times." He eased the wagon to a stop at the train depot at the edge of Springer. "If you can't see any light shining at the end of this tunnel of ours, if the only bright spot in your life is that teaching job, then I don't know what in hell I'm doing."

"I don't know either, Bart," Rosie said as she watched the three-thirty train pull into the station. "I don't know either."

It took about five minutes for Rosie to lose her job as a Harvey Girl. She had barely returned to the dormitory when Mrs. Jensen stormed into the pink bedroom and demanded to know where Rosie had been all day. When Rosie announced that she'd eloped with Buck Springfield, Mrs. Jensen turned on her heel and marched right down the stairs to tell Mr. Gable.

Tom Gable said he had half a mind to keep Rosie on if she wanted to work. He didn't know where he could get as hard and reliable a worker as she had been, he told her. But if she had her heart set on being a farmer's wife, well, there was nothing he could do to dissuade her.

Etta and the other girls flew into a flurry of questions, exclamations, giggles, and sighs when Rosie told them about the train trip to Springer. Though she knew her hands were trembling as she packed her clothes in the trunk she had brought from Kansas City, Rosie kept up a bright voice and a Harvey Girl smile.

Buck was so wonderful, she avowed. The perfect husband! Then she plunged into rhapsodies about the life they would share on his homestead, the plans they had made for their sugar beet farm, and her hopes of getting the teaching position she would apply for later that evening.

"I'll miss you all," she said honestly, when she was standing on the depot platform waiting for Bart to drive his new wagon around to pick her up. "I'll come by sometimes for ice cream."

"I'll have your pay ready for you on Monday," Mr. Gable added. "You can pick it up any time, Miss Kings—er, Mrs. Springfield."

With unexpected tears in her eyes yet again that day, Rosie watched Bart drive his team of horses around from the livery stable and pull them to a stop by the platform. The Harvey House had been a good place for her, she mused. Just what she had hoped for—a quiet home, security, enough money to get by on, and the promise of a future in the New Mexico Territory. Now that future beckoned.

"You take good care of this little lady," Mr. Gable warned Bart as he heaved Rosie's trunk into the back of the wagon. "She's going to make you a fine wife."

"You're lucky to get her!" Mrs. Jensen snapped when Rosie was seated and the wagon began rolling away from the depot. "You just remember that, Mr. Springfield. You're lucky to get her."

Rosie waved a white handkerchief and watched the familiar faces fade into the evening gloom. As the wagon rounded the corner, she could hear Mr. Gable call out, "Back inside and clean up those stations, everyone. We're expecting at least forty omelets on the seven-o'clock from Denver!"

Rosie couldn't help but smile as Bart drove the wagon down First Street and turned toward the schoolhouse on Second. Hard as it was to leave her friends at the Harvey House, it was terribly exciting to think about the moment she would stand on Mr. Kilgore's doorstep and present her new husband.

"Be sure to tip your hat when you meet Mrs. Kilgore," she reminded Bart. "They're very proper people."

"Reckon I should kiss the back of her hand?" Bart drawled.

"No!" Rosie laughed suddenly. "Oh, Bart, I know we've had a rough day, but I'm just beside myself with excitement. I do believe that once I have that teaching job, nothing can hold me down. I just feel positively giddy inside.''

''I sure can't see how trying to ride herd on a bunch of mustang colts can have much appeal for you, Rosie.'' He pulled the wagon to a halt in front of the small house next to the one-room school. ''Looks to me like teaching's a hell of a lot of work and not much fun.''

''Watch your language around the Kilgores, Bart,'' Rosie said as she drew her wrap closer around her bosom. ''And teaching is exactly what I want to do, fun or not.''

He lifted his hands and helped her down from the wagon. Then she quickly stepped away and led him up the front steps of the Kilgores' house.

''Knock for me, Bart,'' she whispered. ''I'm so cold and scared all of a sudden.''

Fighting the urge to put his arm around her, Bart rapped on the green front door. In a moment Mr. Kilgore had drawn it open and was gawking at Rosie from behind his spectacles.

''Why, Miss Kingsley,'' he said. ''I certainly didn't expect to see you at this time of evening. Do come in.''

When the middle-aged man led them into a small front parlor, Rosie could see at once that she hadn't chosen the best time to apply for her new job. The Kilgores had company—a man and a woman and three children were hastily rising to greet Bart and her.

''Miss Kingsley,'' Mr. Kilgore began, ''may I introduce—''

''I beg your pardon, Mr. Kilgore,'' Rosie interrupted, ''but my name has been changed since we last spoke. I am now Mrs. Springfield. And this is my husband, Buck.''

''Howdy,'' Bart said, carefully tipping his hat to all concerned. ''Pleased to meet you folks.''

''Well, this is quite a surprise,'' Mr. Kilgore said. ''I had no idea nuptials were in the planning.''

''Oh, yes,'' Rosie affirmed.

''I've been planning to marry this gal for one hell of a long time,'' Bart put in.

Rosie glanced at him, but he didn't seem to realize he'd

said anything wrong. Instead, he clapped his hat back on his head and nodded at the Kilgores' guests. "And who're these folks?"

Mr. Kilgore cleared his throat. "Mr. and Mrs. Springfield, may I present Mr. and Mrs. Sneed and their children, Abigail, Tom, and Lawrence."

"So pleased to meet you," Rosie said, holding out her hand.

"Indeed," Mrs. Sneed responded. "And congratulations on your recent marriage. I'm sure I'll be seeing a great deal of you once you begin your family."

"Oh?" Rosie asked.

"Certainly, my dear. I'm quite certain I will be educating your children in years to come. I've just been hired by Mr. Kilgore as the new teacher for his school."

*Eleven
. . . .

As hard as he tried, Bart could not get a single word out of Rosie all the way from the Kilgores' house to his homestead, a good long wagon ride. The moment she had been able to exit the scene of her devastation gracefully, she had pulled her shawl over her bonnet and retreated into silence. Bart had tried commenting on the full moon, musing aloud over the probability of rain, even remarking about the uneven gait of one of his horses. Rosie just sat.

Bart felt sure he knew just what she was thinking. A fine mess she's gotten herself into now: stuck with Bart Kingsley, and no teaching job to boot. He knew she had concocted the marriage plan only in hopes of landing that teaching job. Now she had given up her secure position and regular salary at the Harvey House, the whole town of Raton believed she was married, and she'd lost out on her dream.

The worst was yet to come, Bart knew. When Rosie took one look at the barren hills, rocky streambeds, and scrubby brushland he was taking her to, she would go plumb soggy on him. Already he could hear her sniffing under her shawl, and for all the world he wanted to take her in his arms.

But what did he have to offer? Outlaw manners and a wicked reputation. That and a half-dug hole in the ground that was supposed to pass for a house.

Bart tugged his hat down over his brow and studied on the housing situation for a long time. What he had to offer Rosie was pitiful—a fireplace made out of river rocks, a bare plank floor and four plank walls, a bed with no mattress, a table with no chairs, and two windows fitted with paper instead of glass panes.

Bart knew he had a fair hand at carpentry, but he was really cut out for horse work. And with all the plowing, planting, digging, and building he'd had to fit in around his job at the livery stable, Rosie was lucky to have a bed at all.

The more Bart thought about the bed with its hard board bottom and thin blankets, the more uneasy he felt about everything. What would happen to a woman who, all in one day, had made love to a gentleman who turned out to be a wild animal, had seen all her dreams of teaching turn to ashes, and had to start living like a mole in the ground?

Bart glanced at Rosie, but he couldn't make out her face. Lord, he wished he'd had a better family to grow up in. What was a man supposed to do with a crying woman? Most of the men who had lived with his mother—including the man who eventually became Bart's stepfather—wouldn't have had a moment's patience with tears. More than once, Bart had seen his stepfather slap his mother's face for bawling about things.

Bart sure didn't want to slap Rosie. He wanted to hold her and whisper in her ear that he'd take care of her, teaching job or not. But maybe that wasn't the right thing to do either. Maybe if he tried to comfort her, she'd just cry all the harder. That much crying couldn't be a good thing, could it? And if he tried touching her, maybe she'd get scared of him again. Or mad. He sure didn't want to face Rosie's anger.

The best thing to do was just not say anything, Bart decided finally. If he ignored her, she couldn't think one way or the other about him. Maybe he could sort of fade into the background and disappear from her thoughts.

Of course, the wagon was drawing closer and closer to the homestead, and Bart had no doubt Rosie would have an opinion about the dark dugout waiting for her. She'd have a strong opinion. In fact, he ought to prepare himself to haul her back to town and put her up in a hotel for the night. That might be the best solution of all.

Bart's hands grew damp on the reins as the horses pulled the wagon up the incline that led toward the clearing where he had dug the house. The track sure did feel rutted and stony. The pine trees seemed closer than he'd thought when he was chopping out a path.

"Well, all told I've got one hundred sixty acres," he said, hoping to ease Rosie's fears before the ultimate moment when she saw what lay ahead. "It's good land. Trees for lumber. Three streams with fresh water running all year long. After I've lived out here for five years, I can go to Springer to file proof of my claim, and the land will be mine." He paused and glanced at Rosie. "Ours," he amended.

She said nothing in response. The wagon topped the hill and rattled toward the board-and-battan walls that rose a mere three and a half feet above the ground. The house looked more like a half-buried coffin than somebody's home. Bart tugged on the reins to pull his horses to a halt. For a moment he sat staring at the tar-papered roof and the two ground-level windows beside the front door.

"I know this is a far sight from Kansas City," he began. "Probably not what you were used to with that . . . that Dr. Lowell . . ."

"Help me down, Bart," Rosie announced, speaking for the first time since they'd left Raton.

Her words struck him like a bolt of lightning, and he hopped down from the wagon and hurried to her side. When he held out his hands for her, he saw that she had let her shawl slip down from her head. The full moon gleamed on her bonnet, lighting every ribbon and flower. It silvered her shiny blue dress and washed her pale cheeks in alabaster. Lord, she was so beautiful it made his heart ache.

"Thank you, Bart," she said when her feet were on firm ground. "I expect you'll want to unhitch the horses."

"Sure, but . . . well, I'll carry your trunk inside first." To cover his uncertainty about the moments to come, Bart leapt into action. He grabbed the handles of her heavy trunk, heaved it against his chest, and stalked toward the stairs that sank toward the front door of the house.

"This is a half-dugout," he explained to Rosie, who was standing stiff in the mountain breeze. "I got the idea from

Cheyenne Bill. He told me this is the sort of house most homesteaders build to get started. It's warm in winter and cool in . . . Well, it's not much of a house, to tell the truth. . . . I'm digging out a back room for storage and such.''

"Is there a lock on the door, or do we just walk in?" Rosie asked. She turned to Bart and realized for the first time how nervous he was. He had jerked off his hat and was squeezing the brim as if to choke it to death. "You might want to go down first and light a lamp. You do have a lamp inside, don't you?"

"Oh, sure. I've got two lamps." He scampered around her and bolted down the stairs to the door. In moments he had vanished inside.

Alone for a minute, Rosie lifted her head to the sky and sucked in a shaky breath. This was her home now, the place where she would be forced to live and toil until she could find a way to escape it. All her hopes of freedom and independence had come to nothing. If anything, she was more a slave now than she had ever been in her life.

Perhaps this was her punishment for being disobedient to her father. Or for marrying two men at the same time. Or for running away from her husband. Or for making love to Bart Kingsley under the cottonwood tree.

Whatever the cause, Rosie knew she most certainly was being given a stern chastisement. The tiny square house, the empty and neighborless landscape, the utter wilderness that promised backbreaking labor by day and the howls of wild animals by night, the husband she couldn't be sure of—all would be her purgatory. And heaven was nowhere in sight.

"You can come down now, Rosie-girl," Bart said from the doorway. He was holding a lamp in his hand. Only his face was lit, and Rosie could see the worried look in his green eyes. His concern penetrated the layers of hurt and confusion surrounding her. Finally, determined to put on her best front, she stepped onto the first stone of the stairwell.

"It's a real solid door," Bart said as she descended the three-and-a-half-foot drop into the earth. "Oak. I bought the boards in town and built the house to fit the door."

"You dug all this yourself?" she asked, trying to sound interested.

"Manford Wade, that red-haired kid from town, helped out. Soil's pretty sandy around here, which might be a problem for my sugar beets. They like a rich, loamy soil, you know? Anyhow, it took Mannie and me a good long while to hollow out this much space." He stepped back and held out the lamp while she made her way past him into the dugout.

At the first sight of the cramped room with its bare wood walls and floor, Rosie felt a lump knot in her throat. But she had cried enough for one day. More than enough. This was her lot, her castigation, and she would take it the best she could.

"I don't have a cookstove yet," Bart was saying as he gestured toward the cold fireplace. "This'll have to do for now. Guess it's not much like the kitchen at the Harvey House."

"Do you have any pots and pans?"

"I've got a pot and a skillet. They go a long way toward a good meal."

"Where do you keep your stores?"

"There's a pantry back of here," he said, slapping a wooden wall. "I'll cut the door between these rooms once I get things sealed in good. Right now I just keep supplies in there and jump down in the hole when I need something."

Rosie pondered the notion of climbing in and out of the hole in the ground in order to fetch potatoes, sugar, flour, and such. "Do you have a ladder anywhere?"

"I could build one." He hooked one thumb around a suspender. "In fact, I'll build you a set of steps tomorrow so you can get down into the storeroom. I've got tomorrow off from work, being as it's Sunday. And starting next week I'm only going to work afternoons at the livery stable so I can get my spring planting done. See, when you're planting beets, you put out seedballs, and then when the sprouts come up you're obliged to thin like crazy."

Now that he had Rosie on his homestead, Bart couldn't

seem to stop talking about his dream. "I'll rotate my sugar beet crop with potatoes, so they'll stay healthy. I'll have to keep a close watch for blister beetles, too. But if I can raise a good crop, Rosie, we'll sell all we bring in. Beets are bringing five cents a pound these days. Plus we can market the greens for cattle feed. . . ."

Rosie nodded, trying to listen but wondering how she would ever survive the hours alone in this godforsaken place. On the other hand, how would she handle having Bart around her so much? His green eyes, his teasing, his big warm body and gentle smile would put her in a constant struggle to maintain a prudent distance. Oh, everything would have been perfect if only she'd gotten that teaching position. . . .

"How about some supper?" Bart asked quickly when he saw Rosie's face cloud over. "I've got oysters. Bought 'em last week just for you. The grocer over at Huffman's told me they're all the rage with city folk these days."

A smile crossed Rosie's face as she compared this lonely dugout to the luxurious oyster bar where she had attended so many gay parties in Kansas City.

"Oysters would be nice," she said, drawing her shawl from her shoulder. "Do you have a wardrobe . . . or . . . or maybe a hook?"

Bart glanced at the bare wall by the bed. "Well . . . I've got a nail."

"May I hang up my shawl?"

"Sure." He leapt to grab the wool wrap, then quickly stuffed it over the single nail protruding from a plank. "How about your bonnet? You can take it off if you want."

She shrugged. "I'll take care of my things while you fix the oysters. Don't worry. I'm fine."

While Bart opened the tins of oysters, he kept one eye on Rosie, who was digging in her open trunk. Why hadn't he thought about hooks? And she'd want an ironing board, of course. Probably a washtub, too. She might even like a mirror. Of course she'd want a mirror! She'd need a changing screen and a dressing table, chairs, pillows—a hundred things that had never crossed his mind until this moment when he saw her looking so forlorn.

"Here's a stool for you, Rosie-girl," he said, drawing out the only seat in the house. "I've got you a plate of tasty oysters all fixed up."

While Rosie seated herself gingerly on the three-legged stool and made an attempt to arrange her skirts and bustle, Bart took his plate over to the bed. For a long uncertain moment, he eyed the pale gray blobs on his plate. They stank to high heaven, but he knew they must taste delicious, what with all the high-society people craving them these days.

He pulled his knife from the leather sheath that hung on his belt and attempted a stab at the nearest oyster. It shot off the plate and landed with a smack on the floor.

Bart lifted his head to find Rosie watching him, the hint of a grin tugging at her mouth. "Willful little critters, aren't they?" he commented.

"They work best with a spoon. Do you happen to have any spoons?"

"Didn't I give you anything to eat with?" Bart gestured to the mantel. "I bet you'll find a spoon or two up there. Fetch whatever you need."

Rosie stood as gracefully as possible and checked the mantel. Three dusty, bent spoons lay among a tumble of knives, chains, fishing lures, and whetstones. With two fingers, she pulled a spoon from the rubble and wiped it on her blue skirt.

She sat down just in time to see Bart grab an oyster with one bare hand and pop it into his mouth. An expression of vague discomfort instantly spread over his face. He began to chew. He chewed a while longer. Then he chewed some more. Rosie watched, wondering why on earth she felt like giggling at a time like this.

"Is it good?" she asked lightly.

"Mighty fine," he answered around the mouthful of oyster.

While Bart continued to chew, Rosie slipped an oyster onto her spoon, placed it in her mouth and swallowed the delicious morsel whole. It was lukewarm and just out of a can rather than chilled on a bed of ice, but the taste of the oyster transported Rosie to a time of gentility and refinement. If a woman could dine on oysters in such a pit as this house, couldn't she make life a little better for herself somehow?

Rosie lifted her head to discover Bart was still working on his first oyster. "Bart?" she queried.

He finally gave a great gulp and shook his head. "I don't know about your varmint, but mine was as tough as old shoe leather."

Rosie couldn't suppress the giggle that bubbled up inside her. "Oh, Bart, you don't chew oysters! You swallow them whole."

"Swallow them?" As a grin lifted one corner of his mouth, he regarded his plate. "You sure about that? My mama didn't know much about manners, but she taught us kids to chew our food before we downed it."

Rosie swept up her plate and crossed the room to the bed. Sitting down beside Bart, she held out her spoon. "Slide the oyster onto the utensil," she instructed. "Then put the oyster in your mouth and swallow." She demonstrated while Bart studied her.

"I'll be damned." Taking her spoon, he chased a slippery oyster around his plate for a moment before finally nabbing it. Then he followed Rosie's instructions and gulped the creature whole. It seemed to sort of slither down his throat like a live fish, but when it finally landed in his empty stomach, Bart decided it settled pretty well.

"There!" Rosie laughed. "You did it."

At the sight of her happy face and glowing eyes, Bart thought he would eat a hundred oysters, no matter how bad they smelled. "Sure enough, Rosie-girl," he said. "Your turn."

Trapping one of her oysters with the spoon, he slipped it between her lips and watched her face suffuse with ecstasy. She shut her eyes, savored the morsel for a moment, then swallowed.

"Oh," she whispered, and Bart decided he was beginning to like oysters more and more.

As her eyes drifted open, he thought he was going to swell right out of his britches. Her bosom was bathed in the golden glow of the lamp, and her lips were damp. She smiled up at him.

"Your turn now," she said softly.

He dragged his gaze from her face to the plate of oysters. "How about if you snag me one?" he suggested. "You've had more practice."

Rosie scooped up an oyster and slid it into Bart's mouth. "Now swallow."

He obeyed. "Hell of a way to eat, if you ask me."

"Your language would raise the dead, Bart Kingsley." Chuckling again, she ladled another mollusk between his lips. "In Kansas City, oyster restaurants are everywhere. People go to the theater, then they step out for a late-night snack of oysters and champagne, which are said to be the food and drink of passion. So of course it's all the rage to patronize the houses that serve them."

"I reckon I understand about these critters being the food of passion," Bart said as he set his plate on his knees. Taking the spoon from Rosie, he served her another oyster. After she swallowed, he bent and kissed the dampness from her lips. "Not that I knew their reputation when I bought them."

"Or when you chewed on that first one." Rosie smiled as his mouth hovered near hers.

"But I've got the message now." He moved his lips across her cheek, stirring small flames on her skin. "Rosie-girl, you look so good to me right now, I can hardly breathe. And I don't think those oysters have a thing to do with the way you make me feel."

"Oh, Bart, it was good between us this afternoon, wasn't it?" She let out her breath as his mouth slipped down the side of her neck. "But that awful man scared me so much . . . and then I lashed out at you . . . and then Mr. Kilgore—"

"Hush, now, darlin'. There's worse things in this world

than a mean-mouthed little snake like that fellow who tried to rob us. And even though I know you don't think so, I swear there's a good life waiting for you without that teaching job.''

She shook her head. "No, Bart. You just don't understand how I feel about things."

"Maybe not. But I know that I'm doing my best to fill in the empty spaces in your life, Rosie-girl. I'm not much of a gentleman, and this place is no Kansas City mansion, but this is all I've got to give. And everything I have is yours, Rosie. If you'll just accept me, I'm yours."

She looked up into his face and saw the intense light in his eyes. If only she could count on him, if only she could be certain he wouldn't leave her, if only she could be sure his past wouldn't catch up with him . . . then she could face tomorrow with a measure of hope in her heart. But those were such big ifs, and so very heavy.

"I guess it's just going to take time," she said.

"I've got all the time in the world. I'm not going anywhere." He kissed her mouth as if to silence her protest of doubt. "Tomorrow morning I'll be building you a ladder for the storeroom, just wait and see. Now come here, girl, and stop looking so sad." He set the plates on the floor. Easing her into his arms, he spoke against her ear. "I know your luck's been running kind of muddy lately, but I aim to change that right now.''

"I want to make the best out of my own life, Bart. I intend to be strong within myself. I need my independence, and I don't want your charity."

"Darlin', what I have in mind for you isn't what I'd call charity."

She shivered involuntarily as his palm slid down the front of her dress and over her thigh. As tired, confused, and deflated as she felt after her failure to win the teaching position, Rosie couldn't deny the response Bart's touch drew from her body—as though her mind had no connection to her physical self when she was with this man. The need he drew out of her as he slipped her dress up her leg was so strong, so intense, it overwhelmed any argument.

"Are you a betting woman, Rosie?" he whispered as he eased her onto the blankets that covered the bed.

"I did bet once on a game of whist," she acknowledged, "but then my father found out."

"Well, I've been a gambler for years, and I'm willing to make you a bet I know I can't lose." He ran one finger around the tip of her breast. "I'll bet that if you just relax and think about those oysters for a few minutes, things are going to look one hundred percent better to you in the morning. What do you say, Rosie-girl? Do we have us a bet?"

"I just have to think about oysters?"

"That's all." He eased up on one elbow and began slipping her dress off her shoulders. "Think about how wet they were," he murmured, moistening the fragile skin of her bosom, "and think about how they filled up your mouth . . ."

"And how they slid down my throat," she murmured.

"And the way they snuggled down right here in the bottom of your belly." As he spoke, he ran his hand over her stomach and then cupped the mound of her pelvic bone. "I bet you can feel those oysters just curling into you and lighting up that passion they're so famous for. Can you feel them, Rosie-girl?"

"Oh, yes. I sure can." She shut her eyes and relaxed into the sweet pressure of his stroking fingers. "I feel wonderful when you touch me there, Bart."

His heart swelled with the realization that she was succumbing to him once again. He'd dreaded this night for a whole week, expecting her disapproval of the tiny house and certain of her physical rejection of him. But she lay in his arms, welcoming every stroke he had to offer. It was almost as though she had been starving all those years with the man who had used her so thoughtlessly. Now that she had someone to feed her, she craved him with a burning hunger.

The man to nurture and succor her was Bart. As he lifted her skirt and found the soft places she had prepared for him, he swore an oath that went beyond any gambler's bet. He would make Rosie love this place he'd built, he vowed to himself. He'd make her love the land he was homesteading. He'd teach her to see his vision of their future. He'd woo her into trusting him and believing in him. And one day, one fine day, he'd win what he'd been seeking all these years.

One day he'd win Rosie's love.

Rosie slept with sweet dreams . . . beautiful memories of the moment Bart had risen over her and had released the incredible ecstasy of his passion deep inside her body.

Oh, it had been so good to fly with him high above the clouds of desire, to reach out for heaven and to feel it spilling through her flesh. But to know the ultimate height of Bart's seed and to realize that she had driven him there and that her body would fulfill him gave Rosie the greatest contentment she had ever known.

She dreamed of wild violets growing rampant across a sloping hill, of creamy milk sloshing from a silver pail, of golden-leaved aspen trees quaking in the mountain breeze. In her sleep she heard echoes of voices—Bart's deep chuckle, children singing anthems, a baby crying. . . .

At the sound of the infant Rosie opened her eyes and lifted her head from the feather pillow, certain for an instant that she was being summoned. But when she looked around the dimly lit room, she realized at once that there was no baby in this empty house. There would never be a baby for her. The doctors in Kansas City had declared her barren, hopelessly childless. She would never hold a warm bundle or feel the suckle of tiny lips against her breast.

Nor would there be children singing songs in Rosie's life. No anthems. No recitations. Reality sifted over her like heavy sand. She had lost the teaching job to another woman.

Even Bart was gone from their bed. Rosie slipped from beneath the blankets and went to one of the two windows. Though it was daytime, she could see nothing at all through the heavily waxed paper that covered the openings. He had told her he would build steps into the pantry. But she could hear no hammer or saw outside the house.

Sitting on the single stool, Rosie tried to conjure up the

escape she had achieved in Bart's arms the night before. The man's loving could make her forget everything but his sweet caresses. Yet as she looked at the ashes in the fireplace and the dusty floor and chipped crockery, Rosie knew her life could not be filled with dreamy passion forever. This was her lot. This was her reality.

Heavy in heart, she went to her trunk and dressed in a simple blue calico that had hardly a bustle to interrupt a woman's work. She had never really liked the gown, preferring her swishy silks instead. She had never enjoyed a quiet room, either. Rosie liked people, laughter, and chatter.

Who would tell her what to do on this empty day? Who would order her about and schedule her time? She stared at her listless fingers and thought about the succession of tutors who had regimented the Vermillion children after their mother had passed away while giving birth to little Bessie. Those tutors had certainly known what Rosie was to do every single minute.

After the tutors, she had lived by the rules of society ordained by her life with Dr. Lowell: making calls during the morning, taking tea in the afternoon, preparing for evening balls. When she had run away from that life, she had only fled to another world filled with regulations. The Harvey House had been every bit as confining in its own way, with its uniforms, inspections, cup-and-saucer rules, and forced smiles.

And yet those routines had brought a sense of security that Rosie certainly didn't feel now. She looked around the tiny house and tried to accept that, in a sense, it belonged to her to do with as she pleased. The land outside belonged to her, too. She could go where she liked, explore to her heart's content, and never hear a bell to send her running. Her time was her own. There was no one to tell her when to rise, when or how to dress, what to eat, or which chores required doing. The idea of such emancipation both frightened and excited her.

Was this what Rosie had been after all along? She had told Bart she wanted independence. Every night on her

knees, she had begged God for her freedom. Was this the
way He had answered her prayers?

"'For the beauty of the earth, for the glory of the
skies'"—Bart's voice drifted into the house as he sang
somewhere out in the yard—"'for the love which from our
birth over and around us lies: Christ our God, to Thee we
raise this our hymn of grateful praise.'"

Rosie went to the door, opened it, and peeked outside. At
the edge of the clearing just beyond the house, Bart was
burying the blade of his ax in his chopping block. Dressed
in his buckskin jacket and britches, he carried a load of
kindling to a pile beside the steps, stacked the wood, and
started back to his block.

"'For the wonder of each hour of the day and of the
night,'" he sang. Rosie had to smile. Bart might be a terror
at robbing banks and holding up trains. He might be the
handsomest devil this side of the Mississippi, and he could
sure make Rosie feel like an angel when he loved her. But
Bart Kingsley couldn't carry a tune in a bucket.

"'Hill and vale, and tree and flower, sun and moon and
stars of light,'" he bellowed, "'Christ our God, to thee we
raise this our hymn of grateful praise.'" He jerked his
short-handled ax free of the wood stump and set a thick log
on it. In three quick blows he had reduced the log to
kindling. "'For the joy of human love, brother, sister,
parent, child; friends on earth, and friends above, for all
gentle thoughts and mild . . .'"

Rosie shut the door and leaned against it. Bart hadn't
gone away, as she'd feared he might. For this moment, at
least, he was doing exactly what a reasonable, reliable
husband ought to do: he was chopping kindling. So what if
he was wearing buckskins and looked half wild? In the few
weeks that Rosie had known him again, he hadn't robbed a
train or a bank; he hadn't murdered anyone; he'd worked at
a decent job and started his own homestead. If Bart could
accomplish so much, then why couldn't she?

Grabbing the door handle, she marched outside and up
the steps into the sunshine. The moment Bart heard her, he
stopped his chopping, shielded his eyes against the early-

morning light, and gave Rosie a grin as wide as the Llano Estacado.

"Mornin', Rosie-girl," he called, coming toward her. "You look good enough to eat."

She had to laugh as he caught her around the waist and swung her off her feet. "Morning, Bart."

"I've about got us enough wood to start up the fire." He set her back on the ground but didn't move his arms. "Should have done this before you came, but to tell you the truth, I didn't really believe I'd ever get you this far."

"Here I am." She shrugged one shoulder. "So what do you want me to do?"

"Well, for starters you could give me a kiss."

"Me?"

"Don't look so shocked. You can do it if you want."

"I thought the man was supposed to start the kissing."

Bart frowned for a moment. "Darlin', your rules and mine came out of a different book. As far as I'm concerned, you can kiss me any time you damn well please."

Emboldened by his brash talk, Rosie rose up on tiptoes and gave his cheek a quick peck. "There," she announced. "You got the first kiss of the day, Bart Kingsley."

"Now, I know you can do better than that, Rosie-girl. How about I get the second kiss of the day, too?"

She flushed but decided she would just show him she could break rules as well as he could. Wrapping her arms around his neck, she pulled his mouth to hers and kissed him long and hard. At the ripple of pleased surprise that ran through him, she parted her lips and stroked her tongue along his mouth. Instantly he followed suit, and in a moment both were panting for breath as they pressed against each other.

"Lord-a-mercy, girl," Bart breathed. "You're the best thing that ever happened to me."

Rosie quivered as his hands roved down her body, titillating her breasts beneath the blue dress. "I don't think this is how people are supposed to act during the daytime," she whispered when he began licking the side of her neck.

"I don't think anybody gives a damn how we act day or night, Rosie-girl," he answered. "Do you?"

Resting her head on his shoulder, she gazed up at the brilliant blue sky. "I think we're all alone out here . . . except for God."

"I suspect God allows a husband and wife a good amount of leeway, don't you reckon? Especially when they've found each other after six years."

"Yes, I expect so."

"Rosie, last night between you and me . . ." Bart held her head as he spoke. "Last night I knew things were going to be all right. Last night was like a promise."

"Oh, Bart." She ached for his words to be true.

"Don't you believe, Rosie-girl?" he asked as he cupped her hips against his. "Don't you think that our loving was a seal? We're where we ought to be, with each other, aren't we, Rosie?"

"For today we are," she said softly. "I guess for today we're right where we should be."

"You bet we are. And nothing—not one damn thing—is going to change that."

*Twelve
· ·

"So what am I supposed to do?" Rosie asked Bart.

"You can give me another kiss if you want. Or we can go inside the house and—"

"I mean chores. Which chores do you expect me to do today?"

Bart took off his battered Stetson and scratched his forehead. As pretty and fresh as Rosie was this morning, she did look completely out of place on the rugged homestead. Even though he knew she had worked hard as a Harvey Girl, Bart couldn't imagine her ever tending to the kinds of things that needed doing on a farm.

"Don't you have a list?" she was asking. "Or am I supposed to decide by myself?"

The look of barely veiled anticipation in her brown eyes told Bart exactly what he needed to know. "This is your homestead as much as it is mine, Rosie-girl," he said. "That's your house over there, and these are your woods and fields. You can do whatever you damn well please, because I'm not about to hand over a list of chores to a woman with a mind as sharp as yours."

Bart nodded once for good measure, then he bent to retrieve his ax. Rosie knotted her fingers and watched him jerk the axhead out of the log, where it had stood half buried in hardwood. So she *was* free, Rosie thought. Bart didn't plan to boss her around. No one expected anything of her. She could spend the day exactly as she chose.

"I think I'll explore," she announced, testing him just to

be sure. "I want to see what sort of homestead you picked out."

Bart glanced up. He'd been hoping Rosie would decide to cook breakfast. But if she had a mind to explore, he'd have to go along with it. In fact, Bart realized as he carried one last load of kindling to the house, if Rosie didn't want to lift a finger around the place, he was going to have to accept it. He hadn't lured her out here to be a slave to him or to his homestead. He'd wanted her for herself. And if she chose to idle away her days, he'd just abide it the best he could.

Taking a quick look over his shoulder, he realized that she was already sauntering away from the house toward the pine forest. Blue ribbons dangling, her bonnet swung from one hand, and her bustle swayed with a mesmerizing motion.

"You'd better take a gun," Bart called after her. "There are some mean critters out there, you know."

She whirled around, hand at her throat. "What sort of mean critters?"

"Bears, for one. Mountain lions and rattlers, too."

"Rattlesnakes?"

"Well, maybe it's too early in the year for the timber rattlers to be out. Still, they might be sunning on the rocks."

"Oh . . . I hadn't thought about snakes." Lifting her skirts and scanning the ground, she started back toward him. "Are there grizzly bears?"

"Naw, just regular old brown bears. If you don't get between the females and their young'uns, you don't have a thing to worry about."

Rosie brushed past him and headed down the stairs into the dugout. But if Bart thought she was going to hide away in the house all day, he underestimated the woman. Before he had time to select an armful of kindling for the fireplace, Rosie was marching back outside, a little pistol in one hand.

"You reckon you could kill a mountain lion with that, Rosie-girl?" he asked as she set off toward the forest again.

"I imagine I could," she replied before vanishing into the shadows among the trees.

Bart tried to shrug off her casual disappearance. But as he built the cooking fire in the small stone fireplace, he found himself worrying in earnest. Rosie could get herself into a heap of trouble out there alone in the woods. She could get lost, attacked, injured. Indians roamed the area occasionally, and some of them weren't a bit friendly. And there could be folks like that no-good rascal who had tried to rob them the day before. . . .

Slapping a few slices of bacon into his hot skillet, Bart mused over just what he might have gotten himself into by bringing Rosie out to his homestead. He couldn't deny that she was a city gal through and through, and she didn't have a lick of sense about frontier life. Though she'd spent plenty of time on her pappy's farm outside Kansas City, that had been nothing like this. On the Vermillion place, Rosie had had a fine country home with stables, cleared land, horses for riding, and servants to do the cooking and cleaning. The meanest varmint she had been likely to encounter in Missouri was a seed tick.

As he munched on bacon and hot biscuits, Bart felt his stomach tie up in knots. Where the hell was Rosie right now? How would he find her if she got lost out there? What if a hungry mountain lion took hold of her? Bart didn't know whether to start searching for her right away or let her stay gone for a while and risk whatever dangers she might run into.

As he tossed the dishes in a pot of cold water, Bart scowled at the snapping fire. The image of his stepfather filtered into his thoughts. Bart could almost hear the man hollering, "Lydia, get your lazy butt out of bed and fix me some breakfast! You good-for-nothing, don't you know what your job is after all this time? A man has a right to expect certain things from his woman, like clean clothes and three square meals a day. Now, get to work before I bust your head wide open!"

Wincing, Bart felt his hands go damp with sweat at the

memory of his mother struggling out of bed to avoid a beating. *Did* a man have a right to expect such things from his wife? Should Bart drag Rosie back to the homestead and order her to get to work like a decent woman? Did she deserve a good whipping for taking it into her head to go off exploring when she knew damn well there was enough work out here for ten people?

He climbed up the steps into the sunshine. Maybe he was just a sorry son of a gun for letting her go off into the woods. Maybe he would regret not slapping her into shape. But as Bart headed out to hitch the horses to the plow, he buried every instinct his stepfather had instilled in him.

Laura Rose Vermillion had always been Bart's light. And he'd be damned if he was going to snuff her out with the back of his hand.

Rosie sat at the edge of a small pool and dangled her feet in the icy water. Her gun lay in the hammock of dress fabric between her spread knees. Overhead, an eagle soared and drifted on circling currents of cool wind, and its shadow crossed the pool again and again.

Hungrier than she had ever been, Rosie glanced up at the sun and tried to gauge the time. She thought it must be at least an hour past noon. Etta, Mae, and the others at the Harvey House in Raton would be cleaning up their stations as the lunch rush settled into an easier flow. Townsfolk would drift in after Sunday-morning church services. Mr. Adams and his brother in their suits and ties would settle down at the lunch counter and order ham sandwiches. Sheriff Bowman and his young wife would join them. Mrs. Bayne would parade in wearing one of the new spring bonnets her millinery shop girls had created. All of the women in Raton, it seemed, were ordering their summer straw hats from Mrs. Bayne these days.

All the preachers who hadn't been invited to parishioners' homes for dinner would stroll into the Harvey House lunchroom at one-thirty or two o'clock after they'd closed up their churches. The Methodist preacher, Reverend Cullen; the Baptist minister, Reverend Craigmyle; and the

Episcopalian, Reverend Boyle, who drove down from Trinidad each week, would welcome Father Accosini, whose new Catholic church with its glorious bells was the pride of the Gate City; Mr. Adams had documented its construction in almost every issue of the *Comet*.

Rosie herself would have attended church if she'd been in Raton. Every other Sunday she was given the morning off to attend worship services. Though her schedule didn't permit her to take on the responsibility of teaching Sunday school, Rosie did sing in the sanctuary choir.

Now, seated beside the pool, she tried to make herself sing a favorite hymn. After all, she should be grateful, shouldn't she? She was alive, safe, and looked after by a man who cared for her.

On the other hand, Rosie knew she had neglected her nightly prayers of late. She hadn't read her Bible in days. She was skipping church this morning. And worst of all, she had flip-flopped between keeping herself pristine and distant from Bart and making passionate love with the man. How could God approve of such unreliable behavior?

With a sigh, Rosie gave up trying to make the wavering notes come out of her mouth in the right order. The truth was, she felt utterly miserable. Sick at her stomach from hunger, she stared at the swirling pool. She knew she had come out into the woods for no other reason than to prove her independence to Bart. Now he was probably wondering what had become of her. He might even be mad, what with all the work he had to do.

What if Bart turned mean the way Dr. Lowell had? Rosie had seen Bart's anger firsthand, and she sure didn't want it turned on her. Should she go back to the house and meekly do some chores just to avoid Bart's wrath? Or should she set off down the mountain and hike into Raton to look for another job? She *did* have her gun for protection. Maybe Mrs. Bayne would hire her to sew dresses. Rosie was a good seamstress.

Or should she accept the fact that she really had lost the teaching position, that she had physically bonded herself to

Bart, and that she was being punished by God for her many sins? That dugout certainly was a punishment, no doubt about that.

Rosie leaned over and trailed a finger in the water. How long could she sit out here just yards from the house like a stubborn little girl who had run away—but not so far away as to actually risk any danger? How long could she test Bart's patience, as if this were some kind of child's game between them?

She had prayed for freedom. God had given it to her. And now, Rosie decided at last, she had better start acting like an adult who deserved her independence.

Squaring her shoulders, she grabbed the gun, hauled her feet out of the pool and set off through the woods toward the dugout.

Bart whistled a tuneless song as he shrugged out of his buckskin jacket and hung it on a nail beside the door of the small barn he'd built to shelter his horses and cows. Leaning over the trough, he splashed water on his face and chest. He used the tin dipper he'd bought in town the other day to toss water over the back of his head. As it dripped through his hair, he watched the dust sift into the trough. A day of plowing, planting, and thinning his first field of sugar beet sprouts, building a ladder, and moving his two cows to greener pasture had left Bart tired and worn out.

As exhausted as he was from the work, he knew some of his fatigue came from spending the day worrying about Rosie. She hadn't come back to the house for lunch. He knew that, because he'd walked down from his fields just to check on her. He had called into the forest once or twice, but hadn't gotten an answer. Stuffing his anger and fear deep inside himself once again, he had stomped off to water his horses.

The afternoon had gone no better. Rosie hadn't come out to the field to see what he was up to, and he had to assume she was still "exploring." But what in hell was there to explore around these parts? Nothing but a couple of streams near the house, some plowed fields, and a pine forest that went on and on.

As he hooked his jacket on one finger and slapped it over his shoulder, Bart headed for the dugout. What if something had happened to Rosie? What if she'd run off and left him? What if she'd been bitten by a rattler?

Bart squinted at the house and realized that there was no smoke coming from the chimney and no light in the windows. So Rosie hadn't come back, after all.

Humming in a subdued voice, he approached the dugout. As he descended the stairs into the earth, he felt a chill creep around his ankles. Then he laid a palm on the heavy oak door and gave a push.

"Bart!" Rosie jumped up from the stool as the door swung open. A pile of fabric tumbled from her lap to the floor. "Oh, I didn't hear you coming."

For a moment Bart couldn't make his mouth work. He could barely see the silhouetted figure across the darkened room. But she was there, sure enough. His Rosie had come back, safe and sound. All the anger and fear fled in a rush of relief.

"What are you doing sitting in the dark, Rosie?" he asked as he tossed his buckskin jacket onto the table and came toward her. "The sun's almost down."

"Oh, I guess . . . I guess I fell asleep." She bent to gather the flowered fabric from the floor, but Bart caught her shoulders and lifted her to meet him.

"Are you all right?"

"I'm fine." A little dazed, she shook her head and her hands came up to rest lightly on his bare chest. "I was sewing, and I must have drifted off."

"In the middle of the afternoon? How long have you been home?"

Rosie glanced at the cold fireplace and let out a cry of dismay. "Oh, no!"

"What?" Bart gripped her in sudden concern. "What's the matter, darlin'? What's happened?"

"The fire. I fell asleep and didn't get the fire started. Now your dinner will be late, and . . . oh, dear!"

She slipped from his grasp and hurried to the hearth. While he watched in bewilderment, she began stacking firewood and kindling on the iron grate. In moments she had stuck a match on a stone and was blowing the flames to life.

"Light the lamps, would you, Bart?" she asked between puffs, "and I could use some more logs if I'm going to get this fire hot enough to boil water."

Obeying, Bart quickly set the two lamps aglow. When he lifted one of them to carry it to the mantel, his eyes widened. "Well, I'll be damned!"

Rosie turned from the pot of water she had hung over the fire. "What, Bart?"

"Just look at what you've done, Rosie. You've fixed up the place!"

Hiding a grin, she turned back to the iron pot. "A little."

"A little?" With the lamp held high, he strode around the small room. "You set these plates up here on the mantel, didn't you?"

"I had to wash them first. They were coated with grime and grease and who knows what else. Bart, your domestic habits are downright sinful."

"What did you expect from an outlaw?"

She laughed. "Did it ever occur to you to dust this place? There's dirt everywhere. You don't even own a broom. I had to make one out of a branch and some straw. It was just a matter of luck that I found a ball of twine in the barn."

"Dust a dugout?" Bart took off his hat and ran his hand through his damp hair. "I never gave such a notion a thought. Rosie-girl, don't you know that tomorrow this place will be just as dirty as it was today?"

"Then I'll just have to sweep it again, won't I?" She had settled on the stool beside the table and was peeling potatoes quicker than Bart had ever seen anyone accomplish such a chore. "Sweeping's part of housekeeping whether you live in a mansion or a dugout. So are washing and cooking. By the way, you promised to build me a pantry ladder this morning."

"I built it. It's over in the storage room next door." He watched her dump the potatoes into the boiling water. "How long have you been at the house, Rosie?"

"I came back after lunch." She gave her shoulder a casual tilt. "You have a nice bathing pool down the way. Were you aware of that?"

"Sure, I've seen the stream." He glanced at his dusty britches. "Reckon I never gave bathing much of a thought, either."

"Well, if you're going to be a civilized husband to me, Bart Kingsley, you'll have to learn to take regular baths."

"I don't know much about being civilized. But if you want me for a husband, darlin', you've got me."

Rosie gave the potatoes a stir and then turned to face Bart. "Well, I don't know much about being a wife," she said. "My mother died when I was only five, and my father never married again."

"You told me all about your mama years ago. I wouldn't forget a thing like that about you, Rosie."

"You grew up without a father, and I grew up without a mother," she said in a low voice. "So our families didn't give us a whole lot to go on, Bart. But I want to thank you for taking me in when I didn't get that teaching job. Since I don't have any other way of providing for myself, I guess I'll be staying here a little while, and I intend to do my best for you. I'll keep house and fix your meals. I'll wash and mend. If you need me in the fields, I'll help out there, too."

Bart studied the white foam gathering at the top of the pot. "Rosie," he said finally, "if all you want to do is sit around the house and eat Huffman's cream candies and pecan pie, it's all right by me."

Tears sprang into Rosie's eyes as she stared at the pile of beef she had cut into chunks earlier that afternoon. "I don't want to eat cream candies, Bart. I want to clean your house and sew your shirts and . . . and . . . and be your wife."

In an instant he had caught her in his arms and was

holding her against his bare chest. "Oh, Rosie, my Rosie-girl. You don't know how bad I've wanted to hear you say that."

"Bart, I'm scared. I'm just so scared it won't work." She nestled her damp cheek against his shoulder.

"Why not? What's to stop us from making a wonderful life out here on our homestead, Rosie?"

"Any number of things! What if someone finds you out? That—that Pinkerton man could come after you. He could set up a bomb for you like he did for Jesse James's mother. And what if my pappy tracks me to Raton? You did, so what's to stop Pappy? You don't know Dr. Lowell, either. If he makes up his mind to come for me, he'll use his money and his influence. Nothing will stop him. People are after us, Bart, both of us. We won't be able to hide away out here forever."

He stroked her hair. "And what else has got you all worked up, Rosie-girl?"

"I'm afraid that if I start to care about you, Bart . . . to care about you more than I do right now . . . well, what if you get yourself killed? You've already been shot once by Sheriff Bowman." She touched the ridge of scarred flesh on his side. Then she lifted her head and kissed his neck. "And what if you get hauled off to prison and they tie a rope around this neck? What if they decide to hang you for your crimes?"

Bart nodded. "Keep talking, sweetheart. I know that's not all of it."

Rosie shut her eyes tight, trying to stem the flow of tears. For a long time she worked at the lump in her throat, but it just wouldn't dissolve. "I keep . . . keep thinking about that teaching job I lost."

Bart frowned slightly. "I guess I didn't know you wanted it so all-fired bad, Rosie, or how much it meant to you."

"It's not . . . not really the job." She sniffled and swallowed. "It's just that . . . ever since I found out about . . . things . . . I wanted to teach school so I could be with children, you know? But now I know I don't have that teaching job, and I guess I never will. And I'll

never . . . never have any children of my own. . . .
We'll never have babies, Bart. Even if all the rest of it works
out by some miracle, we'll never have children of our own.
Do you realize that?"

He stroked her shoulder, pondering the significance of
her words and wondering how deeply they would affect his
life. "I never let myself believe I'd have *you* again, Rosie,"
he said. "Being a pappy with children of my own seemed
way beyond the range of what a man like me could aim for.
I reckon I would like to have a baby to hold, a son to train
up better than my stepfather trained me, a daughter to watch
out for and love."

"Oh, Bart!"

"Listen here, now. I might like to have children with you,
but I've managed to get this far without them. So have you.
If we don't have babies, we've got each other, Rosie-girl.
We'll be our own company. We'll make our own fun and
laughter and joy. Things will be all right. You'll see."

"Hold me tighter, Bart."

"I'll hold you for the rest of my life. I'll never let you
go."

"Never, Bart?"

"Never, Rosie-girl. Not ever."

Rosie lived in an Eden of her own making. Once she
finally accepted that Bart had indeed offered her freedom,
she set about to create the little paradise of her dreams.

The fabric she had purchased for the schoolroom windows soon brightened the walls of the little dugout. Rosie
fashioned the yards of chintz into billowing curtains and a
tablecloth. Bart built her the framework of a little changing
screen, and she ruffled the cloth to fill in the panels. She
used the remaining yardage to begin cutting triangles and
squares in order to piece together a quilt for their bed.

The bed itself soon sported a new mattress filled with soft
grass Bart brought in from his fields. Of course, the grass
soon dried and grew brittle, but Rosie hardly cared. The
mattress felt soft and comfortable, and it brought a new
dimension to the nights of passion in the little room.

Oh, and they were such wonderful nights! Rosie caught herself reminiscing secretly at various times throughout each day, and always a smile crept over her lips. When Bart was in Raton working at his livery stable job, Rosie would think about him as she baked bread or weeded her kitchen garden or did the laundry.

Every afternoon while he was in the sugar beet fields, she would fall into bed for a nap. Achingly tired, she would doze away the hottest hours. But by evening, when he came down for dinner, Rosie felt fresh and eager to be with him.

No matter how worn out he was from his labors, his face always brightened at the sight of their table laden with freshly baked bread and thick beef stew, chicken and dumplings, or shepherd's pie. Rosie discovered that months of observing Stefan and the other chefs at the Harvey House had given her a head start in cooking skills. With the help of a recipe book Bart bought for her at one of the mercantiles, she produced one hearty meal after another.

After dinner every night, they heated water over the dying fire and bathed in a shallow tin tub. Somehow the evening bath always led into a time of relaxed teasing and play. By the time they tumbled into their bed, both were dancing at the height of desire.

Their sweet passion led them into blissful sleep as they lay twisted in each other's arms. With the first light of sunrise, they woke refreshed and ready to start another day.

Not long after she began her life on the homestead, Rosie decided she would like to have fresh eggs on hand. Not only would this improve her baking, she reasoned, but she could send any extra eggs along to town with Bart when he went to work at the livery stable. With the money from fresh eggs and newly churned butter, Rosie planned to buy herself a real stove. Bart built a raised coop and fetched in a bunch of fluffy yellow chicks one day, and Rosie was off and running with her hen business.

After each day of tending to her chickens, milking the two cows, hoeing her garden, scrubbing laundry on the washboard, sweeping and mopping the ever-dusty dugout, and cooking hearty meals, Rosie expected to feel drained and empty. Instead, the busy life simply sparked her desire to do more and more. She used some of her savings to buy more fabric, and she fashioned several work shirts and two pairs of sturdy britches for Bart. She made herself two sensible dresses and a week's worth of white aprons.

Rosie decided to paint the inner walls of the dugout, and she sent Bart off to Raton with orders for a gallon of white milk paint. In his opinion, white seemed like a pretty loco color for an underground house, but he obeyed. To his surprise, within days the house looked sparkling clean, bright as a new pin, and bigger than it had before.

In fact, the beauty Rosie had brought to the little dugout led Bart to decide that he would not only finish building the pantry room, he would make plans for an upstairs—two fine rooms with big windows and a shingled roof. Once the sugar beet harvest came in, Bart figured, he'd have enough money to buy all the lumber needed to build the upstairs during the slow fall and winter months.

Young Manford Wade visited the homestead on a regular basis. Bart paid the boy a small wage to thin and hoe sugar beets and help with the stump-pulling. Rosie enjoyed the youngster's cheerful banter, though it saddened her to realize that the sound of childish laughter would never come from offspring she and Bart could produce.

"She's as mean as a witch," Mannie confided to Rosie one afternoon when she was hanging laundry on the clothesline that stretched between two aspen trees. "Fact is, she's got red eyes."

"Red eyes!" Rosie laughed at Mannie's description of the new schoolmarm. "People don't have red eyes, Manford."

"I know they don't. But *she* does. Which just goes to prove she's a witch, don't it?"

Chuckling, Rosie jammed a clothespin over the shoulder seam of a wet, flapping shirt that kept trying to slap her in the chest. "Mrs. Sneed is probably just very strict—an essential attribute for a teacher, in my opinion."

"She whupped Minnie yesterday."

"Minnie? Oh, no!" Rosie clutched a dripping tablecloth

as she pictured the responsible young girl who had been left in charge of the recitation. "What on earth did Minnie do to deserve a whipping?"

"Didn't have her composition done. See, Minnie's grandpa up and died last week, and Minnie loved him something awful. Ever since then, Minnie ain't been the same. She missed a lot of school, and her mama told the teacher she was sick. But we all knew she was just sick because she had loved her grandpa so much. Cheyenne Bill gave a speech at Minnie's grandpa's funeral, and you should've seen the tears a-flowin'. Even Tom and Griff came to the buryin', and you know if a dog'll come to a funeral, it must have been for a real good man."

"I'm sorry to hear that he passed away."

"Kicked the bucket is what he did. He had some kind of stomach ailment, you know. Anyhow, Minnie came to school without her composition, and Mrs. Sneed whupped her. Just flat-out whupped her."

Rosie shook her head as she hung up the tablecloth. Whipping a girl who was in mourning certainly didn't sound like the act of a loving teacher. There could be more to the story, however, and Rosie decided she would give Mrs. Sneed the benefit of the doubt.

"Did you hear about the school election in town?" Manford asked. "We got us an independent school district here now."

"Well, that's a good thing, I must say. It's about time Raton came into its own."

"Yep, and there was a charity ball at McAuliffe and Ferguson's Hall last Monday night. Did you hear about that?"

"No, I didn't." Rosie grinned at Manford's flow of happy chatter. "Was the ball grand?"

"I heard they had them a fine dinner. Leg of mutton, capers, mincemeat, roast beef, chicken, ice cream, cake, oranges . . ." He stopped speaking and glanced toward the trail. "Say, look who's coming up the road. It's Sheriff Bowman!"

Rosie swung around and clutched a soggy shirt against her stomach. "The sheriff?" she whispered. "Jiminy."

"Hey, Sheriff!" Manford waved and began trotting down the path toward the trail. "Howdy! What you doin' way out here?"

Suddenly breathless, Rosie looked out into the fields. She could just make out Bart's back as he bent to the plow. Her mouth dry, she turned back to the house and saw the sheriff climbing down from his horse. Rifle in his hand and six-shooter slung on his hip, he ruffled Mannie's red hair and started toward Rosie.

"Afternoon, Mrs. Springfield," he called.

"Sheriff Bowman. This is quite a surprise." After tossing the wet shirt into the laundry basket, Rosie wiped her hands on her apron as she walked over to meet him. "What brings you so far out of town?"

Moistening her lips, Rosie wondered what on earth the sheriff could want. Might he have heard something about Bart? Oh, if only she could send Manford to Bart and warn him to stay away from the house!

"Looks like you and your husband have got things going real good out here," the sheriff commented as he stopped a few paces from Rosie.

"Yes, indeed." She tried to remember her Harvey Girl smile. "We've worked hard on the dugout. My husband has planted nearly thirty acres of sugar beets, and some of the fields are already sprouting. We've got a little kitchen garden growing over here beside the house, too. Would you like to come inside and take a load off your feet? I could fix you a cup of hot tea, Sheriff."

"Mighty kind of you, ma'am. But I'm here on business." He stopped speaking and began to cough. Rosie had heard that Sheriff Bowman had lung trouble, but she had no idea how to ease his suffering. "Let me sit out here on your stoop a minute," he said when he had gotten control of the spasms.

"Sure, I'll fetch you a stool." Rosie grabbed Manford's arm and hauled him down the stairs into the dugout. When they were safely inside with the door shut, she grabbed the boy's shoulders and bent to face him.

"What's the matter, Mrs. Springfield?"

"Manford, I want you to skedaddle up to the fields right this second and tell my husband that Sheriff Bowman is here. Tell him the sheriff has come out to the homestead on business."

"Yes, ma'am. What else?"

"That's all. He'll know what to do. Now run, Manford. Run!" She pushed his shoulders as he bolted up the stairs. Grabbing the stool, Rosie hurried after the boy.

When she broke out into the sunshine, she saw the sheriff had lit a cigarette. Between coughs, he took deep puffs of smoke, held them in his lungs and then slowly exhaled. Rosie set the stool in the slight shade of the tar-paper roof, and waited while her visitor made himself comfortable.

"I hope you'll excuse me, Mrs. Springfield," he said finally. "I get the damnedest coughing spells."

"I'm sure sorry to hear that." Rosie glanced behind her to see that Manford was almost up to the field Bart was plowing.

Clasping her hands together in her lap, she lifted up a fervent prayer that Bart might escape safely into the woods before the sheriff had a chance to go after him. Though she could hardly believe she would want to abet a wanted criminal, Rosie knew she couldn't bear it if Sheriff Bowman hauled Bart off to jail. Their short time together had been so wonderful, so perfect, that it seemed almost impossible her worst nightmare was unfolding right before her at this very moment.

"Would you . . . would you like a glass of water, Sheriff?" she asked, hoping to stall for time. "We have a spring right by the house."

"No, I'm fine." The sheriff took a last draw on his cigarette and tossed it to the ground. Grinding it under his bootheel, he turned to Rosie. "I'll be downright honest with you, Mrs. Springfield. I've come out here with some unpleasant news."

"Oh?" Rosie asked, feigning surprise. "Whatever can it be?"

"There's trouble. Trouble with the law. And I'm afraid your husband is involved."

*Thirteen
. . . .

"My husband?" Rosie asked. "What can you possibly mean by that? I married the most decent, honest, hardworking man in the world, Sheriff Bowman. I don't see how you could ever think he would commit a crime."

"I didn't say he committed no crime."

Rosie flushed. "You didn't?"

"No, ma'am. I said there's trouble with the law."

"Oh, I see." Though she didn't see at all, Rosie nodded her head and tried to think of more things to say to give Bart time to get away. "Well, I know my husband has registered our homestead—one hundred sixty acres—over in Springer, because he showed me the papers just the other day. The claim is perfectly legal, and it doesn't interfere with the Maxwell Land Grant in any way."

"The homestead ain't the problem, either, Mrs. Springfield," Sheriff Bowman said. He reached out and took Rosie's hands between his large callused palms. "It's a different sort of thing. See . . . your husband's been accused of . . . well, of attempted murder."

"Murder!"

"Howdy, Sheriff," Bart called out as he strode around the side of the dugout. "Young Manford here tells me you've come on business."

Rosie's mouth fell open as she watched Bart casually lean one elbow on the dugout roof and adjust his hat against the sun. Mannie stood close beside him, his own smaller elbow propped high on the roof in perfect imitation of his hero.

Clearing his throat, the sheriff rose from the stool and straightened his cartridge belt.

"'Fraid we've got us a problem, Mr. Springfield," he stated.

"Call me Buck," Bart returned. Though his voice sounded calm and easy, every instinct in his body had sprung to alertness. The moment Manford had brought him the news, Bart had assessed his situation. He knew he didn't want to whimper like a kicked mutt and hide out in the woods again. He was through living life on the run.

But Bart also knew he had to be ready to protect himself—and Rosie. He might not be longing to take up his outlaw ways again, but he sure as hell didn't intend to have his neck stretched either. If that meant dealing roughly with the sheriff, Bart knew he wouldn't hesitate.

"Well, Buck," the sheriff was saying, "I hate to have to break such news to you on a fine day like this and right in the middle of your plowing, but we've got a little trouble in town."

"What kind of trouble, Sheriff?" Sensing Rosie's dismay, Bart put one arm around her and drew her against his side. "I don't reckon I've caused a lick of trouble since I set foot in Colfax County."

Bowman shook his head. "I don't expect you have. But we've got a feller in town claims you tried to kill him."

"Kill him?" Bart quickly searched his mind for men he'd winged in the past, and he wondered which of them had finally tracked him down. "How does he figure that?"

Rosie thought she was going to faint. If Bart hadn't been holding her up, she knew she would have sunk right to the ground. So this was it—the moment she had been dreading most. All the dreams she had so tentatively nurtured were about to be destroyed.

"Well, here's the feller's story," the sheriff was saying. "Claims he was out for a ride Saturday three weeks back, and he came upon you and the missus having a picnic. Claims he stopped to ask you for directions into Springer, and you took offense at something he said. Claims you busted up his face and knocked out five of his front teeth.

Then you tied him on his horse and sent him out in the desert to die.''

Bart's eyes darted to Rosie, and he let out a breath. ''Claims all that, does he?''

''It's a fact he's missing every last one of his front teeth.''

''Did this fellow happen to tell you what it was he said that got me so riled I might have knocked his teeth out?''

''He's a little vague on that point. Says he thinks you'd been drinking and were cozying up to the lady here. Says when he interrupted to ask directions, you just jumped him.''

''Directions, huh?'' Bart gave a short laugh. ''Sure, I remember that fellow. I remember him just fine. Short and raggedy with a mop of greasy hair?''

''That's him.''

''He was trying to rob us!'' Rosie exploded. ''He held a shotgun right to my head and threatened to shoot us both!''

''Now, darlin'—''

''Sheriff, that man *did* come upon us that day we were in Springer,'' she continued, heedless. ''We'd gone down on the train to get married. Just ask Mr. Gable at the Harvey House.''

''I already did ask him.''

''We rented a wagon and drove out of town to have a picnic. Then this awful man appeared with a shotgun. He held a shotgun on us and threatened to tie up my husband and . . . and to . . . to *defile* me!''

''Well, I'll be damned.'' The sheriff gave a low whistle and took off his hat.

''My wife is telling you the truth, Sheriff,'' Bart concurred. ''Right off the bat, the fellow spelled out his plan to us. Said he'd followed us out of town because we were dressed so fine, and he figured folk like us would have a lot of cash on hand.''

''But you were just fancied up for your wedding?'' the sheriff asked.

''That's right. Then he declared his intention of robbing us and using my wife in a downright wicked manner. When he was leading me to a tree to tie me up, I got in a swing at him. He didn't offer much resistance, but I sure as hell didn't want him to come back at us wanting seconds. I'll admit I rearranged his face a little and I tied him onto his horse. Maybe that was rough, but I think any man worth a pail of hot spit would do the same to protect the woman he'd married.''

The sheriff nodded slowly. ''I reckon he would. All the same, that fellow's mighty hot under the collar. He checked the train records and found out who you were. He declares he's come to town to find you and make you pay.''

''Pay!'' Rosie exploded again. ''Look around you, Sheriff. Do we look like rich people? My husband works at the livery stable six mornings a week, and he spends every afternoon till dusk in his sugar beet fields. That thief thinks we have money, and he's still trying to steal it from us!''

''Now, calm down, Mrs. Springfield.'' The sheriff coughed again, but managed to contain the spasms. ''Let's all just calm down here. Give me a minute to think this over.''

Rosie could feel her petticoat and corset sticking to her bare skin in the heat. She couldn't live like this. Not with this constant fear. What if the sheriff decided to take Bart into town? How could she bear to lose this man—this *good* man—when she had only just accepted him again?

''I reckon you'd better come into town with me, Buck,'' the sheriff said. ''I'll check out your story and see how it holds up to his. I'll send out a wire to the law in Springer and to whatever town it is you come from. Where *do* you come from, by the way?''

''Mighty hard to say. I lived here and there, up until I found this gal, married her, and made up my mind to settle down.''

''Well, if I can't dig up any problems with your past, then I reckon we can get the feller to back down on his story. With you and the missus claiming the same thing, and with that rascal smelling so thick the lamps won't burn, I reckon any jury would let you off the hook. I sure as hell don't want to haul you in. Not with your homestead up and going, and with the good work I hear you've been doing over at the livery stable.'' He paused and scratched his chin. ''Besides that, you're Cheyenne Bill's cousin. That'll hold a lot of weight in a court of law.''

Rosie shut her eyes and sagged against Bart's hard body. The tangle of lies! This web of deceit they had woven couldn't fail to drag them under. Oh, she felt ill.

''Mrs. Springfield,'' the sheriff said, ''I reckon you'd better come on into town with us, too.''

''You want my testimony?''

''Naw. A woman's word won't hold much water.'' He shouldered his rifle and gave a quick laugh. ''But I almost forgot I came out here for another reason, too. There's somebody in town wants to talk to you.''

''Who is it?'' she whispered, picturing her father and Dr. Lowell waiting for her at the sheriff's office.

''It's Mr. Kilgore. Says he needs to talk to you about that teaching job you've been after. Seems Mrs. Sneed didn't work out so good after all.''

Five times on the rutted track to Raton, Bart had to stop the wagon so Rosie could get off and throw up. He'd never seen a person so sick. From the moment Sheriff Bowman had announced that Bart was wanted for attempted murder, Rosie's skin had turned from its usual soft pink to white to a pale shade of green. Her eyes seemed to sink into her head like big dark raisins. She was shaking so badly that it was all Bart could do to help her off and back on the wagon every time she called out that she intended to be ill.

Not that Bart felt so all-fired dandy himself. He could see Sheriff Bowman's horse just ahead on the track, and it took all his willpower to keep the wagon following that roan. The sheriff was still having his coughing fits, and it occurred to Bart that he could simply do the man in and leave his body on the trail. Everybody would think he'd passed out and died with his lung problem.

But the minute the thought entered Bart's mind, he quickly squelched it. He wasn't about to add another killing to his name, even if no one in town ever found out. Rosie would know. Bart himself would know. The Almighty would know. Those were three he knew he didn't want to have to reckon with.

Although Bart admitted that he had sent more than one man on to the kingdom in the sky, the killings had always been a matter of self-defense. Not one time had Bart actually shot somebody just for spite, or greed, or revenge. He hadn't even been a firsthand party to the killings that the James brothers had committed during their infamous train robberies. Bart had always been in on the planning stage and later served as a lookout during the actual holdups. He knew he wasn't responsible for the careless death of any man.

Difficult as it was, Bart elected to keep the wagon headed straight down the track to Raton and take his medicine as he knew he should. If only he could be sure the sheriff couldn't run down his past . . . if only he could count on no one connecting him with the night the Pinkerton detective had been in town . . . if only he could force that snake of a thief from Springer to back down on his story . . . if only Rosie would stop spitting up her socks!

It was late afternoon by the time the wagon pulled into Raton. Although the sun rested low over the mountains, Sheriff Bowman insisted that Bart accompany him to the courthouse to confront his accuser. Rosie wanted to go with them, but when Bart set her feet on the ground after the wagon ride, she could barely stand.

Instead, he checked her into an upstairs room at the Central Hotel and left her in the charge of Mrs. James Davis, the owner's wife. When Manford Wade had scampered along home, Bart strode down the familiar streets of Raton to the courthouse where J. H. Hunt, justice of the peace, reigned supreme.

"That's him!" the ragged man in the front room shouted the moment Bart walked through the double front doors. "That's the man who knocked out my teeth!"

"Howdy, Jack," Bart responded with a tip of his hat. "Looks like you got loose from that old nag of yours after all."

"My name's not Jack. It's Tucker, and don't you forget it!"

"Ain't likely I'll even remember what you *look* like tomorrow."

"The hell with that, you low-down varmint! I'll make sure you don't forget—"

"Now, settle down, fellers," the sheriff interrupted, coming between the two men. "Mr. Springfield, I'll have to ask you to disarm yourself."

"I'm not armed, Sheriff. I don't much take to guns these days, in spite of no-good rascals like this running around. As a matter of fact, I didn't even have a weapon on me the day he tried to tie me to a tree and violate my bride."

"No weapon!" Tucker exploded. "What do you call them fists of yours—cotton bolls?"

"Now, boys," Bowman interrupted again. "Let's see if you can settle down and tell your stories one at a time."

"You already got my story, Sheriff," Tucker said. "This bullyboy knocked my teeth out, and he owes me the money to get a new set of choppers. That and the cost of my doctor bill and plenty more besides!"

"Tucker, if you don't ever eat corn on the cob again, it'll suit me just dandy," Bart snapped. "Now, what do you need to know, Sheriff? I've got a sick wife to get back to."

"Sit down, Springfield. You, too, Tucker. And if the both of you don't shut your traps, I swear I'll throw you in the same cell and let you work out your troubles thataway."

The threat took instant effect on Tucker, and he plopped down into a chair. Bart settled in a facing seat, took off his hat, and set it on his thigh. As he tried to concentrate on the proceedings, he found his thoughts wandering to Rosie. He had always known she was gentle and kind, the sort of woman who needed tenderness from a man. But he hadn't realized how fragile she was.

More significant, Bart had not understood how deeply Rosie was affected by the repercussions of his past. If a little problem like this Tucker fellow could put her in a sickbed, how in heaven's name would she handle something big?

Bart went cold all over as he thought of Rosie's reaction to some of the things he could be called on the carpet for.

As he sat in the courthouse telling the sheriff his side of what had happened that early May afternoon near Springer, his thoughts roamed over what he could do to protect Rosie from ever having to confront his past. It was late in the evening when the sheriff finally dismissed him, with instructions to be at the courthouse the following morning. But as Bart strode out onto the streets of Raton, he felt lighter of heart than he had in a long while.

Sometime during the evening he had decided what to do. He would write a letter to his closest pal, Frank. The man who had taken him in. The man who had given him the best advice he'd ever known. Frank, the brother of Jesse James.

Rosie was asleep when Bart arrived at the Central Hotel. Mrs. Davis told him that his wife had fallen into bed completely exhausted and had gone to sleep at once. Though Mrs. Davis had checked the room several times that evening, Rosie had never awakened. It was Mrs. Davis's opinion, she informed the worried man in her lobby, that Rosie had eaten something spoiled and that she should never have been taken from her own home that afternoon.

Feeling duly ashamed of himself for having allowed Rosie to make the long wagon ride, Bart climbed the stairs to their room. When he stepped into the lamplit chamber with its thin brocade drapes and uncarved four-poster bed, he could barely see the small mound of bedcovers that defined Rosie's sleeping body.

The chamber pot on the bare wooden floor was empty, so at least her stomach had settled, Bart realized as he unbuttoned his shirt and hung it over a hook. On his pillow he laid the small pistol he'd had hidden in the waistband of his britches all day. As he stared at the gun, he thought of the lie he had told the sheriff about being unarmed. But Bart was not fool enough to go around without a gun when a toothless devil was after him. No, sir.

All the same, as Bart stood by the window and checked the street below for familiar shadows, he decided he'd better do some praying. After three weeks of living with Rosie, he was used to her nightly habit of kneeling by the bedside, and he knew that on a day like this she probably would have been too worn out to take care of matters with the Almighty.

"Lord," he murmured, looking up at the moon so as to fix his focus on something visible, "sorry about telling Sheriff Bowman I didn't have a gun. Reckon I should have 'fessed up to it, but You know damn well . . . darn well . . . what a scoundrel that Tucker is. Anyhow, I suspect You'll work all this out for the best, seeing as how You and I care so much about Rosie."

He fingered the twisted gold fringe on the curtain a moment before continuing. "Lord, I'm doing my dead level best to go straight, You know I am. And You know I wouldn't hurt Rosie for the world. I reckon I'd better turn all this mess over to You to fix up. Chances are, I'll tangle things up worse than they already are with this Tucker fellow. Reckon You could get a letter to Frank James double quick?" Bart watched a cloud drift across the blue face of the moon. "Anyhow, good night . . . and amen."

Spreading on a table the sheet of paper Mrs. Davis had given him, Bart pondered the message he would write. Then he sat down, dipped a pen in the borrowed inkwell, and began to scratch out each letter:

> Dear Frank,
> Howdy from yore old pal Bart Kingsley. Herd the law let you off and a good thing too. You shore didn't deserve to hang no sir. I did what you sed and got me a wife and sum land here in Raton, New Mexico. Things are going real good so far. I'm strate as an arrow.
> Say Frank. Reckun you could do me a favor over there in Mizzuri? I could shore use sum help. . . .

Rosie leaned over the edge of the bed and stared into the empty chamber pot as her stomach rolled in dry waves of nausea. The moment she groaned, Bart's warm hand covered her damp back and the comforting solidity of his body slid alongside hers.

"Rosie," he whispered, "I've got you. It's okay now, girl."

"Oh, Bart, I've never felt so awful in my whole life."

"Mrs. Davis has it all figured out. She thinks you ate something rotten yesterday." He smoothed back Rosie's hair and took her into his arms. "Whatever it is, darlin', you can relax now."

"Did the sheriff let you off?" She gazed up into green eyes threaded with gold. "Are we free to go home?"

"We can leave this afternoon. I've got to go down to the courthouse this morning and clear up the last few details. But don't you worry your head another second. I've taken care of everything."

Rosie shut her eyes and rested her cheek against the hard muscle of his arm. Just the thought of their little dugout sent a feeble wave of calm through her tortured stomach as she relaxed into Bart's warmth. The dresser Bart was building for their dinner plates, the rosebushes that had just begun to bud beside their doorway, the sound of their laundry flapping on the clothesline as the sunshine bleached it as white as the late snow on the mesas, the chickens scratching in the dirt around their coop, the cows lowing . . .

"Bart," she said, "I'm going to talk to Mr. Kilgore this morning. I'm going to tell him I don't want that teaching position after all."

"Rosie." Bart could hardly make the word come out of his throat. "Are you sure about that, Rosie-girl? You've wanted that job for so long. You worked so hard to get it. You even married me—"

"I'm married to you, and that's why I won't take the job," she said, gazing into his eyes. "I'm happy, Bart. Our homestead is a good place for me. You're good for me."

The toothless visage of the man he would face again that morning crossed Bart's mind, and he clutched Rosie tighter against his chest. "I'm doing my best, Rosie-girl. I'm doing the very best I can for you."

"Bart, I just . . . I just . . . oh, no!" Shoving him away, she rolled across the bed and hung her head over the chamber pot. As her empty stomach heaved, she shut her eyes and gripped the sheets. She *would* trust Bart. She would count on spending the rest of her life with him. No matter how often his past reared its ugly head, she would stick by Bart. She could do it; she just knew she could. Oh, Lord, but she was sick!

At ten o'clock that morning Rosie knocked on the front door of Mr. Kilgore's one-room schoolhouse. Back at the hotel she had managed to eat a dry biscuit and sip down a cup of hot tea. Feeling a little more stable, she had washed her face and knotted up her hair. Then she had dressed in a simple green gingham and had set off down the street to the school.

"Ah, Mrs. Springfield," Mr. Kilgore said when he saw his visitor standing on the stoop. "I'm so pleased to see you. Won't you come in?"

Rosie smiled at the warm welcome, and though she had planned to take care of matters with him on the porch, she couldn't resist stepping into the room.

"Good morning, Mrs. Springfield," the children recited from their positions beside their desks.

"Good morning, students." Rosie surveyed the garden of bright faces. "Manford, I'm please to see you in school today. And, Minnie, I see that you're leading the geography recitations."

"Yes, ma'am," Minnie replied shyly. "Mr. Kilgore put me in charge."

"I certainly understand why."

When Minnie's face broke into a brilliant smile, Mr. Kilgore took Rosie by the arm and escorted her to the front of the room. "Students," he said, "Mrs. Springfield has spoken with me on several occasions about her desire to become your teacher. Not only has she passed her school board examination with distinction, but she is qualified to teach every subject we offer, and more besides. Children, Mrs. Springfield has been to *college*."

"College!" The word went up around the room in an awe-filled refrain.

"Although we have only a few weeks of school remaining in this term," Mr. Kilgore continued before Rosie could speak, "I'm pleased to inform you that until the summer vacation, Mrs. Springfield will fill the vacancy here at the free school. And this autumn, if she's willing, she will become our full-time schoolteacher."

"Ya-*hoo*!" Manford shouted. The other students began clapping and stomping their feet on the wooden floor.

"Now, back to work, everyone, while I iron out the details of our agreement." Mr. Kilgore straightened his spectacles and beamed at Rosie. Then he leaned toward her and spoke in a low voice. "Mrs. Springfield, I am prepared to offer you four dollars and fifty cents per week until the summer. For the 1883–84 school year I will pay you the grand total of two hundred and fifty-six dollars—a good deal more than you were earning at the Harvey House, I would think."

"But, Mr. Kilgore—"

"Now, I realize," he said, holding up a hand to halt her protest, "you received tips at the House as well as room and board. I am aware that you were also entitled to free train trips. Of course, I don't have those things to offer. My budget is determined by the school board, as you well know. But I'm certain that, as a married woman, you will be housed and fed by Mr. Springfield. Surely you realize that the salary I've proposed to you is exceptional for anyone working in Raton—especially for a woman."

"Oh, Mr. Kilgore, two hundred and fifty-six dollars . . ."

"And summers off, don't forget. Should you desire to start your own family, my wife has happily agreed to take your baby into our home as part of her little flock during the day while you teach."

"That won't be necessary—"

"And as added incentive, I will allow you to manage the classroom exactly as you please, Mrs. Springfield. I'll rent McAuliffe and Ferguson's Hall for any performances you would like the children to give. I'll even sponsor an end-of-the-year picnic as part of Raton's July Fourth festivities."

As weak as she was, Rosie felt a surge of excitement at

the more than generous offer. Here was her dream, placed in the very palms of her hands! Yet she had told Bart she intended to spend the rest of her days at their homestead.

"I'm honored," she said when she could find the words. "Honored and very touched by your confidence in me."

"Then I'll see you tomorrow morning, Mrs. Springfield. Unless you'd like to start right now?"

Rosie inhaled the strong scent of chalk and old textbooks. "I shall have to speak with my husband first," she said, feeling slightly dizzy again. "You wanted a married woman, Mr. Kilgore, and a married woman must always consult her husband on matters of such importance."

The flicker of dismay that crossed his face was quickly replaced with a smile. "Of course, Mrs. Springfield. I couldn't agree more. Such loyalty to a spouse is highly commendable."

Rosie shook his hand. "I'll let you know my decision, Mr. Kilgore. Until then, thank you very much."

"And thank you, Mrs. Springfield," he called as she made her way down a crooked aisle and out the front door.

Rosie sucked in a breath of lilac-scented air as she leaned against the white picket fence that surrounded the school yard. Clutching her stomach, she shut her eyes and tried to quell the odd excitement she felt. Oh, the classroom could be hers after all! The classroom, the desks, the slates—the children! Even the fine salary. Would Bart possibly want to deny her this dream?

On the other hand, did Rosie really want to give up the days she had come to feel were so precious? She had told Bart she would help him with the farm, and it wouldn't be long before he would need her in the fields. The more land he plowed, the less time he had to care for every single acre. She thought of the dugout, her chickens, her pots and pans. She thought of the vegetables sprouting in her kitchen garden. If she taught all day, those would have to take second place in her life.

But how could she give up the classroom she had longed for since the day she set foot in Raton? To have finally won what she had strived so hard for—and then to just give it up—seemed too difficult a prospect to comprehend. Her own chalk, textbooks, desk! Lesson plans, recitations, music practice! Comforting, disciplining, teaching!

As she made her way down the street, Rosie felt as if she were positively floating. The New Mexico morning seemed lighter and brighter than it ever had, the sky as blue as the pattern on a willowware plate, not a cloud to be seen, the mountains glowing in shades of olive, slate, indigo, and violet.

Raton looked like heaven itself. Wearing fresh coats of summer paint, the clapboard houses, hotels, and saloons fairly strutted in place. The adobe homes, their flat roofs supported by wooden vigas, sported new layers of crusty white caliche. Even the humble log dwellings had been doused with sweet-smelling oil in preparation for the long, dry summer ahead.

Lately the railroad had brought the bulbs and seeds of eastern flowers to town, so every yard was bursting with the vibrant hues of gladioli, freesias, peonies, and hollyhocks. Bees hummed around rose blossoms and honeysuckle vines. Butterflies fluttered among the wisteria. Hummingbirds, their bright wings all but invisible, hovered and darted over crimson trumpet vine flowers.

"Good morning, Mrs. Springfield," Mr. Pace called from the post office as Rosie walked past.

"Morning, Mr. Pace." She gave him a little wave.

"Howdy, Mrs. Springfield." Mr. White, Raton's beloved photographer, tipped his hat as he hurried by with his dog, Tom, close at his heels.

"How-do, Laurie!" Mrs. Bayne tapped on the window of her millinery and dress shop where she was setting up a display of summer calico fabrics and straw hats trimmed with ribbon.

As queasy as she had been that morning, Rosie was feeling perkier than she would ever have imagined as she stepped onto the depot platform outside the Harvey House. The new station was already under construction, and she had to skirt piles of lumber and scaffolding and make her way around kegs of nails.

"Morning, Mr. Gable!" Rosie called when she spotted the manager at the far end of the platform.

"Laurie! Haven't seen you in a coon's age. Get into the lunchroom, and tell those girls to fix you a bowl of ice cream. On the house!"

"Thanks, Mr. Gable." Rosie give him a bright grin and hurried toward the front door. It would be wonderful to see Etta and all the other girls again. Would they notice that marriage had changed her in any way? Would they be pleased with the position she had been offered at Mr. Kilgore's school? Would they admire the new green dress she wore, and would they ask about Bart and how married life was treating her?

Her heart filled to brimming, Rosie almost breezed past the white poster tacked to the wall just inside the door. "Reward," it read in bold black print, "Bart Kingsley."

Rosie swung around and stared:

REWARD: Bart Kingsley—$50, dead or alive. This armed and dangerous criminal is wanted by authorities in the state of Missouri for train robbery and murder. Vitals: Black hair, green eyes, 195 lbs., 6′2″. Half Apache, half white.

As the blood rushed from Rosie's cheeks to her knees, she read the list of offenses her husband was accused of committing:

Robbery: October 7, 1879—Glendale, Missouri, Chicago & Alton line
July 15, 1881—Winston, Missouri, Rock Island line
September 7, 1881—Blue Cut, Missouri, Chicago & Alton line
Accomplice to murder: July 15, 1881—Winston, Missouri
Participated in the shooting deaths of William Westfall and Frank McMillan.

At the bottom of the poster was a notice in boldface type:

Bart Kingsley, alias Injun Jack, Savage Jack, Jack King, was wounded in the territory of New Mexico. Escaped. Believed to have been taken by the authorities in Albuquerque, but it was the wrong man. Last seen alive: Raton, New Mexico.

Someone had drawn a circle around the last three words. Rosie swallowed and touched the letters that formed Bart's name. Then she read the entire poster again. There was no picture, but it hardly mattered. How many men could fit that description?

*Fourteen
. . . .

Abandoning Etta, Annie, and all thoughts of ice cream, Rosie fled from the Harvey House. As fast as her wobbly legs would carry her, she made her way down the street toward the sheriff's office. With the words of the poster fresh in her mind, she suddenly saw the sheet of white paper everywhere. One had been nailed to every post along the depot porch. Three more were glued to the windows of the saloons she passed. Yet another hung fluttering from a pillar at McAuliffe and Ferguson's Hall.

Reward: Bart Kingsley—$50, dead or alive.

"Dear God," Rosie repeated in a breathless prayer as she stumbled over a ridge of dried mud in the street. "Dear God, help . . . help!"

She didn't want Bart to die! She didn't want the sheriff to arrest him and haul him off to jail. Oh, he'd be taken to Missouri where the James gang had left such an evil taste in the mouths of the lawmen. She would fight Sheriff Bowman herself to keep him from arresting Bart. She would!

On the other hand, maybe she should take the first train west. What if Bart really had shot down those two men in cold blood? He had admitted to robbery. Why not murder, too? Rosie knew she wasn't the kind of woman to support the activities of a criminal—she hadn't been brought up that way. She believed in decency, respect for human life. People ought to be honest and hardworking. They should earn their money by the sweat of their brow. Maybe she would be smart to just abandon Bart to the fate he'd earned for himself.

Rosie stopped and grabbed on to a picket of the fence surrounding the sheriff's office. Should she run and hide? Or should she stand by Bart?

Straightening her shoulders, she made up her mind to support her husband, tenuous though their relationship might be. She stepped onto the path that led into the yard. She would tell Sheriff Bowman about their homestead and all the plans they'd made, Rosie decided. She'd tell him how Bart had saved every penny he earned at the livery stable, how every day he plowed and hoed until his muscles ached and he could hardly walk, how he tended his horses and cattle, how he'd bought his wife chickens and built her a coop so she could earn some egg money. As sick at heart as she felt, Rosie knew she would face the sheriff and tell him Bart was a good man. He deserved forgiveness. He deserved a second chance.

As she set one foot on the porch, Bart swung out through the front door. "Come on out for dinner sometime, Sheriff," he called. "My wife makes a great apple pie."

"Sure thing, Buck." Sheriff Bowman stood in the doorway, grinning. "You need anything, just holler."

"Will do." Bart turned and spotted Rosie. "Howdy, darlin'!"

"Bart?"

"Great ghosts, you're as green as a new apple. What are you doing out of bed, Rosie?" He caught her around the waist and swung her up into his arms. "Have you been airin' your paunch again?"

"No . . . no, I've been to see Mr. Kilgore." Rosie stared at the mound of muscle that strained against Bart's shirtsleeve. He was real. Free. As solid and whole as he had been when he left her that morning. "Did you see the poster?" she whispered.

"Damn thing hung right over my head the whole time I was talking to Sheriff Bowman." He chuckled. "I didn't notice it when I first stepped into the office this morning. I had my sights set on that Tucker fellow. But somewhere about midmorning I turned around, and my eye fell on it. I swear, you could have knocked me over with a feather."

As Bart spoke, he carried Rosie toward the Central Hotel. In the golden sunlight his face was more handsome than she had ever seen it. His coal-black hair had grown long again and looked so soft and shiny as the breeze lifted and spilled it over his forehead. Every time he grinned, she caught a glimpse of his strong, white teeth. When he tilted back his head to chuckle, she could see the cords of sinew that ran down his neck. His eyes sparkled, their green depths a startling contrast to his bronze skin.

"I reckon people just see what they want to see," he was saying as he climbed onto the hotel porch. "Sheriff Bowman has me set in his mind as a hardworking family man, the cousin of Cheyenne Bill, and about as honest as the day is long. Shrewd as he is, I don't think it ever crossed his mind to notice that I'm a half-breed green-eyed stranger who showed up in town right after Bart Kingsley ran out."

Bart shouldered his way through the front door and strode across the lobby. "Got me a sick wife, Mrs. Davis," he called out as he started up the stairs. "We're heading back to the farm now."

"About time!" Rosie caught a glimpse of the woman who was scrubbing the lobby floor. "Give her a liver corrective and a blood purifier. Mr. Shroeder's got 'em both over at the Raton Drugstore."

"Thanks, Mrs. Davis."

Bart carried Rosie to their room, lowered her onto the bed, and quickly packed their clothes in the bag they had brought from the homestead. Before she had time to question him about the details of the discussion with Tucker and the sheriff, Bart had slung the bag over his shoulder and scooped up Rosie a second time.

Not until they had traveled some distance away from town did she finally speak up. "So Tucker gave up the fight?" she asked from within the folds of the blankets Mrs. Davis had wrapped her in. Not only was she cocooned in quilts, but Rosie wore a hot linen towel around her throat as well. A sure cure for nausea, Mrs. Davis had insisted.

Bart pondered his answer for a moment. He didn't want Rosie to know how much trouble the old snake had actually been. In fact, there had been enough trouble between the two men that Bart had decided to keep his rifle on his thighs as he drove the wagon down the deserted trail.

"Tucker wouldn't give up," Bart said finally. "He wanted me to give him the money for a new set of choppers. He was asking for ten dollars total, just to make amends."

"Ten dollars!" Rosie exploded, upsetting the hot linen towel. "That's crazy. We don't have that kind of money."

"Hell, don't I know it?" Bart shook his head. There had been times in his life when he'd had so much cash he hadn't known what to do with it all. But it had been ill-gotten—too easily gained and just as easily squandered.

"Anyhow," he went on, "the more we talked things over, the more the situation became clear to Sheriff Bowman. See, Tucker and I both agreed on the exact site where the troubles between us took place. It was about the only thing we saw eye to eye on. Tucker kept insisting that he had just stopped by our picnic to ask directions to Springer. That was when I pointed out there's only one damn road going from there into Springer. Any fool could have made it to town without needing to stop and ask directions."

"Oh, of course," Rosie said with a sigh of relief.

"While we were in the middle of arguing that point, Deputy Catlin came in with a telegram from Springer. The sheriff there had done some snooping around, and he'd gotten witnesses who remembered Tucker sleeping off a drunk on the porch of one of the saloons in town the night before. It was clear as a bell then that Tucker hadn't been on the road heading *into* Springer. Instead, he'd just come from Springer that morning, same as us. That did in his excuse about stopping to ask for directions."

"Did Tucker confess to trying to rob us?"

"Hell, no. About the time Sheriff Bowman was starting to put the picture together, the toothless devil claimed he needed to use the privy out behind the courthouse. Sure enough, off he skedaddled and never came back."

"He got away!"

"Fine with me. I didn't want to fool with him, or with the law, any more than I had to. Tucker didn't manage to rob us or hurt you, and he lost his teeth to boot. That squares it enough for me."

"I guess so." Rosie sighed, snuggled down into the blankets, and shut her eyes. "So it's all settled, then. Everything's going to be okay."

Bart studied the rifle on his thighs for a long time. He sure didn't like what he had to say, but he didn't want to keep anything from Rosie, especially now, when her health was suffering so much from all this trouble.

"Well," he said finally, "there could be one hitch."

Rosie opened her eyes. "Hitch?"

"See, Sheriff Bowman did go ahead and send off telegrams to several places to check up on me. I tried to steer him off the notion, but he does his best to go by the law. Anyhow, I figured he'd come up blank checking on somebody named Buck Springfield, so I went ahead and gave him the names of a few towns to try."

"Not Kansas City . . ."

"No." Bart took a breath. "But he's going to send out queries to every state around."

"Including Missouri?"

"'Fraid so, Rosie-girl. It's a system they have. Sheriff Bowman's going to ask the law in Missouri if they know anything about a green-eyed half-breed who stands six foot two and weighs one hundred ninety-five pounds." He gave Rosie a long look. "I reckon things could get a little interesting, if you know what I mean."

By the time the wagon arrived at the little dugout in the woods, Rosie was feeling better. Her nausea had faded, and her head seemed to have cleared. But with the awakening of her insight came the clarity to see what had actually happened in the past few hours.

Bart was again a pursued man. Not only were those awful posters everywhere, but Sheriff Bowman had sent telegrams all over the territories, and even into the states. It couldn't possibly be long before somebody or something triggered the sheriff's mind to focus on the truth.

She thought of Etta and how much the young woman

knew about Rosie's past and the mysterious green-eyed half-breed she had once married. Would Etta go to the sheriff with her story? And then there was Ezra, the livery stable owner. He saw Bart every day. He knew when Bart had come to town, and of course he knew what his employee looked like. How long would it be before Ezra made a closer inspection of the wanted poster tacked to the depot posts just outside the livery stable?

The one person in town who knew the most, of course, was Cheyenne Bill. How had Bart persuaded the boxer to lie on his behalf? What would it take to make Cheyenne Bill talk against Bart? Would a reward of fifty dollars be too tempting for him to resist?

"You haven't said a word since we left town," Bart commented as he helped Rosie down from the wagon. "You feeling all right?"

"I'm better."

He bent and lightly kissed her cheek. "Come on, Rosie-girl. I'll fix you an oyster supper. How does that sound?"

"*Ughhh*," she groaned. "Just the thought of the smell makes me want to throw up."

"Don't do that!" He caught her up again and carried her down the front steps and into the cool, sweet shadows of their home. "I'm going to put you right here on the bed while I go milk the cow and check on the chickens. I'll be back in a few minutes."

After taking off her boots, he settled her beneath the crisp sheets she had ironed back when their life was golden. He pulled the quilts up around her neck and tucked them under the mattress. When he was halfway to the door, he stopped and turned around. "It'll be all right, Rosie-girl," he said. "Don't you worry your head about a thing."

But when he was gone, worry was all she could do. What if that Tucker fellow had followed them to their homestead? What if he came out of the brush and shot Bart while he was milking? Rosie knotted her body into a ball. Should she go out after him and try to protect him? But she couldn't protect Bart every minute of every day. She couldn't stop him from going to the livery stable the following morning.

She couldn't prevent Etta from talking to the sheriff, or keep the townspeople from noticing how closely "Buck" fit the description on the poster.

Should she just take care of herself and try to put Bart out of her thoughts? If he were carted off to jail in Missouri, should she follow him there and stand up for him against all the odds? Oh, she was beginning to dread every minute of the coming days. The little house felt dank and cold, the unlit room filled with threatening shadows. Even the memory of her kitchen garden and budding roses did nothing to quell the uneasy ache inside her.

One thing, and one thing alone seemed to give her hope—the thought of those rows of small, bright faces, those polished and well-worn desks, that faded flag, the chorus of voices chanting, "Good morning, Teacher. Good morning, ma'am."

Bart's warm body pressed close against hers brought Rosie out of the depths of her sleep. Though she was still dressed in her gingham town clothes, she knew it was almost dawn. The faintest tinges of pink and gold were slanting between the open curtains and through the paper panes of the two front windows. A lone bird, a meadowlark, sang a trilling tune that promised another sun-filled day.

Rosie snuggled closer to Bart, drinking in the scent of his bare skin and enjoying the pressure of his unconscious arousal. Was he dreaming of her? she wondered as she slid her palm down his flat belly and over the long bulge. He stirred slightly, drawing her closer within his embrace.

These were the good times, Rosie thought as she massaged him lightly. These were the moments when she knew how much they belonged together, when the outer world with its chaos seemed so far away. If only she could erase those troubles as she would wipe out the writing on a slate. If only the years between their first meeting and this moment could be blotted out.

"Oh, Bart," she whispered against the smooth round curve of his ear. "Bart, I want you so much."

Sliding out of his dreams, Bart reached up to gather

clumps of Rosie's long hair. His mouth found hers, and he licked apart the seam between her lips. When their tongues touched, she felt an explosion of desire for him more intense then any she had ever known. The force of her need drove her to pull open the buttons on her own dress and release her breasts from her chemise.

Coming fully awake as her nipples teased the bare flesh of his chest, Bart curved his hands around her hips and began to kneed the throbbing pillows of her buttocks. She slid one leg over his thigh and felt his tumescence rise to meet her hot belly. As his fingers worked between her thighs, she allowed her breasts to touch and titillate his skin. But the stimulation only heightened her further, so that she was soon moaning with need to feel the pressure of him deep inside her.

"Bart, please," she whispered, "take me."

"Come onto me, girl," he returned. "You grab the reins, my hot-blooded mare."

Unable to feel the slightest flush at his bold image, she did just as he beckoned. She slipped her legs over his hips and fitted his shaft to the sweet, pulsing hollow of her desire. When she eased down onto him, he let out a groan of disbelief at the intense ecstasy of their morning loving. Her breasts, full and ruby-tipped, swayed above him, and he reached up to flick at them with the tips of his fingers. For hours, it seemed, they rode together, their touches alternately heightening and lessening the pleasurable journey up the mountain of their passion.

Rosie tossed back her head and swayed with each stroke of Bart's hands on her body as he molded his palms to her legs, his thumbs finding the hollows between her thighs. Their mouths and lips and tongues moistened each sensitive curve of neck, ear, cheek, breast. And they climbed and climbed, Rosie's breath ragged in her chest and Bart's flesh damp with need for release. The sheets grew tangled, the mattress poufed and valleyed, the quilts tumbled to the floor.

When it seemed that the sunrise and the bed and the mockingbirds all had vanished in a swift rush of blinding light, Rosie felt poised on the apex of the mountain—a moment of incredible throbbing tension—and then she rolled down and down, cascading with delicious undulations of release. Bart came with her, his own explosion shuddering through him so that he gripped her body in a bruising embrace.

"Oh, Rosie, oh, woman," he mouthed against her breast. "I love you, Rosie. I love you."

The confession ricocheted through her almost as intensely as the moment of their climax had. *He loved her.* Oh, he loved her. . . .

"Girl, you know how to get a man's day off to a fine start," he said as he gazed into her face, his green eyes misty emeralds in the early light. "I love you, Rosie."

"Bart, I . . ."

"Shh, now. I see that worried look creeping across your forehead again and rumpling up that fine smooth skin. Don't let what I say trouble you, darlin'. You just take what you want from me and put the rest of it aside."

"Bart, I don't want the past. That's what I can't live with. I want what we have right now. I want things to be this way forever. But I'm so full of worries—full to the brim."

He shut his eyes and settled her cheek against his shoulder. "If I could take away the past, Rosie, you know I would. But I can't undo it. No man can erase the years gone by. All I can ask is that you forgive me for what I did and how I lived. Forgive me, and let's go on from there."

"Oh, Bart, I do forgive you. But who else will?"

"Maybe no one will ever find out about my past."

"And maybe they will! What then? Bart, I can't let them take you away from me again."

"It's not me I'm worried about, Rosie, it's you. I've been on the run so long the trail feels like home. It won't be anything new for me to be churning up dust and riding for yucca country. Staying two jumps ahead of the law is the life I know best. But I can't take you with me, and I won't. You're no cheap red-light girl used to running with the dregs. You deserve a good life, Rosie. You deserve the best."

He let his eyes trace the smooth pale curve of her bare hip. "Sometimes I get to thinking you deserve a lot better than what I can ever give you, Rosie-girl," he went on. "You ought not to have to live so full of uncertainty and fear that you can't help but get yourself sick as a dog over it. It's damned unfair of me to want to keep you here in this bum dugout, raising chickens and milking cows when you were reared to be a society lady. But no matter how unfair it is, the picture always changes when I think about giving you up. I did that once, Rosie. I'm not going to do it again. I love you, and I mean to keep you by my side come hell or high water."

"Even if it means facing the gallows?"

"I reckon so. I'm sure not going to drag you all over kingdom come to escape what some folks would say are my just deserts. Meanwhile, I'm doing a heap of thinking and even a little praying about all this. I expect it's going to come out all right. The good Lord loves you just as much as I do, you know. Maybe more, though I can't imagine it."

"He loves you, too, Bart."

"Hell, I don't know why." He sat up in bed and swung his legs to the floor. "Anybody who would love a varmit like me ought to have his head examined."

In a moment a stark naked Bart had gone out the front door and climbed the steps into the sunshine.

After a breakfast of scrambled eggs, fried potatoes, hot coffee, and frothy white milk, Bart hitched his horses to the wagon for the ride into Raton. Riding his stallion would get him to town quicker than if he had to haul the heavy wagon, but he needed to buy some more seed and take it out to the farm. He'd be late for work at the stable anyhow, and he decided he didn't care; the time in bed with Rosie had restored his belief in their future.

"I'll see you at lunchtime, darlin'," he called from the wagon. "Don't work too hard, now. You still look a little green around the gills to me."

She tried to smile as she watched him flick the reins and set the horses to pulling the wagon down the bumpy trail.

Her hands still damp from washing the breakfast dishes, she twined them in her apron and studied Bart's broad back as it began to vanish through the trees. Things should have felt normal to her. How many days had she stood just so, waving him off to his job at the livery stable? But she didn't feel normal. The creeping uncertainty slipped back over her the moment the wagon had disappeared.

Bart was gone. She was alone. He could be caught now—by Tucker, the sheriff, or anyone. The sheriff could come for her, too, reasoning that she had hidden him from the law. Why wasn't she braver? She swallowed. Why couldn't she be the fearless pioneer woman she had dreamed up when Bart told her about his homestead?

Because she wasn't fearless. She was human, and she was in love with a man who might vanish from her life as easily as he had just disappeared into the woods. In love with him? Yes, she was. But he had told her she deserved a good life; she deserved the best.

"Bart!" Shouting his name, she ran down the trail after the wagon. "Bart! Bart—wait!"

She tore through the trees and leapt over hummocks of summer grass. Her apron ribbons caught on a briar, and she felt it loosen from her waist. Grabbing the white fabric, she waved it as she ran.

"Bart! Wait for me!"

"Rosie?" The wagon stopped in the middle of the trail at the bottom of a lazy incline. Bart climbed down and started toward her. "Rosie, what's wrong?"

"I'm going with you, Bart!" she cried. "Mr. Kilgore offered me a job at the school yesterday. I'm going to take it. I'm going to teach the children in the morning while you work at the stable."

"What?" He took off his hat and caught her before she could slam into him. "You got that teaching job and you didn't tell me?"

"I wasn't going to take it, Bart. I wanted to stay out here and just be a wife to you. But I can't do that. I've got to have something to fill my time so I won't spend it worrying. And . . . and I need something I can count on."

"You can't count on me?" His face had fallen.

"No, I can't! I can't be sure of anything. But I know if I'm teaching school, I'll have work and I'll have a place to call my own when . . . if anything happens to you."

"Rosie, I've promised to take care of you. If you want to teach so you can make the money, that's fine with me. You know you can do whatever you want. But don't tell me you want the job because you don't trust me."

"I trust you, Bart, as far as I can. But don't you understand? I have to consider myself, my own future. I'm thinking I'll just take that job and . . . and maybe I'll buy that little house, too . . . just until things settle down for you. When I'm sure of you . . . of us . . . then I'll move back out to the homestead. Don't you see?"

He stared at her. "I see, all right. I see that you don't love me the way I love you. You don't trust me to look out for you and build a good future for you. You haven't forgiven me, either. Not the way I asked you to, Rosie."

"I'm trying, Bart. But my life hasn't been easy these past few years, and I've spent a lot of time working to make something better for myself. Don't ask me to give up on that."

He nodded. "Maybe you're right. Maybe you ought to do exactly what you want and to hell with what I'm trying to give you. Lord knows it's not much anyhow."

"Bart, please try to understand."

"Get in the wagon, Rosie. You go make yourself a good life, and if you can ever see your way clear to pardon me for my past, then we'll see what comes of it."

She climbed onto the wooden seat and sat in silence through the long ride. Selfish—that's what she was, she told herself. Bart had risked everything to give her all he had, and she had just flung it in his face.

On the other hand, she had risked an awful lot, too.

She had given up the security of Kansas City and then the haven of the Harvey House, all to make her dream of teaching come true. She had married Bart once, and she'd taken him on again in spite of all that was rational. Just because they had started to build themselves a life, just because they had loved each other and had taken that love to bed, she didn't have to commit her whole future to him. And now that things were heating up for Bart, it made sense to distance herself a little and see how the situation turned out.

Rosie knew she was no naive, lovelorn schoolgirl. Certainly not. She'd seen too many of the harsh realities of life to ever trust in a "happily ever after" ending. If things panned out the way she expected, it wouldn't be long before the sheriff did come after Bart. She might as well start preparing herself for that right now.

"I reckon you want me to let you off at the schoolhouse?" Bart asked when they pulled into Raton. They were the first words he had spoken since leaving the homestead.

"Yes, please." Rosie wanted to look at him, but she was afraid she'd back down on her resolve to keep a distance.

"So, you're planning to stay in town from now on?"

"For a while." She ventured a glance. "I need to get my feet on the ground with my teaching."

"Buying a house sounds pretty glued down to me, Rosie."

"Bart, try to understand."

"I've been trying to understand you all the way from our place to town. I just don't see how a woman and a man can do the things we did this morning and then chuck it out like an old cow chip."

"It wasn't a cow chip!"

He pulled the wagon to a stop in front of the one-room school. "Then trust me, Rosie. I won't do wrong by you, I swear it."

She studied his green eyes beneath the shadow of his hat. "And I won't do wrong by you either, Bart. But I need this chance to give myself some roots, something I can hold on to when things go bad."

"Who says things are going to go bad?"

"Nobody. It just feels that way to me." She slid to the edge of the seat and lifted her skirt. "I'll send word to the livery stable when you can come for me again. It won't be long, Bart."

As she stood on the ground and gazed up at him, he settled his hat lower over his brow. "I never had you figured for a hard-hearted woman, Rosie," he said, "but now I know different."

He flicked the reins and set off in the direction of the railway depot.

Rosie could never have imagined feeling worse than she did when she first set foot inside her new classroom. Not only had she driven Bart away with her selfishness, but she had given up something unbearably precious. To wake up each morning with Bart's big body all warm against hers had become dear. To walk around the side of their dugout and see his tall, strong figure laboring over the plow had always filled her heart to overflowing. To stand in her warm home with stew bubbling over a snapping fire, curtains rustling in the windows, and the scent of wildflowers drifting in through the open door had become heaven itself.

But she had fled from Eden, traded it for a few shekels' worth of security.

"Mrs. Springfield!" Thomas Kilgore hurried through the haphazard rows of desks. "Welcome to the free school! I'm assuming you've decided to accept my offer?"

She turned her attention to the man's bushy eyebrows and bright blue eyes. Nodding slowly, she tried to smile.

"Wonderful!" He clasped her elbow. "Students, Mrs. Springfield is your new teacher." Amid the clapping, he led her to the big wooden desk she had dreamed of so long. "Carry on with your studies, boys and girls, while I hand over the reins to Mrs. Springfield."

Rosie had barely begun to accept what she had done when Mr. Kilgore began loading her arms with books and slates and tablets of lined paper. "Now, the school commissioners have selected these texts for general use," he said, "and their action does help to coordinate the entire area school system. We use Sheldon's English readers, Swinton's Spanish readers, Patterson's grammars and spellers, Robinson's arithmetics, Harper's geography, United States history, and Spencerian penmanship books. As you may know if you've been reading the *Comet*, the commissioners voted to give Mr. Troy three hundred dollars to pay for these texts for the free schools."

"Oh," Rosie said, still in a daze.

"We do use all these materials, of course, but I've found that some of our students need supplemental work. Clark's Drugstore carries comprehensive geography books for one dollar and fifteen cents apiece. I've been thinking of putting Minnie and Lily to work in that; they're so far ahead of the others. But Manford and some of the others may need the elementary geography that sells for sixty-five cents. Clark's also has Dave and Peck's arithmetic at sixty cents and a large selection of readers ranging from a dollar for the fifth reader to a quarter for the first. They also sell spelling books for two bits. You'd think parents would gladly buy these texts for their children. What with the price of whiskey at two bits these days, a schoolbook is not only cheap but a much more prudent purchase."

"Yes, indeed."

"Now, slates cost thirty-five cents, and you'll want to make sure every student has at least one good one. I'm afraid that's not always the case with some of these children. Slates are so easily broken, you know."

Rosie nodded, and hoped her numbed brain was absorbing at least some of what he was telling her.

"Every morning the first, second, and third graders take recitations in reading, grammar, and spelling. They also practice their handwriting. Remember, we are totally Spencerian here at the free school. Nothing less will do. While the younger students labor at reading, grammar, and spelling, the fourth, fifth, and sixth graders are busy with arithmetic, history, geography, and Latin. After the lunch break, the two groups switch subjects. Of course, sometime during the week you'll work in lessons in Spanish, music, and art, too."

"Oh . . . of course."

"School begins promptly at seven. Student tardiness will not be tolerated. Morning recess is at nine. Ring the lunch bell at noon, then start class again at twelve-thirty. Afternoon recess takes place at two, and school is dismissed at four.''

"Four?''

"I know it seems early, but many of these children live in the country, and they do have evening chores. I like to give them an opportunity to help out at home, as well as time to do their homework. You *will* give ample homework, Mrs. Springfield?''

"Yes, sir.''

"I cannot stress enough how important it is that these children catch up with their city counterparts. Under your tutelage I expect them to be able to compete in every educational arena.''

Rosie nodded, though she didn't quite see how these ragged homesteader children who were so far behind and whose parents expected them to spend so much time at chores other than school work could be expected to compete educationally with anyone. All the same, she knew they deserved the very best she could give them—and that meant putting her relationship with Bart behind her for the time being, stiffening her back, and facing her new responsibilities.

"Discipline is a matter of the first order in my school, Mrs. Springfield,'' Mr. Kilgore went on. "Without limits and control, children cannot and will not learn.''

"I agree completely,'' she said, feeling a little better for having made up her mind to focus on the school.

"Good. Here is the switch,'' he said, holding up a long, supple branch that had been stripped of twigs and leaves. He hung its leather loop from a hook by the desk and picked up a thick, smooth stick. "And here is the cane. There in the corner is the stool and dunce cap. Do not hesitate to use them to good benefit.''

"Yes, sir.''

"Suspension and expulsion are acceptable punishments, though generally ineffective. Most students are quite pleased to have the time off from their studies. I've found the opposite to work better: make them stay after school, copy sentences on the chalkboard, and the like. Please consult with me if you have continuing behavior problems with anyone. I'll be next door instructing the high school students and tending to administrative duties. I shall be happy to take any disciplinary matters into my own capable hands.''

"Yes, sir.''

"Any questions?'' When Rosie failed to respond immediately, Mr. Kilgore gave her a broad grin. ''Well, then, Mrs. Springfield—good luck.''

With those parting words, he marched out the front door, and Rosie was left alone to face the fulfillment of her dreams.

*Fifteen
....

Rosie dared to hope that Bart would drive his wagon past the school on his way out of town at noon—but he didn't. As she sat on the front porch steps eating the chicken sandwich Mrs. Kilgore had fixed for her, she scanned the narrow, dusty streets for any sign of an ebony-haired, broad-chested man with his hat pulled low on his brow. Bart didn't come, and by the time Rosie rang the bell to begin the afternoon classes, she had to accept that he had done just as he'd said he would and driven out of town to work alone at their homestead.

If her hopes for Bart went unmet, her classroom more than lived up to her expectations. After Mr. Kilgore's presentation of the switch, cane, and dunce cap, Rosie had expected to run into trouble with some of the students. But evidently the burly pedagogue had molded the children into shape—or perhaps they had simply decided not to put their new teacher to the test on her first day.

At any rate, Rosie had no choice but to slip into the role of facilitator as she noted the texts and stages of learning for each student and each subject, managed the choreographic rotation of six grade levels, learned thirty-seven names, and oversaw both recitations and slate work. In such a busy, crowded classroom, there was little lecturing to be done. By the end of the day, Rosie had begun to feel she was more the director of a large orchestra of various, sometimes unharmonic instruments than the teacher in a one-room schoolhouse.

Exhausted, she rang the final bell and watched the

students gather their homework and file out of the room. Manford Wade held back a moment and gave Rosie his characteristic red-cheeked grin. "Bye, ma'am," he called from the row of coat hooks by the door.

"Good-bye, Manford. See that you practice your script tonight. Mr. Platt Spencer would be rolling in his grave if he knew about the angles in your uppercase *B*."

"Aw, Mrs. Springfield, ain't a soul around these parts cares about my letter *B* but you and Mr. Kilgore."

Rosie brushed a wisp of loose hair into her knot as she walked toward the boy. "Mr. Kilgore and I care that you learn the letter *B*, Manford, because we care about *you*. Any young man who wants to make his way in this world must learn to write properly. And that means practicing your Spencerian *B*."

Manford stuffed his cap over his spiky red hair and gave a little shrug. "Sure, I'll practice some, but us boys have got a game of picket going over in the alley twixt Walley's Saloon and Farley's Bakery. You know, over behind Moshier's Jewelry Store? It's a great place for hide and go seek."

"I know the place."

"Anyhow, we play picket there every afternoon we can. Then I get home and help my mama milk the cow and put up the chickens. And if there's any time left before sundown, I do my schoolwork."

"School should come before picket, Manford," Rosie admonished. "With an education, you can become anything you want in this world. A doctor, a lawyer, a mercantile owner—all those careers are within your reach if you study your schoolbooks. But with picket, all you'll ever learn how to do is hide out and sneak around. Such skills will only serve you if you want to become an outlaw."

"An outlaw? Heck, no. I ain't never gonna do nothing against the law, ma'am. Fact is, I aim to grow up and be just like your husband. Nobody ever saw a finer man than him, and I bet he can't write a Spencer *B* no better than me."

Tipping his cap the way Rosie had seen Bart do a hundred times, Manford took his leave. "Better than *I*," she called after him. But he paid no attention as he ran, kicking a small stone down the street. Rosie stood silently in the doorway, unaware that Mr. Kilgore had emerged from the house next door.

"How did things go for you today, Mrs. Springfield?" he asked as he approached.

She glanced up, startled at his unexpected appearance. "Oh, everything was fine. I . . . I enjoyed the day very much."

"You're going to work out beautifully for us. I feel quite sure of that. Would you like to come over to the house and take a cup of tea while you wait for Mr. Springfield to arrive? You're looking a little peaked. Of course teaching will do that to the best of us!"

Rosie studied the street, wishing she could make Mr. Kilgore's words come true, imagining she could actually see Bart's wagon and team of horses in the distance. But of course he wasn't there.

"Thank you, Mr. Kilgore, but I won't be waiting for my husband today," she said firmly. "We have agreed that I should live here in town during the weekdays. It simply won't be efficient for him to make such a long drive twice each day."

"Oh?" His brow rumpling, Mr. Kilgore took off his spectacles and began wiping them with the large white cotton handkerchief he had pulled from his back pocket. "This is not an arrangement I had expected, Mrs. Springfield."

"We feel it's for the best," she countered.

He frowned and continued polishing. "Hmm."

Rosie swallowed. Surely he wouldn't go back on his word now. No, she had to tackle this issue head-on. "Mr. Kilgore, I'm planning to use my savings from the Harvey House to purchase a small town home."

"Well." He put his spectacles back on, stuffed his handkerchief in his pocket, and stared at Rosie. "Well, well, well."

"Would you and Mrs. Kilgore be so good as to put me up tonight? Tomorrow afternoon I'll speak with Mr. Osfield about the house I'm interested in buying."

"Already picked one out, have you?"

"Yes, sir. It seemed prudent."

"Of course you're welcome to stay with the wife and me for as long as you like. But I would prefer to see you invest your money in a horse and buggy so you can take yourself home to your husband each evening."

Rosie worked up a small smile. "We shall see. In the meantime I'd best collect my texts. I have a lot of preparing to do for tomorrow. I'm planning to begin teaching the students a selection of songs for a spring musical program."

"You are? Wonderful!" With the change in subject, Mr. Kilgore's attitude mellowed, and soon he was off and running over the idea of a second public performance by the students from his school. By the time Rosie had gathered her things and followed him next door, he was positively blathering about patriotic recitations, springtime medleys, piano and violin solos, and even a small operatic play.

The kindly Mrs. Kilgore was quick to support the idea of Rosie spending as much time as she wanted in their home, and she hurried to prepare the attic bedroom for their guest. After a quiet dinner, Rosie climbed up to the small gable room and worked on her lessons until the lamp wick burned low.

Staring at the blurred pages beneath her pen, she reflected on her first day of teaching. It had been everything she had hoped—fulfilling, heartwarming, stimulating. In spite of it all, however, Rosie couldn't help weighing what she had given up against what she had gained. Finally, in the silence of her room, she crawled into the cold, empty bed and fell asleep dreaming of Bart.

A seed sack filled with Rosie's clothes appeared on the school porch the following day, but Rosie never caught sight of Bart. In the following days, she and the students settled into a comfortable schedule that began to chug along like a train on a well-greased track. The troublemakers in the room soon found that Mrs. Springfield would tolerate not a moment of nonsense. No pigtails were to be dipped in inkwells, no secret messages passed back and forth on slates, no pet frogs secreted in pockets, and certainly no backtalk.

Instead of the switch and cane, the new teacher found other methods of motivation. Within a week, the outside of the school sported a new coat of red barn paint donated by one of the farmers. His son had thrown a baseball through the schoolroom window, and not only did he patch the window, but he painted the school as well. The picket fence had been whitewashed by a pair of boys who couldn't seem to refrain from chewing gum like a pair of old heifers at their cud. Three girls who had chosen to whisper and giggle instead of learning their algebraic theorems had been set to stitching curtains from a bolt of plain blue fabric Mrs. Kilgore had found in her attic trunk. As a punishment for tardiness, Manford Wade scrubbed the classroom blackboard. Geraniums, planted by a group of playground fistfighters, flourished in window boxes built by a young man who had dared to test Mrs. Springfield by failing to memorize his Shakespeare soliloquy.

Not that the students minded this extra work. As a matter of fact, word quickly spread that the new teacher's afterschool punishments were the best thing going. She always provided cold lemonade and sandwiches to the laborers, and she regularly joined in the work. Mrs. Springfield was easy to talk to, the story went, and she was nice, to boot. She expected work out of her students, but she was fair and caring.

Rosie knew all about these stories because Mannie Wade made sure to tell her everything that was being said about her, wonderful or not. On the negative side of the gossip was the fact that Mr. Springfield never came to visit his wife and that she looked skinny and dark-eyed from sadness over it. And why was she sick so much of the time, if not from the ill regard of her uncaring absentee husband?

This, of course, only caused Rosie to worry more. She wouldn't have the townsfolk thinking badly of Bart, especially since his absence was her fault in the first place. Besides, she wanted people to know how wonderful he really was.

But as the first weekend approached with no sign of Bart, the gossip grew more intense. Manford told Rosie that everyone in town thought Mr. Springfield was a no-gooder for leaving his bride alone so long. Mannie, of course, continued to maintain that Bart was the most wonderful man on God's green earth. But as he repeatedly told Rosie, what was one eleven-year-old boy's word worth against the griping of a sea of Ratonians?

The last thing Rosie had expected was to become the subject of so much interest. As the new teacher, however, she attracted the attention of every parent in town, each of whom wanted to meet her and express an opinion about one situation or another.

During that first week of Rosie's teaching career, she had put down ten dollars as earnest money for the little yellow clapboard house she had chosen as her town home. But the act gave her little satisfaction, and it was all she could do to keep from running to the livery stable to see Bart. At the same time, she knew she should do her best to keep her mind on the single path of self-sufficiency she had laid out for herself. It would do no good to rush back into Bart's arms only to have him hauled away by the law, leaving her jobless and empty-handed. No, she knew she had to take care of herself until things had settled down for Bart.

Rosie did make it her crusade to remove as many of the wanted posters as she could. On the pretense of needing a scrap of paper on which to write a message, to wipe a spot of mud from her shoe, or to mark a book she was reading, she tore down the posters one by one. She also subscribed to the *Comet* in order to keep abreast of Sheriff Bowman's doings—though of late he had become quite ill with his coughing problem. As much as she hated for the man to be sick, she was thankful if his sickness kept him from investigating Bart's background.

In fact, Rosie began to wonder if everyone in Raton hadn't picked up one sort of bug or another. With the advent of warm weather and blooming flowers, half her students were coughing and sneezing all the way through class. An outbreak of chicken pox felled many of the younger brood, while spring fever in its most virulent form made the older children giddy with puppy love or lost in the land of daydreams.

Rosie herself decided she must have contracted a stomach infection out on the homestead. She just couldn't stop her bouts of nausea, and she certainly wouldn't believe she was still ill from being upset over Bart. On Friday, one week after she had started teaching, she made a Monday afternoon appointment with Dr. Kohlhouser. She knew the man well because his dog, Griff—along with a canine pal, Tom—had made the school's front porch his favorite haunt.

That Saturday morning Rosie was sweeping the walk that led from the school to the street when she spotted Manford Wade and some of his chums sauntering along. She had just hung the newly stitched curtains and was considering whether or not to call the boys inside in order to garner their opinion when Manford broke into a trot ahead of the others.

"Hey, Mrs. Springfield," he called, his thin legs churning up puffs of brown dust. "I just saw Buck over at the stable! He's asked me out to work on your place this afternoon. We're gonna build a refrigerator!"

Rosie clutched the broom handle for support as she took in the first news of Bart. "A refrigerator?" she said, mustering a smile to meet Manford's wide grin. "Sounds like a big job."

"Not for Buck and me. We're gonna dig it wide and deep, straight down into the ground. It'll be so cool you can keep food in there for weeks without it spoilin'. Buck says we're gonna build the refrigerator so it'll work by 'vaporation.''

"Evaporation. My, how complicated." Rosie took a breath. "So, how are things . . . on the homestead, I mean? The sugar beets and all."

"Buck says the beets are growin' like weeds, and come fall he's gonna have to quit his job at the stable to get 'em all harvested. He says he don't mind at all. With the kitchen garden abloom and the beets doin' so good, he thinks the two of you should do just dandy without the extra pay."

"That's what he said?"

"Sure. Get on over to the stable and ask him yourself if you don't believe me."

"I believe you."

Manford squinted up at Rosie in the bright sunshine. "Why *don't* you go see him, ma'am? Do the both of you good. I'll tell you what, if you think you got a bug, you should just see Buck."

"Buck is sick? Mannie, why didn't you tell me!"

"He ain't sick the way you are every morning regular as clockwork. Buck is sick like a man who just lost his best friend. Blue and hangdog day after day. He ain't hardly fun to be around. You better go see him, Mrs. Springfield. I reckon it'd cheer him up mightily."

"Thank you for your advice, Manford. I may just do that."

By this time the other boys had caught up and were shuffling their feet, anxious to get going. "C'mon, Mannie," Joe Foster finally spoke up. "Let's get on over to the alley."

"Playing picket again, boys?" Rosie asked.

"Yes, ma'am. *And* we're aimin' to watch the goin's-on at the shootin' gallery."

Rosie ruffled Joe's dark, sweat-dampened hair. "On a Saturday, I can't think of anything better than a good game of picket. If I weren't all grown up, I'd ask to join you myself."

This comment drew hoots of laughter from the group, and finally Manford crowed, "You're welcome to join us, Mrs. Springfield. I reckon a schoolmarm playing picket would draw a bigger crowd than Charley Baker's shooting gallery."

"I expect you're right. Well, get along with you, then. And be careful around the guns, boys."

"Sure thing, ma'am!" Manford waved as he ran off at the heels of his friends. The redhead was the only one of the older boys who didn't pack his own pistol, and Rosie knew it was only because his mother was far too poor to provide her son with that particular trapping of manhood.

Bending over, Rosie swept the last powdering of dust

from the walk. Her thoughts quickly left the boys and flew to Bart. Was he really so sad that Manford had noticed his mood? Could he really have planned the new refrigerator with her in mind? She glanced at the small gold watch pinned to her bosom. It was drawing close to noon. Should she hurry over to the livery stable and tell Bart she was ready to go home . . . at least for the weekend?

Rosie's fears about the sheriff arresting Bart had not materialized. Most of the posters in town had vanished. That toothless sidewinder from Springer had never returned. As far as Rosie knew, the townsfolk esteemed Bart as highly as ever—except for his mysterious failure to attend to his young bride.

Making up her mind, Rosie propped the broom up by the Kilgores' front door, dusted her hands on her skirt and started across the street. "Bart," she would say, "I've come about that refrigerator you're building. I reckon I'd better head out to the homestead with you to make sure you dig it in the right place. I don't want it too far from my kitchen, you know."

Her kitchen? Rosie shook her head. Why should she expect Bart to build the new refrigerator with her in mind when she had thrown everything he'd done for her in his face?

Oh, but she had missed him so much! The days without him had seemed endless. The lonely nights were even worse. And if she really thought about it, she had to admit that her illness must stem at least partially from the turmoil she felt every day that passed without him.

"Bart," she decided to say, "I've come to talk about us. I've come to tell you that I do love my teaching, I've put ten dollars down on a house, and I'm going to do just fine without you, Bart. But I want you to know how lonesome I've been . . . and how very quiet things seem without you . . . and how much I want to go home. . . ."

Rosie stopped at the corner by the livery stable and tried to swallow the lump in her throat. She *couldn't* stand there and cry in front of Bart. That would never do. But how was she ever going to stay as cool as ice when just the thought of the man tore at her heart so?

She stepped around the corner and scanned the railway platform, with its usual bustle of passengers and baggage boys. Bart was not among them. Walking up the hay-littered ramp into the livery stable, she smoothed her skirt for the hundredth time. "Well, Bart," she would say in a perfectly casual voice, "so how have you been?"

"Rosie?" His deep voice came from somewhere in the shadows, and she stopped, standing as still as stone.

"That's your Rosie?" Another man's voice joined Bart's. Rosie blinked, trying to adjust to the gloom and make out who was speaking.

"If it's not a ghost, it's her. Rosie, what are you doing here?" Bart emerged into a shaft of golden light, and Rosie saw that he was every bit as tall and strong and handsome as she'd dreamed during the long, empty nights. His jet-black hair swept his shoulders, and he wore no shirt. Ropes of muscle shone a coppery red across his chest and down the flat plane of his stomach to his leather-belted denims. His green eyes flickered with a mixture of gladness and wariness.

"Did you come to see me, Rosie?" he asked.

"I . . . well, I . . ." Rosie fumbled, exactly as she'd feared she would. "I just wanted you to know that . . . that my teaching job is wonderful. And . . . I hear you're building a refrigerator."

"Rosie?" Bart reached toward her.

His outstretched arms melted her instantly. "Oh, Bart, I've—"

"*A killin'*, a killin'!" someone screamed just outside the livery stable. "There's been a shootin'!"

Instinctively Bart grabbed Rosie and jerked her against his chest. A stocky fellow bolted from the back of the stable into the sunlight, rifle in hand. "Stay here and guard your woman," barked the man Rosie recognized as Cheyenne Bill. "I'll tend to this."

Bart whipped his own six-shooter from the holster that

hung at his hip. "Bill, look out for your back. No tellin' what kind of outlaws are lurkin' around out there."

The massive man swung around and gave Bart a lopsided grin. "Or lurkin' around in *here*. See you later, Kingsley."

As the Indian ran outside, Bart tucked Rosie more firmly under his arm. "Let's go to the door, darlin'. I've got to see who's stirring up mischief."

Almost oblivious to all but his arm around her waist and the scent of bare male skin against her cheek, Rosie hurried beside Bart to the wide stable door. Outside, the platform was emptying quickly as panicky passengers swarmed toward the safety of the train or the sheltering depot.

When one of the Harvey House kitchen boys ran past, Rosie called out to him. "Jimmy, what's going on?"

"It's a shooting!" he called back, skidding to a brief halt in a low cloud of dust. "I heard tell a kid got killed over by Charley Baker's shootin' gallery. The whole town's astir about it. The men are threatening to lynch Baker for not taking better care of his business. And they say Mrs. Wade's wild with grief."

"*Wade?*" Rosie jerked out of Bart's arms. "Dear God, not Manford!"

Without waiting for a response, she tore down the ramp past Jimmy and joined the crowd headed toward the alley between the bakery and the saloon. Her heart slamming against her rib cage, Rosie elbowed her way through the throng and shoved people aside with a boldness she didn't know she possessed. Mouth as dry as cotton, perspiration streaming down her temples, she fought for air as she ran.

"*Not Mannie! Not Mannie!*" she breathed. But the moment she pushed through the ring of onlookers assembled in the alley behind the jewelry store, she knew her prayers had been in vain.

Manford's mother huddled over the boy, her shrieks of grief piercing the air as Dr. Shuler and Dr. Holcomb examined the small limp form. Deputy Sheriff Heysman and Sheriff Bowman attempted to hold back the crowd while at the same time keeping a close watch on the shooting gallery owner, Charley Baker. A group of men who had evidently been participating in the shooting were studying the bullet holes in the board behind the target while Manford's young friends stood against the alley wall, their eyes wide with horror.

Rosie tried to push her way past the sheriff, but he caught her arm. "I'm Mannie's teacher, Sheriff Bowman," she pleaded, and he let her go. Falling to her knees beside Mrs. Wade, Rosie cradled the hysterically sobbing woman. Manford, his eyes closed and his body completely still without the comforting rise and fall of his chest, lay bloodied and lifeless in the dust. Then a pair of strong brown arms slipped beneath the figure as Bart lifted Mannie against his chest.

"I'll take the boy home," he said. "You doctors can look after him there."

As Bart began to walk out of the alley, the crowd parted. Mrs. Wade clung to her son's dangling hand, while the two physicians hurried along beside them. Dizzy and weak, Rosie started after them, but when she reached the end of the alley, she felt a man's hand clamp around her arm, and she was swung into the street.

"Come with me, Rosie," Cheyenne Bill ordered. "Kingsley won't want you to see it."

Rosie shook her head at the stocky half-breed, whose crooked, flattened nose and lopsided mouth frightened her almost as much as the sight of the heavy cartridge belts and holsters around his thick waist. But if she wanted to escape, he left her no choice. Hoisting her up in his arms just as Bart had done to Manford, he carried her down the street toward the edge of town. In moments, he was pushing through a creaky front door and striding into a gloomy room with bare floors and almost no furniture. He dumped Rosie onto a low, foul-smelling cot with rumpled blankets and torn sheets.

"Rest," he commanded. "I'll get you some whiskey before you up and pass out on me."

"Whiskey? Oh, but I don't—"

"Do you good, woman." He poured amber liquid into a dusty glass and thrust it at Rosie. "Nothing like a shot of panther piss for what ails you. Here—paint yer tonsils with this.''

Shutting her eyes, Rosie took a tiny sip. The whiskey burned its way down her throat, and she shuddered reflexively.

He laughed without mirth. ''That coffin varnish is good stuff, ain't it? It'll eat its way plumb to yer bootheels.'' Not bothering to avail himself of a glass, he tilted the bottle and swilled a long drink. When he had finished, he wiped his mouth with the back of his hand and let out a breath. ''Damn,'' he muttered. ''Damn Charley Baker to hell.''

Rosie shivered as she stared into her glass of whiskey. ''Mannie's not going to die,'' she whispered.

The Indian gave a grunt. ''The boy's dead already, lady, and you might as well get used to the notion. Somebody's bullet plowed clean through that target and the board behind it, and the damn thing put a window in the kid's skull.''

''No!'' Rosie jumped to her feet. ''Don't say such a thing!'' She paced across the sagging floorboards. ''I saw Mannie barely fifteen minutes ago. He was planning to help Bart dig a refrigerator out at the homestead this afternoon. He was laughing and looking forward to his picket game with Joe and the others. He can't die just like that!''

Bill took another swig of whiskey. ''That's how it happens, Rosie: just like that. Better he went quick than he lingered. I've seen folk linger. You don't want that for the boy.''

Rosie shook her head as tears welled up. ''No,'' she whispered. ''No, I can't believe it.''

The big Indian stood and went to the weeping woman. For a moment he stood awkwardly beside her, rubbing his meaty, callused palms together in consternation. Then he let out a breath. ''I'll be damned if I ever knew what to do with a leakin' female,'' he muttered. Finally, taking her shoulders, he settled her on the bed and sat down beside her.

For a long time, Rosie couldn't speak. As much as her mind denied it, she knew Cheyenne Bill had spoken the truth. Mannie had been killed. *Killed.* Skinny Mannie with

his red hair and broad grin, his winsome ways and mischievous smile. Why?

"Ain't no good askin' why," Bill said, almost as if he'd
read her thoughts. "You'll addle yer think-box tryin' to
figure it out."

"I can't . . . I just can't accept it." She pulled her
handkerchief from her pocket and blotted her cheeks.
"Mannie just told me . . . just a few minutes ago . . . to
find Bart. He told me to go see Bart and talk to him."

"What fer?"

"Mannie said I could cheer Bart up because he'd been
feeling blue of late. So I decided to go to the stable—"

"There you go! Hell, don't ya git it? Young Manford was
a angel of mercy sent to earth with a message. When he'd
given it, the good Lord called him home."

"Oh, it's not that simple!" Rosie exploded at the beefy
Indian. "Mannie's whole life wasn't based on telling me to
go to the stable and talk to Bart! He had so much potential.
There was so much that boy could have done. He was a
wonderful child, and he would have made a fine man!"

"All the same, I reckon you better heed his advice. You
never know but what I said was true."

"What do you know about angels? You're a . . . a
fighter. A boxer. Your whole life is glove contests, not
religion."

"No doubt about it—I'm a hard, hard man. But anybody
with a lick of sense knows about angels. Here they be, all
around us, fightin' holy wars with the demons of evil."

Rosie gawked and wondered how she could ever manage
to escape this obviously demented man. She eyed the
whiskey bottle on the table. Was Cheyenne Bill just drunk,
or was he legitimately loco?

"Ain't you never seen a angel?" he was asking.

Rosie shook her head. "No. Nor a demon for that
matter."

"Well, maybe I just got my brains scrambled in all them
glove contests, but the fact is, I seen 'em plenty of times.
Both kinds. Take the kid, Mannie, fer starters. You don't
know nothin' about that young'un before he walks into yer

life and makes a change in ya. Gives ya a message. Sets ya on the straight path when you was headin' off the trail. See what I mean?''

Rosie shook her head again. She wondered where Bart was. Would he have any idea that she was here in this decrepit house with a man who belonged in an asylum?

"Angels is angels, and demons is demons," Cheyenne Bill was saying as he paced up and down the creaky floor. He grabbed the whiskey bottle and downed the remainder of the liquor. "Now, take ol' Bart Kingsley. He let the Devil's brood have their way with him fer a while, sure enough. When your pappy told Bart he weren't no good fer ya, that he was just a dumb half-breed who was never gonna amount to a pail of hot spit, that his family tree wasn't no better'n a shrub, that you deserved a rich life with swishin' silks and satins and a man who could keep you sitting on high cotton, ol' Bart began to listen to them demons a-whisperin' over his shoulder."

"What?" Rosie whispered. "Pappy told Bart *that*?"

"Hell, it didn't matter to yer pappy that Bart could get you as hot as a widowed coyote, and that he was all heart above the waist and all guts below. No, sir, all yer pappy could see was that Bart was half Injun and poor as a hind-tit calf."

"What?" Rosie said again.

"Fact is, Bart hightailed it outta yer life and began runnin' with the Devil's brood. Sometimes it takes the good Lord a might of doin' to set a fellow like Bart back on the right trail. So God sent a angel to shoot him in the side."

"That wasn't an *angel* who shot Bart. It was Sheriff Bowman!"

"Don't split hairs with me, gal. Can't you understand this?"

"No, I can't," she answered bluntly.

Giving her a look of pity, Cheyenne opened another bottle of whiskey and took a swallow. "Gal, ain't you never been to church?"

"I *always* go to church. But I understand Reverend Cullen's been after you for quite some time now."

"Now, there's a man who listens to the angels!"

"I'm sorry, but I have to go—"

"Wait a minute! I ain't done explainin' this. How're you gonna know what to do with yerself if you don't understand that Mannie Wade was a angel?" He gave a snort and began absently swinging the whiskey bottle. "Now, me, I listen to the angels. So, see, here's the story: I'm a-walkin' through the woods one day scoutin' me a rabbit fer my stewpot when I up and see this feller leanin' against a tree bleedin' half to death. Lo and behold, I recognize right off he's a half-breed like me. We jaw awhile and he tells me he reckons he's fixin' to ride off to the great beyond, no matter that he just found the only woman he ever loved. On and on, this feller talks till before you know it I'm blubberin' in my whiskey like a newborned babe. Right then I begin to know that this feller is tryin' to set hisself on the right path. He's tryin' to listen to the angels, see?"

Rosie nodded, and realized that for some odd reason she actually understood some of his garbled speech.

"So I aim to help this feller," Cheyenne Bill continued. "I haul him over to my house and we take up together, him and me. We cook us up a story that he's my cousin, just come to town. We get him a job over at the livery stable, and we commence to takin' the folks by storm, ol' Buck Springfield and me."

He laughed and whirled around, his arms spread wide. "But we was listenin' to the angels, see! So everything works out *perfect*. Then you and him get together, and things is just pretty as peaches . . . till you up and move out on him. Don't you understand, missy, that you wasn't supposed to do that? That weren't part of the plan, see?"

Rosie edged toward the door. "No one ever told me there was a plan."

"Ain't you been heedin' the Reverend Cullen on Sunday mornin's? *Of course* there's a plan. A grand and mighty plan. But you up and wandered away from it. So the good Lord sent a angel to set you straight. A angel by the name of Manford Wade."

"Are you saying that Mannie got killed because of me?"

"Hell, why would I say a thing like that? I'm just tellin' you that Mannie gave you a message, and you better take note. Get on back to Bart where you belong. If that husband of yers is gonna be able to keep on listenin' to angels, he needs you by his side. Fact is, them demons has got loud voices, young lady. Mighty loud. But when Bart Kingsley looks at you, all he ever sees is the angels. Now get home to him, gal. You hear?"

"I'm no angel," Rosie said. "I never have been."

"Hell, don't I know it. What I see when I look at you is a regular woman—pretty as a picture, but scared and ornery, too. But then I ain't in love with you. Bart Kingsley is."

"In love with me." She repeated the words.

"You don't think a man would trek over half the territory, get hisself shot, risk his neck movin' into a town where he was a wanted man, settle a homestead, and plant sugar beets when he'd have a lot better luck robbin' a train for cash—all that—if he weren't in love, do ya?"

"Well . . ." Rosie grabbed the door handle with a damp palm and gave a push. "Well . . . well, good afternoon, Mr. . . . Mr. Cheyenne Bill."

Grinning his lopsided grin, the Indian tipped his hat. "Evenin' to you, too, ma'am. It's been a real pleasure socializin' with you."

*Sixteen
· ·

She had just arrived at the schoolhouse when Rosie saw Bart round the corner in his wagon. Lifting her skirts, she ran toward him. Spotting her, he pulled the horses to a halt, leapt down from the board, and scooped her up in his arms.

"Oh, Rosie-girl," he whispered into her neck, and his words were almost a groan. "He's gone, Rosie. Mannie's truly gone."

"Bart!" she cried. They turned around and around, each wrapped in private grief, yet their tears mingled and their chests heaved as one with racking sobs. "How can it be, Bart?"

He shook his head. "Oh, God, Rosie, I don't know."

As he spoke, Mrs. Kilgore hurried out of the house toward them. "I've packed you a bag, Mrs. Springfield. We've canceled school until after the funeral on Wednesday. Go on home with you, now, honey. You need the rest."

Rosie gazed into the woman's red-rimmed blue eyes. "Thank you, Mrs. Kilgore."

"Hurry now, before the sun goes down and the coyotes come out."

Her words moved Bart to action, and he swept Rosie up into the wagon. Taking his place beside her, he flicked the reins and set the horses trotting down the street.

They were halfway to the homestead before either could speak. Rosie never knew she held so many tears, but the more she tried to stifle them, the faster they flowed. Her nose turned red, and her eyes swelled almost shut. If she had been sick before, she felt ten times worse now. All she could

261

think about was little Mannie and his big grin. Every time she shut her eyes, she saw his cluttered school desk, his inkwell and tattered books, his spiky red hair, his ragged patchwork cap, his green suspenders, his ill-formed Spencerian *B*, and his bright eyes. Then she had to accept that he was gone. Mannie was gone.

"What did the doctors say?" she asked finally.

"There was nothing they could do. He was gone by the time I got him home."

"Did he suffer?"

Bart shook his head. "That job's left to us."

Again, many miles passed before either could speak. Then Bart's words rose up without preamble. "I swear I'd kill Charley Baker if I could get my hands on him."

"Bart!"

"Don't look at me like that, Rosie. So would every other man in town. That sidewinder should have checked his target now and then to make sure the board behind it was holding up. Any half-wit could have guessed it would get shot through—the board was only an inch thick. And Baker sure should have known a twenty-two-caliber target rifle would soon cut a hole in the board. If I'd been running a shooting gallery, I'd have put a sheet of iron behind the target. Any damn fool knows a pine board—no matter how thick—is going to give way in time. Page Palmiter told me he and some of the other men found sixteen bullets lodged in the wall of the jewelry store at the end of the alley. Sixteen!"

"All the same," Rosie said softly, "killing Charley Baker wouldn't bring Mannie back."

"Maybe not, but it would make me feel one hell of a lot better."

She sniffled and dabbed her handkerchief under her eyes. "Cheyenne Bill took me to his house."

Bart sat up straight. "His house? When?"

"While you were at Mrs. Wade's."

"I'll be damned. He didn't make you drink any of that home-brewed rotgut of his, did he?"

"He tried. I couldn't get down more than a swallow, but he was drinking plenty himself."

"I reckon he was talking about angels, then."

Rosie lifted her head. "How did you know?"

"Angels are Cheyenne Bill's favorite subject when he's hitting the hard stuff. Personally I think he's been whacked on the noggin a few too many times."

"He believes Mannie was an angel sent to tell me to go home with you today."

"Does he, now?" Bart shook his head. "Well, maybe Bill has a point. I never knew a better kid than Mannie was. If there ever was an angel on earth, it was Mannie Wade."

"Cheyenne Bill told me how he found you in the woods after you'd left my dormitory room. He said the two of you cooked up the idea to tell everyone in Raton that you're cousins."

Bart gave the hint of a smile. "Bill's a good man, Rosie. A little off center on some things, but harmless as a fly. That's why the whole town loves him so, and he's why they've accepted me. Sure, he swaggers and drinks too much and he's so fierce he wins just about every glove contest in the area, yet the townsfolk invite him to their kids' birthday parties and to every neighborhood picnic they hold. They've made him leader of the hose company, and they write poems about him in the *Comet*. You just mention his name, and everyone sings out his favorite boast: 'Cheyenne Bill is a hard, hard man.' Fact is, I couldn't have a better pal."

Rosie fell silent. There were many things she wanted to clear up with Bart—such as Cheyenne Bill's revelation about the way her pappy had treated Bart many years before—but she couldn't summon up the energy to speak of the past. It was odd how small and inconsequential such things seemed now, in light of Mannie's death.

Issues that once had been so utterly important now meant almost nothing. What did it matter if the Ratonians found out about Bart's checkered past? Let them hem and haw about having a former outlaw in town. Bart was a good man now. Why had she ever thought she needed to run away from him and make her own life? Surely it hadn't taken the death of a little boy to make her see that love and communion and relationships were far more important in this world than having a teaching job or a clapboard house or a pristine reputation.

As the wagon topped the hill and Rosie could see the silhouette of the low dugout walls, she felt yet another pang of grief deep inside her heart. This farm had been one of Mannie's favorite places—and Bart had been his favorite man.

"Mannie thought the world of you, Bart," she said when he had pulled the wagon up to the barn. "He admired you so. I do believe he thought you were just next to God Himself."

Bart gazed at the indigo mesas in the distance. "He told me once that he wished . . ." He stopped speaking and swallowed several times, fighting the emotion. "Mannie told me he wished I was his papa."

At the memory of that tender moment, Bart rolled his big shoulders forward and covered his eyes with his hand. "Oh, God, oh God, Rosie, I should've made him come out to the farm with me earlier today. I shouldn't have let him play picket. I should've . . . I wish . . ."

Rosie wrapped her slender arms around the broad expanse of his back and rested her head against his shoulder while he wept. The gentleness of Bart's character suddenly came to her in a flood of remembrance—cats sitting on his lap while he ate lunch, horses nickering with pleasure as he walked through the stables, the deep cuts of the taunting children. Bart was a man like no other she had ever known. He felt pain more deeply, and he loved more fiercely.

If her father really had said the things Cheyenne Bill had accused him of, no wonder Bart had fled from her. And if Cheyenne Bill insisted that Bart loved her—maybe he really did.

"Bart," she whispered. "Oh, Bart." If it was possible to cradle a massive bullock of a man, Rosie managed it with her grieving husband. For a long time she held him, rocking slowly back and forth on the wagon seat while the horses grazed. She ran her fingers through the long black hair at the back of his neck and stroked the taut muscles of his shoulders and arms. Gently she kissed his cheek and rubbed the side of her face against his.

"Don't go off again, Rosie," he murmured finally. "I want you here with me. Don't you see that? I took care of Mannie the best I could and, by heaven, I'll take care of you."

"I know, Bart." She moved into him as his arms came around her and his hands covered her waist. "I shouldn't have stayed away. I shouldn't have been so scared."

"Nobody's going to get me. Nobody's going to tear us apart. You've got to believe that, Rosie. There's nothing, *nothing*, more important in this world than you and me and what we've built between us. Life's too damn short not to spend it with the person you love."

"Bart, do you love me? Do you truly love me?"

"Hell, girl, don't you know that by now?" He cupped her face and tilted it to the moonlight. "I love you so much, nothing can take me away from you again. Don't you see how it is? Once, I ran off because I thought it was for the best. Then you ran off because you thought it was best. It's not other people who come between us, Rosie; it's *us*. We keep tearing this thing apart. Why? Why do we do that?"

Rosie's shoulders sagged. "Bart, it's not you and I who are doing it. It *is* other folk. Cheyenne Bill told me what Pappy said to you that day after he found out we'd gotten married. That was why you ran away from me, wasn't it? Pappy drove you off."

"I'll be jiggered," Bart muttered. "I told Bill to keep that business quiet."

"Well, he didn't, and now I know how it really came about. Pappy ran you off with all his talk about you being no good for me."

Bart kissed Rosie's cheek and rubbed his nose against the soft strands of brown hair that had tumbled down over her shoulder. "I don't want you ever to blame your pappy for what happened back then. He was just doing what he thought best for you. Besides, he was right. I didn't have a single fine thing to offer you as a husband. You deserved a hell of a lot better than what I had to give.''

''What about your love? That was more than enough for me, Bart!''

''Lord, Rosie, I loved you back then, and I love you now.'' He clutched her and kissed her fully on the mouth. ''Stick close, girl. Now and always.''

''Oh, Bart, I will!'' Her heart full, Rosie met his ardent kisses with an equal passion. She'd been so long absent from this man, it was all she could do to keep from crying aloud with need.

As his mouth claimed her, their tongues met in a wild dance of abandon. His hands worked over her body, cupping and squeezing her shoulders, breasts, hips, thighs, as though to make certain she was real.

Equally hungry, she allowed her fingers to search out the warm skin beneath his collar and the broad, hard muscles of his chest. ''Take me inside, Bart, I've been needing you so much.''

His mouth moved over her neck and cheek and ear with a sweet dampness as he lifted her out of the wagon and carried her across the moonlit yard and down the steps to the front door. Inside the dugout, he laid her on their bed and allowed his big body to cover her. As they lay, kissing and groping, he thought he might pass out from the pleasure of this woman. Her breasts seemed fuller to him than ever before as they swelled against his chest. She wrapped her long legs around his buttocks and pulled them tightly into the small mound of her pelvis. Her breath tasted faintly of the whiskey, and her skin smelled like roses.

With the scent of her drifting over him, intoxicating him, he unbuttoned her dress and began to suck and circle and torment her bare nipples until her hips thrust rhythmically beneath him.

''Bart, oh, Bart!'' she gasped, tearing at his shirt and fumbling with his belt. ''Touch me, Bart, before I faint with the need of you.''

She was wild beneath him, and he hurried to obey the frantic plea. Lifting her skirt, he jerked down her blousy

cotton panties to expose the tender nest of dark curls. His
fingers slid over and inside her, easing, yet raising her need.
Breathing in quick gasps, she tore open the button fly of his
trousers and released him full into her hands.

"I've dreamed of you every night, Bart," she moaned as
she stroked his rigid shaft. "I couldn't bear thinking we'd
never be this way again."

"I needed you so much, but I didn't want to rush you. I
tried to be patient."

"Don't be patient with me now, Bart. Come inside me
where you belong."

Obeying, he spread her thighs with a tingling stroke from
her knees inward. For a moment he hovered over her,
allowing himself to play with the tender damp cushions of
her body. But when she slipped her hands over his bare
buttocks and pulled him toward her, he gave in and entered
her with a thrust that filled her with a wrenching passion.

Crying aloud, she began to rise and fall with him in a
mesmerizing rhythm that lifted them both to unrealized
heights. She stroked herself with her fingertips as his shaft
penetrated and dandled her. His body broke into a sweat,
and his breath became rough and strained.

"I love to watch you touch yourself, Rosie," he whispered as they worked her body into a throbbing pitch. He
bent and lapped at her breasts until her nipples stood out like
shiny red cherries tingling with almost unbearable jolts of
shivering lightning.

When she reached around between his thighs and took his
weighty sac in her hands, he groaned aloud. She began to
gently fondle, teasing the sensitive bulge as he moved in and
out of her. Her hands slipped to his thighs and around over
his smooth buttocks, then traveled back to stroke herself.

She could see him above her, his head thrown back and
his long hair falling onto the straining muscles of his chest.
Oh, he was a beautiful man. His green eyes were lifted
heavenward as he reveled in their union. And then she
raised her head and began to run her tongue around in
circles over the flat brown circles of his nipples. Like tiny

bits of gravel, their tips hardened, and she took them, nipping softly.

"Rosie!" he cried out her name as her head arched backward against the pillow. At the same moment that his body convulsed and exploded inside her, she slipped over the edge of her own dream. For a long time she lost him as waves coursed through her in shuddering, quaking release that lit her body as bright as a torch. From the tips of her toes to the peaks of her breasts, she writhed, prolonging the pleasure that was centered between her thighs.

Then the undulations lessened in their intensity, her body began to surface from the engulfing sea, and she stretched beneath the heavy body that had crushed the breath from her chest. Unmoving, still as a stone, Bart lay atop her.

"Bart?" she whispered.

He turned his head and dampened the side of her neck. "Rosie-girl, I love you better than life itself."

She smiled, wrapped her arms around his chest, and allowed her eyelids to drift shut.

There was a time when it hadn't seemed possible to Bart that he would ever have his Rosie so near his heart again. But as time passed he began to believe that he had been wrong.

Rosie let her option on the house elapse. She took Mr. Kilgore's advice and used her savings to buy a small buggy and a gentle horse. Early each morning she drove her rig to town while Bart rode just ahead on his stallion. At the school she continued to teach the children she had come to love as if they were her own. The death of Manford Wade had affected everyone deeply, and it took time for the students to resume their normal carefree behavior. But eventually they were back to their usual antics, and their teacher was obliged to cook up a whole new round of after-school punishments.

Bart's sugar beet crop promised a good income. Thanks to his careful thinning, good irrigation, and diligent prevention of blister beetles, leaf spot, black root, root rot, and curly top, the plants had flourished. During the cool nights and warm days of the New Mexico summer, the long, fleshy silver-white taproots were growing toward a prime weight of two pounds or more each. Their crowns had sent out brilliantly rich greens, each leaf a good two feet long. Bart planned to sell the protein-rich leaves for cattle feed and the crowns as food for all types of livestock. The farm demanded so much of his time and energy that he knew he would soon have to quit his stable job just to keep up with his own fields.

With Rosie's earnings, they bought another milk cow and the lumber to build a two-bedroom addition onto the top of their dugout. Bart finished digging the refrigerator alone and gradually filled it with venison, wild turkey, quail, and rabbit. The kitchen garden began to yield a bountiful harvest, and the eggs Rosie sold in town brought in enough extra income to fence off the garden from hungry varmints.

Rosie started to grow healthier almost right away. With Bart's teasing and her own comforting home so close at hand, she perked right up. As she felt better, her worries about Bart being carted off to jail subsided for the most part, and the "newlyweds" began to make their presence felt at the Gate City's social functions.

May brought frequent rain, but they drove into town on the twenty-first for the grand charity ball at McAuliffe's and Ferguson's Hall. The New Mexico Live Stock Association hosted a ranch dinner four days later, and Bart and Rosie ate their fill of baked pike, boiled mutton, capers, roast beef, brown potatoes, stewed tomatoes, sweet corn, chicken, and a desert of blancmange, ice cream, and cake.

The *Comet* announced that the building of the new Atchison, Topeka and Santa Fe Railway passenger depot would commence within two weeks. The cattle roundup in the area ended. And, sadly, on the fifth day of June, Sheriff Bowman died suddenly of a lung hemorrhage. He had been married scarcely two years and was but thirty-six years old.

Although the town mourned the county lawman, it quickly turned its sights to more uplifting news, such as the new soda fountain that was being added at O. C. Huffman's, where Rosie bought her favorite cream candies. As sympathetic as Rosie felt toward the sheriff's young widow, she couldn't deny her relief that any investigation of Bart's background would surely cease.

The rain ended, and the town began to gear up for a hot summer. By mid-June three men had tossed in their hats for the vacant position of county sheriff. Thike Stockton, Wally Wallace, and George Geer all hoped to wear the silver badge, and Rosie made sure to find out how much each of them knew about a James gang outlaw, Bart Kingsley, who had passed through Raton earlier that spring.

As Bart's sugar beets grew and Rosie's children learned their parts for the recital, the town sailed along on an even keel, a mixture of scandal and blissful anticipation creating a healthy potpourri. Though engineer Robert Henderson was shot and killed by a man whose wife he had slandered, Senator Stephen Dorsey was acquitted of mail fraud in the Star Route trial. A big hunt was scheduled for late June, a town football club was formed, and plans were made for the coming Fourth of July celebrations.

With all these public events to attend, Rosie decided it was high time for Bart to work on his manners. She stitched up shirts, trousers, and ties, and taught him to wear them properly. As she learned to cook, she taught him how to eat bluepoint oysters on the half shell, English pea soup au gratin, roast sirloin of beef au jus and salmi of duck.

At night in bed they rehearsed polite conversations about the weather, current local and national news, and the state of political affairs—anything to keep Bart from regaling polite company with his favorite ribald jokes, as he had been known to do on more than one occasion. Usually, however, Rosie's nightly lessons on morals and manners deteriorated into teasing and laughter, tickling and playing, and finally long forays into succulent purple ardor.

On Sundays they went to church. They even managed to haul a grumbling Cheyenne Bill along with them. Rosie agreed to teach Sunday school, and Bart volunteered to landscape the church property.

In fact, Rosie realized one noon as she was driving her horse and buggy away from the schoolhouse, she and Bart had settled into a life so full of contentment and peace that it almost frightened her. Every day held more promise than she'd ever known in her life. Each night in Bart's arms she felt more and more at ease with the world they were building.

In fact, the only wrinkle in the whole picture was her health. Due to Mannie's death, she had missed her earlier appointment with Dr. Kohlhouser but now today she had scheduled a quick lunchtime visit just to clear things up. While the children played tag and picket under the supervision of Mr. Kilgore, Rosie drove her buggy to the doctor's office and pulled it up outside the small frame building. She hitched her skirts up over her ankles and climbed down. After lapping the reins over the hitching post, she bent to give Griff a pat on his massive head, then stepped over the dog and pushed the door open.

"Well, Mrs. Springfield," the physician greeted her as she entered the office. "What can I do for you today?"

She gave the burly man a smile and accompanied him into his examining room. "Thank you so much for seeing me at noon, Dr. Kohlhouser. I've been putting off this appointment far too long."

"No trouble at all. Glad to do it." He gestured to a chair, and she seated herself demurely, hands in her lap. "Now, how would you describe this problem you've been having, Mrs. Springfield?" Picking up a notebook, he adjusted his spectacles and stared at her.

She took a deep breath. "It's a . . . a feminine problem, sir."

"I see. Of what nature?"

"Well," Rosie said with a flush, "I was ill some time ago, and ever since then my monthly flow seems to have stopped altogether."

"What sort of illness did you suffer?"

"I suppose it was influenza of the stomach variety. I was quite nauseated for several weeks, you see. That went away finally, but my cycles never resumed."

He lifted his head and gave her a tender smile. "I'm

assuming, therefore, that you believe you may be with child?''

''What?'' Rosie sat up, startled. ''Oh, no, of course not. That's quite impossible. I can't have children, you see.''

''You can't? How do you know?''

Rosie fiddled with the folds of her skirts. She had known this was going to be difficult, but she hadn't expected it to be quite so hard. Finally she cleared her throat. ''I was . . . I was married once before.''

''I see.'' He made a note in his book.

''I trust this is a confidential conversation, Dr. Kohlhouser.''

''Of course, Mrs. Springfield. And when did your former husband pass away?''

Rosie glanced at the doctor's desk, wishing for a fan. ''He . . . um . . . didn't. Pass away, I mean. The marriage . . . it ended.''

The doctor was staring at her with a new look on his face, a look of utter disapproval. ''So, you are a *divorced* woman?''

''I am a married woman,'' she snapped. ''Mr. Springfield is my husband, and that's all there is to it. The point is, because of my past experience, I know I can't conceive. So will you please tell me what's the matter with me?''

He placed his notebook on his leg and tapped the tip of his pen against it, making small blue dots. ''I'm going to have to ask you some more questions, Mrs. Springfield— about your first marriage.''

She bristled. ''I don't see why. That is none of your business.''

''It certainly is if I'm to learn why your monthly cycles have ceased.''

Rosie sank back into the chair. The last thing she wanted to have to recall at a time like this was her horrible marriage to Dr. Lowell. In fact, she had put that part of her past so far from her thoughts, she was reluctant to dredge it up.

''How long were you married before, Mrs. Springfield?'' Dr. Kohlhouser asked.

''For three years,'' she answered glumly.

"And I'm assuming you had a normal conjugal relationship with your first husband."

"Yes." But what she really thought was how different, how *abnormal* that experience seemed in comparison to her lovemaking with Bart.

"In those three years of marriage, did you ever conceive or did you ever experience the symptoms you're experiencing now—nausea, followed by cessation of your menstrual cycle?"

"No. I never did. And I went to several doctors, too. They all said the same thing—I'm barren."

"Will you permit me to send to these physicians for your medical records, Mrs. Springfield?"

"Absolutely not." Just the thought of contacting men who would rush to her husband and tell him where she was sent a chill into Rosie's bones. "That's all in the past. Why don't you simply take what I say as fact, Dr. Kohlhouser, and then tell me what else could be wrong with me?"

He shrugged. "I'll try my best. But a healthy young married woman with your symptoms certainly would seem to call for a diagnosis of gravidity."

"I'm not going to have a baby," Rosie whispered. "I can't. Please don't mention it again."

At the look on her face, the doctor's own visage fell into tender lines, and he patted Rosie's knotted hands. "There now, I know how very much you do love little ones, Mrs. Springfield. Your work with the school has been exemplary. I'll see what I can do for you."

Rosie bared herself to the humiliation of a thorough exam. All the while, the doctor questioned her about the size and tenderness of her breasts, the color of her nipples, the appearance of her cervix. Had this or that changed? Was she always so emotional? Had her husband noticed anything different? Finally he allowed her to dress, then asked her to accompany him to his study.

"Mrs. Springfield," he said when she was seated in yet another chair, "I can arrive at only one diagnosis, and it's based on twenty-five years of medical practice. You are with child."

A tingle washed down Rosie's spine as she stared at him. "Are you sure?"

"As certain as I can possibly be. You have every classic symptom. Based on what you've told me, I would say you're about two months along. Maybe more. If I'm correct, you'll deliver sometime around . . . oh, next January."

Rosie couldn't speak.

"Now, I could be wrong."

"Yes," Rosie breathed, certain he must be, and fearful he might.

"I could be mistaken, and you'll deliver in December. Or February. We'll know better as you progress."

"But I . . . I . . ."

"If I were a betting man, Mrs. Springfield—and I am—I'd swear you're going to have yourself a baby in a few months. I've been wrong only twice in my career, and I've delivered nigh onto three hundred babies."

"A baby . . ." she whispered.

"Congratulations. I hope you're happy."

"Happy! Of course—oh, a baby!" Rosie jumped out of her chair and ran to the window. She felt light-headed, fairly dancing with joy. But when she looked out at the reality of the bustling street, she had to turn again to the doctor. "How?" she asked. "How can I possibly have conceived, Dr. Kohlhouser? All those doctors examined me, and they were good men, too. Friends of my husband. Well, he examined me himself, and he should know—he's a doctor, too."

Thunderstruck, Dr. Kohlhouser stared at Rosie. "Your first husband was a physician? And he diagnosed you as barren?"

She nodded. "So did all his friends."

He cleared his throat. "Did any of them ever examine your husband, Mrs. Springfield? Just to make certain that *he* wasn't the cause of the infertility?"

"Oh, no." She shook her head. "It couldn't have been him. He's a very . . . forceful . . . strong-willed man."

"A man's *character* has nothing whatsoever to do with his production of the male seed, Mrs. Springfield." He adjusted his spectacles again. "I am going to record my assumption, therefore, that your first husband was unable to provide you with children due, in all probability, to a problem with the quantity or viability of his spermatozoa. Your second husband, on the other hand, has no trouble whatsoever in that realm. And you, Mrs. Springfield, are as fertile as the good springtime earth."

Rosie's hands slipped down over her belly. For a long moment she stood in silence, trying to absorb the doctor's words. She had conceived. Through their loving, she and Bart had created a child. Even now the living baby was growing inside her body—developing, strengthening, forming into a beautiful child, the essence of each of its parents.

"A baby," she murmured again. "A baby."

Dr. Kohlhouser laughed. "Or maybe two. Now, Mrs. Springfield, here's what I want you to do."

She listened in a fog as he explained how important it was that she rest and eat properly during the months to come. She mustn't wear herself out, and she must take in plenty of fresh air. In spite of fashion, she mustn't corset herself too tightly; she had to allow the baby room to grow and expand. She mustn't be alone much, and toward the end she should move into town to be close to the doctor when her time came.

"Yes," Rosie replied to everything he said. "Yes, yes, of course."

But as she walked out the front door, her head might as well have been a blank slate. She was going to have a *baby*!

Forgetting all about her horse, her afternoon classes, and the doctor's admonitions, she began running down the street toward the stables. Bart! She must tell him right away. How happy he'd be! Oh, she couldn't wait to see the expression on his face when she told him they were going to have a child of their very own!

"Bart!" she murmured aloud as she rounded the corner of the depot. "Bart, a baby!" She whispered the refrain as she ran across the platform in front of the Harvey House, oblivious of the late lunch train and the arrival of the passengers who were startled at the sight of a woman hurtling past them, her blue dress flying around her knees, her booted feet churning.

"Bart!" she shouted as she pounded up the ramp into the livery stable. "Bart, where are you?"

"Rosie!" He emerged from the shadows and caught her before she could slam into him. "Rosie, what in the hell are you doing here?"

His voice was harsh, angry, and as cold as steel. She blinked at him, trying to fathom the hard look on his face. At the same time, it dawned on her that he was hiding something. Something he didn't want her to know about.

"Bart?" she asked, flashes of secret liaisons with women or covert illegal transactions or criminal plots darting through her mind one after the other. "Bart? What's going on?"

"So this is the little woman you've been telling me about," a man announced, striding out into the middle of the stable. "Rosie, is it?"

She stared at a face worn into crags, at blue eyes hard and glittering. "Who are you?"

"Ain't you told her about me, Injun?" the man asked, jabbing Bart in the side with his drawn gun. "You better introduce us, pal."

Breathing hard, Bart pushed the barrel of the six-shooter away from his once-injured side. "Rosie, this is a partner of mine from a long time back. We used to run together in the old days. His name's Bob Ford. Bob . . . Bob is the man who killed Jesse James."

"Not only that, but I saved Bart's butt from a bullet a time or two." As he spoke, two more men emerged from the shadows. "And now me and my buddies have come to town to pay you folks a friendly visit. For old times' sake, if you know what I mean."

As Rosie turned to Bart, Bob Ford began to laugh.

*Seventeen
. . . .

"Rosie, get on back to the schoolhouse," Bart said, his voice still hard. "And stay with the Kilgores tonight. We'll talk in the morning when I come to work."

"Hell, you mean we rode all this way and we ain't gonna get us a home-cooked meal?" Bob complained. "Now listen here, Miz Kingsley, don't pay your husband no heed. You head on home tonight and whip us up somethin' dandy to eat. We been livin' on frijoles and tortillas for almost a month now."

Rosie glanced at Bart. To the best of her knowledge, she'd never seen him truly angry until this moment. Now she understood, just by the stance of his body, what had become of men who had tried to cross him. His bare biceps were bunched and knotted into bulging mountains. Big fists clenched, his knuckles had gone white as bone. The muscle in his square jaw worked as he gritted his teeth, and his eyes sparkled with a burning green flame.

"I told my wife to go on back to work, Ford, and she'll do as I say," he growled. His head snapped toward Rosie, but his eyes stayed on the intruder. "Get out of here, woman. *Now.*"

Her hand protectively covering her stomach, she started for the door. But when she had crossed into the shaft of afternoon sunlight, she stopped and swung around to address Bob Ford. "Tell me one thing," she demanded. "I want to know how you found Bart."

"Shoot, that's easy. Injun writ a letter to Frank James a couple months back. Frank mentioned the news to some of

277

the other boys, and word leaked around. Now everybody knows where he's been hidin' out."

Rosie stopped breathing. "Everybody?"

"Damn right."

"Watch your language in front of my woman, Ford," Bart cut in. "She's no lowlife like you."

"I ain't a lowlife, Injun. I'm famous, don't ya know?"

"Yeah, you pulled the trigger on Jesse. That sets you real high in people's books."

Bob frowned. "For your information, Injun, I *am* famous. I'm makin' a name for myself as the man who shot the most wanted outlaw in the United States of America. Hell, once I get rollin', folks will line up and pay good money just to get a gander at me. I'm fixin' to get plumb rich off my reputation."

"Well, why don't you get your famous butt out of Raton and take it someplace where people give a damn?"

"Watch *your* language, Injun!" Bob hooted, and his two companions joined in the laughter. Sobering after a moment, the outlaw nodded at Rosie. "Don't worry, Miz Kingsley, we ain't gonna cause you folk no trouble. We just got tired of Las Vegas and thought we'd head over your way to visit a spell. Ain't that right, boys?"

"Tired of gettin' run out of places on account of your famous reputation, Ford," one of them countered. Then he tipped his grimy hat at Rosie. "They call me Snort, and this here's Fancy. Pleased to meet ya, Miz Kingsley."

Rosie gave the two men a quick scrutiny. Snort, a skinny brown-haired fellow with a big nose and an enormous walrus mustache, wore a pair of six-shooters strapped to his thighs and cradled a rifle in his arms. Fancy, the dirtiest, greasiest, smelliest man Rosie had ever laid eyes on, had a mane of thick black hair and a stomach twice the size of his hips.

"Good afternoon, gentlemen," she greeted them in as polite a tone as she could muster. "Bart, I'd like to speak with you a moment, please."

"Better do what the lady says, Injun," Bob admonished.

"You don't want to get yourself in trouble with the law now, boy."

Accompanied by derisive laughter, Bart strode across the stable and took Rosie by the elbow. As soon as he had hauled her outside, he placed his big hands on her shoulders and gave her a quick shake.

"I want you to stay away from the homestead, Rosie," he whispered firmly. "Don't even think about going out there. It's clear Ford's not having much success at cashing in on killing Jesse, and he may even be on the dodge from the law. The boys may want to stay at our place a few days, but I'll run 'em off as quick as I can."

"Bart, that man could ruin you!"

"My reputation's the least of my worries, girl. No telling what these fellows have up their sleeves."

"But what if the law finds out about you? They'll come for you and take you away to Missouri, and they'll *hang* you."

"Rosie, stop worrying about that and let me handle things. Now just get on over to the school and act like nothing's going on. I'll let the boys ride out to the homestead and stay with me for a couple of days. I'll feed 'em up good and liquor 'em down, and then I'll send 'em packing. It'll be all right. But I don't want you around, hear? They're rough men. Killers."

"Oh, Bart!"

"They're not going to kill *me*, Rosie. I'm their pal." He shook his head and studied the cloudless sky for a moment. "I'm their damn *pal*."

"Bart, there are things I need to talk to you about. Important things. I need to tell you—"

"We'll talk later, darlin'. Now go on, before Ford and his sidewinder buddies get itchy feet."

He gave her a little push that sent her down the ramp. On the platform she turned to call him, but Bart had already vanished back inside the stable. Breathless, she stood immobilized for a moment as passengers and baggage boys scurried around her. Then, without warning, the stable's side door slid open, and four men on horseback thundered

down the ramp. As they galloped out of town in a cloud of
dust, Rosie realized that one of them was Bart.

Having blamed her tardy return on the doctor visit,
Rosie managed to get through the rest of the school day. She
claimed an illness she truly felt, and the Kilgores were more
than happy to put her up for the night. The next three days,
however, were an endless hell.

Rosie couldn't concentrate on her teaching, and though
Bart had promised to come to her, he didn't. She went to the
livery stable after school one day and learned from the
stable owner that Bart hadn't come back to work since he'd
ridden away with the "friends" who'd come to visit. As
much as the man had hated to do it, he said, he had been
forced to replace Bart on the job.

If Rosie had briefly dreamed of a happy family—herself,
Bart, and their baby—she discarded that image the moment
she realized the seriousness of her situation. The men who
had invaded her life were outlaws. Killers, Bart had said.
And although Bart had denied it, Bob Ford *was* famous.
There wasn't a soul in the Territory who hadn't heard of the
killing of Jesse James by a member of his own gang. If Bob
Ford made Bart's background known to the town, that
would be the end of everything.

Sick at heart, Rosie drew the curtains in her classroom
that hot Friday afternoon after the children had gone home
for the weekend. The blue light dampened the usual cheer
that seemed to settle in the quiet room at the end of every
day. After dusting off her texts, she drew her summer shawl
around her shoulders and tried to imagine what Bart was
doing.

Had he been too worried about exposing himself to return
to town? She knew he wouldn't easily give up the livery
stable job that had supported them so well, not when the
sugar beets were still this far from harvest. But what if he
had been kidnapped by those outlaws and taken off to
participate in some heinous crime—a bank or train robbery?

Straightening desks as she went along, Rosie made her
way to the door. What if Bart wasn't even out at their

homestead anymore? Maybe the lure of the old life had drawn him away. What if he'd just gone off and left the cows swollen with milk and the chickens unfed? Bart wouldn't do a thing like that . . . would he?

Maybe Bob Ford had killed him! Maybe he'd shot Bart to get the money they'd saved and buried beneath the cottonwood tree by the stream . . . or lynched him for refusing to go along with him and his boys on some outlaw scheme . . . or strangled him in an argument.

If Bob Ford would shoot Jesse James in the back of the head for reward money, what would keep him from doing the same to Bart? Dead or alive, Bart was worth fifty dollars!

"Dear God!" Rosie prayed as she ran out of the school yard. She had been so preoccupied with the news about the baby, the attempt to conduct her lessons with some semblance of normalcy, and the worry about why Bart hadn't shown up that her mind hadn't sorted through everything clearly. Until now. Bart was probably dead—killed for the fifty-dollar reward!

Rosie rushed into the house beside the school and grabbed Mr. Kilgore's rifle from the top of the cupboard in the kitchen. Just as Mrs. Kilgore was descending the stairs, Rosie flew out the back door. Faster than she ever had, she hitched up the buggy, climbed onto the seat, and whipped the horse into a trot.

"Mrs. Springfield!" Mrs. Kilgore called from the kitchen door. "What's the matter? Where are you going?"

Rosie turned briefly and gave the kind woman a quick wave. "I'm going home for my husband! If I'm not back Monday morning, send a deputy out to the homestead."

"A deputy? Oh, my!"

But Rosie had already rounded the corner and was speeding out of town. The poor, mild-mannered mare didn't know what had gotten into her mistress as Rosie drove like a demon along the rutted trail. The buggy bounced and jounced into ruts and over hummocks. Rosie's hair tumbled from its knot, fell around her shoulders, and slid down her back. Her stomach began to ache and then to tighten, and then to cramp. Oblivious, she crashed through the forests and up the bumpy track. The buggy seat swayed, its springs tossing her this way and that with the unfamiliar speed.

Perspiration streamed down Rosie's temples. Her dress dampened and stuck to her body. Her corset seemed to pierce her fragile ribs and pelvis. The cramping in her stomach increased in intensity, but still she didn't stop.

"Bart," she cried as she finally drove the mare up the last hill toward the dugout. "Bart, please, please don't be dead!"

When she crested the rise, she could see the light of lamps burning in the paper windows. The sight calmed her a little, but she kept the horse at a canter until the buggy was almost up to the dugout.

At the sound of the creaking wagon and the mare's hoofbeats, the front door flew open and three men dashed up the stairs.

"Rosie!"

"Bart!" She recognized him right away, though he was in silhouette. "Bart, you're alive!"

After catching the mare's reins, he set the buggy brake. "Rosie, what are you doing here? Didn't I tell you to stay gone?"

Though his words admonished her, his voice was soft with relief. He lifted his arms, and Rosie slipped down into them. "Bart, I was so worried about you. You said you'd come back to town, but you didn't. Your boss gave your job away to somebody else! And I've been sick with fear."

"Aw, Rosie," he held her, and she could smell the hint of whiskey on his breath. "I thought I told you not to worry. Everything's going to be all right."

"How can you say that? Those men are still here, aren't they? You've lost your job. And I'm . . . I'm . . ." Convulsing with a sudden sharp pain, she bent over double. "Oh, Bart!"

"Rosie? What is it?"

"Bart, I'm sick. I'm—"

"Oh, darlin'." He picked her up in his arms and pushed past Fancy and Snort, who had been standing at watch through the whole thing. "Get your damn hides down there and put fresh sheets on the bed," Bart growled at the two men. They sprang into action, following him into the house.

"Well, if it ain't the missus!" Bob Ford rose from the little table Bart had built. Swaying, he held up a half-empty whiskey bottle. "'Bout time we had a woman to entertain us."

"Shut up, Ford," Bart barked. "Rosie's sick."

"Sick? Hell, how're we gonna have a fandango with a sick woman? I'm in the mood to kick up my heels, and I sure ain't gonna do with it *you*, Injun."

"You're not going to do it with my wife, either." Bart laid her gently on the rumpled sheets and knelt beside her, taking her hand in his. "What's ailing you, Rosie?"

"Oh, Bart," she whispered. "My stomach hurts. It really hurts. You may have to fetch Dr. Kohlhouser."

His green eyes narrowed. "Fetch the doc? Rosie, what's wrong?"

Biting her lip, she forced her eyes away. How could she tell him about their baby now—here in the midst of this chaos? In the past three days, their tidy little house had been turned upside down. The table was littered with empty whiskey bottles. The floor was buried under an inch of dust and trash. The room smelled of rotting food, liquor, and unbathed men.

"Rosie?" Bart asked as he shook her shoulder lightly.

When she looked at him again, what she saw startled her. Gone was the clean-shaven man whose broad shoulders haunted her dreams. Bart looked almost as bad as he had the day he'd crawled out from under her bed at the Harvey House dormitory. His chambray shirt and denims were stained. His hair hadn't been washed or combed, and his breath might have wafted in from a distillery.

"Bart . . . what's happened to you?"

"Me? I'm fine. It's you I'm worried about." He rubbed the backs of her hands with his thumbs. "Listen, you just rest now. I'll brew you a pot of tea, how's that?"

"I don't want tea, Bart. Why haven't you shaved?"

He scowled. "I haven't been thinking about shaving, Rosie. That's the last thing on my mind."

"Obviously. How many of those empty bottles are you responsible for?"

He turned his head, as if seeing the mess for the first time. "The boys must have been here three whole days," he said.

"Have you milked the cows and fed my chickens?"

"Yes, Rosie."

"What about the sugar beets?"

Smoothing a hand over her damp brow, he gazed down at her with a soft smile on his face. "Why don't you get some rest, darlin'? It's plain you're overwrought."

"I am not overwrought!" She rose up on her elbows. "Just look at my house! You and those damned criminals have made a pigsty of it!"

"Hush, now, Rosie," he whispered, attempting to calm her. "I've been working as hard as I can to . . . um . . . entertain Bob and the fellers. Would you just settle back until they get ready to leave?"

"I'll *run* them off. Hand me that rifle!"

Before she could bolt out of bed, Bart grabbed her shoulders and thrust her back onto the pillow. "Rest, Rosie," he commanded. "We'll work things out in the morning."

Cramping again, she curled up into a ball of pain as he rose and walked back to the table where the others were engaged in a hand of poker. Rosie buried her face in the pillow to keep from crying out. What if she lost the baby? How terrible, how devastating it would be to feel the tiny life being wrenched away from her body!

Forcing herself to calm down, she tried to control her breathing. Bart was alive, she reminded herself. The house was still standing. The crops were still in the field, and the stock had been cared for. Maybe things weren't so bad.

On the other hand, just look at her home! Rosie opened her eyes to half-mast and gave the room another quick study before shutting them again in horror. But if the house was disturbing, the conversation that drifted her way was downright appalling.

"I reckon we're about two jumps ahead of that low-down Las Vegas sheriff," Bob Ford was saying. "Whatcha think, Snort?"

"Hell, that posse was campin' on our trail till we had saddle sores." Snort took a swig of whiskey, then struck a match on his boot and lit up a cheroot. "Anyhow, I suspect we lost 'em. Nobody's gonna figure we come to Raton. Who'd ever want to wet his whistle in this hellhole?"

"Hey, watch what you say about my abode," Bart put in as he slapped a card onto the table. "Raton may have been named for a varmint with yellow teeth and a hankering for rotten cheese, but it's been paradise to me."

"Sure!" Fancy said with a laugh. "You got yerself a dandy double-breasted female to warm yer blanket. Shoot, I'd settle myself down for a few months, too, if I had me some hot drawers like them to get inside of at the end of the day."

The men chuckled, and Bart glanced over his shoulder. Rosie quickly shut her eyes. Squaring his shoulders, Bart lit up a cheroot of his own and took a deep draw. "That little gal is as sweet as barnyard milk, if you want the truth, boys. We're making us a home here, and I aim to live the rest of my life inside the law."

"Like hell!" Bob chuckled. "Injun, you wouldn't know the law if it hit you up side the head. Your name don't exactly tally with the Bible, and I reckon you're just wastin' the talents the Devil gave you, sittin' out here on this mesa, no matter how hot that gal's britches are."

"Quit your jawing, Ford." Scowling, Bart glanced at Rosie again, then lowered his voice. "Anybody ever told you you're damn mouthy?"

"I reckon Jesse might have, and look what it got him."

The room fell silent. As the pain in her stomach gradually subsided, Rosie listened to the sound of cards being flipped onto the table and the swish of liquor in the bottles as the men swilled it. Finally Fancy gave a loud, gusty belch as if to announce that he was ready to change the subject.

"So what about the Sante Fe line, Injun?" he asked. "You reckon we could pull us off a good one?"

"What? You're joshing me."

"Like hell. The minute Bob heard you was in Raton, he says, 'Injun'll have the inside stuff on the Atchison, Topeka and Santa Fe, and we'll make us some dinero. Let's head on over there and find Injun and have us a good time.' Ain't that right, Bob?"

"Now that you mention it, I reckon I did say something like that. So why don't you tell us what you know, Injun? I reckon with the trains hauling all them heavy passenger cars up the pass, we ought to have an easy time pulling off a job on one of them slow movers."

Rosie watched through the pall of gray smoke as Bart tossed his cheroot to the floor and ground out the glowing cinder with his bootheel. "I'm not a train robber anymore, fellers. You might as well get that set in your noggins right off. I'm not going to get myself strung up for aiding and abetting neither."

"You gone yaller on us, Injun?" Snort jeered.

"I'm no coward, boys. I just made up my mind to go straight."

"Yeah, straight as a snake in a cactus patch. What's the matter—you plannin' a deal on yer own, Injun? Don't you want to cut us in?"

"I'm telling you, Snort. I'm not interested."

"You trying to say yer plannin' to dig sugar beets till yer gray and wrinkled?"

"Naw, he's just airin' his lungs," Fancy said. "Come on, Injun. What you got up yer sleeve?"

Bart gave a shoulder-bulging stretch and scooted his chair back from the table. "What I got up my sleeve is a good-loving woman and one hundred sixty acres of land so quiet I can hear daylight coming."

"Shoot," Snort said.

"To add to it, I got decent food to eat, a good horse, and just enough religion to set my soul at ease. No sheriff's breathing down my back; no posse's licking at my trail; and my butt's not saddlesore from churning up the dust for weeks at a time. I got honest work, honest pay, and—yep—a warm bed to come home to at night. And if you boys don't mind, I'm aiming to settle myself in with my lady right now.''

"I'll be damned if I don't think he means it," Fancy declared as he watched Bart head for the dressing screen.

"He's a little addlepated is all," Bob Ford said, gathering up the playing cards. ''Damn female will ruin a good man ever' time if you give her half a chance. Just leave it to me to set him straight. Come on, fellers, let's roll out and get some sleep.''

Rosie watched through the blur of her eyelashes as the men kicked aside whiskey bottles and tossed saddle blankets on the bare floor. In a moment Bart pulled back the edge of the quilt and slipped into the bed beside her. Sliding against her body, he drew his hands up her arms and over her shoulders.

She didn't move a muscle. The last thing she wanted in a situation like this was for Bart to get amorous, so she tried her best to pretend she was asleep. The time away from him had been hard, though, and when he slid his hands under her arms and around her breasts, it was all she could do to keep her breath steady.

"I missed you, Rosie-girl," he whispered in her ear. ''If you're still awake, I want you to know I'm sorry you got scared and rushed out here looking for me. Try to understand that I couldn't come back into town. I couldn't get away from them, see?'' He let out a deep breath. ''I wish to hell you weren't so sick over things all the time. You've got to trust me that it'll turn out okay, hear?''

She shut her eyes as his fingertips brushed the tips of her breasts. No, she didn't want to hear him. She couldn't listen to his gentle words, and she couldn't let herself be swept away by his touch. She had more to think about now than ever before. It wasn't just her own future and her own hard-fought freedom that were at stake. It was the life of an unborn child.

"Rosie, can you hear me?" he was saying against her cheek.

She waited a long time before nodding.

"The boys have drunk up what little liquor I had around

here, and they've spent all their loose change. I know they're starting to think about moving on now, and I reckon they'll be heading out tomorrow or the next day."

"To rob a train?" she whispered, still turned away from him.

"Whatever they do, the point is, they'll be gone. Long gone. It'll just be us again here at home."

"Until the next outlaws come hunting down their old pal."

Bart was silent, his breath stirring the strands of hair around her neck. "Maybe so, Rosie," he said finally. "Are you going to give me up because of it? Or do you love me enough to stay with me, whatever comes our way?"

"Do you love me enough to put the past behind you, Bart? That's what I want to know."

"I can't just run Bob Ford out of my house. He saved my life, remember? Ornery as the man is, if it wasn't for him I wouldn't be here today. I'd be dead as a can of corned beef. I owe him, Rosie, don't you see? A man stands by his pals, and that's just the way it is."

"I know that," Rosie whispered. "But sometimes . . . sometimes a man has to choose between his friends and his family. And Bart . . . Bart, you have a *family* now."

She waited, breathless, as he absorbed her words. Did he know what she meant? Could he see the changes in her that she already felt? Were his hands on her breasts aware of the swollen tenderness beneath them? Could he sense the soft weight in her belly? Did he know by the tears in her eyes that she was not the woman he had married, that she was different now? Different and new and blossoming inside. *Oh, please, Bart! Please understand.*

"Rosie," he murmured, turning her shoulders so that she faced him in the bed, "you're all the family and friends I'll ever need or want. I've promised to take care of you and protect you with my life, and I aim to do just that. Now I want you to quit your fretting and snuggle up here in my arms. Get yourself a good night's sleep, and things will look a darned sight better in the morning. I swear it."

Before she could speak again, he had tucked her head

against his shoulder, let out a deep breath, and fallen sound asleep.

It hadn't taken four nights in the same house for Bart to figure out how Snort had gotten his nickname. If the roof of the dugout hadn't been nailed down, Snort would have sent it a mile high with every one of his thunderous snores. When Bart rolled out of bed that Saturday morning, he could have sworn the walls were shaking.

He studied Rosie's sleeping form for a long time as he stood pulling on and buttoning his buckskin jacket. She sure looked innocent and frail to him. Her skin was as white as the underbelly of a rabbit, and just as soft. Long brown hair fell in thick, shining ropes over her shoulders and across the pillow. Her fingers lay spread across the quilt, relaxed as though they hadn't worked as hard as Bart knew they always did.

But it was her parted lips and dark lashes that stirred his soul. Lord, he loved the woman. He'd give every inch of ground he owned, every sugar beet he'd planted, everything he possessed just to make sure she stayed with him, content and as peaceful as she looked right now.

So how in heaven's name was he going to get rid of Bob Ford and his pair of no-good saddle tramps? He'd mentioned several times that they might want to head on out, but they'd just made themselves more at home. None of them lifted a finger to help with the cooking, washing, sweeping, and such. Instead, they had made a filthy mess out of Rosie's beautiful little home.

If politeness hadn't worked, Bart was sure force would never do the trick. Trying to order Bob Ford off his land would bring a hailstorm of bullets at the worst. At the very least, Bart knew, the men would rob him blind, tear up everything they could get their hands on, and ride off with his horses and cattle. There was no telling what they might do to Rosie, woman-starved as they were, and Bart knew he would have to keep an eye on her every minute.

Rubbing the back of his neck, he thought of the time she'd given him a haircut. He had to smile. In those days he sure hadn't been much better put together than the fellows snoring on the floor. But there had been one difference between Bart Kingsley and Bob Ford: Bart wanted to make a respectable life for himself, and he had; Bob, on the other hand, was still footloose and bent on making trouble.

Well, Bart thought, if politeness wouldn't get rid of the three moochers, and if forcing their hand would cause more trouble than it was worth, he'd just have to think of another way to run them off. Quick.

"Get your fanny up and quit shaking down my house, Snort," Bart said, giving the sleeping outlaw a swift kick in the hindquarters. "You know anything about milking cows, boy?"

Snort rolled over and began rubbing his behind. "What the hell . . . ?"

"We got us a woman in the house now, Snort. Time to whip yourself into shape." He nudged Fancy's backside with the toe of his boot. "Rise and shine, dude. If you want breakfast, you better fetch some eggs."

"Breakfast?" Fancy worked his dry tongue around the inside of his mouth. "All I want is another shot of rotgut. I got a headache as big as Lincoln County."

"Your breath is strong enough to bust a mirror. Come on, I'll boil you up some strong black coffee, and you can get to work sweeping."

"Sweeping!" Fancy glanced at Bob, who was just stirring. "Hell, that's woman's work. Put yer wife to the job, why don't ya?"

Bart looked at the bed. Rosie had sat up and was staring at her disheveled house with a look of horror. "Rosie darlin', settle back now and rest a spell," he called. "Us boys'll take care of you, won't we, fellers?"

"Not me," Fancy cut in. "I'm headin' outside to water the daisies."

Before Bart could say another word, Fancy and Snort had fairly run to the door and were vanishing up the stairs. Bob sat up on his haunches and laughed. "Got rid of them two, didn't you? Just mention honest work, and they hightail it out of here.''

Bart hunkered down beside the man who had once saved his life. ''Bob, I've got to speak plain with you,'' he said in a low voice. ''It's time you boys hit the trail. We've had us some good laughs jawing over the past, but I meant what I told you about my life these days. I've gone straight. That means I've got to tend my crops and my stock. I've got weeding and irrigating and hoeing to do, and unless you boys want to join me, I'm going to have to ask that you head out.''

''I'll be damned,'' Ford spat. ''Some thanks you show to a man who saved your life. I reckon you owe me more than a few drops of hair oil, Injun. And I aim to collect.''

Bart eyed Rosie, who had risen and was stepping over whiskey bottles on her way to the dressing screen. ''What is it you want, Ford? Speak plain.''

''I want the Atchison, Topeka and Santa Fe, *hombre*. I want me a nice, fat bankroll. You don't think I came all this way just to catch up on old times, do you? No, sir, I tracked you down for one reason, Injun—with Jesse gone and Frank living the clean life, you're the best there is at setting up a train haul, and I aim to let you back into the business.''

''I'm not robbing any trains, Ford!'' Bart hissed. ''I made that clear last night.''

''Now, don't get riled. You just put that brain of yours to work figuring out a plan of action, while me and the boys skedaddle into town for some more whiskey. When we get back, we'll set ourselves down and put all the details in place. It'll be just like the old days, don't you know? Jesse, Frank, me, you—all the boys in it together. Pals.''

''Yeah, and you shot Jesse in the back. Some pal.''

Ford jumped up and grabbed Bart's collar. ''Jesse was a bastard, and you know it! Every one of us considered plugging him for the reward. I was the only one man enough to do it!''

''You were the only one low enough to do it,'' Bart snapped, knocking Ford's hand away.

"Like hell. Now get your butt to work planning that train heist before I blast you to Kingdom Come."

Bart had no doubt that Ford meant what he said. He also knew Ford wouldn't stand a chance if it came to a showdown between them. Bart could outdraw most of the boys in the James gang, and Ford had never been much of a deadeye in the first place. He'd managed to plug Jesse only because the outlaw had been hanging up a picture and had had his back to his killer. And if it came to a fistfight, Bart could fold Ford up like an empty purse.

But there was more to consider than the conflict between the two men. First, there was the undeniable fact that Bart *did* owe Ford his life. Such a debt could never be looked at lightly. Second, there was Rosie, who had to be taken out of the situation before it blew sky high. Third, there were Snort and Fancy, both of whom would stick by Ford. With three men against him, the battle would be tougher, and Bart sure was hoping it wouldn't come to that.

"We'll talk over your damned train robbery," Bart stated bluntly, "after I take care of what's important."

"You do that," Ford responded as he walked toward the door. "Meantime I'll join my pals in that piss-patch of a garden you got out there."

"Stay out of my wife's vegetables!" Bart hollered.

"If you don't rake in her crop, Injun, we will!" Laughing at the innuendo, Bob Ford climbed the stairs and banged the door shut behind him.

*Eighteen
· · · · · · · · · · · · · · · · · · · ·

While Bart did his morning chores, Rosie worked to put her little home back in order. To her relief, she discovered that the cramps she'd experienced the night before had not led to any spotting, and she knew that she still carried the tiny life inside her. Fierce with determination to protect her unborn baby, she made up her mind to do whatever it took to keep the child safe and to restore peace in her own world. After all, how well could the baby grow if its mother was constantly fretting, worrying, and scared to death?

With this aim in mind, she ran Bob and Snort out of the house the minute they tried to come back in. When Fancy elected to disobey her orders, she took her broom to his backside until he ran howling up the stairs. The sweeping didn't take as long as she had expected, but setting the house to rights required much more than a lick and a promise. Bart's shirts and britches lay in a heap by the dressing screen. Not a single dish, cup, or spoon had been washed in days. A ring of some undetermined scum encrusted her fine black iron pot, and she couldn't bring herself to ask what it was. Worst of all, the house smelled to high heaven of stale cigarette smoke and whiskey. If she hadn't known better, Rosie would have thought she was walking around in a low-class saloon.

She had just filled the cook pot with boiling soapy water when she heard the front door open. Thinking it was Fancy again, she grabbed her broom and swung around.

"It's time to go," Bart announced. "I'm taking you back to town."

Rosie stiffened and propped the broom up against the table. "I'm not going back to town until Monday morning. If you want to run somebody off, get rid of your pals."

"This isn't something to argue about, Rosie. While I was out tending the stock, I made up my mind."

Planting her hands on her hips, she lifted her chin. "You made up *your* mind? Don't *I* have a mind to make up, Bart Kingsley?"

"In this case I've made the decision for you. I've thought it all through, and it's for the best."

"What's best is me living with you in our house—by ourselves. See, I've done some thinking, too, Bart. There was a time when just the thought of your outlaw days scared me so much I wanted to run away from you. The very notion of Sheriff Bowman searching the Missouri law records sent me scampering off to Raton to hide out with the Kilgores."

"I remember. That was just a crazy notion you took into your head, girl. I knew the sheriff couldn't track me down on the little information I'd given him. But this is different. Bob, Snort, and Fancy are real mean men, Rosie. They've got a bad streak in them a mile wide, and I want you to stay clear of this place until they're gone."

"You don't seem to understand that I'm not afraid anymore, Bart." She wiped her hands on her apron and came to stand before him. "More than a year ago I decided I wanted—and deserved—a better life for myself. I left Kansas City to find it. I gave up a marriage to a wealthy man to go after my dream. I left my good job at the Harvey House so I could keep the dream alive. I've been scared; I've been poor; I've worked my fingers to the bone—all for that dream, Bart. And just when I thought I'd lost it forever, I realized I had found it—right here in this little dugout with you. So don't tell me to start running away again. I'm through with that. This is my house, those are my chickens out in the yard, that's my kitchen garden those outlaws are defiling, and you're my husband. It's my dream, and I'm not turning my back on it. Do you understand me, Bart Kingsley?"

"Plain as day. But the fact is, that little dream of yours is in danger of getting blown sky high if you don't do what I say. You're coming with me to Raton if I have to hog-tie you, Rosie.''

He reached out to take her hand, but she jerked away. ''Bart! Don't do this.''

''I don't have a choice,'' he said, grabbing her around the waist and slinging her over one shoulder. ''You've got a city-girl way of looking at things, but dreams just don't work out as neat and pretty as you paint them.''

As he spoke, he hauled her up the steps into the sunshine and deposited her on the seat of the wagon. When she started to squirm away, he jerked a rope from the bed and whipped it around her ankles.

''Bart!'' she cried as he tied her feet together and then knotted the rope to the wagon seat. ''Bart, no!''

''Better gag her, too!'' Snort laughed when he and the others saw what Bart was up to. ''We don't want no female squallin' all the way to town.''

''Just shut up and get in the wagon,'' Bart snapped.

Rosie sat in utter shock as her husband pulled his hat low on his brow and gave the reins a quick flick. Ford and his boys scrambled onto the moving wagon bed, but Bart hardly seemed aware of them. Glowering darkly, he grabbed his rifle and set it across his thighs. Then he lit a cheroot and smoked it with an intensity Rosie had never seen.

She couldn't believe he had actually *tied* her to the wagon! Despite her fine speech about her dreams, he had tossed her around like a sack of potatoes! To think that the man could be so rough—never mind that he had no idea of her delicate condition. She glared at him from the corner of her eye. Maybe he was worried about the outlaws, but that gave him no right to treat her worse than he treated his cows and horses!

She crossed her arms and sat fuming as the wagon bounced down the track. Once those men had gone, she would give Bart what-for! If he truly loved her as he said he did, he would have listened more closely to what she was saying. He would have taken her feelings into account. Most of all, he would have run off those *pals* of his a long time ago!

"So tell us about the Atchison, Topeka and Santa Fe, Injun," Bob Ford said from the back of the wagon.

"I'm busy," Bart growled.

"You told me you'd talk once you got them chores done. So talk."

Bart hurled his cheroot onto the track. "I said, I'm busy."

"You want us to ask little Rosie? She used to work at the Harvey House, didn't she?"

"Leave her out of this. We'll talk later."

"How're us boys gonna rob us a train if we don't plan it out, Injun? You know better'n anybody how important it is to line up a good scheme. Now, when's the richest train roll through town?"

Bart had clamped his jaw shut, and Rosie had never seen him look so dark. Was he angry with her? Or was he mad at Ford and his boys? Or was Bart actually considering robbing one of the trains that passed through town? A chill washed into her bones when she heard him begin to speak.

"Any one of 'em could be loaded," he said. "You've got three or four a day pulling up from Albuquerque and Lamy. They go through Las Vegas, Wagon Mound and Springer picking up passengers and freight on their way east. Then you've got the trains down from Denver. They've come all the way from Kansas City loaded with goods and settlers."

"You reckon we could take a bigger haul off the westbound traffic?"

"Probably. Hard telling, though. There's some good money going east these days. Gold and silver coming out of the territories. Rich cattlemen taking their profits to banks in Missouri."

"Sounds like a pretty good flow both ways."

Bart nodded. Rosie could hardly believe her ears. Was Bart just trying to pacify these outlaws, or was he actually discussing which train to rob? For all she could tell, he was helping them plan an armed robbery! Was he going to join them, then? Had her worst fears come true, that Bart had been lured back into his old ways by the temptation of easy money?

For a moment she considered grabbing the rifle off his lap and peppering all three of those filthy criminals in the wagon bed. But she knew she'd never get away with it. Instead, she bent and began untying the rope around her ankles. At the very least, she intended to be free to escape if the need arose. How awful to think of needing to escape from Bart!

Tears of anger and dismay filled her eyes as she struggled with the knotted hemp. It wasn't fair! Just when they had begun to build a normal life, a life more fulfilling and passionate than she'd ever dreamed possible, everything had come crashing down.

Bart had slid back into the role he'd worked so hard to leave behind him. When Rosie had freed her legs and had taken a closer look at the man she loved so deeply, the sight of him sent a curl of panic shooting through her stomach. His long black hair blew away from the angles and planes of his face. The sharp Indian cheekbones, his father's legacy, had bronzed to deep mahogany. Instead of the clean, starched white shirts she had sewn for him, Bart wore his rugged buckskin jacket. His faded denims and boots, the holsters on his thighs, the cheroot clamped between his teeth, and the smell of whiskey on his breath forced her to see what she wanted so much to deny: Bart looked every bit the gunman he was.

Even if he didn't really intend to rob one of the inbound trains, he wouldn't stand a chance in town if he showed up looking like this. Sheriff Bowman was no longer around to identify him, but there were three deputies who might. Besides, a whole town full of people no doubt had read the wanted posters describing a green-eyed Indian. To top it off, Bart was in league with a man who loved to boast that he'd shot Jesse James. That would seal Bart's fate.

"We want to stop a train that's pulling into town, don't we, Injun?" Ford was asking. "Ain't I right about 'em bein' slower comin' in? There's that switchback and all."

"The switchback isn't used these days," Bart responded.

"The train used to have to climb all the way to the summit with six percent grades and sixteen-degree curves. That was an eight-thousand-foot climb. But there's a tunnel now, so the trains aren't so slow coming in, but they're not so fast going out, either."

"So either way might work?"

"Might."

"Any bridges?"

"There's a trestle at Raton Pass. It's pretty shaky."

"Hey, boys, how about that? We could stop the engine while it's on the trestle. It'd only take one of us to keep it in line while the rest of us could work the safe and the passengers."

"Sounds good to me," Snort said. "Whatever Injun thinks."

"What do you say, Injun?"

"I say we just hit the city limits, and you boys better shut your gates if you don't want the whole town in on this."

Rosie wanted to shrink into her boots as the wagon jolted down the street past stores and restaurants filled with people she had come to love and respect. How would they react if they knew of the conversation she had just heard? Oh, there had been a time when she was just as pristine and pious as any of them. But now, thanks to Bart Kingsley and his pals, she was party to a crime. Just for having listened to their plans she could be brought before a jury! Especially if she didn't run straight to the sheriff's office and tell the deputies everything she knew. Yet Rosie knew full well that if she did, she'd be turning Bart in, too.

She studied his handsome profile as he pulled the wagon up to the hitching post in front of the Central Hotel. How grim he looked. The light had died in his green eyes. His face was as dark as she'd ever seen it. As he came around the wagon to help her out, she remembered what he'd once told her. He'd said that his life had become black—as black as a tunnel with no end in sight. And she was the only light he'd been able to remember. Rosie was Bart's shining light! Now he seemed ready to snuff it all out again.

"Bart," she whispered as she slipped into the cup of his hands. "Bart, please—"

"Stay here at the hotel, Rosie," he cut in. "You'll be safer where there're lots of folk around you."

"Safer? Bart—"

"Don't go to the law, Rosie. I don't want to complicate things, you hear?"

She stared at him as he lowered her to the ground. "Bart, what's become of you?"

"Just do what I say, and don't ask questions."

"Oh, Bart."

"C'mon, Injun," Snort called. "Time's a-wasting. Let's head over to the Bank Exchange Saloon and bend our elbows a spell."

"Rosie, get inside the hotel quick," Bart said in a low voice. "Take this and keep it hidden so Mrs. Davis and the others don't see." He thrust a small revolver into her hands, jamming the butt against her stomach. "I'll come back for you when I can."

Clutching the gun, she watched him stride away and swing up into the wagon. Without a backward glance, he pulled away from the hotel and set off toward the nearest saloon.

Rosie stayed up in her little room all the rest of the day. She didn't feel up to going downstairs for lunch, and she knew she didn't stand a chance of putting on a cheerful demeanor for Mrs. Davis and the other hotel guests. Instead she sat in a rocking chair by the window and watched the trains pull in and out of town.

All the while she rocked, she held her hands over her stomach as if to protect the tiny life within her body. Visions of small hand-smocked linen dresses, knitted booties tied with white ribbons, quilted flannel coverlets, and lacy crocheted blankets flitted through her thoughts and mingled with memories of whiskey bottles strewn about, coarse language, and the cold steel of a six-shooter.

Maybe Manford Wade had been an angel sent to tell Rosie to stick by Bart. But what right did she have to bring a child into the world of outlaws with their foul smell and rough demeanor? A baby, no matter what its heritage, deserved the very best life had to offer. She wanted picture books and sun-gilded tea parties, puppies and tender gardens for her baby. She wanted the child to go to school and to learn manners and decorum. She wanted fine clothes and good healthy food, and clean skin for her child. And most of all, she wanted loving parents to nurture and guard the baby until the time was ripe for opening windows and setting the child free.

If she told Bart about their baby, would that make the difference for him? Would it pull him back from the brink on which he now balanced? Or would a child even matter to him? How well Rosie knew that Bart had never experienced the love of a father. His mother had not given him the affection and gentleness he needed. So why should she think Bart would suddenly be filled with glowing images of fatherhood, as she was?

With a sigh born in the very depths of her being, Rosie stood and went to the mirror over the washstand. As the dinner bell rang from the floor below her room, she brushed back strands of loose hair around her neck. What hope was left for her and the seed of life inside her? Even now Bart might be completing the plans that would destroy any dreams for happiness they had ever cherished.

With a weight of sadness heavy on her shoulders, Rosie left her room and made her way down the carpeted hall to the stairs. She descended to the foyer and followed the rest of the hotel guests into the small dining room. Seated at a small table by a window, she tried to make herself read the menu but the words were all a blur. She had just settled on soup and chicken when a shout from a nearby table snapped the frayed threads of her composure.

"By God, Vermillion, there she is!"

Rosie's head shot up at the familiar voice. In the dining room, not ten feet away, sat her father and the man she had married three years before in Kansas City.

"Laura Rose?" Dr. Vermillion was on his feet in an

instant. "Good Lord, girl, what in heaven's name are you doing here?"

For a moment Rosie couldn't speak. Her mouth fell open, and she clutched the menu to her breast. "Pappy," she said softly.

"Stand up, young lady!"

Her urge to bolt was quelled by the sharp command. Accustomed to obeying every word from the man's mouth, she jumped to her feet, nearly knocking her chair over. Dr. Lowell was at her father's side in a second, his frowning visage glowering at her.

"She's my wife, sir," the physician snapped. "Allow me to address the matter."

"I beg your pardon, but she was my daughter first. Laura Rose, you will march out of this room at once, and we shall speak with you in our private quarters." Dr. Vermillion grabbed Rosie's hand and jerked her away from the table behind which she had been standing as if for meager protection.

Humiliated in front of the other diners, Rosie hurried out of the room and across the lobby with both men gripping her arms. After practically being carried up the stairs between them, she fairly flew down the hall. In moments Dr. Vermillion had unlocked the door to his suite and hauled his daughter inside.

"Now, young lady," he stated, "your husband and I have been searching for you for almost six months. We've employed the Pinkerton National Detective Agency from New York City, and we've scoured the entire state of Missouri. We've spared no expense in tracking you to this godforsaken outpost. Our worst fear was that you had been abducted for foul purposes. But our most unhappy thought was that you might actually have run away as you stated in the cruel note you left behind when you vanished. Am I to assume that you actually did flee your loving husband and the fine home he built for you?"

Rosie wished the floor would open up and swallow her. "My note was accurate," she said.

"Why?" Dr. Lowell bellowed. "Why in the name of

God did you do such a thing? Have you any earthly idea of the ramifications of your actions? Do you know what I've been subjected to? Why, it's taken every ounce of my fortitude to hold up my head in public. Your behavior threatened not only my standing in polite society, but my professional reputation as well!''

"I'm sorry," Rosie murmured. "I didn't mean to cause your practice any harm, Dr. Lowell." She tried to make herself look at the man who had verbally threatened and cowed her so many times. But when she lifted her head to meet his uncompromising glare, she saw the short, stocky body that had dominated her every night of their marriage. Noticing the thick hands that once had grappled her, she felt herself shrink even farther inside herself.

"When I finally learned you had been observed laboring as a common waitress in this pitiful stink-hole of a town, I could hardly believe my ears!''

"Why? Why, Laura Rose?" her father repeated the query. "Why did you ever commit such a despicable action?"

She clamped her hands over her stomach. "I . . . because . . . I . . . don't love him," she fumbled. "I don't love Dr. Lowell and I never have."

"Love!" the physician exploded. "What does love have to do with anything! We contracted a marriage, if you recall. You agreed to tend our home, manage the servants, make the proper social calls, and see that our calendar of events was adequately filled. In return, I agreed to pursue my career and to provide you with everything your heart could desire."

"Not everything," she said, lifting her chin. "I wanted children, a family. I wanted compassion. I wanted a life of fulfillment. I wanted to be a teacher. And that's what I am."

"A teacher! Good God, you can't be serious."

"I most certainly am serious. Upon obtaining my certification two months ago, I took a position at an excellent free school here in Raton. I earn a fine salary, and in a few weeks I shall sign a contract for the 1883–84 school year."

"You will not!" Dr. Lowell shouted.

"Yes, I shall, sir! You don't know anything about my life, and you never have. I've always wanted to teach school, and I'm *good* at it. You won't take that away from me!"

"I'll do with you exactly as I please. And if you intend to continue sassing me with your smart mouth, I shall have no hesitation in turning you over this bed and lashing you with a hickory switch."

Rosie stiffened. "I'm a grown woman, not a child. You'll do nothing of the sort!"

"Now then, William," Dr. Vermillion intervened, his brows lifted in surprise. "You certainly don't need to take such an extreme measure. Granted, Laura Rose has been difficult at times, but I've never felt the need to punish her physically."

"You have no idea of the trial she has been to me during the course of our marriage, sir," Dr. Lowell stated. "This is merely the worst in a long series of rebellious, ungrateful acts your daughter has committed against me."

"Please!" Dr. Vermillion held up his hands. "It's not my place to hear out the difficulties of your domestic arrangement. Laura Rose, I'm assuming your previous statements concerning a desire to remain in this town as a teacher were merely made out of provoked hostility. And I trust, Dr. Lowell, that you never have and never will resort to physical abuse of my daughter."

Rosie and the man who had struck her more times than she could remember stared at each other across the room.

"As you wish, sir," Dr. Lowell said finally. "Now, if you will allow me to escort my wife to her room, I shall settle the matter of our travel arrangements by return train to Kansas City tomorrow."

"Of course." Dr. Vermillion gave Rosie a look she knew all too well. *Obey*, it said. *Obey, or else.*

In moments Rosie and William Lowell were sweeping out of the room and down the hall to Rosie's chamber. He took the key from her hand, unlocked the door, and pushed her inside.

"You," he uttered, "have humiliated me beyond endurance."

"And you drove me away with your irrational anger!"

"Silence! I will countenance no argument from you. You will stay in this room until morning, at which time I shall come for you and escort you to the train. You will return with me to our home in Kansas City, where you will resume your duties as if nothing scandalous had happened."

Trembling with anger, Rosie stared at him.

"We shall spread the news that in desperation to have a child, you left Kansas City and went to a noted doctor in the East, where you have been receiving special treatments for some months now. This will garner sympathy for you from the women in our society. They, in turn, will pass that emotion to their husbands. You will then simply carry on as before. Do you understand?"

"I am not stupid."

"I had begun to wonder." He lifted one thick blond eyebrow and regarded her coldly. "At least your adventure in the West has had some benefit, my dear. You are looking quite passable, and I find myself considering something I have had to do without in the past months. I believe I shall find it acceptable to resume our conjugal relations, after all." He gave her the hint of a smile, then walked to the door. "Good evening, Mrs. Lowell," he said.

Rosie watched the door shut behind him, and then she heard the key turn in the lock.

"Oh, God, oh, God!" Rosie cried, falling to her knees at the side of her bed. After hearing the man's footsteps fade away down the hall, she had drawn her curtains and turned down her bedding. Unable to make herself perform the most common tasks of washing her face and unwinding her hair, she could think only of rushing to her bedside to implore the Almighty. "Dear Lord, if You ever loved me," she breathed, "if You ever cared for me at all, help me now! He's come for me . . . that . . . that hideous man. . . ."

Unable to go on, she struggled to control the tears that had begun to flow. Against her cheeks, her hands grew wet, and sobs tore from her chest in agony. "Oh, God, I can't . . . can't do this! I'm so confused. So scared! Dr. Lowell wants to take me back to Kansas City, but . . ." She broke into tears again. "Oh, I want Bart so much. I don't know what to do, dear Lord. I want everything to be the way it was. What shall I do? Where's Bart? Where's Bart?"

As she spoke, a warm hand suddenly covered her thigh. "Here I am—under the bed."

"Bart!" Stifling a scream, Rosie scrambled backward.

Sure enough, a familiar pair of legs appeared, followed by slim, hard hips, then a broad chest and shoulder. Finally, with a last shove, Bart's head slid out from under the bed frame. "Howdy, Rosie." Beaming, Bart rolled up on his haunches.

"Bart, what are you doing here?"

"Just answering your prayers, I reckon." He took her hand and gave it a quick kiss. "I love you, girl."

Undaunted, Rosie pulled her hand away. "How on earth did you get under my bed?"

"I was just climbing through your window to bring you these." He held up a small brown sack.

"Huffman's cream candies!"

"They're tasting mighty good tonight, Rosie. Here, have a taste."

How could she possibly think about sweets at a time like this? In spite of everything, his kind gesture made her want to smile. "Bart—"

But as she said his name, he popped a tiny candy into her open mouth.

"When I heard the key in the lock," he explained, "I scouted out the best hiding place I could find in a hurry before you and that man could walk through the door." He paused and regarded her evenly. "Is that the fellow you married, Rosie?"

She nodded. "Dr. William Lowell."

"He tracked you down, did he?"

"He and Pappy are both here in Raton." She got up off

her knees and sat on the bed. "They've hired the Pinkertons, too."

"Dad-gum." Frowning, Bart eased up beside her. "Did
they say anything about me?"

"No. But it won't be long before they find out."

"Hell's bells, if this ain't a pickle."

She glanced at him as she swallowed the last of her
candy. "At least you smell better than you did."

Laughing, he threw one arm around her shoulders. "Me
and the boys got into a tangle with some fellows at the
saloon, and I wound up in the horse trough. Good way to get
a quick bath, I found out."

"You were *fighting*?"

"Just a friendly scuffle. Seems Bob's reputation as the
killer of Jesse James doesn't make him as popular as he'd
hoped. I tried to warn him about that."

"So, the town knows who he is now? That means they
know about you! Oh, Bart, you'll be arrested. Is that why
you came to hide in my room like before? Are you running
from the law again?"

"Rosie, you're just as jumpy as a speckle-legged frog,
did you know that? I've never seen a woman who could
worry as much as you."

"I have reason to worry!" she said. "Pappy and Dr. Lowell
are planning to haul me back to Kansas City tomorrow. Bob
Ford, Fancy, and Snort are stirring up all sorts of trouble. The
Pinkerton detectives and the deputy sheriffs are sniffing all
around you. And there's more . . . other things you don't
even know about."

He drew her close. "I know all I need to know. I heard
your prayer about us when I was under this bed, Rosie. You
said you wanted me, and that's all that matters now. God's
going to take care of us, don't you know that? After all these
years of going to church and teaching Sunday school, don't
you trust the Lord, girl?"

"I trust God, Bart, but I don't know if I trust *you*."

"If you don't trust me now, I don't reckon you ever will.
I promised to take care of you. I promised to work things out
for us, and I aim to do just that."

She shook her head, wanting to believe him but so uncertain. His hand on her shoulder felt big and warm, so comforting that the memories of their happy days together on the little homestead flooded into her heart. Yet despite sun-filled images of sweet pies baking in the fireplace, fragrant primroses blossoming in a pitcher on the table, damp sheets flapping in the mountain breeze, Rosie couldn't quite shut away the threatening clouds that had gathered overhead.

"I want to trust you, Bart," she whispered. "It is as I said in my prayer: I want things to be the way they were before. But life isn't like one of the slates in my schoolroom; I can't just erase the parts I don't want."

He bent and kissed her cheek, his touch soft and endearing. "I hope you don't want to erase me, Rosie-girl. I told you once, you're the light of my life, the bright spot in all the dark years of my past. That still holds true—truer than ever. You've got to believe that I won't do anything to risk snuffing out that light."

"Oh, Bart, I need light, too! Things are crowding in on me, and I can't . . . I just can't seem to . . ."

"Come here, darlin'. You've done enough crying for fifty folks lately." He took her up in his arms and settled her on his lap. Drawing her face against his, he kissed the tears that had started down her cheeks. "Don't cry, Rosie. It's going to be all right, I swear."

"Don't swear, Bart," she said in a muffled voice. "I can't abide any more broken promises."

"I haven't broken a single promise to you since I found you here in Raton," he answered, but as he spoke the words, a stab of uncertainty ran through him. For all the comforting words he had to give this beautiful woman in his arms, he knew darkness hung like an ominous storm all around them.

The things she had outlined loomed and hovered in his thoughts as he worked to ease her mind. He'd done his damnedest to run off Ford and his sidekicks, but they were still in town. At this very moment they were plotting the train robbery that might seal his fate forever. The townfolk now knew that Jesse James's killer was in their midst and that they had welcomed "Buck Springfield" into their company like an old pal. How long before one of the deputies remembered those wanted posters? How long before Snort or one of the others called him by his real name? If the Pinkerton men had tracked Rosie down, how long would it be before they followed the trail straight to him?

Then there was the matter of this cold-as-ice doctor who claimed to be Rosie's husband. Only moments ago he had locked her in this room, leaving her with the intimation that it wouldn't be long before he would claim a right to share her bed.

"God!" He cried aloud at the thought of any man touching his wife. "Rosie, I love you. I'm not going to let anything come between us!"

As he spoke, he couldn't help gripping her tightly against his chest. Seemingly comforted by the intensity of his promise, she rested her head in the curve of his neck and allowed her lips to touch the sensitive skin below his ear. The damp caress sent an unexpected glow through his body, and he struggled with it for no more than a moment.

"Rosie," he said, taking her head in his hands and lifting her face to meet his. "Rosie, say you love me! Give me that tonight."

A tear trickled out of the corner of her eye as she shuddered against him. "I do love you, Bart. I love you with all my heart. If the darkness comes, Bart, remember that!"

*Nineteen
. . . .

With a groan of anguish, Bart crushed Rosie to his chest. She flung her arms around his shoulders and kissed his neck, his cheek, and finally his mouth. Oh, his breath was warm and sweet, and his skin smelled of rainwater! She tangled her fingers in the long hair that hung down to his shoulders as he pulled the pins from the soft knot at the nape of her neck. Hunger and fear and need the threads of their passion, they fell across the small bed in the weaving of a tapestry of love.

But if their ardent desire was quick to blossom, they took their time to nourish it into bloom. Erasing all thoughts of the tempest gathering at their door, they cherished and nurtured the fragile flower of love that had grown up between them. With whispered avowals of undying devotion, they slowly slipped away fettering garments until they lay entwined, bare hard flesh against tender petal-soft skin.

As the long hours of the night drifted away, they explored, renewed, and finally united their bodies in an expression of promises neither could completely trust. They rose and fell with caresses born of hope, yet their passion held a note of desperation that took their loving even higher.

When Rosie slid over Bart's long thighs and allowed him to pleasure her as she gazed down on his beloved face, it was almost more than she could bear. But her hunger for his touch stole away her fears as quickly as they slipped into her thoughts, and she succumbed to the incredible joy of his hands cupping and teasing and stroking her body. As she rose to the crest of a high wave, she felt him ascend with

309

her, his head thrown back on the bed and his flesh barely leashed.

"Bart, I love you, I do!" she cried out at the ultimate moment, and his body shuddered beneath hers.

"You're mine, Rosie," he groaned as his release filled her and touched the cords that had held her away. "And I'm yours."

As she broke loose with a trembling surrender, her body convulsed onto his undulations of ecstasy. She sank against his chest, her cheek damp on his hot naked flesh. Her hair covered them like a cape as she stretched out her legs along his length and rolled with him to her side.

Together they lay rocking as the last of the waves curled through them. And then, with dawn flushing the mesas of the Sangre de Cristo Mountains, they slept.

"Laura Rose!"

The rattle of a key in the lock sent Rosie bolt upright in bed. "Oh, no!" she cried in a hoarse whisper. In half a second she had given the sleeping Bart a mighty shove and sent him thudding to the floor on the far side of the bed.

"What the hell—" he began, sitting up in a tangle of sheets.

"Hush!" Rosie's hand covered the top of his head, and she pushed with all her strength.

"Laura Rose? I expected you to be up and packed by now." Dr. Lowell walked into the room just as Bart's head disappeared beneath the edge of the bed.

She jerked her sheet up to her neck and regarded the man coldly. "You have entered my room without permission, Dr. Lowell, and I'll thank you to turn around and march right back out."

"I beg your pardon!"

"Do as I say," she commanded, stretching out a long bare arm.

"You little wench! How dare you presume to order me around?"

"Out!" she shouted, using her foot to hold an angry Bart under the bed. "I'll be dressed in fifteen minutes."

"You're my wife, and I can stay in this room as long as I damn well—"

"You get out before I holler for the deputy!" Rosie scrambled out of bed, dragging the sheet with her. Reaching the burly physician, she thrust her hand against his chest and pushed him backward until he was just beyond the threshold.

"And don't come back until I say you can!" With that, she slammed the door in his face and set a chair beneath the knob. "Bastard!" she added as a final note.

"Rosie, good golly," Bart said as he clambered out from under the bed. "You'd better watch your language, girl."

She couldn't help but grin, but as quickly as it had started, her smile fell away. "Oh, Bart, that man puts the fear of God in me."

"Him? He's as full of wind as a bull in a corn patch. If you wouldn't have kept pushing me under the bed, I'd have kicked his britches up so tight around his neck they'd have choked him to death."

Rosie shook her head. "He may look fat and weak, but he's mean, Bart."

"Shoot, you stood up to him pretty good if you ask me."

"Only because I knew you were in the room. If he ever gets me alone—"

Bart caught her by the shoulders. "He's not ever going to get you to himself, Rosie! I swear it. Now, you get yourself dressed and keep that chair under the doorknob. I've got to take care of a few things with the boys, and then—"

"The boys! Bart, you aren't going back to Bob Ford, are you?"

"Rosie, I've got to settle things. What I have in mind won't take more than an hour or two, and then I'll come back here for you."

"My father will tear down this door in five seconds, Bart. I can't hold him off for an hour."

"If you have to, hold him off with that gun I gave you."

"But why can't you take me with you? What are you going to do?"

He put a finger over her lips. "Don't ask and then you

won't know the answer. If you don't know what I'm up to, you won't worry. This business is between me and Bob Ford. I'm going to take care of our future, Rosie—in every which way.''

''Bart, what are you going to do?'' As images of Bart robbing a train flooded through her, Rosie tried to grab him while he shrugged on his buckskin and denims. But he was already making for the window, and by the time she reached him he was halfway out.

''Let me go, Rosie,'' he said, taking her hand away from his jacket. ''It's got to be this way.''

After kissing the back of her hand, he climbed through the window and bounded like a mountain lion across the sloping roof. As she watched him leap down and disappear into a tangle of honeysuckle, she felt a thick lump form in her throat.

''Oh, Bart,'' she whispered, ''you don't know what you've just asked of me!''

She shoved down the window against the morning breeze, but for a long time she stood gazing out at the mesas that ringed the tiny town of Raton. It would be a blistering day, unbearably hot—a Sunday, the first day of July. After morning church, children would linger in the cool shadows of their homes. Mothers would read from the Bible until their young ones had fallen asleep for afternoon naps. Fathers would sweat like horses as they tended crops or worked their stock. Dogs would lie panting under wagons. Chickens would scurry beneath houses. And rattlesnakes would bask on burning stones.

Would this be the day Bart Kingsley robbed a train? Was that how he intended to settle his future with Rosie—in a flurry of bullets, a life on the run, and easy money taken from others who had earned it the hard way? Did he think that her love would bind her to him, no matter what he did?

Gazing down at the opened box of cream candies, Rosie tried to picture herself living in such a world. Plenty of other women did it, she knew. There was nothing so unusual about falling in love with an outlaw and following him on the trail until the law caught up with him. Could she do it? Did she love him enough?

She certainly did love Bart. There was no question in her mind about that. And she didn't want to go back to Kansas City with Dr. Lowell and her father. If the word about Bob Ford got out, and if people learned about Bart's past, she would lose her teaching position. Traveling with an outlaw gang would be the only choice she had.

But when she considered all the options, one thing dominated every possibility: her child.

Never, never would she bring a baby into a world of guns and fists, a life of tobacco smoke and whiskey, a home filled with cussing, quarreling, and threats. Bart had not been brought up with a father and mother who loved and nurtured him and she was raised by a man who treated his children no better than he treated his inanimate assets, but this baby, this innocent life inside her body, deserved the best she had to offer.

As Rosie stood by the window, she knew what her choice must be. There was only one place where this child could receive love, security, nourishment, clothing, education—a *future*.

Clamping her jaw tight against threatening tears, Rosie went to the bed and began to dress. "Let me go," Bart had begged. For all the love he vowed, he couldn't escape the truth about himself. He wanted to be set free. He wanted his old ways, the life he knew best. "Let me go," he had pleaded.

"Yes, Bart," she breathed as she drew her shawl around her shoulders and pulled the chair out from under the doorknob, "because I love you so, I'll let you go."

At seven forty-five the Atchison, Topeka and Santa Fe engine pulled out of the Raton station. Steam blanketed the windows, and chunks of burning coal shot from the firebox as the train gathered speed on its way to Denver. The whistle blew, and the rattle of the wheels settled into a rhythmic click on the tracks.

Rosie sat wedged in the corner of a seat in a passenger

car, her eyes shut and her throat working hard to swallow the thick lump lodged in it. As hard as she tried to block all sound, all sight, every sense in her body, she couldn't help but hear the voices of the men who sat in her berth.

"Railroad stocks are up, you know, Vermillion," Dr. Lowell commented from his place beside Rosie. "I'm thinking of investing some capital myself, and the Atchison, Topeka line has impressed me greatly."

"With round-trip tickets to Kansas City at twenty-five dollars, she'll be bringing in a pretty penny." Rosie's father cleared his throat. "You should speak with Mr. W. F. White. He's the general passenger agent and a good friend of mine. He could give you the inside story."

"What about this Harvey fellow? I hear he's taking over the restaurants all along the line. Clever idea, if you ask me."

"Indeed. He used to service his eating houses with men, but it seems they haven't worked out as well as the women he's using now. Mr. Davis, the hotel proprietor, told me that Raton was where Harvey first hired women. It seems he was having a deuce of a time keeping his male employees in line. But the changeover worked so well, he's converting all his staff to women."

"Makes sense, of course," Dr. Lowell interjected. "Women belong in roles of servitude. It suits them best."

"Naturally. Of course, Harvey will want to retain his male chefs. I hear he imports them from the Continent."

"The Continent! Maybe the Harvey Houses would make a good investment. You can't deny he's positioned to expand."

Rosie wished she could fade into the upholstery of her seat. It was obvious the men hardly remembered she was there. Having accomplished their aim of rounding her up like a lost cow, they'd switched their focus back to business. They didn't even have the good grace to recall that she herself had worked for Fred Harvey and would have an insider's view of his operation.

Oh, she felt ill again! Though she wanted to look outside, she couldn't bring herself to sit up. It had been terribly difficult to see for the last time the townspeople she loved so dearly. Mrs. Davis had accosted her in the hotel foyer with word that a message had come for "Buck." Rosie had forced a smile to her lips and said she'd let him know. But of course she wouldn't. She knew she would never see Bart again.

Etta had waved at Rosie from inside the dining room of the Harvey House, where she was serving breakfast. The baggage boys had called her name as they scurried to load the train with trunks and parcels. The owner of the livery stable had passed by and inquired as to Buck's health. She'd given him a brief greeting and hurried on.

They were all behind her now—Raton and the people who had brought her the only real freedom she'd ever known. Somewhere behind her, Mr. Kilgore and his wife were dressing for church. They would check in on the classroom before climbing into their buggy. Reverend Cullen would be studying his sermon notes one last time. Cheyenne Bill, now a regular at the Methodist church, would button on his new white collar and comb his hair the way Rosie had taught him. Mrs. Wade would visit her son Manford's flower-strewn grave. Father Accosini would ring his new church bells. Tom and Griff would sniff out the ground around one of the saloons, then dig beds in the bare dirt and settle in for a long snooze.

It had been a good life, hadn't it? Rosie thought. In spite of the ups and downs, the uncertainties and worries, she had been happy in Raton. Very happy.

And the best and most poignant memories were of her days with Bart Kingsley. She thought of their little homestead. Were the chickens up and scratching in the dirt? Had the morning glories bloomed on the tree by the river? Were jackrabbits peeking covetously through the fencing around her kitchen garden as dew evaporated from the round heads of lettuce?

"Butchers' cattle are scarce this summer," Dr. Lowell was saying, his words interrupting Rosie's thoughts. "Thirty-five to forty dollars, I hear. Milk cows run from thirty to sixty according to quality, and yearlings are going for eighteen to twenty-two.''

"Your stock will be up, then.''

"Well up. As a matter of fact, I'm finding myself constantly on the lookout for new investments. I'm considering purchasing some fine art pieces for the house. I may make an excursion to New York or possibly even Paris. I imagine I can solicit any number of suitable traveling companions from the club. The only problem I'll have is taking time away from my office.''

"I see our little trip has whetted your appetite for adventure, Dr. Lowell.''

"A trifle." The man laughed, and Rosie remembered how deeply she had come to despise that whinnying sound.

In contrast, she had loved to hear Bart's deep chuckle. They had had such fun, teasing and playing together—never mind that they were fully adult and led a completely responsible life on their farm. Oh, those sun-sprinkled days! What would Rosie ever do without them? What would she ever do without Bart?

And the child . . . never to know a true father, one who tickled and romped and laughed. Rosie squeezed her eyes shut and laid a warm hand on her stomach. Bart would make a good father, no matter if he had fallen back into his outlaw ways. He was a tender and kind man, despite his earthy qualities, and he knew just how to ease a troubled spirit. It was true, too, what Bart had promised Rosie—he *had* protected her. He had provided for her. And he'd kept her secure. He would do the same for a child; she had no doubt about that.

"Hams are running eighteen to twenty cents a pound out here in the Territory,'' Dr. Lowell was saying, "and dressed pork is at ten.''

"No!''

"I should say so. If I had my books here, what I couldn't do! The love of money may be the root of all evil, but it keeps a man climbing to the top, you know.''

"Yes, indeed!'' Rosie's father laughed as the train chugged into a tunnel and darkness fell over the car.

It was a long tunnel, and the intensity of the gloom silenced the passengers and made Rosie open her eyes. Utter, utter blackness. A shade of ebony she could not recall in the darkest of her dreams. And this was how Bart had described his life without her.

Oh, Bart! Nothing he could ever do could make her own life as bleak and empty as this fathomless void.

"Father," she announced, sitting up and grabbing the edge of the window. "Dr. Lowell, I will speak with both of you."

"Laura Rose, what are you up to now?"

She stood, swaying in the darkness. "I've come to a decision. When the train stops at the next station, I will get off."

"I beg your pardon?"

Somebody's hand clamped over her wrist, but she shook it off. "There are things you don't know about me. Things neither of you understand and never will. Pappy, for six years you have denied the truth that I was already married when Dr. Lowell spoke for me."

"What!" the physician exploded as the train emerged from the tunnel.

"Laura Rose, you're imagining things!" her father implored.

Rosie saw their faces as light filled the car. "I married Bart Kingsley six years ago, and you know it," she stated firmly. "I'm a married woman, and what's more I am now carrying his—"

"*A holdup!*" someone screamed from the front of the car. "It's a holdup! We're being robbed!"

"Robbed!" Cries of dismay flooded the car as the passengers scrambled to the windows. The train began to shriek to a halt, and great clouds of steam billowed forth. With the jerking stop, the passengers in the crowded car were tossed back and forth, jerked and shaken like rag dolls.

"A holdup! Look—gunmen!"

Rosie elbowed Dr. Lowell aside and stuck her head out the window. Sure enough, three men on horses had surrounded the engine. The engineer was climbing down from

his station, and the fireman had leapt from the box. Looking
for strangers with bandanna-covered faces and armloads of
weaponry, Rosie was shocked to see men she recognized
instantly.

"Bob Ford!" she gasped. "And Snort and Fancy! Oh,
no—not *this* train, Bart! Not this train!"

But her hopes were short-lived as the door to her car
banged open and Bart Kingsley climbed aboard, his six-
shooter drawn. Striding past the cowering passengers, he
doffed his hat.

"Mornin', folks," he said, handling the gun with an
absent air. "Sorry to trouble you. Hey, there, Rosie-girl."

"Bart!" Wide-eyed she watched him walk toward her,
his towering form a startling contrast with the smaller men
who hovered protectively around their wives and children.
"Bart, don't do this!"

"Don't do what?" He stopped, puzzled. "I've come to
save you, darlin'. Don't you want to be rescued?"

"Save me?" She glanced at her father, who was trembling like an aspen leaf in autumn. "From what?"

"You don't mean you went willingly with these two
sidewinders, do you?" he asked as he took off his hat in
bewilderment.

"Well, I . . . I . . ."

"Of course she came with us willingly," Dr. Lowell
stated. "Who are you?"

"I'm Bart Kingsley. I'm her husband."

"*I'm* her husband."

"Like hell you are." Bart flipped back the edge of his
buckskin jacket and drew a folded sheet of paper from his
britches pocket. "I've carried this certificate here every day
of my life. A true and verified marriage license from the
state of Missouri."

"Marriage!" Dr. Lowell exploded. "Dr. Vermillion,
what is the meaning of this outrage?"

Rosie glanced at her father, who had gone as white as a
sheet. "Well . . . er . . ."

"It's true," Rosie said, squaring her shoulders and
staring into the eyes of the man she had come to love so

deeply. "Bart and I are married, and we have been for six years. I've loved him every day of those six years, and I love him now more than ever." She turned to Dr. Lowell. "My father and I were wrong to deceive you, but I didn't do it out of malice. I meant to make a good life for both of us out of the arrangement. And when I boarded the train with you this morning, I fully intended to try it again. But I was wrong."

"Laura Rose!" her father whispered. "You're ruining every chance I ever gave you in life."

"No, Pappy." She moved to stand at Bart's side. "I belong with this man, no matter what comes our way. I trust him to protect me and keep me safe. I trust him to see to my livelihood and my happiness." Glancing up at the tall man whose green eyes shone, she placed her hands over the softness of her waist. "And I trust him to provide a good home for our baby."

"Baby!" Bart grabbed Rosie's shoulders and swung her around. "Baby?" he repeated.

She laughed. "If God's willing, I'll make you a papa in January, Bart Kingsley."

"Hot damn!" He swung her up in his arms and planted a big kiss on her lips.

"What's going on here?" a voice said behind Bart's shoulder. "You still holding up this train, Mr. Kingsley?"

Bart turned, and Rosie saw two of Raton's deputy sheriffs striding down the aisle. But before the chill of fear had a chance to wash through her, the man clapped Bart on the back. "Gonna be a pappy, huh?" one of them said. "Well, good thing. You can set that kid on the right track so he don't steer off it like you did."

"Sure enough." Bart laughed again and gave Rosie a bruising hug. "Come on, girl, we've held this train up long enough, don't you reckon?"

"You're not . . . robbing it?" she whispered.

"Now, why would I do a thing like that? Beets selling for five cents a pound, chickens laying so fast I can't keep up with them, cows so fat they're practically giving buttermilk, and . . . and a *baby* on the way! I'm the richest man in the world, Rosie-girl.''

As he turned to escort her down the aisle, he gave her father a backward glance. "So long, Dr. Vermillion. Don't you worry yourself, now. I'll take care of Rosie. I always said I would, you know."

The morning sunshine hit Rosie full in the face as she and Bart left the shelter of the passenger car. "Hey, boys, I got me a young'un coming!" he called to Ford and the others. "How about that?"

"Yahoo!" Snort shouted and fired off two rounds as the train whistle blew and the engine began to build up steam.

"How'd we do that, anyway?" Bart leaned close and whispered to Rosie on his way to his horse. "I thought you couldn't have babies."

She gave a happy shrug. "Looks as if I was wrong about more than one thing."

"I'll be."

"So how did you manage to sweet-talk the deputies," she asked, "*and* get Ford to help you stop the train? Bart, what's going on?"

He set her on her feet by the stallion he had ridden into a lather all the way from the livery stable. Patting the horse on the neck, he waved and hollered his thanks as Ford, Snort, Fancy, and the deputies rode back down the track toward Raton.

"When I left you this morning," he explained when they were alone at last, "I went to the boys and laid out the straight line. I told them they could do whatever they wanted, but I wasn't going to be party to holding up any trains. Ford was mad as a rattler on a hot skillet. He was jawing at me while I walked back to the hotel to fetch you, but I wouldn't give him heed. When we got into the lobby, Mrs. Davis handed me a letter that had come in the mail a few days back. It was from Frank James."

"Jesse's brother?"

"Sure enough. He allowed as how after he got my letter, he talked to his pals in Missouri—and he's got buddies in high places, you know. Seems the law decided to check out my role in the train robberies, and Frank volunteered to vouch for me. It didn't take too long before they'd cleared my name off the books. Only thing—they don't particularly want me back in Missouri. Fact is, they said if I set foot in the state, they'd arrest me."

"That's fine with me!" Rosie explained, relieved at the thought of never again having to face the man who had tormented her so.

"I reckoned you wouldn't care. Me and the boys had started up the stairs after you, when lo and behold, Mrs. Davis said you'd up and gone off to the depot with those two men who'd marched you out of the dining room the night before. I'll be damned if it wasn't Bob Ford who came up with the notion to round up the deputies, hold up the train, and haul you off."

"But you didn't know I'd left Raton on purpose," Rosie said, mentioning the one barrier left between them.

"Why'd you do that, darlin'? Why'd you leave me again, after all we've been through?"

She sighed. "It was the baby, Bart. I want a good life for this child, and I could only think how awful it would be to bring up our little one in an outlaw's world. But once I'd gone a short distance on the train, I knew I'd been crazy to do it. I made up my mind to get off at the next station and come home to you, no matter what kind of life we had to live."

Bart softly kissed her cheek. "I promised you a good life, Rosie," he said. "When will you trust me to give you that?"

She gazed up into his green eyes. "Now, Bart. I'll trust you now."

"Then hop on this horse, girl, and let's head for home. Those poor milk cows are probably about to bust their britches."

Laughing, Rosie set her foot in the stirrup. Bart cupped her bottom with his hands and pushed her up into the saddle. He climbed on behind her, took the reins, and spurred the horse down the hill toward Raton.

As they rode along, Rosie leaned her head back on his

shoulder and shut her eyes in the warmth of the golden morning sun. "It's a bright day, Bart Kingsley," she whispered, "a bright day after a long, dark night."

Placing his hand over her stomach, he kissed her lips. "A bright, clear, shining day, and not a cloud in sight, Rosie-girl."

*Author's Note

. . . .

The mesa-rimmed town of Raton, New Mexico, saw many prosperous years to come with farming, stock-raising, railroading, and coal mining as profitable industries. According to *The Raton Comet* and other publications, the historical characters in *Gunman's Lady* went on to lead peaceful lives.

Mr. Thomas Kilgore's successful students began attending school in a brand-new building in the fall of 1884. Charles Adams sold the *Comet* in 1886, and the newspaper was renamed *The Raton Range*. It continues to publish today. The Reverend J. A. Cullen resigned his pastorate of the Methodist church in 1883, and his position was filled by the Reverend J. W. Sinnock. Dr. Kohlhouser's beautiful home on Third Street was converted into Saint Patrick's Academy. His dog, Griff, no doubt joined the rest of Raton at the funeral of W. A. White's beloved canine, Tom, who was laid to rest beneath a beautifully carved tombstone in March 1885.

Cheyenne Bill, the popular boxer, came to be called "the Terror of the Wicked West." Despite his reputation as "a hard, hard man," he rigged himself up in fine new clothes, got a haircut, and continued to be the subject of humorous but good-natured poetry published in the local newspaper.

Mathias Broyles Stockton became the new sheriff of Raton in June 1883. That same year, Charles Baker was found guilty of criminal negligence in the shooting death of eleven-year-old Manford Wade. Robert Ford ran into trouble with Raton's deputy sheriff, Jack Miller, and challenged him to a gunfight. Ford failed to appear, was branded a coward, and was run out of town. After roaming the West in a failed attempt to capitalize on the killing of Jesse James, he was gunned down in a saloon in Creed, Colorado, in 1892. In Missouri, Frank James succeeded in his goal of living a quiet life with a home, wife, and children. The brother of Jesse James died a natural death in 1915.

On a more chimeric note, it should be recorded that on the evening of January 10, 1884, Mr. and Mrs. Bart Kingsley became the proud parents of a bouncing nine-pound boy whom they named Buck. And, of course, they all lived happily ever after.

To learn more about the factual basis for *Gunman's Lady*, the author suggests:

Conway, Jay T. *A Brief Community History of Raton, New Mexico: 1880–1930.* Raton: Smith's Printing & Stationery, 1991.

New Mexico Magazine (various articles). Sante Fe, New Mexico.

Poling-Kempes, Lesley. *The Harvey Girls: Women Who Opened the West.* New York: Paragon House, 1989.

The Raton Comet (all issues from 1883). Raton: New Mexico.

Stanley, F. *Raton Chronicle.* Raton Historical Society.

I love to hear from my readers. Please write to me care of the Publicity Dept., Berkley Publishing Group, 200 Madison Avenue, New York, NY 10016.

Diamond Wildflower Romance

A breathtaking new line of spectacular novels set in the untamed frontier of the American West. Every month, Diamond Wildflower brings you new adventures where passionate men and women dare to embrace their boldest dreams. Finally, romances that capture the very spirit and passion of the wild frontier.

__BANDIT'S KISS by Mary Lou Rich
1-55773-842-4/$4.99

__AUTUMN BLAZE by Samantha Harte
1-55773-853-X/$4.99

__RIVER TEMPTRESS by Elaine Crawford
1-55773-867-X/$4.99

__WYOMING WILDFIRE by Anne Harmon
1-55773-883-1/$4.99

__GUNMAN'S LADY by Catherine Palmer
1-55773-893-9/$4.99

__RECKLESS WIND by Bonnie K. Winn
1-55773-902-1/$4.99 (June 1993)

__NEVADA HEAT by Ann Carberry
1-55773-915-3/$4.99 (July 1993)

__TEXAS JEWEL by Shannon Willow
1-55773-923-4/$4.99 (August 1993)

If you enjoyed this book, take advantage of this special offer. Subscribe now and...

Get a Historical
No Obligation

If you enjoy reading the very best in historical romantic fiction...romances that set back the hands of time to those by-gone days with strong virile heros and passionate heroines ...then you'll want to subscribe to the True Value Historical Romance Home Subscription Service. Now that you have read one of the best historical romances around today, we're sure you'll want more of the same fiery passion, intimate romance and historical settings that set these books apart from all others.

Each month the editors of True Value select the four *very best* novels from America's leading publishers of romantic fiction. We have made arrangements for you to preview them in your home *Free* for 10 days. And with the first four books you

receive, we'll send you a FREE book as our introductory gift. No Obligation!

FREE HOME DELIVERY

We will send you the four best and newest historical romances as soon as they are published to preview FREE for 10 days (in many cases you may even get them before they arrive in the book stores). If for any reason you decide not to keep them, just return them and owe nothing. But if you like them as much as we think you will, you'll pay just $4.00 each and save at *least* $.50 each off the cover price. (Your savings are *guaranteed* to be at least $2.00 each month.) There is NO postage and handling—or other hidden charges. There are no minimum number of books to buy and you may cancel at any time.

FREE
Romance
(a $4.50 value)

Send in the Coupon Below

To get your FREE historical romance and start saving, fill out the coupon below and mail it today. As soon as we receive it we'll send you your FREE Book along with your first month's selections.

Mail To: **True Value Home Subscription Services, Inc.** P.O. Box 5235
120 Brighton Road, Clifton, New Jersey 07015-5235

YES! I want to start previewing the very best historical romances being published today. Send me my FREE book along with the first month's selections. I understand that I may look them over FREE for 10 days. If I'm not absolutely delighted I may return them and owe nothing. Otherwise I will pay the low price of just $4.00 each: a total $16.00 (at *least* an $18.00 value) and save at least $2.00. Then each month I will receive four brand new novels to preview as soon as they are published for the same low price. I can always return a shipment and I may cancel this subscription at any time with no obligation to buy even a single book. In any event the FREE book is mine to keep regardless.

Name _____

Street Address _____ Apt. No. _____

City _____ State _____ Zip Code _____

Telephone _____

Signature _____
(if under 18 parent or guardian must sign)   **893**

Terms and prices subject to change. Orders subject
to acceptance by True Value Home Subscription
Services, Inc.